Spring 1998   Vol. XVIII, no. 1
ISSN: 0276-0045   ISBN: 1-56478-178-X

THE REVIEW OF CONTEMPORARY FICTION

Editor
JOHN O'BRIE
Illinois State Un

T0166460

Senior Edit
ROBERT L. McLAUGHLIN
Illinois State University

Associate Editors
BROOKE HORVATH, IRVING MALIN, DAVID FOSTER WALLACE

Book Review Editor
CHRISTOPHER PADDOCK

Guest Editors
NORA IKSTENA, RITA LAIMA KRIEVIŅA

Production & Design
TODD MICHAEL BUSHMAN

Editorial Assistants
MELISSA DEMKOWICZ, KRISTA HUTLEY, KENT D. WOLF

Cover Photo
"La Dolce Vita"
BY FRANCESKA KIRKE

Copyright © 1998 *The Review of Contemporary Fiction.*
No part of this periodical may be reproduced without the
permission of the publisher. Address all correspondence to:
The Review of Contemporary Fiction,
ISU Campus Box 4241, Normal, IL 61790-4241 USA.

The Review of Contemporary Fiction is published three times a year
(February, June, October) by The Review of Contemporary Fiction,
Inc., a nonprofit organization located at ISU Campus Box 4241,
Normal, IL 61790-4241. ISSN 0276-0045. Subscription prices are
as follows:

Single volume (three issues):
    Individuals: $17.00; foreign, add $3.50;
    Institutions: $26.00; foreign, add $3.50.

DISTRIBUTION. Bookstores should send orders to:

Dalkey Archive Press, ISU Campus Box 4241, Normal, IL. 61790-
4241. Phone 309-438-7555; fax 309-438-7422.

This issue is partially supported by grants from the Illinois Arts
Council, a state agency.

Indexed in *American Humanities Index, International Bibliography of Periodical Literature, International Bibliography of Book
Reviews, MLA Bibliography,* and *Book Review Index.* Abstracted in
Abstracts of English Studies.

The Review of Contemporary Fiction is also available in 16mm
microfilm, 35mm microfilm, and 105mm microfiche from University Microfilms International, 300 North Zeeb Road, Ann Arbor, MI
48106-1346.

This issue is dedicated
to the memories of

Kathy Acker

&

James Laughlin

il miglior fabbro

THE REVIEW OF CONTEMPORARY FICTION

FUTURE ISSUES DEVOTED TO: Rikki Ducornet, Curtis White, Milorad Pavić, Richard Powers, Ed Sanders, and postmodern Japanese fiction.

BACK ISSUES

Back issues are still available for the following numbers of the *Review of Contemporary Fiction* ($8 each unless otherwise noted):

DOUGLAS WOOLF / WALLACE MARKFIELD
WILLIAM EASTLAKE / AIDAN HIGGINS
ALEXANDER THEROUX / PAUL WEST
CAMILO JOSÉ CELA
CLAUDE SIMON ($15)
CHANDLER BROSSARD
SAMUEL BECKETT
CLAUDE OLLIER / CARLOS FUENTES
JOHN BARTH / DAVID MARKSON
DONALD BARTHELME / TOBY OLSON
PAUL BOWLES / COLEMAN DOWELL
BRIGID BROPHY / ROBERT CREELEY / OSMAN LINS
WILLIAM T. VOLLMANN / SUSAN DAITCH / DAVID FOSTER WALLACE

WILLIAM H. GASS / MANUEL PUIG
ROBERT WALSER
JOSÉ DONOSO / JEROME CHARYN
GEORGES PEREC / FELIPE ALFAU
JOSEPH MCELROY
DJUNA BARNES
ANGELA CARTER / TADEUSZ KONWICKI
STANLEY ELKIN / ALASDAIR GRAY
EDMUND WHITE / SAMUEL R. DELANY
MARIO VARGAS LLOSA / JOSEF SKVORECKY
WILSON HARRIS / ALAN BURNS
RAYMOND QUENEAU / CAROLE MASO

SPECIAL FICTION ISSUE: Fiction by Pinget, Bowles, Mathews, Markfield, Rower, Ríos, Tindall, Sorrentino, Goytisolo, McGonigle, Dukore, Dowell, McManus, Mosley, and Acker

NOVELIST AS CRITIC: Essays by Garrett, Barth, Sorrentino, Wallace, Ollier, Brooke-Rose, Creeley, Mathews, Kelly, Abbott, West, McCourt, McGonigle, and McCarthy

NEW FINNISH FICTION: Fiction by Eskelinen, Jäntti, Kontio, Krohn, Paltto, Sairanen, Selo, Siekkinen, Sund, Valkeapää

NEW ITALIAN FICTION: Interviews and fiction by Malerba, Tabucchi, Zanotto, Ferrucci, Busi, Corti, Rasy, Cherchi, Balduino, Ceresa, Capriolo, Carrera, Valesio, and Gramigna

GROVE PRESS NUMBER: Contributions by Allen, Beckett, Corso, Ferlinghetti, Jordan, McClure, Rechy, Rosset, Selby, Sorrentino, and others

NEW DANISH FICTION: Fiction by Brøgger, Høeg, Andersen, Grøndahl, Holst, Jensen, Thorup, Michael, Sibast, Ryum, Lynggaard, Grønfeldt, Willumsen, and Holm

THE FUTURE OF FICTION: Essays by Birkerts, Caponegro, Franzen, Galloway, Maso, Morrow, Vollmann, White, and others

Individuals receive a 10% discount on orders of one issue and a 20% discount on orders of two or more issues. To place an order, use the form on the last page of this issue.

contents

When Will Latvians Witness Those Times? _____ 7
Nora Ikstena

The Week of Golden Silence _____ 11
Paul Bankovskis

Beckett Is Alive: Texts to Myself _____ 17
Guntis Berelis

*Cucuimber Aria, The Wonderful Bird, Fate, Etude with a Bullet,
   Nice Guy Moon, Dundaga Mornings* _____ 45
Jānis Einfelds

Pleasures of the Saints _____ 55
Nora Ikstena

Veronica, the Schoolgirl _____ 65
Arvis Kolmanis

The Stairs _____ 84
Aija Lāce

Summer Log (The Zone) _____ 92
Andra Neiburga

Tale No. 13 _____ 111
Aivars Ozoliņš

From Stigmata _____ 125
Gundega Repše

Eventide _____ 145
Jānis Vēveris

Storm Approaching _____ 153
Mārtiņš Zelmenis

The Flying Fish _____ 165
Rimants Ziedonis

The Bookstore in America: Woodland Pattern _____ 193
John O'Brien and Christopher Paddock

William Eastlake (1917–1997) _____ 216
W. C. Bamberger

Book Reviews _____ 221

Books Received _____ 257

Translators _____ 263

Critical acclaim has been unanimous in declaring PAUL METCALF a newly rediscovered genius.

"The publication of Metcalf's Collected Works . . . is nothing less than an event." *—Library Journal*

"Metcalf maps an invaluable literary landscape, unrestrained by any form or geography. At last, it is open to the general public."
—Publishers Weekly (starred review)

"[Metcalf] echoes Ezra Pound's facility with disparate sources and William Carlos Williams's fascination with the history of place . . . while remaining coherently centered within the vortex of the writer's immense vision." *—CUPS*

"The great-grandson of Herman Melville and [one of the] last of the Black Mountain writers, Metcalf possesses a passionate and dramatic sense of American history. . . . He has worked within a deep zone of privacy and artistic integrity. It is now time to make his work available." *—ALA Booklist*

"Often startling, sometimes grotesque and always amazing." *—Columbus Dispatch*, selected as one of the ten favorite books of 1996

"Metcalf is an American original." *—artsMEDIA*

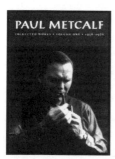  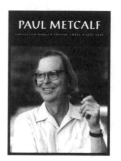

COLLECTED WORKS, VOLUME I, 1956-1976 CLOTH / $35.00
Introduction by Guy Davenport. Includes: *Will West, Genoa, Patagoni, Apalache,* and *The Middle Passage.*

COLLECTED WORKS, VOLUME II, 1976-1986 CLOTH / $35.00
This volume is comprised of: *I-57, Zip Odes, Willie's Throw, U.S. Dept. of the Interior, Both, The Island,* and *Waters of Potowmack.*

COLLECTED WORKS, VOLUME III, 1987-1997 CLOTH / $35.00
Of particular note to Metcalf collectors is the debut of his latest two significant works—*Huascarán* and *The Wonderful White Whale of Kansas,* available exclusively in this edition. Also included: *Louis the Torch, Firebird, Golden Delicious, ". . . and nobody objected," Araminta and the Coyotes, Mountaineers Are Always Free!, Where Do You Put the Horse?,* and *Three Plays.*

COFFEE HOUSE PRESS
WHERE GOOD BOOKS ARE BREWING

Available at fine bookstores or send VISA/MC/personal check (add $3.00 handling) to: Coffee House Press, 27 North Fourth Street, Minneapolis, MN 55401 / 612-338-0125. Distributed by Consortium Book Sales & Distribution / 1-800-283-3572.

When Will Latvians Witness Those Times?

Nora Ikstena

When will Latvians witness those times,
Which other nations are seeing now . . .

These wistful lines, written in 1841 by Latvian writer Jānis
Ruģēns, are often quoted when speaking of Latvian self-esteem.
Even now, as the twenty-first century draws near, this question remains valid. The twentieth century was not favorable to Latvia and
its neighbors Lithuania and Estonia. Only now American readers
can acquaint themselves with a selection of stories written by contemporary Latvian writers whose collective memory emerges from
the history of hard life, wars, occupations, exiles, and deportations.
These experiences, although not first-hand for these young authors,
comprise the common experience of the Baltic peoples. These writers' visions are rooted in a rich culture which has miraculously
withstood the tests of time and a mostly ruthless history. And now,
they are attempting to tame the new era, writing in a language spoken by fewer than 1.5 million people but which is alive and has
something to say about the persona of its people.

Surviving seven hundred years of slavery under the German
landed gentry, who called the Latvians *die Bauer,* "the nation of
peasants" created over two million *dainas*—four-line stanzas which
expressed poetic and often philosophical reflections on the phenomena of life—man's relation to the natural and spiritual worlds, human relations, and the cycle of life from birth to adulthood to death.
The *dainas* were rescued from obscurity for posterity by Krišjānis
Barons, active during the time of national awakening of Latvians in
the late 1800s, who took it upon himself to immortalize these
unique examples of oral tradition in six massive volumes—almost
1.5 million *dainas,* or one *daina* per Latvian. These are now popu-
larly regarded by many Latvians as something comparable to the
Bible.

Up until their declaration of independence in 1918, Latvians had
put up with the dictates of not only the German "lords": the Poles,
Swedes, and czarist Russia had also planted their flags on Latvian
soil. The twentieth century brought enormous changes to this part
of Europe which affected millions of people for many years to come.
As the last Russian czar Nicholas II was toppled and Russia was

swept away by the chaos of its revolution, and with the German army defeated and driven out of Latvia, Latvians struggled to build up their fledgling state.

Latvia recovered rapidly from the effects of World War I. In the scant twenty years of its sovereignty, Latvian culture flourished and its European context was easily recognizable. Latvia's capital, Rīga, with its gems of turn-of-the-century *art nouveau* buildings, was fondly deemed the Paris of the North. Rīga was considered an international city where many ethnic minorities coexisted peacefully.

Visions of pre-World War II were immortalized in the poetry of Aleksandrs Čaks (1901-1950), a romantic modernist, whose oeuvre still lingers in the minds of Latvian readers and continues to be a source of inspiration for contemporary Latvian poetry.

The secret Molotov-Ribbentrop Pact of 1939 signaled for Latvia the end of its brief but vivacious era of rebirth. In 1940 Latvia was annexed by the Soviet Union. Tanks rolled in and arrests began. The majority of Latvians were tragically affected—losing family, friend, and neighbor to the Siberian wastelands. The Soviet wave of terror was followed by the Nazi German occupation which annihilated Latvia's Jewish population. The final wave—the return of the Soviet army following the fall of the Third Reich—left Latvia behind the Iron Curtain for half a century in the postwar division of Europe.

What, then, comprises the collective unconscious of the Latvian nation? Latvia's newly independent state lies over the layers of history: a former freedom short-lived, a hard agrarian way of life, the eternal struggle to survive in a master-serf relationship—one can tread deeper and deeper into ages tarnished by Time, receding into pre-Christian pantheistic times.

The Latvian language embodies the Latvian soul or consciousness. Oral traditions carried the Latvian language into the nineteenth century when it sprang to life in the written word. Stirred up by the winds of the Russian revolution, Latvian journals, books, and newspapers increasingly disseminated the notion of freedom. Once independent Latvia came to life in 1918, words invoked the common experience.

Latvian literature came under fire as history changed its course under Adolf Hitler and Josef Stalin. Under the long Soviet occupation, words were twisted or destroyed, misconstrued and made malleable by "the authorities," and poets learned to write between the lines.

The dual proximity of lies and truth, which permeated both art and life in the Soviet era, eventually led to a golden age in

Latvian poetry—beginning with Ojārs Vācietis (1933-1983), Vizma Belševica (1931), and Imants Ziedonis (1933—see *Flowers of Ice,* trans. Barry Callaghan [Toronto, 1987]), and later enriched by the social irony of Uldis Bērziņš (1944), the intellectual poetry of Jānis Rokpelnis (1945), and the popular works of Māra Zālīte (1952), rich in references to folklore and infused with national sentiment. On this side of the Iron Curtain, the consumers of works by Latvian poets and writers were, although bent under the hardships of Soviet rule, wise and avid readers who knew how to read between the lines.

On the other side of the Iron Curtain, émigrés in exile sought to preserve their language while integrating into new cultures in the United States, Canada, Germany, Sweden, Australia, England, Venezuela, and other host countries. During the 1960s, New York's "Hell's Kitchen" group of Latvian writers (Linards Tauns, Gunars Saliņš, and others) soaked up the spirit of American modernism. They sought to maintain their national identity while living as strangers in a strange but comfortable land.

American-Latvian writer Agate Nesaule's autobiographical work *A Woman in Amber,* published in the United States in 1996, received excellent reviews and for the first time brought to the American public what could be called the Latvian experience—that is, the experiences and consequences of World War II.

In this issue we present twelve writers of prose from modern-day, post-Soviet Latvia. Their prose does not give the impression that these—for the most part young writers—are weighed down by the burden of the past. Stylistically diverse, the authors use dreams and stream of consciousness to express themselves, often merging reality with the world of the irrational, the mundane with the metaphysical.

The advent of postmodern theories has been accompanied by a skeptical attitude toward realism in writing on the part of young writers, thus in a way confronting them with the older generation of writers. One of the reasons for such skepticism comes from the association of realism with social realism, which during the Soviet occupation imposed on writers the demand for one ideologically correct approach to representing reality. However, nowadays Latvian authors do not shy away from a realistic approach to writing, choosing to merge it with the postmodern elements of game, fixations of the inner world, and layers of parables and metaphors.

Latvian literature needs time and considerable effort to reach an international audience, mostly due to a lack of funding and qualified translators. This is one of the first attempts to bring to a wider public works originally crafted in the Latvian language.

Note from Rita Laima Krieviņa

I seem to recall being wrapped in sweaters and shawls and drinking gallons of hot tea to keep myself warm in a cold Rīga apartment while working on this issue. I recall being surrounded by papers, books, diskettes, and children leaning over my shoulder. This issue has had me stooped over an old PC with a clogged memory in late evenings, going through the work of other translators, struggling to refrain from meddling with their interpretations of the prose. I took a democratic approach. There are works where diacritical marks, so characteristic of the Latvian language, have been tediously put in, and there are works where Latvian names have been anglicized and I chose to leave them that way. I have my favorites in this selection, like anyone. Some works have gone to sleep with me, invading my dreams. This selection is only the tip of the iceberg. Latvian literature has much to share with the world.

Acknowledgments

The Guest Editors and the *Review of Contemporary Fiction* would like to thank the following for their contributions to this issue: Ingūna Beķere, Jānis Ikstens, FORTECH Company, and Jānis Bergs.

We also gratefully acknowledge the Soros Foundation Latvia, whose generosity has made this issue possible.

Paul Bankovskis

Pauls Bankovskis (1973) was born in Sigulda, one of Latvia's most pictur-
esque towns. He studied at Latvia's School for the Applied Arts and at the
University of Latvia. Bankovskis made his literary debut with his collection of stories, *Svētā Bokasīna koks* (St. Bokasin's Tree), which attracted
the attention of critics and readers alike. Alongside his work at Latvia's
principal daily *Diena,* Bankovskis is a fervent writer of prose, and his
Laiku grāmata (Times Book) was published in 1997. Bankovskis says that
his world has been made more colorful by modern English-language literature. One of his favorite authors is Roddy Doyle. Bankovskis's prose is characterized by an intellectual toying with knowledge and an ironic and skeptical perception of the world.

The Week of Golden Silence

Monday

It was a very common type of bet. We made it Sunday evening, yesterday. Pedestrians and cars slid by the window of the café. Like fish in an aquarium. Coats hung on the rack near the entrance like stuffed scarecrows. Darkness was descending, and the lights left an oppressive and indelible impression on the sky.

"Say neither 'yes' nor 'no,' nor 'white,' nor 'black'. . . ," you whispered the children's rhyme in the dusk. "The first of us to speak, will the porridge eat."

"Silence is golden," I chimed in. It didn't occur to me then that nursery rhymes, teasers, and proverbs are the inevitable harbingers of misfortune. If what happened really was a misfortune.

We didn't even mention porridge made of ashes, the classic fare of nursery rhymes, as the stake in this bet. We wagered on something much more prosaic—a few bottles of *demi-sec,* a bar of bittersweet chocolate, a can of pistachio nuts, or the cream candies that you eat with such gusto.

The loser won't be the one who first initiates a conversation with the other, but the one who first responds. The bet is on! We invited to our table the waiter who, with a hesitant smile, bore witness to our wager.

Afterward, I stood at the door of the train, and we exchanged awkward gestures. Just like all the strange people who seem to be carrying on final discussions through the windows of departing trains, trams, and buses. You were standing on the station platform, and the end of your cigarette flashed together with the rings on your lively fingers.

Even before we had agreed on the stakes and had invited the waiter to our table, you told me that you loved me. And exactly for this reason—you thought it would be interesting to test the power of our love or to discover the extent of our endurance.

With a graceful gesture, you waved farewell, and the embers of your cigarette disappeared. The train jerked forward and started to slide away. But the doors remained open. Obviously they were broken. The wind ruffled my hair, and a strange thought entered my mind—why not jump out? The answer was simple. Because there was no reason to make the leap. And I turned around to enter a train car occupied by a few sleepy passengers.

I wanted to call you first thing in the morning. Still, I suddenly realized the senselessness of it—you wouldn't have answered me anyway. And so I refrained.

I took the morning train in to work—together with workers who were either hung over or already drunk. I didn't think about you until evening. And it was only around eleven o'clock that I called you to reassure myself that it was your breath I was hearing at the other end of the phone. I didn't say a word as you impatiently repeated "Hello, hello" in my ear. We had survived the first day.

Tuesday

We met in the very heart of the city without, of course, exchanging a word. I caught up with you at a crosswalk when the light was red, and touched your elbow lightly. You didn't look back—you merely smiled. Hand in hand, we set off. It was impossible to understand who was leading whom—we were like two dumbstruck blind men. A thunderstorm had died down a while before, and the damp streets smelled of cooled tar. Water was steaming off overheated cars, and some sort of sadistic music descended upon us from an open window.

After walking for about an hour we arrived at a bridge. Beneath it were small family gardens, single-family homes, an asphalt lot with huge piles of tires. You leaned against the rail of the bridge and squinted at the railroad tracks winding and bending ahead. At the horizon they fused with power lines and the bluish haze. Small blue signal lights twinkled above the tracks, and the switches clanked.

I felt a growing disquiet which was totally unfounded. The two of us were alone. Cars hurtled by and, beneath our feet, a freight train rattled toward its destination. In the tire-laden lot, someone was welding.

Suddenly, I recognized that the source of my restlessness was this plain and unfamiliar place. I became angry and nervous because you were standing here, engrossed in this stupid, industrial landscape. Yes, you even dared to smile at me and look into my eyes.

Then you stretched out your hand and hailed a passing taxi, which I hadn't even noticed.

"I love you," you murmured quickly and jumped into the car. The door slammed shut, and you were gone. Your fingers—frozen in the act of blowing a kiss—flashed in the window of the taxi. This was, actually, an unfair provocation. Fortunately, I didn't have the time to respond. Otherwise, I would have lost the bet.

Wednesday

Today, I longed to meet you. Failing in my search around the city, I went to your house. We drank fruit juice and listened to a new cassette which, I gather, you bought yesterday after leaving the bridge.

Setting off from the house, we stepped into a bus which was heated and dusty like a small greenhouse or some building in Sun City. We rode without speaking until we realized that we had gone full circle.

We pointed out objects and events, smiling incessantly at each other. It's quite possible that to bystanders we looked like idiots. Some unkempt boy at a bus stop made fun of us. Before parting, by some divine chance, we managed to come to an agreement about the next day's plans. It required half an hour's worth of effort.

On my way home, I was overcome by the strange restlessness once again. Now I was sure that our self-imposed silence was to blame. In childhood, we hid small flowers, pebbles, and broken dishes in holes dug in the sand, covered the secrets with broken glass, and carefully evened out the ground. Even then, we felt compelled to share make-believe secrets about the whereabouts of the treasures with someone. A secret unknown to anyone isn't really a secret at all. *Love is a secret and no one to tell* are the words to a song. It's almost as if the song is about us.

Thursday

When I arrived at our arranged meeting place near the Daugavgrīva lighthouse, you were not there. Tired waves clunked against the concrete blocks and rocks dumped into the sea. Ships clanked in the port, and some sort of construction work was taking place out on the breakwater. Every once in a while, trucks filled with rocks drove out to the site, only to return much later, empty. I sat there until twilight, but you never came. Maybe I had misunderstood.

Friday

I disconnected the telephone and spent the entire day in the confines of my room. I observed the passage of sunlight and the shadows of the tree in the yard. The feeling was one I had forgotten since my youth—so many desires culminating in indifference. In order to overcome this sensation, I acted as though I was sick. I found a thermometer and—lo and behold—my temperature really was a few degrees higher than normal. That was the perfect excuse for a day of loafing—and smoking a whole pack of cigarettes.

Saturday

You actually did come to the designated meeting place near the lighthouse. And you wrote in the sand that you had also been there yesterday. Of course, I kept silent. The wind blew fine grains of sand across the beach; the sand stuck to our fingers and heels. Our skin grew sticky from the salty sea air, and for a long time afterward our ears, like small seashells pinned to our heads, retained the sound of surf.

It must be the end of summer. It can get chilly even at noon, although it is still hot where there is no wind. Indian summer. *Atvasara. Babje ljeto.* To each his own.

Slipping behind the rusty buoys, we allowed ourselves to go sunbathing. You took off all your clothes, but I wasn't even tempted to touch you. I got dressed and headed home. You stayed there and didn't say a word.

Sunday

Our bet has ended. We are sitting in the same place where we sat exactly one week ago. You're telling me something, but I'm not listening. I should probably reply, but I have no desire to do so. My mother used to say—one betting partner is a fool, the other, a cheat. This case is a little different. Both of us are losers and both—winners. I'm embarrassed to admit it, but I simply cannot remember the stakes we played for. I should ask you, but I don't really feel like it.

You are watching my fingers as they stir the pieces of ice in my glass. Remember to hold the glass by the rim with the palm of your hand so that it completely covers the top, and make a toast. The sound is like pebbles in the sea. It's an old joke. Maybe I should be ashamed of the fact that, following a week of silence, the only thing I can think of are stupid bar jokes. Your gaze touches me around the ear, the temples, or the base of my nose—in order plausibly to imitate a direct look into my eyes. This was a trick invented by the author of an etiquette book. We bought the book about a year ago and read it together in the evenings.

"There's nothing to say," one or both of us admit. We get up to pay the check and go. We still haven't exchanged a word.

Translated by Māra Sīmanis

Guntis Berelis

Guntis Berelis (1961) is Latvia's most productive literary critic of the 1990s. His reviews have always caused a stir among his followers and opponents. Berelis's "theoretical fathers" are Roland Barthes, Jacques Derrida, Jean Lyotard, and Ihab Hassan. Ludwig Wittgenstein's work has had a profound effect on Berelis, and he writes, "From Wittgenstein I have both a deep distrust and worship of language. A tendency to perceive any given expression not as 'truth' but as the end result of the game of language." It is in this context that Berelis's brilliant essays *Klusums un vārds* (Silence and the Word) and *Autora dzimšana* (The Author's Birth) were written.

Although Berelis feels that the writing of literature is a public-intimate or intimate-public activity, similar to the antics of an exhibitionist, he nevertheless continues to write fiction. *Mitomānija* (Mythomania, 1989) is Berelis's debut book, and in its introduction he writes: "All of literature is a grandiose system of lies. Do not believe the written word." Recently, Berelis has published a children's book, *Agnese un Tumsas valdnieks* (Agnes and the Ruler of Darkness, 1996) and a collection of literary theory and critical essays, *Silence and the Word*. Berelis lives in a secluded spot in the Latvian countryside. Recipient of a stipend from Latvia's Culture Foundation, he is devoting his time to writing a history of Latvian literature.

Beckett Is Alive:
Texts to Myself

Somebody once maintained that somewhere at some point in time Beckett had died, so he'd heard or read somewhere, he couldn't remember exactly where, but I haven't managed to clarify whether or not he's right. Anyone whom I happen to ask, "Is Beckett alive?" either replies by asking, "What's a beckett?" or else shrugs his shoulders indifferently; there are also those who ask suspiciously— "What do you need to know that for? What difference does it make if Beckett's alive or dead? Words, they're just words." To tell you the truth, at times I feel rather uncomfortable: encountering an acquaintance on the street, at the theater or somewhere else, I feel inclined to ask them, "By the way, do you happen to know whether Beckett's still alive?" But I've already asked so many people that I can't keep track anymore, and so I'd better just drop the whole Beckett thing or else my acquaintances will begin to think I'm some kind of weirdo, or even a pathological character, if every time we meet I'll try to slip the Beckett question into the conversation with a feigned nonchalance.

One day I went to the library and asked the librarian if she could find out what the story of Beckett was: was he alive, and if not then when did he die? The librarian disappeared into a maze of stacks for a moment; upon returning, she informed me that she nevertheless thought that Beckett was alive. "What does 'nevertheless' mean?" I asked with a pang of perplexity. "Nevertheless—it means," the librarian explained that she had looked through all the available encyclopedias, including the hefty *Oxford Encyclopedia of English Literature,* and that all of these sources indicated only Beckett's birth date—1906. "However," she added quickly, "By no means does that mean that Beckett is alive at the moment. Yet, according to the information on hand, he's alive," she asserted. It was possible that Beckett had died within the last two or three years, since the library didn't have encyclopedias that recent. Perhaps, the librarian continued to develop her train of thought, at the very moment when I had posed my question Beckett was still alive, but now—at the very moment she was speaking these words—he could be dead and gone. Maybe he'll die tomorrow after dinner, but maybe he signed off already last year around midsummer's eve. Anyhow, he'll have to die sometime soon, he's an old man, after all. Wasn't it all the same to me? "No, it isn't it all the same to me!" I snapped back. "Then it's very important to you?" "I don't know," I admitted. I really didn't know whether it was important to me, "I just wanted to find out if Beckett was alive." "Well, then, in fact you don't really *need* to find out whether Beckett is alive or not," she uttered with noticeable relief. "I don't know," I faltered once again. "In that case, if you don't know whether it's important to you or not, and if you're not sure whether you really want to find out whether Beckett is alive or dead, then what are you doing here anyway?" the librarian suddenly snarled. "I don't know," I was forced to admit once again, overcome by confusion. The librarian appeared to be formulating her next question, the pupils of her eyes floated upward and vanished behind her eyelids, I was staring at the whites of her eyes. I feared she would either hammer me into the ground or strangle herself with morbid strings of subordinate clauses, so I quickly departed. Actually, there was a grain of truth in what the librarian had said: if we assume that Beckett isn't dead, then we can never be completely convinced that he isn't dying at this very moment. Hence the following eerie and beautiful conclusion: Beckett is continually dying.

Imagine: on the street in broad daylight—a day like any other day, nothing special except that maybe it's sprinkling a bit—a man approaches you, someone you're probably seeing for the first time in your life, he suddenly grabs your hand (limp from surprise), shakes it sincerely, maybe even pats you on the shoulder and cries out, "Hello, I'm Godot!" He must be nuts, you'll think to yourself. "But I can do that, I can take the liberty of shaking your hand and tell you that I'm Godot without being crazy and/or uttering a single untruth." He must be nuts, you're deciding at this very moment. Well, no, no more than you, sir! What's more, let's also take into account that I have no intention of declaring that I'm Godot's prototype (that would be a shameless lie), or that my parents, being great admirers of Beckett, named me Godot (a credible theory, but wrong all the same). There are moments when I really *am* Godot, the Godot created by Beckett, and it's been inscribed in documents and certified with a seal. But there are also times when I'm not Godot. Well, now, can you guess what this all means?

Beckett was Joyce's secretary. Not everyone can have a secretary like Beckett, and not everyone can become a secretary for a man like Joyce. Joyce was a terrorist and a dictator. He terrorized both time and his readers. On June 24, 1921, right after midsummer night, without displaying the least bit of shame, Joyce announced in a letter that he had wasted something close to twenty thousand hours on *Ulysses*. But this alone wasn't enough for Joyce. To this outrageous figure we'll add on the hours the poor readers spent attempting to get through the first part of the monster book. Let's also add the hours stolen from the lives of the readers—true, there weren't too many readers who succeeded in conquering *Ulysses* in its entirety. Let's add on the hours, months, years, and decades squandered away by translators intent on rendering Joyce into other languages (I wonder if *Ulysses* has been translated into the language of the Kru people, an African tribe) and by scholars researching, criticizing, analyzing, summarizing, explaining, commenting on, reviewing, generalizing about, and paraphrasing *Ulysses;* and, even more, writing monographs, biographies, bibliographies, biobibliographies, topographies (i.e., essays on the topic "Joyce's Dublin"), and heaven knows what else, not even to mention the pettier manifestations of literary masturbation to be found in the publications of various countries, in journals and collections of scholarly articles devoted to literature. And, of course, Joyce's imitators and followers—a few tons. Let's get back to the poor innocent reader (forever the author's victim), and let's add on a few more centuries that the reader wasted reading all these monographs, biographies, and bibliographies. Let's subtract the final figure from world history and for a moment review the dreadful results. Beckett had many moments to review these results. Therefore, it's no coincidence that Beckett wrote precisely in the manner that he wrote, and not even the Nobel Prize was of much help here. But Beckett's secretary probably went insane, and then he no longer needed a secretary.

In the evenings, returning home from the theater, I have a bite to eat, make my bed, and sit down in the easy chair by the window (I live somewhere on the second or third floor). I wait. There's a dilapidated two-story house on the other side of the street; behind it—a courtyard, in the courtyard—another house; I've no idea what the address is but it's supplemented with the letter "b": a seven-story, angular block of stone, bleak and grayish-blue (a rhinoceros grayish-blue). Gradually, it becomes dark. The lights in the windows of the gray block go out one after another. Only one window on the seventh floor directly below the roof remains illuminated—it goes on shining with a wan, yellowish light night after night. There have been nights when I've tried to compete with it: what will expire first, the window or my consciousness, and yet consciousness has always lost the contest—toward morning I usually can't hold out and fall asleep, or, having grown completely stiff from sitting, I collapse into bed. There is something about this window that attracts me—in a completely mystical way it rivets my attention and won't let go. And so I pine away by my window—every evening, I pine away lost in thought, struggling with strings of unanswered questions. Why are the lights always on in the window on the seventh floor? Is such crazy insomnia possible—night after night, the whole year round? Maybe an artist is at work up there? Yet this is highly unlikely, for, as they say, an artist needs natural daylight. Maybe a writer lives up there—one of those who writes only by night, sitting up there and rattling away on his typewriter? Or perhaps it's a sex maniac?

I had a good friend, a writer, who wrote mystery novels. He dreamed of writing a mystery novel in which at the beginning the reader would be confused by the fact that a murder has taken place, but that, contrary to all the principles of a mystery novel, there is no murderer. But at some point, in a sudden moment of illumination, the reader would understand that *he himself* is the murderer. "Just imagine, what a catharsis!" my friend would cry out, having expounded his idea for the nth time, toward which I had a rather skeptical attitude. After that, he would usually give a disgusting laugh and go on: "Then the entire police department would get sidetracked! Imagine, the number of readers would equal the number of murderers! The investigator reads it—after all, he needs to acquaint himself with the facts and circumstances—and he discovers that he's the murderer! Fine, he gets thrown in jail. The next investigator, a fellow of superior rank investigating the crimes of his colleagues, reads it, and *he* lands behind bars! The attorney general, for instance, reads it; he can't understand why all the investigators have gone mad, they've all started murdering—and pow, he goes straight to jail! The president or someone like that reads it—he gets a kick in the ass and is sent off to jail! That, you see, is what I call a catharsis. The whole nation is catharted!" "In your opinion, is writing mystery novels taking revenge on the world?" I asked him sarcastically. "Definitely! Especially if they're lousy mystery novels. Look, Dante wrote his *Divine Comedy* as a mystery, and it's an exceptionally lousy book, isn't it? He piled all his enemies and ill-wishers into hell's frying pans. And not only with the living; he filtered through all of history and picked out those characters who seemed culpable to him. Isn't that revenge on the world? Dante couldn't take revenge any other way. If you'd give Dante a regiment then you'd see what a mess he'd make in his fourteenth century, a mess like never before! You see," my friend returned to his idea. "It's simple to establish a logical chain of events and then point your finger—see, there's the murderer. Those are blatant lies that don't provide any catharsis. But it's necessary for you to believe it—that you yourself are the murderer, not some made-up character from a book. That will be art; that will be a catharsis!"

I mulled this over, finding my friend's logic rather spotty. "Hold on," I exclaimed, "What about you? Won't you, in the process of writing the novel, being the very first reader, believe that you're the murderer? Your happiness will be rather short-lived; you'll be the first to sit in jail, and you'll have to wait a while before the president and his gang arrive." "Oh!" he murmured, grinning enigmatically. "There's a particular trick involved, a specific convention of the genre, so to speak. There's no way I can be the murderer. I've been allotted a *different* role. But you'll see for yourself when you read it."

After a few months, I called the writer to find out how he was doing and where he'd disappeared to for so long, but my friend seemed very busy and cut the conversation short, saying that he was working hard on the new mystery novel. "The same one" was how he put it. He would be wrapping it up and handing the manuscript to a critic he knew, but afterward—maybe (again he stressed *"maybe";* it sounded like he wanted to say "if nothing unforeseen happens") to me, as well. After a short time, I read several obituary notices in the paper eulogizing my friend in all respects as the most distinguished writer of mystery novels of the "post-Kolberg era"; here and there rather obscure parallels had been drawn between his books and his tragic death. The writer had been found in his apartment, comfortably reclined in an easy chair, an unfinished cup of coffee and a cigarette that was a stick of ashes next to him. The murderer had smashed his skull open, and the manuscript of the new mystery ("the same one") had disappeared. Well, my friend had played the role he chose out to the very finish. They say that even in death he had smiled triumphantly, though I think his lower jaw was simply dangling open, typical of a corpse.

Beckett is roaming the city aimlessly, who knows whence and who knows where to, as is Beckett's wont. He sees Ionesco walking toward him wearing a rhinoceros mask. At first Beckett doesn't recognize him. He's thinking it's just some rhinoceros, nothing more. Beckett rounds the corner and suddenly comes to his senses—a rhinoceros! Could it be . . . ? Of course, it must be Ionesco! As alive as they get!

Meanwhile, Ionesco, who's managed to remove his mask, saunters slowly ahead, humming to himself. Suddenly someone careens into him, nearly knocking him down, and without a word of apology gallops away. It's Beckett. But Beckett no longer recognizes Ionesco now that he's taken off his mask. Ionesco is carrying the rhinoceros mask in his bag with just the horn sticking out. Ionesco hides himself in an alley and watches the hopelessly confused Beckett stop at the intersection, shuffle his feet for a moment, and then turn into a side street. Ionesco puts his mask on again and begins to roar with laughter, so loudly that all the passersby stop and begin to laugh along with him. If he'd known that Beckett was going to capture the Nobel Prize he wouldn't have laughed.

At night, sitting by my window, gazing at the illuminated window on the seventh floor of the house across from me, I'm thinking: always the same thing, that which I cannot and don't want to say out loud, that which I want to hide inside myself. The yellowish square lures thoughts from their hiding places, thoughts swirl, I'm muffled in a cloud of thoughts, and for the most part they are acrid thoughts that refuse to leave me in peace. They blame me, these writers, they all blame me; true, they don't spell it out, as professionals they never spell anything out, as if that weren't the simplest way—for once to say something concisely and precisely without superfluous and roundabout talk—it's as if they deliberately drag everything out, maybe really deliberately; every letter is only a pretext for the next one so that again they can continue to crumble me crumb by crumb, never adding the finishing touch that would make everything clear to me. To tell you the truth, I'm not sure what to think—nor do I know who they are or where they are, why they're turning against me, what they want from me, these damned scribblers. Hopeless ignorance is maddeningly torturous; of course, I can soothe myself in a completely banal way by saying that I always know that I know nothing, but that doesn't change anything, doesn't even come close to satisfying me. To dispel my uncertainty I could go on endlessly asking questions, but if there's no one to ask, except perhaps myself; then I myself would supply the answers to my own questions. These questions and answers—if from time to time I succeed in luring them out into the open—clearly mean nothing, they are only fairy tales that I tell myself, an illusory little world that I have created for myself and where I dwell, modestly and humbly.

It's a shame I didn't keep the first letters, but I recall the way I inspected envelopes that had no stamps, no cancellations, no return address; obviously the writer (or writers) had tossed them into my mailbox directly. I couldn't make anything of the first letter, though it seemed to be written with a conviction that everything would become clear to me from the first glance (or maybe it was written with the opposite idea of taking me for a ride). It went something like this: "Well, hi there, I won't ask how you're doing, we both know anyway, what's more, I know a little better than you do, you've probably already realized who this letter is from, and I can already sense what you'll do after reading it—or at least you'll start to think about doing it, but that's really of no importance, and, to tell you the truth, this letter isn't important either, or more precisely, this notice or, let's say, announcement, if it already exists—everything has the right to be, if it already is—to be more open with you, I don't really feel like writing, what should I write about—well, I'm, well, I'm writing, well, read on, since this letter has reached you, and of this I'm now certain." And so on, for a couple more pages. With no signature. I'll admit, contrary to the conviction expressed by the letter's author, I had no idea who he was and why he'd wasted so much time and paper in order to fill up these few pages with absolutely nothing. I even reread the letter several times, trying to decode some hidden meaning, trying to unearth a kernel of rationality in the roundabout jibberish—but there was neither meaning nor any kernel, only empty babble, for some reason embellished with silly venomous irony. It would have been understandable if the author had offered one of those idiotic letter games to me—even in idiocy one can find some splinter of a kernel of rationality; however, the letter had no offer in it, didn't ask me to do anything like, for example, find three or seven more addressees. Similarly, it didn't remind me of a joke, for every joke has some point to it—for instance, making a fool out of me so that someone could have a good laugh. I remained as I was and didn't hear any snickering. In fact, the letter didn't change anything, and I threw it in the garbage.

The sound of the doorbell yanks me out of my musing, and I go to open the door. There's a man, an ordinary man, the kind the world is full of, standing there, and he says, "Hello, I'm Vladimir!" Another man is standing behind him staring; it's written on his forehead that he's Estragon. No, not like that. A man overtakes me on the street, a thoroughly average fellow, grabs me by the hand, shakes it and says, "But we're waiting and waiting for you and you're just not coming. Listen, where did you disappear to? Estragon was also looking for you and couldn't find you!"

I write on the tiled walls of public restrooms—*I will come soon.* And sign it *Godot.*

But those are merely dreams. Actually, every evening I'm forced to kill time in the small theater, always somewhere in the middle so as not to be too conspicuous—fidgeting in a seat worn out by many derrieres watching Vladimir and Estragon waiting for Godot. I admit, it's possible that waiting for Godot is interesting and at moments may even seem useful, but to watch two absolute idiots wait for Godot for at least an hour and a half-dozen times is a good way of losing your mind. I admit, initially I felt marvelous: I sat in the very middle, small and inconspicuous, and relished a private feeling of superiority: no one, not a single soul, not even Vladimir or Estragon, not to mention the audience, knew that I WAS GODOT. They suspect nothing; later they have long and clever conversations (at times I've overheard them as they passed by) about "the inevitability of the absurd" or something of the sort. That's the catch—that there isn't anything absurd, there's no deep philosophy here—may the madcap Vladimir and Estragon continue to vegetate till doomsday or until the show is discontinued; everything is very clear and mundane: Godot, the guy they're so diligently waiting for, to be precise, the actor who plays Godot, and that's me—is simply sitting here in the audience and grinning in his beard (in order to grin in your beard you don't necessarily need a beard, and, actually, you don't need a grin either); Godot is not on his way, he cannot arrive *because he has already arrived,* yet no one knows it. I get paid for the fact that no one suspects anything (and they pay well; I'm paid for my leading role, but only I, the director and the accountant know this; upon receiving my salary I have to sign a separate piece of paper that the accountant keeps in a safe for fear that someone may accidentally read it and discover our secret). The performance's finale is always the most beautiful part: the final moment of silence fades as the clapping begins, and I get up and stride nobly out, listening to the applause that in reality is for me; again I succeeded in fooling them, all of them! Again they waited for me, not knowing I'd already come. Never before has anyone waited for me so long, although those who are waiting are only a bunch of crazy idiots. Actually, I must be a master of the art of acting, for no one has succeeded in guessing that I'm acting or what my role is; they consider me to be just a common spectator; that means that my role and my essence have melted into one integrated whole. At times I feel like God (the etymological analogy stressed by naive theoreticians: *Godot = God;* maybe *Godot = good;* but maybe *Godo = o, dog!*).

But I'm sick of this; I feel tired; I know why they say that an actor's work is exceptionally difficult, and it becomes even more difficult when it doesn't cross anyone's mind that you're an actor. To endure this waiting for Godot dozens of times, to live for months knowing that they waited for you, they are waiting and will continue to wait, not to permit this absurd waiting to drive you crazy—that's no laughing matter. At times I barely succeed in repressing the desire to bring it all to a crashing finale—a big, fat, profound finale: for instance, standing up in the middle of the performance, squeezing past the confused spectators (they're all pretty mediocre imitations of Vladimir and Estragon) to the stage, pushing aside Vladimir and Estragon, opening my arms wide as if I wanted to hug the whole theater, and melodramatically crying out, "Hello, I'm Godot! Have you been waiting long?" It's difficult to picture what the reaction would be. Maybe Vladimir would fly into a rage and call the police; maybe Estragon would punch me in nose and throw me out on the street; maybe they would both pretend not to notice me and continue the performance in exaggeratedly loud voices. But maybe for a split second they would succeed in overcoming their stupor; they would pretend that everything was happening just as it should, they would start improvising along with me, and together we would present an unprecedented masterpiece—*The Coming of Godot*.

I had a good friend—a writer. To tell you the truth, he was a pretty mediocre writer—one of those who cook up a fat volume just about every year and love to tell you that in their novels "everything is true to life." For some reason when uttering these words my friend's eyes become moist. When I tried to tell him that nothing in his books bore any semblance to life, that all of it reeked of pulp, he would pull bundles of readers' letters from his desk drawers and start quoting the blunt apologias which he'd underlined with a red marker. All the same, let's leave his scribblings alone; we speak only well of the deceased. My friend was put in jail, where he slashed his veins, unable to endure the humiliation. But he ended up in jail because he had murdered his son (true, nothing was mentioned in the charges about the son; Karlis Krammaus was identified as "unemployed and without a known address"; furthermore, when the prosecutor was questioned as to who had actually been murdered, he could only helplessly shrug his shoulders).

One day, when my friend was sitting at his desk, scribbling one of his many novels, someone knocked timidly at the door. He opened it and saw (he later told me this) a noticeably agitated young man standing in the stairway; he seemed both familiar and not. He stood there quietly for a considerable time, and then the writer asked him who he was looking for. Suddenly the young man burst into a flood of tears, moved as if he wanted to throw himself around my friend's neck, and hoarsely exclaimed, "I'm your son!" He uttered this and then vanished from sight. The young man's display of emotion had been so genuine that the writer had believed him at once. Why would anyone want to deceive him? No one could have anything to gain by posing as his son.

The writer recollected the sins of his youth (there weren't too many; later he complained to me that he'd missed so many opportunities). But no, all the women he had slept with twenty years ago (that's about how old the young man had seemed to him) he had met later and was assured that he hadn't produced any sons. Then my

friend began to think about why the young man had seemed so familiar—not someone he might accidentally have spotted from the
corner of his eye, but someone he had known for a long time. He
thought about this all evening, couldn't sleep that night, and in the
morning skipped breakfast—but he couldn't come to any conclu-
sions.

The following afternoon the young man was back. He stood in the
stairway and flexed his jaw muscles tensely so as to restrain himself and not succumb to tears. And then he cried out, "Dad, I'm your
son! My name is Kārlis Krammaus!" My friend nearly collapsed
from surprise. Of course, he instantly realized why the young man
had seemed familiar to him, as well as why he was presenting himself as his son. Krammaus really was the writer's son—not physically or genetically, but spiritually. Twenty years ago he himself
had made up Krammaus; Kārlis Krammaus—that was the name of
an exceptionally pleasant young man who was unlucky in love in
one of his friend's first novels. "Creating a son is no problem, you
can create rows of them," said my friend. "But I labored over
Krammaus for a good couple of weeks. Just think how much work
the last name alone required: not the banal Krāmausis nor
Kramauss, but Krammaus, with two 'm's' and one 's.' Not to speak
of all the rest—the little scar on his forehead, the birthmark on his
back. . . . Krammaus turned out true to life. And you're still saying
that I'm bad writer. Krammaus is an argument for the opposite!"
my friend finished triumphantly. Yes, Krammaus had presented
himself not "true to life" but very much alive.

Around that time, a couple of sharply critical articles, in which
my friend was, to put it mildly, panned along with all of his novels,
appeared in the press. Considering the attacks undeserved, he was
terribly hurt by the criticism. However, he had Kārlis Krammaus,
living proof of his talent, and my friend decided to take his creation
by the hand and escort him to all of the editorial offices, introduce
him to the obnoxious critics, and let the critics draw their own con-
clusions. But Krammaus resisted adamantly—"Not on your life!
Dad, I'm your son, but you can't ask *this* of me," he said, putting a
special emphasis on "this," as if the writer were suggesting that he
perform an indecent act. My friend even thought up a trick: he invited a number of his colleagues over just at the hour when
Krammaus was expected to arrive. But Krammaus, somehow having sensed the trap, didn't come; only later he said, "Dad, I never
expected *this* of you!" He uttered these words in such a voice that
the writer felt ashamed. Even I, his best friend, had never seen
him, not even once. I didn't even believe in the existence of
Krammaus and I remember dropping some ironic comments about

my friend's "primitive metaphors."

If even I didn't believe that he existed, then what could be expected of others? I can imagine that my friend had been driven to despair: testimony to the veracity of his life's work existed but was completely useless, serving solely as a private little joy. The writer hesitated for a long time, then decided on an extreme solution: he would murder his son and then invite a number of writers and critics over—those who having taken a look at his novel would be able to identify the corpse and attest that Krammaus had actually existed. Undoubtedly, a heroic step; although I found his attitude toward Krammaus disturbingly similar to that which he bore toward his manuscript—if it's no good, it must be destroyed. And my friend did destroy Krammaus. But the terrible irony of fate was that on that day everyone he knew, including me, was either out of town or busy; there was no one who could serve as a witness. Instead, the police arrived. What happened next, you already know. My friend acted as befits a real writer: he sacrificed himself in order to prove that his work was sincere.

You see, one Beckett has just been searching for Ionesco. Another Beckett is taking a stroll at the zoo right now. Having gone up to the rhino's cage, he stares in great surprise at the cage's inhabitant and then whacks himself on the head. "Ionesco!" Beckett cries. The rhinoceros shakes its head in denial and sighs. But Beckett protests, "If I want you to be Ionesco then I say that you are Ionesco and you will be Ionesco!" Ionesco removes the rhinoceros mask and replies, "But I am Ionesco. Truly." Beckett takes fright and runs away.

A variation: all that you have just read is nothing but a dull parable, an allegorical game about the mysterious power of the signifier. The rhino really was Ionesco, objectively, as well as subjectively, for some overly erudite and not particularly witty zoo-keeper was immersed up to his ears in Ionesco's *Rhinoceros* at the time of the rhino's birth and named the animal Ionesco.

Another variation: the second variation is also nothing but a literary-historical allusion. What if *Ionesco* (for example, *ioohnheschoo* sounds African, doesn't it?) really means "rhinoceros" in the language of some African tribe? Who can know them all, these languages? There have been cases like this. In 1916, some Frenchified Romanian (by the way, the spitting image of Ionesco), who went by the obscure name of Tzara, substituted for all possible languages the lone word *DADA*. Later, he was completely crushed, having found out that *dada* means "the holy cow's tail" in the language of the African Kru people. He was crushed not because of "the tail," but because the word that in his understanding encompassed *all* possible words in *all* possible languages actually signified *one* mere tail of one mere cow. Tzara was also crushed because he had understood *dada* to signify a grand and all-encompassing nothing, but now, as it turned out, it wasn't nothing but solely and precisely the holy cow's tail. The whole world, everything and nothing, was under the cow's tail—it was enough to drive you crazy! But, then again, what a cow!

The rhinoceros-gray, angular, gigantic, seventh-story, bright and yellowish square tempts me: one day I must clarify what is actually hiding (is it hiding?) behind this window; why the lights are on night after night; yet I sit gloomily and do nothing to solve the mystery; I'm thinking about the letters, these damned letters. Maybe the interest of the letters' author is to entangle me in my thoughts so that I can't disengage myself from them, so that I can think of nothing else except the letters. I didn't save the second letter, either, for I still don't understand anything; having established the fact that the second letter was written by another person (the handwriting is different and the language has a different intonation, somewhat flattering, somewhat ironical; I tossed it in the garbage). "Hello again," it said. "We already know how you, our pride and joy, settle accounts with our letters, we knew this even before you, we know many things before you do, but that's just foolishness, dear, the lovely nonsense which constitutes most of what we do or what has happened to us, is it clear to you now, well, nothing is really clear, we know this too, we're always one step ahead of you, you'll probably be waiting for the next letter impatiently, again we know about all this before you do, don't worry, you'll get it, the little letter will come, it will come, this I promise you right away so that you don't risk anticipating in vain." And so it continued for two whole pages; once again some joker had taken pains to dirty the white page's innocence with gibberish. However, if the first letter seemed absolutely senseless and incomprehensible, then I detected beyond the apparent nonsense and flattering irony something more than cautionary—it was threatening. I felt these threats but all my efforts to thoroughly analyze the text with which he (or they) was threatening me, to determine what sin I had committed to deserve his agitation, even which words were the threatening ones, were unsuccessful; there was nothing concrete, all my efforts were fruitless. I didn't like the letter, not at all. I wouldn't want to say that I was frightened—I even let an ironic grin creep across my face as I threw the letter into the garbage, but actually the grin was only a mask, a mask to protect me from my own thoughts. The letter with its unintelligible and insignificant rigmarole took root in me, and so profoundly that all efforts to rid myself of it were in vain. It wasn't really fear; it was more a fidgety, expectant restlessness. Possibly, this was what the anonymous author was waiting for, which, let me remind you, he didn't conceal one bit: to induce me to think about him; to reach a state in which his shadow dwelled within me continuously; to force me to wait for the third letter day after day—and, I must admit, he succeeded in achieving this by marvelously simple means, with an emptiness filled with words. I gave up all efforts to detect any clues with the help of logic; I comforted myself with the thought that somehow everything would clear up: I'll receive the third letter, the problem will resolve itself. By the way, the stamp on the second letter wasn't canceled, either. I still remember my reaction to the first letter: at first I waited for the next one nervously, peering into the mailbox every day, rationalizing my behavior by pretending that I was rushing to get my hands on the latest newspapers, not admitting to myself that I was actually looking for the letter; later I decided that it was really a silly joke and my measly brain couldn't see the humor. I chose the most credible explanation, even though it didn't explain a thing; I gradually began to forget the letter. But now, along with the second letter, the first one reemerged, and everything started all over, but with the difference that now I knew a third letter would follow. I ran down to check the mailbox every day; sometimes I would decend several times—the letter's author could toss it into my mailbox at any time; he could deliver it even after midnight. And just before going to bed I would go down to check one last time, for the image was vivid in my mind—the letter's author emerges from the dark and, looking around, he slides the envelope stealthily into the mailbox and quickly disappears. In a word, I had fallen under his power.

Is Beckett alive?—It's not just curiosity, it's a matter of principle: it's one thing to act in the plays of a deceased master when you are certain that the author won't play any more jokes on you, but to play a role created by a living person—that's something entirely different. If Beckett is alive, he could, for example, write the play *The Coming of Godot,* which tells the story of how the long-awaited Godot suddenly appears from the crowd of spectators and triumphantly climbs onto the stage, sweeping away Vladimir and Estragon with a single wave of his hand. Even more: Beckett could publicly admit that *Waiting for Godot* is a grandiose mystification spanning many decades, bait for intellectuals which they've obediently swallowed; according to his (Beckett's) design, the person named Godot hasn't disappeared anywhere—for forty years already he's been hiding in the audience. That would mean that Beckett knew about me even before I was born, and I would have to feel like both a component and victim of Beckett's plan.

What part (how much) of me belongs to Beckett's Godot and what part to myself? If I die, will Godot die as well? Am I the only Godot in the whole world? Or maybe all directors, who knows how long ago, have decoded Beckett's plan, and in each production of the play there's a Godot sitting among the spectators, who signs a separate receipt upon receiving his salary? Maybe there are even performances where all spectators play the part of Godot, even though they don't know about each other's existence. Maybe in his twisted mind, Beckett has even foreseen that a time will come when one of the many Godots won't be sitting in the audience anymore and he'll climb up onto the stage and create *The Coming of Godot* with the participation of Beckett himself?

Should I buy a dog and name him Beckett? Then I would know with 100 percent certainty the year, month, day, hour and minute of Beckett's death, unless the creature kills me first. Or should I name the dog Godot?

I had a good friend, a writer, who shot himself to death; to be more precise, he shot himself but died a good while later. He had the tendency to polish his works to perfection; more precisely, he made an attempt, for he never really understood what perfection was. My friend tried to find out through experimentation: he wrote a story, read it, said it was garbage but that he'd struggle with it a bit more. Then he rewrote the story, read it, scratched his head and said that he hadn't reached perfection yet, that it still required work. Then he rewrote it again, read it over again, and announced that it was complete rubbish and still a long way from perfection. Etc. And so he would toil and tamper with the work until disgust overwhelmed him; then my friend could no longer touch it, much less think about perfection anymore. Finally, he threw his composition into the garbage. "Tossing a manuscript into the garbage," in my friend's jargon, meant handing the manuscript over to the publishers. By the way, the critical reviews, or, as my friend used to say, "God's voice from the garbage can," were usually favorable and at times even full of praise, lauding especially his professional approach to language. Having spent a great deal of time on short stories, writing one or two a year, my friend began work on a novel entitled *Muteness*. It was about a family: one day, a husband finds his wife in bed with another man, and from this moment on he stops talking to her. Understandably, the wife no longer talks to him either. And thus they remain for thirty years. The husband's inner monologues alternate with the wife's in the novel; however, interestingly enough their mutual muteness doesn't interfere with their harmonious coexistence. Eventually, they both come almost simultaneously to the conclusion that talking makes no sense anyway; a person can only harm himself by uttering words, because in response he is barraged by a reciprocal flood of words that literally knocks him to the ground. And so they seclude themselves in their silence; they cease to talk to others around them; even their inner monologues become more and more fragmentary and vague until they break off altogether. The novel ends with an episode in which the neighbors call the police, alarmed by the fact that this couple is never heard, nor has anyone seen them emerge from their apartment. Breaking in, the police discover that the apartment is empty. The couple's belongings haven't been touched; clothes are still hanging in the closet; their passports and a large wad of money are still lying in the drawer of their desk, but the couple has vanished without a trace. One of the policemen who is preparing to write a report carelessly brushes a moldy slice of bread still showing teeth marks off the kitchen table. The novel comes to an end with this scene. But the slice of bread mentioned so casually is eloquent enough for the observant reader: the very last fragment of the husband's inner monologue has consisted of one single word—"bread"; on the other hand, the wife's train of thought comes to an end with the words "he. mouth. teeth." (It should be explained here that as the novel comes to a conclusion both the wife and the husband have begun to think in simple, fragmented sentences—their vocabulary dwindles and more complex logical connections between words disintegrate; this process reaches a climax in the last pages, which consist only of nouns in the singular and plural.) The conclusion is obvious: they've stopped talking, they've imperceptibly lost the ability to be conscious of themselves; no longer conscious of themselves, they dwindle into nothingness. The husband doesn't even get a chance to finish eating his bread.

But my friend didn't like the novel. "Even a piece of shit has to possess the elegance of perfection where language is concerned," he used to declare. He worked for a year, two years, five; he rewrote the novel dozens of times (the first page—at least a hundred times), and there was no end to his profuse talk about "his rough drafts," as he put it. My friend detached himself from the world more and more; on the rare occasions when we happened to meet up, he fidgeted nervously and babbled, then came to an abrupt stop, announcing that he must "work," and rushed home. After that, my friend lost his mind. What else could he do? He battled with the novel like a true writer, but in the long run it beat him: he couldn't force the novel to stop, couldn't find the true course; the novel overmastered him. He attempted suicide, but this procedure, too, was far from perfect. He didn't have enough money, nor was he connected well enough to buy a real pistol; he went to the market and bought a frightening shooting apparatus that some locksmith had assembled from an electric hammer he had stolen at work. A detent and a cocking mechanism were welded to it. The bullet didn't blow his brains out; it lingered between the lobules, cerebral hemispheres and folds of his brain for a long time until it came to a stop somewhere in the back of the head—amid the nerves of the speech center. The surgeons patched him up a little, but they were afraid that digging around in the brain to extract the bullet would kill him. And so he came to after his unsuccessful suicide and realized that he'd lost his ability to speak. He was completely dumb.

But my friend's wife had no intention of following the example of her spouse; on the contrary, she wouldn't keep her mouth shut; she talked and talked and talked, not stopping even in her sleep, as if she wanted to vent everything that had built up in her soul during the long years when my friend was working on his novel *Muteness*. To keep from losing his mind, he tried to keep his wife from talking. It's hard to imagine what my friend was thinking then about his novel and ideal perfection; if you ask me, he became even crazier by failing to shut up his wife. She, on the other hand, disappointed about their never-ending lack of money, stole the novel, which was clearly a far cry from perfection, and submitted it for publication. Soon after that, my friend died—supposedly from a stroke that was a consequence of his suicide attempt, though I suspect that what he was really doing was trying to protest by choosing the most extreme kind of dumbness. His wife requested the following inscription on his tombstone: "Now I must be forever silent." If you ask me, the hint of a sneer lurked behind these words.

Yet another variation: once again Beckett is looking for Ionesco in order to brag to him about his Nobel Prize. He looks for Ionesco at his home—it's vacated; he looks for him at the Writers' Union; he looks for him in the cafés—nothing; he runs through the city, wanders through all the side streets, walks through courtyards, sneaks into basements, up stairways into attics; peers into elevator shafts, under bridges, in the murky waters of the city canal; he goes to the theater, the cinema, the opera, the ballet (God forbid he ever might have written a ballet!—Beckett thinks with horror), calls the hospitals and the morgue. Ionesco isn't anywhere to be found; he's vanished into thin air. Who knows in what circles of hell the bastard's hanging out! But then it occurs to Beckett that he hasn't tried the zoo. Wandering through the zoo from cage to cage, he looks and sees a rhinoceros giving a heavy, doleful sigh. "Ha! So that's where you've been hiding!" Beckett cries out joyfully, climbs over the fence and starts to pull dollar bills out from his pockets, wads of them. The rhino shakes his head skeptically, sighs, and spears Beckett with his only horn, tossing him back over the fence. Then it eats the dollar bills.

At the time, Ionesco was shooting rhinos not far from Nairobi. He was accompanied by a professional hunter, a mute member of the Kru tribe by the name of Dante.

The illuminated square tempts me irresistibly. One evening, I gathered my courage and decided to find out once and for all what it was about. To tell you the truth, I couldn't admit my intentions to myself; I buried my plan somewhere behind the glittering curtains of other thoughts; I didn't let it materialize into words. I was afraid of being disappointed—what if there was nothing on the seventh floor? Nothing like *that?* I wasn't sure what I was hoping to see there; in any event, not a common hack sitting at his typewriter, or an artist who, noticing me, would try to hide behind his easel in surprise, or, for example, a mundane group of bums who were boozing it up night after night in their attic. Still, I left my apartment precisely because of the illuminated window, even though I had almost convinced myself that I would just go down to the mailbox to take a peek and see whether a letter might have popped up. No letter. *Such a lovely evening,* I said to myself, *as if it were created especially for a little walk before going to bed.* Actually, it was only a pretext; I don't care for aimless wandering through the streets, not even on lovely evenings; I'd much rather sit by the window drowning inside myself and not seeing what's happening on the street, peering at the gray giant's seventh-floor window. I walked a considerable distance, making a detour of several blocks; later I realized that I was initially maintaining a rapid pace, almost a half-trot, but that as I neared the place where I believed I would find the entrance to the courtyard of the gray house (only from the other side), I slackened my pace. I lingered for a moment by the gateway through which I could see the poorly lit courtyard and some of the windows on the first floor of the gray house; I told myself I'd just gone out to take a walk and that I would have nothing to do with the lighted window on the seventh floor this evening. However, when I spotted a narrow gap between two houses on the way, like a little side street, I couldn't hold myself back and entered the courtyard, nervously looking around to see if some latecomer living in one of the surrounding houses wasn't out and about—someone who might ask me what I was looking for, who'd stare after me to see whether I pissed on a wall. There was a gigantic truck parked in the courtyard, so huge that I wondered how it had squeezed through the narrow gap between the two buildings. *The driver must be a real professional,* I decided; I suddenly recalled that I'd noticed the truck's grille from my apartment window, for the dumpy building in front of it couldn't conceal everything; apparently, the driver lived somewhere around here and left his vehicle in the courtyard at night. I looked up. The seventh-story window emitted a wan, yellowish light. With sudden resolution I went up to the building's door, which for some reason was unusually wide, a double door, just like a garage door, and I discovered that it was locked but that the locking mechanism could be disengaged by punching in a code. How long was I to hang around in this courtyard? There was nothing left to do but return home.

A letter—the third—was waiting for me in the mailbox. At first, having skimmed it, I didn't notice anything peculiar, just monotonous babble as in the first two letters. Having reread it more carefully, I still didn't really notice, didn't really catch the hints, but I did catch hints indicating that hints were possible—something tangible was emerging through the babble, as if the author had wanted to say something but his message always slipped off to the side, one empty word would pull along with it an entire string of similar words—and so on to infinity, an endless shuffling around and around. But there were hints, separate words that brought to memory a friend of mine, a writer of mystery novels—he's dead now. A few trifles were mentioned in the letter, completely trivial and meaningless; but the fact that these trifles were known only to the two of us (for instance, an aphorism that my friend had once uttered and then forgotten—"The head is an unusual and unnatural extension of the spine"), this bestowed upon them an unexpected significance in the letter. Of course, I didn't believe for a moment that my friend could be writing me letters from the grave; I did not allow such thoughts. However—and this is the strange part—it's not that I ruled this possibility out entirely, but that I tried to break it down logically by asking myself things like: where could he get paper there? envelopes? writing utensils? how could the letters reach my mailbox? how did he move the pen if his hands had long since decomposed? (A frightful sight: yellowish-white finger bones holding a pen.) And why is he writing this rubbish? Why can't he put everything down simply and clearly? Foolish questions, of course, but in such ridiculous circumstances a person becomes a fool himself: three absurd letters had driven me to the point where I was asking myself questions that were impossible to answer. If I had two or let's say five answers, I'd have my doubts for a long time, hesitate, but in the end I would choose one anyway, and in the meantime I would try to forget the others, persuading myself that from the very beginning there has been only one correct answer. However, I had only one answer—that letters were coming from beyond the grave, and this answer was useless, dismissable without hesitation. I live a rather lonely and secluded life to begin with, but these letters cut me off from the world even more; they locked me in a cage whose bars consisted of the hours and days of waiting for the letters, and with every letter the cage became narrower. But maybe all people receive similar letters, and this is precisely why they are so reserved and unsociable, because no one wants to admit that he's become a fool because of a foolish predicament. Everyone remains silent and thinks that he's been chosen to be the victim of words that come from beyond the grave. Therefore, I can't be sure of anything—as soon as I'm sure of anything, as soon as I divide the world into little squares and begin to play hopscotch on them, I'll have lost myself; I'll have succumbed to the oppression of words.

I had a good friend, a writer; he was not only a writer but also a member of parliament, and on top of that he had a very popular, I'd even say common, first and last name—at one time in the same parliament there were about five or six MPs with the same names. This time let's call him Jānis Bērziņš (here I would like to stress that any connection with any real Jānis Bērziņš is purely coincidental). Jānis Bērziņš was blown to pieces by a Kurdish terrorist when my friend was sent to Turkey in order to arrange the purchase of three tons of fezzes. Jānis Bērziņš was very fond of fame; for example, he greatly enjoyed making TV appearances; he impaled himself on the microphone the moment he noticed a TV camera; thus my friend could be seen on the screen every night, wiggling like a plump fish under the heat lamp of an aquarium. That's probably why he wasn't satisfied with the short-lived popularity that the role of MP offered. My friend wanted to achieve immortality as well, and wrote a wonderful novel. The novel was about an artist who was carried away with painting nudes and for many years painted only one model, his lover. When the woman finally aged and her physical resemblance to the paintings faded, the artist strangled her so that she wouldn't compromise the paintings. The novel begins with an episode in the cemetary, where the artist has arrived soon after the funeral in order to bid farewell to his model in private; the plot takes shape in the form of memories that pass through the artist's mind as he sits on a bench by the grave. Having left the graveyard, the artist suddenly sees a woman who he thinks would make an ideal model; he rushes over to her, introduces himself, strikes up a conversation, and asks her to let him paint her in the nude; and the woman, after hesitating for a moment, agrees. Actually, the plot isn't even important—it was more important that the author's first and last name was on the cover—Jānis Bērziņš. But there are hundreds of Jānis Bērziņšes in Latvia! Which of them was the author of the novel? It even crossed my mind that the so-called Jānis Bērziņš was an obfuscation, that someone else was using this name as a disguise, some author who was already well-known, who had put on the mask of Jānis Bērziņš with the elegant and respectable élan of an honorable literator, placing himself in line with hundreds of other Jānis Bērziņšes just for the fun of it, to make fun of the readers. If it suddenly occurred to some beginner by the name of Jānis Bērziņš to write a novel, the first thing he would do would be to rid himself of the preposterous first and last name. But then a certain journalist turned up (by the way, a good friend of mine whose name was Jānis Bērziņš), and loudly asked the parliament member in an interview—could it be that MP Jānis Bērziņš was also the writer Jānis Bērziņš? I have a feeling that my friend—the parliament member—couldn't control his lust for fame, although he tried to preserve his anonymity as the novel's author, for he proudly declared that he himself was not the novel's author but that Jānis Bērziņš (the writer) was a good friend of his, and that if Jānis Bērziņš (the journalist) so desired, he'd try to convince Jānis Bērziņš (the writer) to agree to an interview with Jānis Bērziņš (the journalist). Soon afterward, the phone rang in Jānis Bērziņš's apartment. It was Jānis Bērziņš himself on the phone. (Later my friend told me that in order to disguise his voice he had smoked a whole pack of cigarettes within an hour, thereby acquiring a strange hoarseness, and during the conversation he had chewed on hard candy to the point of nausea.) But Janis Berzins' cooperation with Jānis Bērziņš didn't end with this interview: it turned out that Jānis Bērziņš's life story was absolutely fascinating, and Jānis Bērziņš convinced him to write his auto-biography. It's possible that without the persuasion of Jānis Bērziņš this truly absorbing book might never have come to be. I remember that there was a wonderful part where Jānis Bērziņš told the story of how, in order to get from Munich to Hamburg, he had stopped a small truck on the highway. It turned out that three Catholic monks had been transporting a traveling exhibition in the small truck—holograms depicting the best-known sculptures of the Virgin Mary. In the course of the trip, it emerged that all three monks were gay (Jānis Bērziņš related in detail some piquant scenes of jealousy and attempts to seduce him), and, having gotten to know the monks better, Jānis Bērziņš found out that they had formed a sect that was preparing to reform the Christian faith (one of the monks liked to be called Dr. Mr. Luther, Jr.). The essence of the new religion was rooted in the thesis that the Virgin

Mary was the world's first transsexual, and that she had become one not with the help of the surgeon's scalpel but of God's personal finger. Actually, that is, Mary had originally been a man—and the miracle wasn't that Mary had become pregnant as a virgin (such incidents have been frequently noted in history and can be explained in purely physiological terms without the intervention of God); the real miracle was that a man had turned into a woman (via this man-woman, the monks also explained the Holy Trinity), and in those days this could not have been possible without the intervention of God. But that's not what I wanted to tell you about. To make it brief, my friend wrote Jānis Bērziņš's autobiography, and it was so brilliant that it would make any writer jealous. The last sentences of the book were the following: "I have always known that someday I would write the story of my life. Now this has been done. There's nothing more wonderful than living out one's own novel." However, after this, when Jānis Bērziņš was blown sky-high by Kurdish terrorists, the new version of his auto-biography came out. There it was indicated that he was not Jānis Bērziņš at all, the author of the book about the maniac artist; he had been urged to pose as Jānis Bērziņš by Jānis Bērziņš with his interview's absurd question; furthermore, Jānis Bērziņš didn't have the faintest idea who this mysterious Jānis Bērziņš really was. Who cared? His invented Jānis Bērziņš was so real that if some Jānis Bērziņš were now to show up claiming to be more real than the real one, no one would believe him (the words of Jānis Bērziņš turned out to be prophetic: a journalist by the name of Jānis Bērziņš, a good friend of mine, really did try to expose Jānis Bērziņš as an impostor, but in comparison with the wonderful autobiography his protests seemed feeble and contrived). In his new autobiography, Jānis Bērziņš gave a tedious and detailed account of his life, set against an historical background, starting with his first childhood memories all the way to his gloomy premonitions on the eve of the tragic trip to Turkey; the book ended with: "Even though I've never felt any special calling to pursue writing, I've still always known that someday I would write the story of my life. There's nothing more wonderful than living out one's own novel."

Beckett isn't alive; at least this Beckett isn't alive; he's a little figure cut out of paper (true, brightly colored paper). Besides that, he's fictitious—just like Ionesco, just like the rhinoceros; little figures on a white piece of paper on which were I to feel like it, I could imagine more—for example, an admirably regular street and network of side-streets, or a zoo. The figures could be arranged in varied combinations, forming a handsome, geometrically precise triangle—Beckett, the rhinoceros, Ionesco—to invent symbols of correlation, names that would bring my games to life. These flat little figures are extremely attractive because you can do whatever pops into your head; you can write, for example, Beckett, Ionesco, The Rhinoceros (or, even better, b(B)eckett, i(I)onesco, t(T)he r(R)hinoceros; you can cut out another little figure—Godot, who would introduce the element of chance into the relationship between Beckett, Ionesco and the rhinoceros: let's say that Beckett is waiting for Godot (or at least for the idea of Godot), but the rhino comes, strangely similar to Ionesco (or Ionesco suddenly loses his mask, and it turns out that he's the rhinoceros, who, driven by starvation, has come to try to squeeze some money out of Beckett). You could also do the following: make the little figures even more alive than the real Beckett, or more precisely, more alive than my conception of Beckett, which has been formed from the remains of all kinds of myth and legend. Actually, the only real way of bringing Beckett to life would be to kick him out of all these myths and legends so that it would be impossible to decipher where the real Beckett is hiding and where my conception of him is hiding—and the little paper figures are wearing mysterious names instead of clothes; that could mean a great deal and at the same time nothing at all. In other words, having taken down what Joyce dictated, and having replied to all the letters addressed to Joyce, Beckett sat down at the table and started thinking about where he should hide Godot.

The world could probably fall apart, but the window on the seventh floor of the gray block house would continue to shine night after night. This time, I deliberate and decide to go and check out the situation there, to set myself at ease, bring an end to my delirious and senseless nights in the chair by the window; it was a little after midnight; in the house with the number that I can't remember appended with the letter "b," the rest of the windows had already become dark, even casual passersby wouldn't give me much trouble, and I prepared for my walk just as I would for an expedition to the other side of town: I dressed carefully, wrapping a shawl around my neck; I put a pack of cigarettes and a lighter in my pocket, brushed my hair, inspected myself in the mirror, felt satisfied with my appearance (I even thought: *everything's in order, now I can go*). Having gone through the dumpy two-story building along a narrow, unlit corridor, I came out into the already familiar courtyard where the huge truck was still standing, though now it was parked close to the gray house's entrance, but both the back doors of the truck and the house's wide doors were open—as if some large object had just been carried from the truck into the house, but the movers hadn't returned to shut the doors and move the truck off to the side. I looked up: sure enough, all windows were dark; only the window on the seventh floor was shining with a wan yellowish light, which meant that the object was obviously carried straight to the mysterious room where night after night the light never went out. (Maybe the truck stops by here every night, I thought to myself, and every night the movers carry all kinds of objects up the stairs, big, heavy things that can fit only into the gigantic truck; and maybe precisely because these things are delivered every night the light never goes out on the seventh floor.) The last time I was in the courtyard, the entrance to the gray house was locked; therefore, having decided not to pass up a favorable opportunity, I squeezed into the narrow gap between the truck and the wall of the house and came out in a stairwell that was lit by a weak lightbulb; for some reason the place seemed wastefully huge, like a meeting hall, so spacious that the doors of the apartments and the top of the staircase were hidden in the dark. I was already preparing to make my way toward the stairs when a man, or, more precisely, a dude, a big strong dude wearing a plaid shirt with rolled-up sleeves and a rubber apron, came trotting down, skipping every other step. *A real butcher!*—I thought. Having caught sight of me, he appeared as confused as I, but in a moment he regained his senses and almost threateningly, with his left shoulder thrust forward, marched toward me. "What are you doing here!" he whispered ferociously. "I've never seen you here! What are you doing here!" I stepped back a little, but then I realized that the thick-set man had no right to ask me what I was doing here; maybe I'd come here to visit a friend, or maybe I was an architect who was interested in buildings of the first half of the century, and so I snapped back: "What's it to you! I'm looking for something, and if I feel like it, I'll look for it until I find it!" "There's nothing for you to look for here!" the big guy continued to hiss and nudged me step by step toward the door. "There's nothing for you to look for here, get lost while there's still time, the quicker, the better! Out, out, out, do you hear me?" I must confess, the man scared me a bit; after all, it's no fun rubbing shoulders after midnight in a murky stairwell with a big, threatening, hissing man who looks like a bona fide butcher, and I quickly squeezed back into the courtyard and hurried home. Glancing over my shoulder, I noticed that the big guy had come out into the courtyard and was eyeing me suspiciously. I couldn't fall asleep for a long time that night and tossed and turned in my bed, feeling ashamed that I'd run away; and the light in the window on the seventh floor continued to shine all the way to the crack of dawn.

I had a good friend, a writer; for many years he worked on a novel, if that's what it could be called, and its name was simple and straight-forward—*The City* (my friend explained that this was a temporary title, that the real title would materialize with time). It was a strange novel—no plot, no action, no characters. The gargantuan manuscript, many thousands of pages long, was a description of some gigantic City. Every day, with enviable diligence, my friend set aside a couple of hours for the novel, adding one or two pages in which he described yet another place of interest in the City, and so year after year he created his City building by building, block after block (it's hard to imagine who'd have the strength to conquer this unimaginably boring monster; even I could not get through more than a couple dozen pages in one sitting, and there were thousands of pages). And the City was completely empty; it was not known who had built it, whom it was meant for, or, in general, whether anyone had ever lived in it. As my friend used to say, the City is "ru-ins hidden in the future." To a certain extent, the City really did resemble a mass of ruins, but it wasn't clear whether it had crumbled from the passage of time or from the efforts of man, or whether perhaps it had always been in ruins; furthermore, it was difficult to make out whether the City was really in ruins or merely something similar to ruins; I never quite managed to comprehend whether the City was a city at all, and, if it wasn't, then what on earth was it? In any case, the buildings whose descriptions I had enough patience to read were, for the most part, uninhabitable. Some were shaped by slabs of granite or marble dumped into piles, and they reminded one of gigantic stone anthills with passages so low and narrow that a human being could move around in them only by crawling. Others consisted of uniform windows of various shapes, so many that it seemed that the walls had been erected for the sole purpose of serving as window frames. Still other buildings contained four high walls that enclosed countless little interior courtyards placed at various levels (some were so small that it was possible to stand in them only on one foot), which were connected by stairs; there were also buildings that were composed entirely of stairs, without a single horizontal span; in some you couldn't find one right angle—even the floors were aslant; then there were rooms without entrances or exits; there were countless blind alleys and circular passages or streets; there were, of course, labyrinths and dead-end stairways; there were vertical streets and squares, and horizontal building walls from which green grass sprung. In other words, the City was a fantastic chaos into which my friend crammed everything he could possibly imagine (or had stolen from books and paintings). About the City's dimensions my friend wrote: "The

City's space was constant: no matter what hill you climbed, you would always see the same view—the City stretched from horizon to horizon." With this phrase my friend was saying that the City was endless and that the novel he had written was endless as well, and on top of that you could write this novel's beginning from any point—depending on your mood. Once, bewildered by the work's immensity, I asked my friend whether he even remembered the buildings that he had described in the beginning of the novel so many years ago. He shrugged his shoulders, chuckled, and replied, "Why should I stuff my memory full of such nonsense?" And, placing his hand on the voluminous manuscript, he said, "My guidebook is always at hand." "In that case, yours is the most useless guidebook in the world," I noted, adding, "There's not even the tiniest bit of order in it, no system, everything's topsy-turvy. You'd never be able to find your way around in the City with the help of your guidebook. You could have at least sketched out a plan. . . ." "What do I need a plan for?" he asked. "Who has any need for planned chaos? You see, if I had a plan, I'd lose all interest in my novel and in the City. It would be an insanely boring undertaking, to be writing ten years from now what you'd planned ten years earlier. On the other hand, now I don't know what I'll see . . . what I'll write tomorrow evening, not to mention what will come to be in a year. I don't even remember what I wrote a few weeks ago, and sometimes I re-read what I've written before with great interest. The City lives inside me. . . ." Soon after this conversation, my friend began to vanish—at first for a day or two, then later he couldn't be found for weeks at a time, and I figured that he had found himself a lover. Then he vansihed altogether—he left the apartment, left his belongings, and was gone, taking with him only *The City*'s manuscript. Somewhere at the bottom of my heart, I believe that my friend moved to the City: day after day he wanders around, losing his way in the jumble of streets, always discovering something never seen before, and this is even more attractive because it brings to memory something vaguely familiar created by him somewhere back in his past; he spends the night in marble anthills or in halls with slanted floors; he meditates outside buildings that are impossible to enter; he arranges expeditions to the peaks of immense pyramids or into the labyrinths of fantastically senseless basements, and he never knows what he will see when he peeks around the next corner. But it's possible that my friend has simply moved in with his lover, that he's burned *The City*'s manuscript in the stove and begun a new life.

Of course, there are no letters, and what's even clearer is that there's no beyond-the-grave mysticism. More precisely, there are letters, but they're not written by dead or failed writers; what's more, for some reason they just don't want to die, they're all living life to the fullest, if not in some other way, then in your consciousness: you're the one writing letters to yourself; desperately you try to compose a letter that won't disclose the fact that you yourself have written it, and so you write around in circles, attaching words to one another senselessly and stubbornly striving to say nothing; you sneak over to the mailbox and slip the letter through the narrow slit, and in a few hours you'll pull it out in foolish surprise. But games with oneself are always unsuccessful, and even the corps of corpses possessed with graphomania can't be much help here. Actually, there's nothing left for you to do but wither away night after night in your dusty apartment, on a chair by the window, peering at the illuminated window on the seventh floor of the building facing you, reciting to yourself endless texts that you never know how to finish properly, and trying to fill up the horrifying emptiness within you that no one else can fill. This emptiness within you is voracious: cheerfully it gobbles up everything that you feed it; it gobbles up all your stories—everything disappears into it as into a bottomless pit, and your efforts to fill it up with your experiences, your ideas, your illusions, the games you play with yourself are all fruitless; the emptiness doesn't get any smaller; in fact, it is growing, swelling, widening, threatening to gobble up what little is still left in you. What will it be called, that which is left over when the emptiness has gobbled up everything within you; what was the creature that concocted you without the slightest recourse to fantasy?

The world is becoming stifling, obtrusive; the world shoves me out of my apartment; in a moment I'm across the street, shuffling through the dark hallway, and then I'm in the courtyard, approaching the door of the gray house. This time, the truck has been parked in the corner of the courtyard, and the big man wearing a rubber apron is nowhere to be seen. Having looked up, as usual, and convinced myself that the window on the seventh floor is still lit, I give the door a nudge with my shoulder. The door, either by mistake or by mere chance, is unlocked. I step into the enormous stairwell and once again find myself amazed at its size; its proportions seem ridiculously spacious; the stairs are so wide that there's enough room to carry a grand piano easily up and down (there just might be a musician in the seventh-floor apartment, plunking away on his grand piano night after night; this thought hadn't occurred to me until now; perhaps the house was built specifically for pianists and composers so that they could move their instruments upstairs easily). I'm ascending, and I can't stop being impressed at the generous landings between the flights—enough room for a passenger car to turn around with relative ease—and I'm thinking about how huge the apartments must be if they're proportional to the landings. I climb slowly, constantly asking myself whether it's worth the effort; wouldn't it be wiser to put the window on the seventh floor out of my mind, go home, and go to bed? But I keep climbing. There's only one doorway on the seventh floor—an impressive double door, wide and high, with metal fittings like a barn door's. I push the handle cautiously, expecting it to be locked, expecting to turn around and head down back. But the door obeys the pressure of my hand and opens. I find myself gazing into a spacious attic crisscrossed with dusty beamwork; the floor is caked with a layer of pigeon droppings and slag; the only window is covered with paper, and a few bare light bulbs hang on long wires from the beams. An immense table nailed together from enormous wood planks sprawls under the lights in the middle of the room. It is encircled by ten or twenty heavyset men wearing identical rubber aprons. Among them I recognize the big dude in the plaid shirt who chased me out of the building. Large tin tubs, pots, and bowls have been placed near the table; a number of impressive cleavers have been propped up against the beams. A rhinoceros—a wonderful, gray-blue rhino, complete with horn and wrinkled skin—lies on the table, trussed up with ropes. With its legs wrenched apart, the beast has been rendered completely helpless; its snout is tightly wrapped in ropes; he can't open his mouth to bellow. The rhinoceros blinks his eyes; he's panting and twitching, struggling to free himself. The table shudders. One of the men is bent over the rhino; he's wielding a large knife, preparing to pierce the rhino's heart, or to slit its throat; two men hover nearby with bowls, waiting for the blood; the rest smoke in silence a little farther away. Having heard the creaking of the door, the men turn their eyes to me. I feel terribly uncomfortable; their gazes pierce me with cheerful curiosity.

Before I can manage to escape, the fellow with the large knife calls out to me, "What are you staring at? Come here and give us a hand!"

Jānis Einfelds

Jānis Einfelds (1967) arrived on the Latvian literary scene five years ago, taking readers and critics by surprise with his extraordinary view of the world and his original metaphors. The short prose published here is from his first book of stories, *Mēness bērns* (Moon Child). Einfelds creates a virgin cosmos of metaphors where gravity is void in terms of finding a "theme, subject, method," and the only time that exists is that of tales and myths.

In 1995 Einfelds's *Cūku grāmata* (Pig Book) was published and was met with conflicting reviews. According to one, Einfelds was writing what God was dictating to him, or, as another review mused, his writing was "clinical literature." *Cūku grāmata* is more or less autobiographical—an enormous parable about the life of pigs and human existence through the past, present, and future.

Jānis Einfelds lives with his mother, composer Maija Einfelde, and is still being treated for an injury sustained while serving in the Soviet army.

Cucumber Aria

On the national holiday, the flags flew from the flagpoles, even I could see that from the hospital ward. The holiday passed like a shudder. A couple of intoxicated voices sang during the night. Later I heard somebody had been stabbed over by the Freedom Monument. And somebody else had lost his concertina. Next day there was frost.

At the hospital everything seemed unhurried. The treatments stretched out useless and sticky, like putty. From the window of the ward I could see a meadow where foals with big clumsy feet were grazing. I like them, I can't help being the son of a thief. My father, who did time in the pen six times, died of bad homemade booze. He was buried in Kroni. Right after the wake everybody forgot him.

My older brother is also a thief. He ripped a handbag out of a woman's hands. Got caught. Served time in a penitentiary.

But I'm sitting here torturing flies on the windowsill. It's warm in the ward. I wish I had a jar of black currant jam, then my stomach would stop going on strike. Porridge and gruel stimulate your imagination, I vomit them up soon after eating. My brother is a chip off the old block—he and Dad both knew how to use a knife. It's a tool a guy has to know how to handle. Like it says in the song: "Oh knife, oh knife, light of my life! Cheeooo!"

In the sky I saw a dead starling. This might mean that the times are going to change; if you've been drinking homemade booze, you know the table is right.

They discharged me on the fifth. Did they cure my stomach?— Like hell they did! I don't have any place to live. I sleep in a woodshed. During the day, I sit by the river and spit in the water. I eat at a neighbor's house, her husband is an ex-con, too.

One day the woodshed turned out to be occupied. My brother was lying on the box. He jumped up and yelled:

"Great to see you!"

"I'm hungry! I'm very very hungry!"

We crawled into the garden of some kind of high-ranking government official, where a dog with an ungodly smell attacked us. Slash! My brother drew a razor across the dog's throat. A howl. Silence. Fur. A heavy body and lots of blood.

We picked cucumbers. Big. Green.

"Let me!" I said.

My brother nodded. I felt one of them. Wrinkled. I took a tentative little bite. Peel. Bitter. Hurriedly, bite by bite, I ate it all. The seeds in the middle were very sweet. The cucumbers were good, I often think of them. Especially tasty with sour cream. And with buttermilk. You can even make tea from the leaves. I can't, I don't have a hotplate. You can love cucumbers, only I don't know how. Voices. My brother got antsy. And I shit my pants. He dragged me by the collar. I was embarrassed, I'd have to wait till it dried.

He got arrested a week later. His hand had been wandering around in somebody else's pocket. It didn't bother me. I was hungry. But the cucumber season was over.

Again it's a national holiday and the flags are flying, as weak as the blood in my veins. I live in the woodshed. And chew on fir logs. I got splinters in my tongue. It swelled up. There was pus. But my stomach demanded its due.

I got caught when I smashed the windows of a kiosk. Then a cucumber-shaped vehicle took me somewhere. I don't know where. Maybe to the wonderland where everything gets shared—food, candy. As I thought about it and the sound of the car lulled me, I dozed off.

The Wonderful Bird

It happened at school. During breaks. That's when all the grades, all sorts of faces, mix in the hallways.

We were separated from the youngest kids of all. Starting with fourth grade, though, we met the little buggers face to face.

I was in eighth grade, and that year we were supposed to take these big final exams. The story is not about me, though. . . .

As a rule, we didn't pay much attention to the little kids, except for one, and you couldn't help noticing him. He was a fifth-grader. Between two little eyes that looked like the eyes of an old Chinaman, a big crooked nose jutted out as though it had been stuck there. The top row of his teeth was out of place and came down over his lower lip. The boy always tried to hide his "misbehaving" teeth, but when he forgot, there they'd be again. His thin arms were long, like whips.

He reminded me of a bird. A wonderful bird. I used to love watching titmice and sparrows. But he was different. He had flown here on a summer night, when the sun left a pink shadow in the sky.

Other kids in my grade also noticed him.

"Where did you fly in from? Is your mother an alligator or what?" they roared.

"He's a bird!" somebody said.

"No, a Pterodactyl!" everybody roared again.

That's how he got his nickname.

During recess, the Pterodactyl would flutter around, and we all felt like we had gotten lost in a prehistoric era.

Later I found out he lived in the boarders' dorm.

One time the Pterodactyl got a mark on his forehead. Here is what happened: he went into the toilet, and some smoker put a kiss on the Pterodactyl's forehead with his cigarette. After that, a razor danced around on his wretched little suit of clothes; the seam of his jacket opened its mouth wide. This was the last straw. His father came to school. Just as ugly, and plastered. Tiny red veins ornamented the father's cheeks and nose.

"When he grows up, the Pterodactyl will be just like his dad!" I thought and turned away.

After that, the weird-looking kid disappeared somewhere. . . .

Years passed. I was working as a clerk in a government office. One day, on my way home from work, I noticed somebody towering above people's heads. I hurried closer. And saw—the Pterodactyl. He hadn't changed a bit, still the same bird.

"Take me with you!" I called.

He shook his head, receded in the distance and vanished in the sky.

The Ice Age began. None of us had time to crawl into our caves. We were buried by gray snow.

Fate

Each of us has a different fate. That's what Grandma told her grandson, little Charlie. He could hardly understand what she had said, for he was little. All he knew was that everybody—Grandma, Dad, and Mom—lived happy lives, except that sometimes an argument would be touched off. They lived on the first floor of a wooden house. An asphalt-covered street wound past it. Now and then a car came humming along. The word *fate* alighted in Charlie's head, bounced back and forth uneasily. It was something scary.

Then Edward appeared in their neck of the woods. He had a goatee, and he wore a dark tattered trench coat, a hat with holes in it, almost as though a bullet had pierced it, and boots so old that they "showed their teeth." Edward had a habit of creeping up to the house from the street side and looking in the window to see what was going on inside. Charlie's parents said that Edward, who had been lost, was back again. And they chased him away from the window. When Charlie saw him, he got scared and thought that this was what fate looked like. He was terrified: What if fate climbed in through the window? That would be the end. And the boy clung feverishly to his grandma's skirts. That's how Edward got the nickname "Fate."

Charlie got older, and his fear of fate subsided. It was funny when Edward tried to pal around with Charlie's friends. Once a wind sprang up and tore Fate's hat from his head. Fate rushed after it. But Fate—why, Fate was bald on top. How they all laughed!

Now, when Fate peered in the window, Charlie would stick out his tongue. Before he even reached his teens, a tattooed Mickey Mouse appeared on Charlie's chest. His parents scolded him. What else could they do?

Life went somersaulting furiously along, though to Charlie it felt slow. He didn't even notice that his feet would often carry him to places full of fun—where there were adventures that made your head spin, and sleepless nights. Often the devil's brew would go to Charlie's head. It felt as if mountains would be moved and Charlie would be the mover. Afterward, though, he'd return home—like the prodigal son. He would look contrite as his mother's reproaches came crashing down on his head. His father would sit there in silence. Charlie didn't have the courage to look his father in the eye. The avalanche was followed by his grandma's words:

"Don't let fate carry you piggyback!"

"Fate? Good idea!" said Charlie.

The next time he disappeared, Charlie caused a ruckus: he jumped piggyback on Edward's back. The little man fell down and hurt his nose. Grandma's prohibition had been heeded, besides which Charlie successfully eluded the guardians of law and order.

Later, Charlie disappeared for a much longer period. Rumor had it that Charlie had lost his head.

Soon the time came for him to go into the army, and Charlie gave Fate a blue windbreaker, for which Edward was mutely grateful.

Charlie was brought back in the fall . . . in a coffin. Without a head.

The room where the coffin stood resembled an upside-down testtube. Just as narrow, with high ceilings, no windows. An officer, smoking one cigarette after another, humming a tune and taking a look at his watch from time to time, paced around the coffin. It was obvious that the recumbent figure was a young man. His head had been torn away, neck and all; in its place were layers of gauze, affixed with worm-shaped steel hooks that penetrated the young man's shoulders. The gauze was stained, red as a Young Pioneer's tie.

Nobody noticed the arrival of the father and mother. "Gray and silent, like mice," thought the officer after a glance at them. The officer kept quiet. The father was the first to go up to the coffin, which looked like a huge and open can of sardines. The father tried to caress the sleeping figure, but he seemed to have gone blind—his hand caressed the edge of the cut. It was sharp, and blood appeared on his palm. The silence was interrupted by the officer; he asked if they recognized their son. There was no head so it was hard to say. The mother unbuttoned the supine man's coat and jacket. A smiling Mickey Mouse met their eyes. Charlie! Suddenly Charlie seemed to move.

The father bent down and whispered:

"Where're you gonna run to without a head, son? Your hands and feet won't obey you!"

Grandma wasn't there. She was irrevocably senile.

Charlie is dead and buried, but the family silently sits in their little wooden house, as though in a coffin. The father has gone crazy with grief and booze. He has no idea what goes on around him.

Fate, having crept up to the window, stands there in his blue windbreaker. Nobody sees him. Nobody chases him away. Yet Fate can feel: grief is gnawing at the foundations of the house—it wouldn't surprise him if the house collapsed altogether. There'd be shattering glass, splintering boards. Terrified by his own imagination, Fate flees. Galloping, galloping.

Etude with a Bullet

They say there is no God. That's not true.

There is. And everybody's got one.

There are craggy mountains on both sides. Once, two gods encountered each other here.

The young man's weapon reminded him of a fiddle. The fiddler played and received a bullet in his chest. He fell heavily and didn't get up. There was noise everywhere. God hovered above him. In the mountains dark men were scurrying—Afghans. They cursed the fiddler and his playing. But the fiddler's God won't allow them to sneer at the dead soldier, or to defile him. God drives away everyone.

Allah laughs in heaven. Not for long though. Having shown his teeth—a string of white pearls—he vanishes.

The fiddler lies there for several days. God keeps watch over him. He permits only insects to attend the dead man. Far away in the mountains a mortar roars and flashes its lightning. Nearby, a demolished tank dissolves in the dark.

In the gaping mouth of the fiddler, worms crawl about. His eyes are covered with flies. But God is with him. In his uniform pocket there is a snapshot and sediments of memories out of which an étude springs up.

The teddy bear blows a trumpet. The little rabbit skips and dances. The cars and tiny tractors drive around—they can be wound up. The teddy bear wants honey. But there is no honey. It's a windless day. The teddy bear is soft, and the teddy bear falls in love. He falls in love with a snapshot on which a boy with a white shirt is playing a violin. The walls are covered with posters and bright national flags. God allows everything, and the teddy bear blows the trumpet even louder. The rabbit has stopped dancing—the spring is broken. The teddy bear blows and waits for the boy. They wait so long they are all gradually covered with dust. Finally a spider comes to call and beats a slow tattoo on his belly. IIe's come to prepare a shroud.

The toy weapons are off to one side. A shell whizzes past the teddy bear. The teddy bear knows only honey and sweet pea bullets.

Nice Guy Moon

The Moon is a nice guy. I realized that right away, as soon as he arrived in town. He didn't go to the ear-splitting bar, but came to my house—climbed in the window of my room.

"Hallo there!"

"Hallo, hallo," he replied, went over to the mirror, and examined his pimply features. After a while, with chubby fingers, he squeezed white and dark pimples from his face, which resembled crumpled paper.

"What do you want?" I asked.

"Me? . . . Coffee with cream," he answered and licked his lips.

While I was busy at the stove, he studied the slightly yellowed photographs on the shelf. And uttered an occasional: "Ahem, ahem. . . ."

I brought the steaming coffee, slipped yesterday's paper under it, placed it on the slanting desk.

The Moon added his own cream, wouldn't let me do it. Having taken a sip, the Moon began to pant and unbuttoned his shirt collar.

"Do you love your sister?" I asked, looking at him slyly.

"Which one?" his eyes widened.

"Night!"

"Night? . . . Yes, I do. Only she's too old-fashioned. As soon as the watch begins, she begins to play her old part, as though times hadn't changed. Everybody's supposed to close their eyes and fall fast asleep—that's what she thinks as she walks through the empty streets. If she sees a light anywhere or any people having fun, her pressure goes up, she starts shaking as though she was having convulsions. Poor night! What I think is, her black velvet cloak is worn out, and the seams are splitting, too. . . ."

"Yes, night certainly does seem brighter, with some white gaps."

"Okay, I've had my coffee. I'm not going to talk anymore."

And the Moon started to rummage around among my books.

He was only interested in picture books and studied them till morning.

Toward morning I tugged at the Moon's whiskers, and he left me.

For a while he'd visit every night. Then he disappeared. I expected darkness, night, but there was no night. The magician with the three-cornered hat said the Moon had fallen on sad days.

I went looking for the Moon. I traveled through many countries, saw different cities, all kinds of forests, until I reached the holiest mountain cave. That's where the Moon lived.

The cave was narrow. A long velvet blanket lay on the ground. Bent over like a sickle, the Moon sat by a sooty, old-fashioned lantern.

"What's the matter? Why did you disappear?" I asked.

He looked up, eyes full of a red rain, and answered that his sister had died. I tended my sympathies. Apparently the Moon had inherited the worn-out black cloak.

"And now go away," he sighed. "I want to be alone!"

Night was gone. The constant light pretty nearly drove me crazy. Then I actually did go insane. I was locked in a cage—that's what they did to a great many people. I wasn't alone in the cage; I shared it with a stranger wrapped in a black cloak. I recognized him, but he didn't recognize me. Before the cage was sunk, I tugged at his whiskers one last time. After they sank the cage, everything became silent, including the river.

Only the children would point at the river and say: "That's where the Moon sank!"

As for me, nobody remembered me.

Dundaga Mornings

Summer shimmered like something about to overflow. Milk ran in streams. In the lakes and ponds, ducks fluttered around and the local boys went swimming in the raw. Among the reeds, past their feet, slid fish, eternally inaudible, expressing the essence of the depths.

In the meadows, there was the fragrance of hay, and in the barns was the fragrance of hay that had been harvested. In the valleys, you could hear the haymakers' songs. Along the highway, the wind carried sand, and spotted dogs led herds of cattle with due solemnity. All over Kurzeme there was sunburnt work, a witness to all truths.

Mākulis arrived one of those mornings. Everybody knew about it. They just didn't know where he had been wandering all this time. He spit on his hands and dove into the middle of haymaking, with all the neighbors helping each other. Morning—sleepy men, day—the heat of work, evening—fog and the fellows walking young girls out to the sound of concertinas. Some time later, Neimale had a boy, the spitting image of Mākulis. She called him Jānītis. Lots of people came for the baptism. The farmhouse was decorated with birch boughs, you could have a taste of Papa Miķelis's home-brewed beer. In the back room, one-eyed Jāzepelis tugged at the bellows of his concertina, you would have thought he'd tear its soul out. He could easily have struck up a dance.

But Dundaga wouldn't hear of it, for the morning was near.

Soon Neimale gave birth to little Olga, a second child for Mākulis. A daughter. Mākulis, eyes half-closed, sucked on his pipe with a cool smile.

As time went on, Neimale grew stout. Then Mākulis began fluttering around some of the livelier young women. And then wombs opened, babies came, midwives ran around in a lather; yet Mākulis never pitched in.

Little Jānītis and little Olga grew older and looked on their little brothers and sisters with hatred. Countless babies were born, and hunger began to establish itself in the village. Mākulis became stooped, Neimale drowned herself, grass grew over her grave—the one outside the cemetery gate. The Dundaga mornings turned into creatures with chapped lips, empty eyes, and bellies distended with want. Bread was rationed. Children succumbed. Jānītīs became a truck driver and took off for good. Little Olga pursued intellectual concerns. There were so many children they were like vermin—the old farmer's house teemed with life. Everything was compromised and befouled. The roof of the farmhouse had been torn off and burned for fuel during a bad winter. Mākulis became gaunt, but his seed became even more profligate. The children covered the sun. The meadows vanished. The Dundaga mornings died, and Mākulis let slip a little laugh, drowned in the mass of children. Arms outstretched, he blessed himself against the days to come. But the Dundaga mornings wouldn't let Mākulis into paradise. Now he is a tramp roaming our native land.

Translated by Ilze Kļaviņa-Mueller

Nora Ikstena

Nora Ikstena (1969) represents Latvia's young generation of writers. She studied the Latvian language and literature at the University of Latvia. In 1992 Ikstena published her first book *Pārnākšana* (The Homecoming), which is a literary and historical exploration of the life of Latvian diplomat and writer Anna Rūmane-Kenina. Ikstena's first collection of stories, *Nieki un izpriecas* (Trifles and Pleasures), was published in 1995, and critics called it "modernly romantic." Ikstena has named Dzintars Sodums, a Latvian writer and translator living in the United States, as well as writers Angela Carter and Karen Blixen as her mentors.

Ikstena spent 1995 in the United States, in Columbia, Missouri, together with her husband Jānis Ikstens, a political scientist. In 1996 she was a writer-in-residence in Ghent, New York, at the Ledig House International Writers' Colony, where she wrote her second collection of stories *Maldīgas romances* (Misleading Romances), which was published in 1997. Ikstena is presently working on a biography of Latvian émigré Brunis Rubess. She is an editor at the literary magazine *Karogs* and serves as Latvia's PEN Club secretary.

Ikstena's stories have been published in Finland, Germany, Russia, and Slovenia. "Pleasures of the Saints" is from *Trifles and Pleasures.*

Pleasures of the Saints

Theresa opened her eyes in a round bed. With each new awakening, she was surprised to be lying there like a raindrop. And right next to her—Augustine, another raindrop in the round bed. Augustine was not awake. Since they never woke together, Theresa and Augustine had never met. They had only watched each other in sleep.

Theresa liked the moments of awakening. It seemed to her that a creaking lever was lifting a bramble-choked cover to release a stream of memory. She enjoyed the weightlessness in her head, where giant fragments of events roamed. She was awake; she could move, join, or even destroy these fragments. In sleep, Theresa was helpless—events took place, but she was forced to rush through and merely take note of them. She had awakened to tell Augustine everything. It was so good to see herself and Augustine in the round bed. And understanding that this mound of dry land was eternal, Theresa could forget her recent fear of getting blindly lost amid blossoming flowers and many-angled figures. Theresa could now touch Augustine and collect her thoughts. He slept so peacefully—this giant raindrop, Augustine. Theresa knew that he now wandered in the cosmos of flowers and many-sided figures, yet his face appeared luminous, and Theresa knew the reason for it—he could sense the small spot of dry land, his awakening, seeing Theresa. . . . Theresa kissed him—the long-awaited moment of contact—she felt how gently Augustine permeated her via her lips. At that moment she realized that everything she had experienced before waking had actually been Augustine. And now she was kissing all of it, even as Augustine roamed and, perhaps, betrayed, sold, or murdered Theresa. But they were fated to it—two raindrops in this round bed. Theresa kissed Augustine, thus asking forgiveness for the night's events, which, though merely fragments, obediently filed into the order of recollection.

"Augustine!" was the first word that Theresa uttered. "I felt wonderful when, having wandered to the point of exhaustion, I discovered a bathhouse. Smooth shelves, a worn clay floor, wooden tubs filled with water moving almost imperceptibly below swirling vapors, a red-hot stove panting for the water's hiss. I stood in the doorway and watched its parched mouth. The thought of how desperately the stove longed for a splash of water irked me. Yet I was afraid to destroy this taut moment of suspense. I looked back. On the other side of the threshold, in the darkness surrounding the bathhouse, bright-green flowers glowed. I longed for rest, Augustine! I stepped into the mild vapors, dipped vessels into the water, and splashed the stove's hot stones, I dove into the steam and listened to the stove's satisfied gasps. . . .

" 'Stop it, I'm out of breath,' I suddenly heard someone say. The steam gradually settled, and I noticed a naked Woman with short gray hair on the sauna's upper shelf. She was so beautiful, Augustine! Small drops of water glistened on her hot skin.

" 'It's not so bad, the vapors tickle my armpits,' she said, banishing my confusion with a smile. I felt drained and miserable in my rags. 'You're like a cocoon,' she laughed and climbed down to help me undress. Her fingers brushed my timid skin. She poured water over me, and my sufferings and delusions, the rancid odor of life, oceans of sorrow, ashes of passions, fear of the truth, the satisfaction gleaned from lies, the insomnia of denial, the fevers of desire, fields of emptiness all flowed away over my eyelashes. . . . With the last drop falling to the floor, I gave a laugh.

" 'In another moment you're going to be real,' the Woman said and gently cut off my long, wet hair. I didn't regret it, Augustine! I felt relieved watching the strands curl up and vanish on the hot stones. I forgot my timid body and kissed the Woman out of gratitude.

" 'You are so gentle,' she whispered. 'I'd forgotten. You are from the gentle world, but life here is quite different.' I noticed that the moment of gentle peace was making her slow and sorrowful.

" 'Do you know what it means to wait?' Her sorrow suddenly gone, the Woman nearly frightened me. She was addressing me harshly, hatefully, squinting her eyes, her eyelashes trembling. I wanted to tell her that I knew what longing for awakening was. But she did not want me to speak. She placed her hands on my shoulders and squeezed my shoulders together painfully. She kept me locked in her embrace and went on: 'Forever lying on the narrow shelf, listening to the stove gasp, relieving it from time to time with a splash of water, waiting for the white, humble vapors to climb up and tickle my armpits, making me laugh—an unnatural laughter that rattles my dry body. . . .' The Woman breathed faster and faster, and it seemed that her eyelashes would flap their wings and fly away into dark space populated with green flowers and figures of countless angles. And then she let go of her grip on me, smiled, and said calmly, 'I'm waiting for the Chestnut Baker. He comes rarely— when he's tired of standing by his huge stove. He lets me wash him, takes a nap, and makes love to me afterward. He almost never speaks, but as he's leaving, he always says the same phrase—'I'm going back to bake chestnuts.' And I begin waiting for his next arrival, nurturing sinful thought; like destroying his stove, quenching the flaming ruins with tubs of water, laughing hideously in the scalding vapors.' The Woman was gazing into nowhere; everything had abruptly vanished for her, Augustine—the bathhouse, the stones, tubs, shelves, tickling vapors. She didn't see me anymore, either. Perhaps she was bathing the Chestnut Baker in an enormous lake? His stove was destroyed, but was he happy? He had no shop to return to. Was he to tire himself only by making love?

" 'Can we watch him bake chestnuts and perhaps taste one?' I asked, wanting to protect the Woman from a mendacious nowhere. The Woman came back to her senses and gave me a look full of gratitude and sorrow. 'That requires courage,' she said pensively, but with an undercurrent of excitement. 'Courage, courage, courage,' she muttered, trying to encourage herself. Finally, she calmed down—I could stare at her incessantly, excitedly; the bathhouse and the vaporous solitude had taught her to solve dilemmas on her own. Up until I showed up in my tattered rags, the only phrase the Woman had heard was, 'I am going back to bake chestnuts.' In the bathhouse, Augustine, reality was an illusion and vice-versa—everything happened simultaneously; one could forget oneself and regain one's senses, but it was not possible to wake up because there was no distinction between reality and dream. The Woman emerged from her mendacious nowhere where a happy Chestnut Baker swam in an enormous lake, oblivious of the smoldering ruins of his stove. 'It demands courage', she repeated blandly, 'but when will someone else like you visit me from the gentle world and propose such bold ventures?' The Woman took me by the hand, and we crossed the threshold to enter a corridor with a dim light at the end of it. 'It is from there that he comes. That glow must be coming from the coals of his stove,' she said, and we continued to walk. It was getting colder, and the light was becoming brighter—it certainly wasn't the light of any coals. Strange noises floated toward us. Suddenly, Augustine, we found ourselves in the midst of a mob of people, animals, things, lights, and noise. We were naked and confused, but nobody had time to notice us. We mingled with the heaving mass and smiled about what the glow of coals had turned out to be:

"... *The Merchant haggled over his wares, he knew how to buy and sell, he smiled his obsequious smile at anyone whose pockets had no holes, he was wealthy and amiable, he pinched the buttocks of chubby little girls and from time to time sang 'Money rules the world–la–la–la–la, da–da–da–da,' the Beggar, a toothless, limbless old man flicked his tongue like a sly snake, crying every ten minutes out of habit, the Beggar, who was a barefoot child, earned his living by praying for mankind, his parents had recently been admitted to*

*The True Fraternity—its members were busy maintaining Distance
from the World with the help of a sacred drink, there was no time for
anything else, the Minister had climbed on top of a gleaming car, yet
he couldn't get up on his feet, he had very good shoes but their soles
had no traction, but he had to stand up, stand up in order to announce with confidence and conviction—'I had a hard childhood,' at
that moment the Godfather, who possessed wealth galore, purchased
some sort of tomfoolery attached to a string in order to produce a
popular play—free admission—with only two actors, one dialogue,
and an eternal catharsis—*

1st actor: 'Peter says the right thing!'

2nd actor: 'Peter has it right!'

"A drunken Poet got tangled up in the words and wrote a poem
about John Brown, the Poet who did not drink anymore was forsaken by his words, the Minister said he'd seen God, in the middle of
the heaving mass he publicly promised his illegitimate children that
they would inherit from him the Transcendental Reality, having
struck a thrilling pose, the Prostitute lay in the middle of the square
with her legs spread, she'd lost her job because she had not adjusted
to a Bisexual Orientation, the Murderer cut his victim's ears off,
thus depriving him of a last chance to hear the voices of the angels,
the Vagabond was stirring up garbage cans and the rumors of the
mob, mixing them together carefully, a cocktail like that was held in
high esteem, being a Vagabond was his life's. . . , the Thief taught his
trade to the Apprentice-Thief, after their first success they cut their
fingers with a Korean knife, mixed their blood, and whispered a
beautiful word they'd heard somewhere before—silentium—to each
other, the Doctor was sitting in a glass cage, but patients were describing their complaints with fine brushes and bright colors—they
were hopelessly incurable, yet it was a beautiful sight, the Artist
could not be distinguished, since everybody was drawing. . . .*

"Such was this mob, Augustine, but its raucous qualities were in
reality a thousand times more colorful. If they were given the liberty, they would swallow the whole universe, sucking in the green
flowers, the figures with countless angles, and the tunnel we had
walked through; watching the Chestnut Baker's deceptive firelight,
they'd break into the Woman's bathhouse, upsetting the wooden
tubs and replacing gentle vapors with a coarse trail of dust. We
were still unnoticed by the mob, and abashed at our nudity. Suddenly, the Woman rose up on her toes, her gray eyelashes trembled;
despite the light, she opened her eyes wide. Augustine, can you
imagine light-green eyes beneath gray lashes? I forgot that I was
standing naked in a mob, I forgot everything, I tried to cement the
Woman's eyes in my mind. But the Woman started walking, she was

seeing smoke, she felt the fragrance of baking chestnuts. She had tried to wash this scent away so often, but it had resisted the wondrous qualities of her bathhouse waters. The Chestnut Baker was standing to one side, his eyes smarting, and snakes of sweat wound about his brow. He did not see the Woman. He was poking the coals under an old tin pan, attempting to keep the flame burning. The slightest movement would have caused the pan to disintegrate. The Woman squatted down next to him and blew on the coals. They glowed brighter, emitting a fan of flames, and the Woman ate hot chestnuts, singeing her fingertips. She watched the Chestnut Baker closely, his palms bore the red imprint of the poker, he was trying to protect his few remaining eyelashes from the hot smoke, but they fell into his eyes like the leaves of wilted plants. Having eaten, the Woman took me by the hand and we went back into the corridor. It was getting warmer and more comfortable. Having returned to the bathhouse, we sat down on the threshold. "How miserable are those dark-green flowers unfolding in the dark space around my bathhouse,' the Woman exclaimed. 'They cannot be picked, so I cannot make tea for the Chestnut Baker when he comes.' It was time for me to go, Augustine. I picked up my clothes, which had become clean and fragrant, and I left. The Woman remained seated on the threshold, hating the green flowers which could not to be picked."

Theresa stopped speaking. It seemed to her she had recalled a great deal. The fragments of events were obedient and let themselves be woven into words. Theresa smiled, imagining the events to be like hobbled horses neighing at pasture in the night. She had once been in a fragrant night meadow during her wanderings. She had lain down by a sputtering fire. A gentle incense with an unusual fragrance made her indolent and pliant; horses neighed softly, subdued by their ropes and the mist of incense. Theresa wanted to succumb to the temptation of the sputtering fire, not return as a raindrop to Augustine in the round bed. Yet, if ever there was an Eternal Return, it was Theresa's to Augustine. Momentous, perhaps beautiful, maybe even unforgettable wishes were dispersed in it like dandelion seeds. Therefore, Theresa was in the round bed next to Augustine, finishing her story. Augustine would wake up soon, but Theresa had to continue her wanderings. She kissed Augustine—it was the much-expected and everlasting touch—and she felt Augustine permeate her through her parted lips. . . .

Augustine opened his eyes. He enjoyed that moment of awakening. Theresa breathed quietly next to him. Her eyelashes did not tremble, she was far away. So white was she, this huge raindrop,

Theresa. Hesitating, Augustine touched Theresa's neck with his clumsy fingers. He drew labyrinths on the white skin, nobody could disturb him, he was awake, the events taking place in the darkness within him continued to unfold without his presence. Sometime and somewhere Theresa would be joining them—was she murdering Augustine or saving him? Augustine knew he had little time to recount to Theresa the many events he had experienced. Yet he hesitated—his gaze lingering in her hair, the corners of her eyes, the sloping shells of her ears, the arcs of her eyebrows, the lines of her lips, the webs of her eyelids. . . .

"Theresa," Augustine started quietly. "My wanderings were a war. Something had happened to the cosmos's chilly peace. It was full of fires, people fleeing, the noise of victory and defeat. The roaring songs of a feast could be heard—this is what it had to be like. Somewhere, living and dead bodies were being bulldozed—it had to be that way, too. I walked through the chaos in silence—how could I possibly speak to people who found happiness in destruction? They were cleaning the dark space enthusiastically, they felt alien, unhappy, unfulfilled. . . . Can you imagine, Theresa, their happiness was death, and it did not matter who died—divine temples or little children, old manuscripts or dusky, passionate women, painted sunflowers or fresh red irises, the countless strata of things, or old men who knew something about meaning and harmony. In this chaos of destruction, I met only one man with a zest for life. His marching in the streets was a motley, joyful vision.

"Flames, burning trees, blood—and suddenly, the shy sounds of bagpipes rise out of the smoke. The man's companions are playing their pipes off-key and are laughing at themselves, there are no woman, they are drinking wine with abandon. The old man looks foolish. Two chestnut blossoms like horns in his hair, he was eating big, juicy, dark-blue plums. He appeared lighthearted in this world of devastation. Noticing my clean, white clothes, he waved to me and exclaimed joyfully, '*Urbi et orbi*. Barabas greets you, fellow traveler!'

"This is how I met Barabas, the cause of all the unfortunate mess. Barabas was kind, he invited me to join him on his journey to a place of peace. He assured me there would be enough wine to get us through the piles of bodies, stones, and smoking trees. I knew nothing about this man with chestnut blossoms in his hair. But he had bagpipes, he smiled, and I felt something more akin to joy than to the horror surrounding me. So this is how our journey commenced, Theresa. He gave a sly smile when he learned my name. You know, he treated me benevolently, as if I were a harmless lunatic, when I told him about our round bed, our separate awakenings, our dream stories.

" 'Augustine, you come from a completely different world, so I can talk to you. It will make the trip shorter, although you are used to wandering alone. Drink the wine—you will never savor anything like it in your round bed!' Barabas stopped laughing for a moment and poured the wine with such gusto that it splattered redly on my white garments.

" 'Khaaa-rrr-e!' Barabas gave a roar, his companions retreated with their bagpipes, and we started our carefree journey through the war zone to the place of peace he'd promised. He talked, and I have to admit that I completely forgot myself in listening to him. Only the acrid smoke reminded me of what was going on around us.

Barabas's Story

" 'I was born in a disgusting place. I was a strange infant because immediately I took note of everything—the dirty bed, gray rags, my mother's calloused feet, the crooked fingers of the old woman holding me, wet and feeble, and slapping my back to elicit a cry of recovery from the hypnosis of birth. When I started wailing, the old crone's face broke into a smile—of course, she had only a few teeth. My mother died, I remember that. She did not open her eyes; she just took a deep breath, and smiled. My mother was beautiful, though she slept amid rags and filth. I remember the old woman crying. So sad and disgusting was my birth. I became used to the old woman, so it took me a long time to find out what beauty was. When I was a child, I thought notched pots, thin soups, and half-baked simmering on the side of the stove were the epitome of love and perfection. The old woman never left me alone. She tied me to her and often went into the forest. We ate wild strawberries and the fresh sprouts of fir trees, chased snakes that dozed on the hummocks, let marsh tea put us to sleep, hid behind trees to watch elks eat beautiful death-cups and survive, we sought frozen birds in the snowed-covered forest, brought home ice-coated twigs that melted their beauty away in the warmth of our house, we gathered lichen that looked like the old woman's eyebrows, we fled from rabid foxes, cut saffron milk caps with the orange blood, scattered the dew from the grass, mourned flies devoured by a strange flower. . . . When I grew older, the old woman turned me out of the house, saying that the moment of my ingratitude was nearly at hand. I didn't know at the time what ingratitude was. I loved her very much and kept turning around and coming back, weeping with grief. But the old woman bolted her door and threatened to kill me if I did not leave. I knew what death was. Although my mother had smiled on that occasion, she had also disappeared. I did not want to disappear, so I retreated from the old woman's door. . . .'

"Barabas had become pensive, somewhat sad, and it did not suit him on this merry journey. Then, it seemed his memories did a wild somersault. Once again, wine flowed generously.

" 'Khaaa-rrr-e,' Barabas gave another roar. 'I almost grew sad, Augustine, over my own story! What can be more perverse in this kingdom of nightmares than sadness?' He halted and called one of his men imperiously. The man kneeled down, and Barabas climbed up on his shoulders. He rose above the others, stared around, and exclaimed, *'Vita brevis!'* Standing in military bearing, his companions shrieked, *'Est!'* For a while, the shouting continued—*'Vita brevis!'*—*'Est!'* Barabas was in high spirits; we continued the journey, and he continued his story.

" 'When I left the old woman, I encountered expanses that made me laugh at notched pots, mushrooms, elks, foxes, and lichen. The expanses were inhabited by people, things, and ideas that tormented but could not destroy one another. Gradually, I realized that they did not want to be separated—like you, Augustine, and Theresa. An eternal vigil hung over people; they returned from their short dreams with no memories. Being awake, they believed anyone who promised happiness. So I put chestnut blossoms in my hair, gathered my companions—who, though they played their bagpipes off-key, were faithful and cheery—and began to promise happiness. This is how my perpetual gaiety started. I ate, drank, devoted myself to the fine arts—my men cheered when I painted wings onto an ermine held by a plump lady, or an ear on a man who had cut his own off and gazed in confusion and fear at me from the canvas, I added black dots to a well-known music score, or I promoted symmetry by hewing off the other arm of a white sculpture. There wasn't a single woman who did not believe in my eternal love, which lasted as long as the meadow dew. You know, Augustine, if somebody happened along who asserted that happiness was not possible, people invariably chose me. They did not want to hear about suffering, they adored me fanatically, attaching themselves to me like the thistles in the old woman's hair. I can confess, Augustine, that blind faith is most difficult to stomach. I arranged another Feast of Waiting for Happiness, and declared—"Happiness is death." And you can see how diligently they're preparing for it. I'm waiting for the silence to set in and then I will plant forests—the elks will come and eat the beautiful death-cups and survive; the flower will attract flies, and they will die; I will gather lichen that looks like the eyebrows of the old woman.'

"Barabas finished his story, he was sad again, he did not drink any more wine, he did not call upon his men.

" 'Where is that place of peace? Is it far?' I asked sad Baraba cautiously.

" 'You want to reach the place of peace, Augustinus?' Barabas gazed at me with compassion. 'Escape by waking up, you can do it. My journey will be long, the silence will not come soon, and forests grow slowly.'

" 'Khaaa-rrr-e!' I heard Barabas roar wildly.

Augustine fell silent, he was tired of talking. He kissed Theresa—the long-awaited, perpetual touch. He felt Theresa permeate him through his lips. Lying next to each other, the two raindrops, Theresa and Augustine, breathed almost imperceptibly.

Translated by Jānis Ikstens and Rita Laima Krieviņa

Arvis Kolmanis

Arvis Kolmanis (1959) earns his money selling cosmetics. His first collection of stories, *Greniāna jeb ceturtā versija* (Greniana or the Fourth Version, 1995), vividly unveiled the essence of his texts—something akin to proving the meaninglessness of meanings and phenomena. Kolmanis is a product of his time: he believes everything has already been said and nothing remains to be proved. Therefore, one can devote oneself to depicting the uselessness of meaning(s). Kolmanis's prose is very visual—possibly due to his studies of film as art. Kolmanis is presently writing a horror book which he calls *Žūpa Amors jeb Mirušais dievs* (The Drunk Cupid or the Deceased God). Kolmanis lives in Rīga with his wife and two sons.

Veronica, the Schoolgirl

I was dicing an onion and crying when Victor entered the room. He sat down at the kitchen table, produced a pack of cards and began to play solitaire. I chopped eggs, squid, added sour cream and salt, and suddenly remembered I didn't have any black pepper.

"Is that such a big deal," said Victor.

"Squid salad without pepper is inedible," I replied. "Bring me some pepper."

"For some two days now I've been wondering about it," said Victor as he shuffled the cards. "And I can't make head or tail of it, why they should. . . . Yesterday someone tried to convince me that it was because those creatures don't like it. They don't like it, period. And just try to do something about it!"

"The pepper, Victor."

But Victor went on, "An inanimate thing is just an inanimate thing, right? So, what's the use in hating something inanimate. Arcady, are stones living things?"

"No."

"Well, then, isn't it foolish, for instance, to hate stones?"

"I hated stones when I was little," I replied. "The neighborhood boys used to throw them at me. I thought—if there were no stones then everything would be all right. But the stones were there, and I hated them simply because they existed. Are you bringing the pepper or what?"

"Right," said Victor. He got up, went to his flat, and brought back the pepper. I mixed it into the salad and went to get Veronica.

"She won't eat it," my brother said.

"She has to eat. She can't just sit by some dying Sophia day after day and not eat anything."

"A couple more days," my brother said. "What difference does it make if she eats or doesn't eat."

"It's squid salad, really good."

"She doesn't eat squid. You'd forgotten?"

I had forgotten.

"I'll think of something else," I said and went back to the kitchen.

"There's no way she'll eat!" my brother called after me.

The refrigerator was half-empty. Yesterday's spaghetti. A little of this and that. I cut bacon into cubes, fried it in a pan and added the spaghetti. While that was slowly heating up I beat some eggs and added grated cheese, salt, pepper, diced onion, then slopped the mixture over the spaghetti, drizzling the whole thing with ketchup.

"Didn't she want the salad?" Victor asked.

"No."

"I'm wondering why they cling to those Sophias so desperately," said Victor. "Okay, nice-looking. But why such overwheming affection for them, such affection that later . . ."

"Have some squid."

"I'm not really up to it," Victor replied. He picked up his cards. "There's nothing to do. Feel like a drink?"

I didn't want to drink so Victor went away. I finished off the squid salad and went to the room to get Veronica. She refused to eat spaghetti. Refused to eat anything at all.

"Dad, just leave me alone," she said. "It's no use. You can't do anything about it anyway."

Why can't I, I thought, why not. . . . You simply don't have to do it. You mustn't do it. Oh, hell, what a life. . . . I felt for the switch, the motor started to hum quietly, it calmed me down, my reflection in the mirror by the wall misted.

"Switch it off," Veronica said meekly. "I know it's easier for you this way, but switch it off. Please. . . ."

I sighed. Switched off the motor.

That creep was dying.

The bell rang briskly, class doors were flung open, the corridor quickly filled. As the principal—a tall, slim, razor-faced man—emerged, I managed to slip into the restroom. He went by with heavy steps, I waited for a moment, then I returned to the corridor and saw Livia. I called her name. She seemed surprised but didn't stop, her face darkened, she continued her pace, I followed in her footsteps, she glanced back across her shoulder once in a while, as if to make sure I was following. We walked like this for a while, the corridor was a long one. Livia stopped by the principal's door and waited for me to catch up.

"What are you doing here?" she asked softly, looked around, then raised her hand in a brief caress. "You shouldn't come here."

"I'm her father."

"That's irrelevant."

"Veronica. . . ."

"You can't do anything about it. I can't, nobody can. She has to cope with it on her own. And she knows it."

"I wanted to see you. It's been so hard."

She looked at her watch, unbuttoned a button on her blouse, then another one.

"I'm in a hurry," she said. "The break is about to end. They expect me in there. If you want to, there's a window on the other side. I'll meet you out there in ten minutes."

She vanished into the principal's office.

For a while I watched the children running amok in the corridor. Not one of them stood aside, or shrunk into a corner, everyone was in a reckless frenzy. There were no teachers to be seen, nobody paid any attention to me. I walked out of the school, went around to its other side, and began to calculate which one might be the principal's window. I went up on my toes, peered inside, I'd made a mistake, I saw an empty classroom, its walls were decorated with portraits of women.

The principal's window was the next one over. The principal was standing with his back to it, a ruler in his hand, he was leaning over Livia who was stretched out on the table, her hands under her head, her legs dangling on either side of the table, my hand glided into my pocket, the little motor started to hum, the windowpane colored red as though by the setting sun, Livia's legs and the principal's naked buttocks were tinted red as well, everything in the office became red, I switched it off, everything regained its former appearance, I switched it on. Switched it off. Switched it on. I became bored and retreated from the window, waiting for Livia. I didn't have to wait long.

She walked toward me with wide strides. Kissed me. We stood under the principal's window in silence. Tiny flecks of mica glistened on Livia's neck. I put out my finger to brush them off, she recoiled, shuddered. "It's nothing," she said, but a hint of defiance shone in her eyes.

"Livia," I said. "Tell me, what. . . ."

"The same as usual," she replied. "I love you."

"I love you, too. . . ."

"He saw you. Didn't I tell you not to come here?"

"He can't tell me what to do and not to do!"

"Switch it off," she said suddenly.

I obeyed her.

"Come and live with me," I said. "Livia, come and live with me. Not right away, but afterward."

She gave me a questioning look, smiled, puckered, licked her lips, crossed her hands over her breasts. A teacher.

"What about your whiny brother. . . ."

"Livia, he loves Veronica as much as I do. I can't just throw him out. He's going through hell as it is. . . ."

"You said—afterward. . . ." Then she became a loving woman again, closed her eyes, and offered her face to me. "Kiss me."

I kissed her, watched her fix her lipstick, the principal opened his window, leaned out and appeared to be looking somewhere far over our heads, his mouth was compressed into a thin line. I pretended not to notice him, he pretended not to notice me.

"The party tonight. . . ."

"I'll be there," she said and walked off. I set off in the opposite direction. The principal's stare dug into my back, I started to run and managed to jump into a trolleybus. The trolleycar was overcrowded. The day wasn't particularly cold, but many women had scarves around their necks. Patterned, pretty, and bright. Striking bright. Visually striking.

We were waltzing, I hadn't danced in a long time, I had actually forgotten how to waltz, but Irene danced wonderfully, soon we were spinning until Irene was wet with perspiration and I lost interest. I was drinking heavily, Irene was drinking, that evening everyone was drinking hard. A teacher from Veronica's school who sat down next to me was completely drunk.

"You're an intelligent man," she started to mumble. "And yet you're letting your own daughter, a minor. . . ."

"What's that have to do with intelligence. . . ."

"No, Veronica could never have thought of that herself, she's such a sensible girl, but you. . . ."

I was rescued by Robert, we started talking about our work, it was impossible to get coolers anywhere, Robert couldn't find coolers anywhere, hell, there was everything except for coolers. Robert was desperate. Livia arrived in a black dress, blew out all the candles as the Sophia around her neck began to glow, women gave squeals of delight, some of them had the greenish bands around their throats, up until now concealed in their purses, encouraged by Livia they had put them on, giggling as though it were a conspiracy. Too many lately, too many, I thought. Livia sipped from the glass that glinted greenishly in her hand, voices softly droned, after a while the teacher still sitting next to me started to shout that I had had no right to show up at the school, the principal had forbidden it, there was bound to be trouble because of me, some parents had already told their children not to play with Veronica, then Livia flung the contents of her glass straight into the woman's face.

"I'm a teacher, too," said Livia. "But I've never screeched in an obnoxious voice like that! How can you teach children if you're bellowing like that, you fool!"

"Right," Robert exclaimed and dragged the sobbing teacher away to some remote corner. Irene was whispering in my ear not to worry, she thought I was right in going to the school, she was very sorry for Veronica, too, Veronica was a good girl, she was managing so nicely, Irene was proud of Veronica and proud to be her mother. Livia came up and they struck up a conversation, Livia asked when Irene was going to agree to a divorce, she wanted to come and live with me but Irene was still formally my wife, if Irene were to divorce me and Livia could marry me then she'd be entitled to throw my brother out of the flat, I calmed Livia down by saying that my brother would presumably come to terms with the situation and leave the flat as soon as everything was over. "Yes," Irene said, "listen, dear, hasn't the principal broken his ruler yet?" Both of them started to giggle but I went over to Victor, Victor was on all fours on the floor looking for his screwdriver but it was too dark, the Sophias' illumination didn't reach that far, I tried to light a candle but the women started protesting and Victor got sore. We squeezed ourselves into a corner and continued drinking, it was his last screwdriver, he was muttering incoherently, we drank and drank until the others began to dress, I roused Victor and we dressed, too. The crowd poured out into the street and tried to catch taxis but none would stop, I realized what the problem was, I shouted to the women to take their Sophias off but they ignored me, we set off on foot until we got to the principal's house, all the windows in his house were dark, I fumbled in my pocket for the switch, the windows lit up a cadmium yellow, more yellow than the stars, which couldn't be seen anyway because the sky was full of clouds. We climbed the stairs to the second floor where the principal had come out to meet us, he was standing in the doorway, sleepy and disheveled, he had probably just crawled out of bed.

"To tell you the truth, I wasn't expecting any guests," the principal said. "I don't have anything to drink."

Irene had a bottle with her, she gave it to the principal, we went into his room and seated ourselves wherever we could, the principal sat down in a chair in the middle of the room and took an occasional swig from the bottle Irene had brought along with her, shortly his wife emerged, sleepy, rubbing her eyes, she started talking to Livia, both of them laughed, I was wondering how to help Robert, I had come up with something, I found the telephone and called home. My brother picked up the receiver.

"Sorry, if I woke you up. . . ."

"I wasn't sleeping," my brother said. "You can guess why."

"I know," I said. "Listen, you once had a friend. He was one of the first guys to start doing business with motors."

"Andrejs."

"Whoever," I said. "I need some coolers. Can you. . . ."

"Maybe," my brother said. "It's good you called. In another minute . . . everything will be over." He started to cry.

"I'm on my way," I said and put down the receiver. I told Robert

I might get him the coolers. He didn't believe me, he probably thought I was raving. Livia was still chatting with the principal's wife. I interrupted the conversation.

"It's over?" Livia asked.

"Maybe," I said.

"Wait a minute," said the principal's wife. "I'll go with you. I can't let you go alone at a time like this."

"My brother's home."

"Nevertheless," she said adamantly. "It'll be better if I go along with you. I'll just go put on something warm."

"I'll call you tomorrow," Livia said and kissed me.

On the street I realized that the motor had been humming in my pocket all this time. Nobody had objected to it. Naturally—everyone was too drunk. I switched it off and the windows of the principal's house grew dark.

"We've got candles," the principal's wife said. She latched on to my elbow. "They won't stay in the dark. And probably somebody else took one along. . . . You want to know?"

"I don't know what I want. . . ."

"You have to know that I don't judge you. Not for one moment. It doesn't matter that Veronica is underage. It's not the issue. Your going to the school really amazes me, I admire you. But I'm not coming with you because of this. I'm coming with you because I don't think it's good to let you go off alone at a time like this."

"Thanks," I replied. "I already said I wouldn't be alone. My brother's at home."

"He's got problems of his own," the principal's wife said. "Isn't he suffering? Sure he is. Besides, when Livia moves in with you, he'll have to go. I don't want to say anything, but . . . Livia has never been. . . . Well, you see for yourself, she wears her Sophia so openly. . . ."

"She sure does," I said.

"She's never been conservative," the principal's wife went on. "Not me. I can't forget myself. I'd like to but I can't. And it's not because of my husband, no. I just can't forget myself, my inhibitions."

A taxi approached, I raised my hand, it stopped, both of us took the backseat, the taxi accelerated jerkily, and the body of the principal's wife exerted a slight pressure against mine. She was short and fat, but her face was exceptionally delicate, it didn't match the rotund body. I could feel a goodness radiating from her. Strangely enough, I felt much more relaxed at the moment than when I was alone with Livia.

"You're comparing me with Livia now?" she asked.

"Yes."

"Don't."

"Why not?"

"It doesn't make any sense."

"I'm often thinking about senseless things. Especially when I've been drinking. I drank a lot today."

"No, no, you don't seem drunk at all."

"Maybe I just don't show it, but I am. But I can still think. I'm even trying to anticipate what will come next."

"Everything will be fine. Livia is an intelligent woman, she'll help you regain your balance. She's good at it. And soon enough you'll. . . . If only. . . ."

"If only. . . . And what if the same thing happens again? What then?"

"Are you comfortable?" she asked suddenly. "I'll give you more room."

"No, no. . . . Stay there. . . . It's soothing. . . ."

"That's nice to hear. You're the first person to tell me that my presence is soothing. My husband is a very reserved man. He gives the impression of being arrogant but actually he's very gentle and easily hurt. . . . He told me that at school, well, when you. . . ."

"I'd rather not talk about it."

"No, let me speak. He told me about it because he knew that I could calm him down, but he's never actually told me that I could soothe him, he just feels it and goes through the emotions inside himself. . . ."

"You're a good person."

"Thank you. I brought something along with me, my husband doesn't know I had it stashed away back home. I thought we might need it. . . ."

She took a half-empty bottle out of her bag and handed it to me, I took a gulp, she took a gulp, and then the taxi pulled up to my house.

Nothing was over. It dragged on for an excruciatingly long time, it seemed it would continue forever. The room filled with a mist, windows and mirrors dripped, the motor was overheated, but I needed it, simply needed it. Otherwise I couldn't bear it.

"I'd mop it up," said the principal's wife. "If you give me a rag I'll mop it up."

"Leave it," I said. "What's the difference. Nothing makes sense anymore."

"You're worried," said the principal's wife. "But don't be. Give yourself up to sorrow. There's nothing you can do about it. Reconcile yourself to the inevitable." She sat down at the piano and started playing, her stubby fingers touched the keys with incredible alacrity, light, soft sounds mingled with the mist and muffled the hum of the motor.

"You play wonderfully," my brother said.

"Chopin should never be played badly," the principal's wife said. "My husband taught me how to play. He was the one who said—'Chopin may only be performed wonderfully.' You like it, don't you? You see, you're not crying anymore. Music heals. . . ."

"Arcady," my brother ventured to say, "I'm seeing such a nice woman for the first time. You know, if it weren't for Livia, I'd tell you to. . . ."

"I was actually beginning to think about it myself," the principal's wife said. "I feel awkward saying this, but . . . maybe it would be much better if I. . . ."

"I love Livia," I said.

"Is that always enough?" the principal's wife countered.

"Isn't it?"

"Well . . ." the principal's wife spoke up slowly. "I suppose you haven't read Nietzsche?"

"No, I haven't."

"Neither have I," said the principal's wife. "But he exerts an influence anyway. I hate Wagner, for instance. And I believe that God is dead."

"That's ridiculous," I murmured.

"No, it's absolutely possible," she said. "I can discuss it with Livia myself, Arcady, if . . . if only you'd want me to."

"Arcady, you should agree," my brother nudged me. "That way it'd be better. It'd be easier for you, and me, too."

"Undoubtedly," the pricipal's wife added. "I would never make you leave."

She played on and on. My brother and I did nothing but listen. Veronica came out of her room.

"Dead," she said when the principal's wife had stopped playing for a moment to wipe the perspiration from her forehead.

"You told me you'd phone me," I said into the mouthpiece, but Livia remained silent. I waited.

"I tried to call you but I couldn't get through," said Livia's voice. "How's Veronica?"

"It's all over now. . . . Why don't you ask me how I'm doing?"

"Forgive me," said Livia's voice. "So-o-o . . . it's over. . . ."

"Yes," I said. "It's over."

"Wait a moment," said Livia's voice. She seemed to cover the receiver with her hand, I could hear only muffled unintelligible sounds, she was speaking to someone. Then she came back to me again. "I guess you don't have any money, do you?"

"A little bit," I answered.

"I just spoke to the principal. He. . . ."

"Livia," I said. "The principal's wife. . . ."

"I know," Livia's voice replied. "If you really think it would be better. . . ."

"Livia, I love you."

"I love you, too," her voice said. "But it's up to you to make the decision. After all, I'm a teacher, I have my classes, I have the principal, you're not a child anymore, you have to understand. Wait. . . ."

She resumed talking to someone at the other end of the line.

"Arcady," Livia's voice floated back. "The principal is leaving the school. He feels—although I disagree with him—that after what's happened he has no right to work with children anymore. Because Veronica isn't the only one. There's another girl. But the school is ready to cover all funeral expenses. The principal will see to it."

"Another girl?"

"Arcady, they've got as many arms and legs as we do," Livia's voice was saying. "And everybody's got the right to choose. Everybody."

"Don't give me that crap! If only I knew who was the one who decided that Sophias. . . ."

"Leave Sophias alone," said Livia's voice. "There are some things you just don't argue about. The right to personal choice, for instance. Including mine. Veronica's, too. And yours, for that matter. Let's not talk about it anymore. I know it's not easy for you, you're upset, but. . . ."

"Livia," I struggled to remain calm. "Livia, if you and the others hadn't. . . ."

She hung up.

The park, benches, trees. Colorful leaves were falling. Swings went back and forth by themselves, untouched by anyone. A group of children were trying to outwail the wind. They were running around, shouting, falling to the ground, rolling in the leaves.

"Andrejs," I said. "What's going on? If it's impossible to test coolers for three hours. . . ."

"If you're not thinking of buying them just tell me," Andrejs snapped back. He had connected a cooler to the massive motor, but it wasn't working, it sputtered and fell silent over and over. The leaves were scattered only by the wind.

"I'm not going to throw my money away on useless coolers," I said. "Okay, hook them up to mine. If they don't work for mine, they're not fit for anything." I took my little motor out of my pocket, Andrejs glared at me, shrugged his shoulders, and snapped the wires off the motor.

"The screw," he said after a moment. "You need a different screw."

"That's absurd," I said. "Up until now I've managed to change coolers without any difficulty."

"You want to test them, don't you?" Andrejs glanced at me.

"Of course."

"Then you need a different screw. That can only be done at the service station."

"All right, let's go to the station," I said and got up. I was suddenly giddy. The wind wailed. Swings careened. Children yelled. Leaves whirled. Livia had thrown down the receiver.

"We can't go anywhere," said Andrejs. "The truck is coming later. I didn't think we would need a screw. And we can't leave the big motor in the middle of the park unattended. That's just what they're waiting for. . . ."

A couple of boys weren't taking part in the general amusement, they stood aside silently watching Andrejs's manipulations with the motor as though enchanted.

"I can't wait that long," I said. "I'll be late for the funeral."

"It's up to you," Andrejs replied and hooked the cooler up to the big motor again, turned it on, listened to it rumble for a moment and fall silent. He spat. "If you stay here. . . . Give me your motor, I'll be quick, I'll get a new screw and be back in a moment."

"Are you in your right mind?"

"I swear, everything will be all right," he said. "Nobody'll find out."

"It's out of the question," I replied. "Only. . . . If you're willing, I could find someone to look after it while both of us. . . ."

" 'Someone' is no good," said Andrejs.

I was thinking of whom to phone. Livia won't do it, my brother won't leave the house, Robert's at work, Victor is on a drinking binge, isn't going to leave the house, Veronica, no, how could I think of Veronica, Irene. . . .

"My wife," I said.

Andrew grimaced and shrugged. Agreed. I ran to the phone booth. Irene was at home, Irene wasn't asleep, Irene was kindness incarnate, Irene promised to come and sit in the park and keep an eye on the motor. I suspected she was wondering why I had chosen her. In fact, she even seemed a little surprised.

"If anybody else asked me do it . . ." she said. "But, we'll be late for the funeral."

"I'll call you," I said. "I'll call Veronica, see if they can start later. A lot of them will be late anyway. Then it'll be better to start later."

"Well, well. . . ." said Irene.

I called home from Andrejs's garage.

"Robert was asking for you," my brother said, and I could tell from his voice he'd been crying. "And Veronica can't seem to get in touch with the minister."

"The minister is coming. I spoke to him myself."

"She doesn't want any minister. She's changed her mind."

"Nonsense. How can you do without a minister. . . ."

"It really makes no sense. In the end she herself. . . ."

"What a pity," I said. "What a pity that nothing ever happens normally. Hasn't the principal's wife left yet?"

"No," said my brother. "She thinks she should be here. And it's good she's here."

"Maybe you're right. Get Veronica. Or maybe just tell her. There's a minor delay. Irene and I won't make it on time. Ask Veronica to start later."

"Tell her yourself," said my brother. "Arcady, only you can tell her this. I'll go get her. And please call Robert."

I waited.

"Dad?"

"Darling. . . . You must understand, your mother and I can't possibly make it on time. Can't you. . . ."

"If you wish," Veronica said. "All right. Can you make it in an hour?"

"Sounds good. An hour from now—definitely. Then we'll even be early. Anyway, why don't you want a minister at the service?"

"No, I don't want anybody . . ." Veronica's voice broke. "Can't I decide for myself this time. . . ."

"All right, all right," I said. "If you wish."

"Thanks! Listen, uncle is saying you have to phone Robert."

"I won't forget," I said.

"Then I'll be seeing you in an hour? Don't be late."

"In an hour, dear," I said and wanted to hang up, but I heard the voice of the principal's wife: "Arcady? Don't worry, I'm not going anywhere, I think I should stay right here, it will be better that way. I can't just abandon both of them like that, you do feel better when I'm here, right, Arcady?"

"I won't know how to thank you," I replied. "I feel uncomfortable about the whole situation. . . ."

"No, no, Arcady," she said. "Don't talk like that. I'll be at the cemetery, too, I will most certainly be there. But you take care!"

"I'll take care," I said. I put down the phone. Only then did I notice that Andrejs's garage had no windows. The air was heavy and rancid. The floor was dirty, no mirrors, no paintings on the walls. He probably didn't have enough money. An unshaven beard, matted, dirty hair. He felt my scrutinizing gaze, raised his head, and looked at me with vacant eyes. Pity overcame me.

"I just don't understand," said Andrejs. "I made a new thread but they still don't fit."

"Forget about it," I said. "I'm buying them."

"But we didn't test them. What if they don't work?"

"It won't be my fault if they don't work," I said, and I was right. "Give me back my motor."

He handed it over to me. I switched the motor on and put it in my pocket.

"What a waste of time," said Andrejs. "You could have told me right away."

"Leave me alone," I said. I dialed Robert's number, but nobody answered. "Let's go. I don't have time."

Nothing in the park had changed, leaves were falling from the trees, children were shouting and rolling on the ground, Irene was huddled on a bench with her coat collar upturned, her hands in her pockets, she looked chilled to the bone. She was very beautiful.

"Sorry," I said. "It wasn't my fault. Am I late?"

"Everything's fine," she replied. "Everything all right with you?"

"I guess so."

"That's good," she said wrinkling her forehead. "Switch it off, please. It's disgusting."

"Is that why you left me?" I asked, turning it off.

Andrejs was rolling up the cables, unscrewing the supports from the big motor, fastening the springs with pieces of styrofoam, the wind snatched a piece away, sent it rolling through the grass, one of the boys who was still standing and staring at the motor ran after it, caught it, dashed back to Andrejs with it, handing it over reverently, with beseeching eyes. Andrejs gave in: "Well, come on, you can help me, but don't say a word to anybody!" The boys' faces lit up in ecstasy. I gave Andrejs the money for the coolers, the money the school had bequeathed me was nearly spent, but, thank God, everything had been paid for already, except the minister's fee, but there would be no minister. . . .

"No, no, not because of that," said Irene.

The cemetery was empty. The wind waited as it had in the park a moment ago, I felt giddy again, I felt nauseated, I staggered and sank to the ground by the fresh grave. Irene helped me up quickly and guided me to a bench, asked if I often experienced these spells of weakness, suggested that I see a doctor. I promised to take care of it as soon as I could find the time.

"So be it," Irene murmured thoughtfully. "Life has its demands. If you want to live a full life then there's no time for anything else. You can't stand still, you have to stay on the move. Listen, about that divorce. . . . I've thought it over. Let's not divide our things, it will take an awfully long time to settle the matter and will make us both uncomfortable. I don't need anything. I've been offered a good job with a decent salary, I'll be able to buy everything I need. It'll be easier for you, too, Livia will be able to move in with you that much sooner."

I answered that I wasn't so sure about that.

"I wouldn't recommend the principal's wife," said Irene. "Livia suits you better. Of course, it's your choice."

"I love Livia," I replied. "But the principal's wife. . . ."

"She hates everything new, just like you," Irene said. "That's the only thing that appeals to you. You're of the same breed, prepared to sit in your dens until judgment day. But you can't live like that, darling. What would happen if everyone started behaving like you? Have you ever tried to fathom this? Besides, you're nothing in terms of individuality, sorry I have to tell you. So, think it over. And the fact that you allowed Veronica to have a Sophia simply points up your laziness. You were too lazy to tell her no. Livia wouldn't let you be so complacent."

"Irene," I said. "Those Sophias, the idiocy of it all."

"I know, it's hard for you, you're upset," said Irene. "There's no sense in talking to you now. And this isn't really the right moment. Get yourself together. I think they've arrived."

A bus pulled up to the cemetery gate.

A violin played softly, the violinist was a young boy with a weary face and eyes rimmed with blue, I doubted if he was much older than Veronica but he played marvelously, the people stood listening transfixed, then the coffin with the Sophia was opened, the creature was lying stretched out amid minuscule flakes of mica like an enormous white slug. Nobody spoke. Many people had come to the funeral: Irene's colleagues, Veronica's girlfriends, Veronica's teachers, I detected the principal, his wife and Livia next to him in the crowd. I saw Robert, Robert caught my glance and shook his head. The minister was standing next to Veronica but he shouldn't have been there, I cautiously made my way through the crowd of mourners and touched the minister's shoulder, he glanced at me inquiringly, recognized me, greeted me with a nod, and we moved off to one side.

"No, no, I'm not going to speak," he said. "If your daughter doesn't want it. . . ."

"I didn't know," I said. "She changed her mind at the last moment but couldn't reach you."

"It's all right," the minister replied. "It wasn't possible to reach me on the phone. All morning I've had . . . a lot of work."

"You've come," I said. "But I don't have any money at the moment to pay you."

"I didn't come here for money," the minister said.

I looked into his eyes, he did not avert his gaze and waited.

"You . . . you ought to know, can you tell me . . ." I muttered.

The principal's wife grabbed me by the hand, the wind was wailing, the violinist played, the minister kept silent.

"Come," she whispered. "It's time to start, come. . . . Arcady, dear, are you perfectly calm? Come. . . ."

Tears were shining in her eyes.

I looked back over my shoulder, the minister remained standing, did not follow us—a motionless, black figure, the crowd let me pass, I went up to Veronica, the coffin with the Sophia was closed and being lowered into the grave, Veronica pressed herself to me, I embraced her, my head was spinning again, I didn't understand what I was supposed to be doing, Robert came up to us, patted me on my shoulder. "I couldn't get you on the phone," I said, "I kept calling but you didn't answer." "Later," he replied and patted my shoulder again. "Take care, Dad," Veronica whispered. "You'll take care, won't you?" I shook my head, still not understanding anything, caressing Veronica, a woman cried out hysterically, Veronica detatched herself from me and stepped into the grave, lying down beside the Sophia's coffin, someone offered me a spadeful of soil, Veronica stared at me with wide-open eyes, looking at me from below, I took a handful of soil and threw it into the grave, trying not to hit Veronica's pale face, when the first handful of soil hit her body she shuddered and closed her eyes, I turned away and didn't see where my second and third handful of sand landed, after that they started to fill the grave with the help of spades, the soil fell softly, made hardly a sound, there weren't enough spades to go around, the men took turns, the principal's back bent in front of me, when he began to pant I took his place, but then I grew dizzy again, someone took my spade, I was led aside, Livia made me swallow some tablets and drink something from a bottle that scorched my throat, I came to my senses just as the grave was being covered with wreaths, Victor walked over to me and took me by the shoulder, he didn't speak, the principal's wife was fretting her handkerchief nervously, looking at me with sorrow, Irene came up, caressed me and kissed my cheek, I noticed Robert walk away, recede deeper into the cemetery, I shouted after him but he didn't seem to hear me. I ran after him.

"Are you upset that I didn't call you?"

"Arcady, don't talk like that," he said. "I understand you perfectly."

"I nearly forgot," I said and handed him the coolers. "Here. But I don't know if they're working. I didn't have time to test them."

"It's all right," Robert said. "The main thing is that you got them. Thanks. You were a great help. How much do I owe you?"

I named the sum and he counted the money into my hand.

"You're coming to the banquet, aren't you?" I asked.

"Of course, I'm coming," he said. "I only. . . ."

"Just make it quick."

"Quick as I can," Robert promised. I went back.

There was nobody left at the grave, everybody had boarded the bus, the principal's wife stood by the door, the wind tossing her hair.

"I was starting to worry," she said. "We have to go, Arcady. Let's not make the others wait."

We were drinking beer, nibbling on pieces of rye bread fried in fat and rubbed with garlic. The principal emptied the mug of beer in one gulp, a piece of toast lodged in his teeth, he brushed crumbs from his lips.

"So, wasn't it nice of me to bring you here? Those funeral meals are so unbearable."

"You're right," I agreed. "I didn't have the slightest desire to sit there. Still, I don't think I would have left on my own. After all. . . ."

"It's just a formality," said the principal. "An oppressive ritual that doesn't ease the pain, just makes everything more difficult. I've never enjoyed funeral receptions."

It was evening. The bar was slowly filling up with people. Wet snow was falling. It was warm and cozy here. Nobody bothered us. The waiter wandered around the hall carrying mugs of beer, soft music played, some people were dancing. Formless shadows slid through time and space. Peace reigned on earth, peace was bread for the dead.

"Are you thinking of what's next?"

I didn't answer.

"Don't think I'm just forcing myself on you. You're depressed, you have to talk about it, Arcady. It will ease the pain.

"I'd rather drink."

"We really should have a drink," said the principal. "To

Veronica."

"May she rest in peace."

"May she rest in peace."

We drank. The toasted bread crunched.

"You know," the principal said, "if my wife really moves in with you, then, as far as I know, it will be a good thing for your brother, as well. Understand me, I don't want to influence your decision, but I don't think you'll ever be happy with Livia."

"Maybe I don't want to be happy."

"Are you thinking. . . . Oh! If you think I'd give you my wife in order to get Livia for myself, Arcady, you must be crazy! What would I do with Livia even if she'd agree. . . . No, I don't want to divorce my wife at all. Not at all. Nature is not capable of creating another woman as exquisite. But I wish you happiness, Arcady. Because of you I feel guilty all the time."

"I sincerely . . ." I murmured.

"I'm no longer a principal," the man said. "Now I've got only my name."

I didn't even know his name. I was looking at the people in the bar, people who didn't have anything to do with me or the principal. Men were ogling women with dreamy eyes. Sophias were softly clinging to the women's necks. People were relaxing. Loving each other. A girl reached for the microphone and started to croon. The clamor subsided. The soft voice wrapped itself up in music and whispered strange words. Syllables pattered like falling chestnuts on the concrete floor. Womens' legs stiffened under the tables, no longer feeling the touch of boots. I wanted to close my eyes. The voice opened the ceiling. Spotlights came on aimed at the girl's frozen face. Exploded and faded. Sophias began to gleam on her naked body trembling in the darkness. They clung to her neck, her breasts, her thighs, her ankles like jets of phosphorus belched out from some dead sea. Clung to her virgin skin, pulsing feverishly, as if sensing the proximity of death. I wandered far away. Somewhere between the stars and the southern islands. Where there was no snow. Where lemon juice poured from the sky. Where women sat silently around huge bonfires. Humming without a sound like bees in pain, gazing into the past with bright eyes. The ocean was smashing shells against the rocks. The children of deep-diving coral hunters, drinkers of dew collected by the wind in the hollows of the stones, dwelled there in caves. The voice carried me rapidly onward. Through herds of whimpering birds with broken beaks hungrily snatching at words lost by crusaders along the roadside. Grieving wolves forsaken in fields of red slime howling their praise to the sun. My brother was lying in a reed hut. Dressed in a suit for the first time in his life. Unbreathing, without a single frozen tear in the corner of his eye. Without a trace of disappointment in his face, gnawed by termites. I shouted loudly. The banal melody I had been humming left me in my fear, like steam from a chimney. My stare grew wet. A lump rose in my throat. The fairy tale snapped. I was alive, I recollected in fear. Tears streamed down my face. Fell tinkling into the beer mug. As if cast in metal. The people sitting at nearby tables cast glances at me. The principal reached out and patted my shoulder. But I didn't care, my beloved, I didn't care. I pushed his hand away. I felt for the switch in my pocket and flicked it on. Nobody noticed anything until the glasses started to melt. A waiter came up.

"He buried his daughter today," the principal said to the waiter. Threw a couple of banknotes on the table. "It's not something that happens every day, right, my friend? Glasses are just glass. . . . Thank God, the beer mugs are resistant enough."

The girl stopped singing and threw her mike away. She stood there with her head lowered. Men waited. I had a premonition about what would follow. I was right. She started to detach the shining bands covering her body. Unwound Sophias from her throat, breasts, ankles.

"Let's get drunk," the principal said as if having guessed my thoughts. "Let's get completely drunk. I've never been completely drunk before."

"I don't want to drink beer anymore."

"Then we have to go somewhere else," said the principal. "They've only got beer here."

"What a stupid place."

"Just like everything else," said the principal. "Let's go?"

The girl touched the last Sophia covering her hips. Smiled and caressed it. Gave it a sudden jerk and screamed. The little creature was biting into her stomach. The girl pulled at it as hard as she could. The Sophia broke in two, its intestines mixing with flakes of mica dripped to the floor. She screamed again.

We rose and left. I looked back when we reached the door. The girl had rid herself of the Sophia, she was standing naked and crying, holding her wounded belly. The people seemed confused. Some were getting up to leave, too.

The music was loud. I had to ring the bell for a long time before the door finally opened.

"Ha!" Victor bellowed as he saw the principal and me. "Here they are! I told them you couldn't get lost just like that." He started doing a wild dance in the middle of the doorway. "Ha!" he yelled. "Ha!

We've got the same blood, you and I!"

Livia was also there at Victor's place. As was the principal's wife. And Robert. Later we dragged my brother out of his bed, too.

What a time we had. We got drunk as lords.

Translated by Mārtiņš Zelmenis

Aija Lāce

Aija Lāce (1947) has published only one book—a collection of stories entitled *Nāves piedzimšana* (The Birth of Death, 1994). Lāce has a degree in biology and is the daughter of Latvian writer Ēvalds Vilks. She has worked for many years as prose editor for *Karogs,* a literary magazine published in Latvia, and for the weekly newspaper *Literatūra. Māksla. Mēs* (Literature. Art. We). Lāce made her first appearances in the press with her poems and translations of Russian classical literature. Lāce's prose is intimate and, like Doris Lessing's prose, reveals that "future utopias" can only take place in the human soul.

The Stairs

I do not know and am not capable of understanding what is happening to me, or what has, perhaps, finally transpired. I cannot find a name for it, short of calling it madness. This might, of course, represent the only solution, but for obvious reasons, it is an option neither pleasant nor convenient. Maybe my malady has been assigned a completely different name or has no name at all; possibly, what is happening to me has never happened to anyone else. In any case, I have found nothing analogous either in scientific literature or in that literature which deems itself scientific. Probably, I should be exploring fiction, which I've ignored until now, postponing such research for a state of utter despair and hopelessness, since I'm fully aware that it's fiction which deals with the subject of madness seriously and truthfully. For this very reason, my turning to fiction would mark me as a not-so-respectable outsider at least according to the standardized canons of thought shared by most people. I've lived my whole life as if what was happening to me were not happening at all, passing over reminders with feigned bravado and indifference. Who can tell what twist my life would have taken were it not for my deplorable cowardice?

Presently, I feel confused not so much by the inevitability of my condition as by its recent reversal. I still would like to try to comprehend at least a part of it all, but I am distracted by this new offer of hope which fate, or something else, has confronted me with; it's an offer I can perceive only as a second variant, replacing the one I rejected. It worries me, because secretly I had already begun to reconcile myself to some form of a gradually progressive, not particularly bothersome madness. But madness, as I understand it, is a steady and one-sided quantity, a particularly limited obsession in which the narrower the range of possible oscillations, the more severe the disorder.

However, my madness has acquired a new form, and if I imagine that I safely avoided going mad from that first offer thrown at me by some external force, then I'm afraid that this time I won't have enough time to adjust to this new phenomenon so easily.

It all started a long time ago, in childhood. I was at an age when all things are perceived as self-explanatory, as though they existed solely for my sake, or, if they were independent of me, then for the sake of just existing—they were unnecessary, a part of the world, nothing more.

It was a bright spring day, I'm absolutely sure of it, although many years were to pass until a sudden and violent fear triggered by what was happening made me rewind time like a reel of film to locate a similar chain of events in my memory; they lit up as if marked by a radioactive isotope. So, it was an exceptionally bright spring day, and I was on my way home from school. My route took about half an hour, and I covered it on foot. We lived and still live in a resort town which stretches like a bent sausage along the coastline; the distances are short if one's route is perpendicular to the coast, but long if one has to get from a point A, located at one end of the sausage, to a point B somewhere at the other end.

My mood was as bright as that spring day—I suppose I might have been bringing some good grades home to my parents. Humming and skipping, swinging my bag in the air, I was trotting down the hill of a sandy side street and was about to gallop up the next hill when suddenly my attention was arrested by a stairway. I knew very well there should be no stairs there. This was a stretch I covered every day. But, as I already mentioned, I was at an age when—"Stairs, so what? What's the big deal?"—was about the only reaction to expect of me.

To be sure, I paused for an instant, but that was just a reflex evoked by the unexpected situation, nothing more. I stopped and stared blankly at the stairs, which led up the very hill I was about to climb, though a little off to one side. I am not sure if the way the stairway looked that day was cemented in my memory. It's more likely that the very incongruity of this sandstone structure in this spot, this town, this hill covered by sand and tufts of sharp grass, dawned in my memory later, at a more reasonable age.

Thus I paused for a moment; there was a stairway next to me. Long, rather steep, the stairs gave the impression of reaching up to the clouds. Without thinking about it, I sensed there was something wrong: the clouds were high in the sky, the stairs ended off a bit lower. It must have been just an impression that the stairs were endless. They also appeared much higher than the hill itself.

Having paused to react to the unexpected obstacle, I shifted from foot to foot, threw my bag from one hand to the other, and raced away, not giving the stairs a second thought.

My scatterbrained head forgot about the occurrence. I forgot to wonder about these stairs, where they'd come from, what it all meant. This level of thinking—"what could it all mean?"—was not available to me.

The stairs were gone the next day, and I realized this only after I'd skipped past the spot; only then I felt myself wondering what it was that had surprised me the previous day, that had vanished today.

I would have forgotten the stairs altogether, since my memory had no intention of burdening itself with things for which I had no use. Perhaps the stairs were too real, and what was too real was incapable of enchanting and stimulating my imagination. I can't recall whether I was at my prince and princess stage then, or whether I was raiding faraway places in the company of adventurous pirates. Maybe I was spending my days in the company of a sweetly decadent higher society of days of yore, who can remember, but what could a real stairway in my own home town mean to me?

But the stairs wouldn't relent. They came back again and again. Gradually I got used to them, regarded them as familiar, although I always stood at the bottom, roving with my eyes, peering, listening, as well, since I noticed that with each of their appearances the stairs were accompanied by a whole complex of phenomena. For instance, the stairs appeared only on sunny days. Bright and alluring, they offered up every nook, every pore of their sandstone structure to my inspection. Moreover, I felt I could sense that the stairs wanted me to touch them. Cautiously, I refrained, afraid to touch even the bottom step. My awkward shyness in unusual situations kept me back. And I was too afraid even to consider ascending the stairs.

It was only later that I realized that the music which my imagination had associated with the stairs' appearances, like a movie sound track, was actually a gentle humming that took the shape of a melody in my mind; perhaps it was my nervousness or the heat, or perhaps it was the stairs themselves that hummed.

In any case, the stairs did everything in their power to overcome my reticence, and my periods of lingering at their foot became more and more extended; it was getting harder and harder to leave. Finally, out of sudden fear that I might actually make an ascent into the unknown, I would mumble a few excuses to the stairs and, whirling around, race off, afraid to look back. My fear was strange, a mixture of terror and sweet temptation.

And then, one day I drifted off on my dreamy wanderings, roaming farther and farther away. Up until then, I'd thought that I knew the town like my own pocket, but I suddenly came to, finding myself on a completely unfamiliar street which led me to a narrower and equally unfamiliar street, and so on. The only thing I could detect in my new surroundings was an unusually heavy, intoxicating scent from an unknown flower. I went on as in a dream, as though floating on clouds, until the narrow path led me down to a calm and peaceful southern sea shimmering in the heat. Yes, it was southern, although our sea, our geographic latitude, where you and you reside, as well, in no way coincides with what I encountered. I had never seen a southern sea, but I knew without a doubt that this was one, right in front of me. There was no sense of surprise, no sense of wonder; I accepted without thought everything that my senses offered. As though on a string, I clambered down the path toward the very edge of the water, enjoying the southern scents with my eyes half-closed. Seashells cracked under my feet, the insides of my eyelids became a movie screen on which I watched jellyfish dancing like transparent parachutes. I recognized them, just like everything else, from descriptions and drawings in books.

I was sobered by the proximity of the water. It was probably an instinctive fear of getting my feet wet that caused me to stop so suddenly—I was jolted from my reverie—I could feel the suddenness of my stop—I felt the solidity of the ground under my feet. I was that close to having stumbled against the bottom stair.

What would have happened to me if the spell had not broken? Never, until then, nor ever after, had I come so close to the stairs. If I hadn't faltered at the water—would I have ascended? Would the trancelike state have lead me all the way to the top? Maybe for once in my life I would have seen what was up there?

I won't relate how I fled without looking back, arriving home breathless and with wet feet, incapable of sane behavior, watching my mother wring the water out of my socks, stuffing newspapers into my squeaking sneakers. . . .

As usual, I was afraid to tell anyone about the stairs. Again I felt that this phenomenon was to be kept a secret; I was afraid of being accused of fantasies and lies—the adults considered these great sins—I was afraid for myself—even at that early age I was beginning to worry that I was confusing reality with something else. I wondered where I actually existed—in reality or in that other somewhere—the adults had occasionally given me hints—*that* could be contained only within me, although the soles of my feet preserved memories of the hard ground a while after, and my eyes—the never before so sharply perceived lacework of scars and crevices in the sandstone, all illuminated by the slanting rays of a low southern sun. And the scent, yes, the scent delivered up its name only in the evening, at home, in my bed under many blankets—they were wisterias that bloomed in the narrow seaside streets, no question about it, although I still don't know until this day what wisterias look like, or whether they smell the way *my* wisterias smelled.

I tried to forget this event—it was too cumbersome to keep in mind. It was so inexplicable that if it lodged in my head, I would be forced to think about it incessantly. Instinctively I tried to run away from, to avoid this disaster—this is how I began to view it—as a disaster in which no one could help me, one which I could relate to nobody, and which only I could attempt to render unreal.

For a while, the stairs left me in peace. As I now recall, it visited me most often during my early youth and adolescence. Finally, I had to come to terms with the fact that I suffered from this *ailment,* as I deemed it, for what other name could I give it? But I reasoned that it was not fatal, and I resigned myself to bearing it like a cross until the end of my days, rather as one would put up with enlarged tonsils or flat feet.

At times I imagined that other people were also visited by the stairs, but that they were unwilling to tell anyone. I tried to test my theory, but I suppose my attempts were naive and clumsy, or, perhaps, too direct and intrusive, because when I spoke up in a careless and nonchalant tone—"Yesterday I saw those stairs again"— my companion, whoever it might have been, always responded by asking, "What stairs?" Thus, I was unable to ascertain whether I was a poor actress and my pretense was fumbled, whether maybe other people had never seen the stairs; yet I was convinced, due to the absolutely identical answers I received from everyone I mentioned the stairs to, that everyone had the same problem, but that it was impossible to react differently—it was a programmed response perfected long before, a mechanical retort. . . . The rules of the game.

I tried not to think about the stairs. Obviously, they came to mind every once in a while, but not so much their physical appearance as a feeling of sweet temptation and the promise of something lovely and good. I regretted never having tried to climb them, but my regrets were eased by my conviction that it was an impossible feat.

My youth came and went, I put my school years behind me, I married, had children. . . . The stairs faded from my memory. In time, I completely forgot about them. They came back briefly to me once when I was discussing dreams with my grown children—how often we dreamed, what kind of dreams, were they good or bad, did they repeat. We got to dreams which come more than once, and then I told my children that when I was young I often had a recurring dream about a sandstone stairway overgrown with green vines, mysterious and alluring, inviting me to ascend. "And you never did," my children said in a mournful tone. "No," I said, "I never did. I'd always wake up." "Too bad," the children said, "Too bad that you never went up, that you never found out what was at the top. . . ."

I would probably have spent the rest of my life believing that the stairs really were just a dream had they not visited me once more. And now what I spoke of at the beginning of my story came to pass—*they* threw a new choice at me.

One day, I was walking at a brisk pace along the same route I'd taken time and time again since early childhood. I was going to pick up my youngest grandchild. My entire life had been spent in the same seaside town, but I wasn't complaining; there had never been a time when I'd longed for anything bigger or better. It was a beautiful, sunny day in September, the loveliest time of the year, when it is as warm as in summer but the air is clearer and the sky seems much higher. It is a time that I've always associated with the greatest clarity of thought I'm capable of. It is also a time that I associate with a feeling of being uplifted, bordering on unreality, and with what I might call an apocalyptic lightness. Can lightness be apocalyptic? Probably not, but I understand it as a certain state of being when the border between the earth beneath my feet and the boundless heavens above my head disappears, when I feel equally at home both here and there and wouldn't feel the slightest confusion in answering a call from either direction.

It's a miracle I didn't tumble down then and there, actually; it should have happened as I hurried down the hill—there was absolutely no warning that the road would suddenly turn into a stairway, which, as far as I could in my astonishment discern, descended steeply, reaching somewhere far below the foot of the hill. It was *my stairway*. I couldn't think; I stood still and dumb, like a post driven into the ground. I was incapable of either turning back or taking a few steps to either side to pass around the stairs. I stood there transfixed, barely sensing that I was rocking slightly—more forward than back; the stairs exerted an almost magnetic pull. I was guided by an instinctive thought—to hold my ground. I won. I felt the oscillations of my body become weaker; the tension in the almost real and straining bond binding me to the staircase gradually eased; I opened my open eyes—that is, I started to see again—the stairs had vanished; I could continue, but I couldn't move. No, it wasn't fear; it was as though someone else had just signed a contract against my will, as though something important had been decided in my place. I hadn't won.

I came to. I went where I intended to go and did what had to be done. But I was aware that *it* had started again, but now in reverse, and that I wouldn't get rid of *it* as before, because there was no third variant—I hadn't wanted to climb so now I was being offered the opposite. But why was the offer so aggressive?

At one point I was beginning to think that nothing unusual had taken place—maybe I had climbed up once, am up here at the top, and now it's time for the dream to end, to descend—I'll come down, the nightmare will end, this is the dream's second series, nothing more. . . . My daily life continued—household chores, stairs, the vegetable garden, stairs, the burden of grandchildren, the stairs; it continued to be so tangibly real that there was no sense hoping it was a dream I would wake from. I hadn't climbed anywhere, hadn't reached anything.

The stairs appeared more and more often. I had had a good look at it. It was the same stairway. The only difference was that when I had been looking at the stairs from the bottom up, I could see every single step, of which there were very many, and ascension had seemed rather hard and difficult; viewed from the top, the steps merged into a slippery children's slide, and the whole length of the stairs could be covered in one breath.

These days, I dwell on such details with strange delight. I think hard and long—too long, as though I could distend time, stretch it out, stretch it, stretch it eternally . . . yet in my mind the slide beneath my buttocks seems slathered with soap, and I know there's no turning back—the stairs will force me to succumb.

Obsession. Stairs in front of me, stairs behind me—that wasn't the worst part—I could still escape on either side. Even horseshoe-shaped stairs left room for escape, but what can I do now when descending stairs have surrounded me on all sides, when my own space is becoming smaller and smaller? So what if I'm permitted to move myself, my space, and my stairs—it's nothing; this baroque combination doesn't seem to interrupt my usual life, my only life. And yet I no longer sleep—I'm afraid to fall asleep because I know that as soon as I do, I will tumble away into the void without even having found a name for what has happened to me. I have never felt so sleepy in all my life.

Translated by Ieva Lešinska

Andra Neiburga

Andra Neiburga was born in 1957 in Rīga. In 1986 she graduated from the
Latvian Academy of Art's design department. While studying, she began to
write. Her first and only collection of stories, *Izbāzti putni un putni būros*
(Stuffed Birds and Caged Birds), was published in 1988. Neiburga's
children's book *Stāsts par Tilli un suņu vīru* (A Story about Tille and the
Dog Man), was published in 1991. It was well received and was later produced as a play.

   Neiburga's prose is marked by a fine feeling for style, colorful and paint-
erly portraits of people and places, and a kind-hearted melancholy. Some of
Neiburga's stories have been published in English: "Stuffed Birds and
Caged Birds" (*AGNI* 33, Boston University); and "Mosy Death—Description of a Struggle" (*The Picador Book of Contemporary East European
Prose*). This issue features "Zone," excerpts from Neiburga's summer diary.
Neiburga is presently involved in Rīga real estate, managing her family's
numerous properties. She is married to artist Andris Breže and has a
daughter and son.

Summer Log
(The Zone)

Normunds is back from Germany, Gundega from Australia, Inese from Sweden, but Jānis—from the countryside. He's spent a month there alone with his dog, he's transformed. His hands don't shake anymore, he's stopped stammering, his muddled thinking and sloppiness are gone. True, he's grown a little belly.

And what if he needs his shaking hands for writing poetry?

I'm out in the countryside, too. I don't count the days, I sleep and eat, I do laundry, and I weed.

That great life worthy of literature is, thank God, somewhere on the invisible horizon.

The wires are cut, the phone is silent, the radio is broken.

When there is absolutely nothing else to do, I write for myself.

I log.

A bit of self-discovery: in the countryside, I am not afraid of death. At least not the way I am in the city. Death in the city is too unnatural. That is all I can say on this.

When I watch a lizard sunbathing on a rock, I don't think—"it exists in order to exterminate vermin." I think—"it exists in order to sunbathe on a rock." The lizard is older than me and older than the rock, I can't explain the lizard.

I don't want to understand anything. I just want to feel.

I don't like to make use of steroetypes. One just came over to my house, Šūmanis by name. In his shopping net, a three-liter jar of muddy swill. He's been officially registered as an alcoholic. Reddish violet, coarse. Plastered. Cheerful and benign. He knows how to build houses and brick stoves, raise fences, clean chimneys, tar boats, glaze windows, cut firewood, slaughter cattle, catch fish. Forty-seven years old. Looks sixty. A hat shiny with grease on his head. Loves to curse the Slavs, sticking a juicy Russian obscenity on the end of every sentence. One eye is glass, it's clear and motionless, the other permanently squints. This peculiarity puts a fixed, cunning smirk on the man's face.

"I'm no fool!" Šūmanis says. "Fools are them what digs in the mud, I'm not digging no mud!"

An absolutely unverifiable statement, but I like it.

You could make a hero out of this Šūmanis, even a protagonist. Put together a comedy or a tragedy or a farce.

You could reveal his child's soul in all its sensitivity, its naïveté. You could work hard to condemn the nasty life that has made him what he is. And—to dodge the banality so scorned by critics—you could make poor Šūmanis murder his wife in the end, after all.

But Šūmanis doesn't ask to be explicable. He leaves happily, swinging his net with the jar. He lives just past the swamp here.

Once the pain of labor is forgotten, it turns into something akin to pleasure in the mind. Summer, not spring, is the best season, really, for adult love.

I could make a story out of that as well, but it probably wouldn't be about Šūmanis.

Painter Heinrihsone's large fields of color are extremely sensuous. My schoolmate Sarmite's pale and narrow fingers are also sensuous, which Heinrihsone described so wonderfully in the magazine *Zilite*. Cucumber plants and peonies and the fat grubs in cabbage are sensuous. Poppies in their brief bloom. But with marigolds, only the seeds are sensuous.

Life, too, can lack a theme.

Sure, there's birth and death, but they are just the top edge of the first page and the bottom edge of the last.

Oh, if only I were Max Frisch!

Even better—if I were Gantenbein.

I'm not.

The woman at the mirror by twilight—that's me too.

(I have to stop writing, a butterfly has strayed into the room accidentally, I have to help it get out, outside it's a glaringly bright day, tomorrow, in a week at the latest, there'll be a storm.)

By twilight at the mirror. The mirror has some kind of connection with death, because only the past is hidden there. You must not look into the mirror too long, especially at dusk. Your eyes become hollow and eerie, the lips draw back and bare the teeth (they're not mine), damp shadows cover everything, and sticky fingers paw the soul. The woman unravels in slate-colored shadows, paralyzed, and there is someone standing behind her.

But outside it's a glaringly bright day, the sun melts the sky, pours it into the room, and the mirror becomes only your reflection, for now. No, the mirror becomes the bridge to a fairy tale. (All fairy tales, though they begin with the words "Once upon a time," speak of the future—they model endless possibilities for your life and invite you to choose your role therein.)

The sun melts the sky and pours it into the room, you're all golden in the mirror, in the quivering light, your hair fine gold and your lightly gilded skin, a brocade mantilla on your shoulders—silver and violet, and the fragrance of lemon thyme.

A beauty.

You melt in the light, and mercury drips from your fingertips onto the worn planks in the floor, smashing into a million brilliant bullets.

The choir sings Hallelujah.

(However, the mirror lies.)

Washing the floor on all fours, you happen to glance in the mirror—an unfamiliar face, moist and flushed, hair stuck to the forehead.

Who's that?

Yourself.

The mirror must not be broken. The images of the sun and the twilight continue to live in the mirror, as long as it's whole.

When the mirror cracks, they're set free and scatter about the house, they will never leave you again.

Summer, as I said, is by far the most sensuous time of year. The yellow flowers of the cucumbers. Bumblebees. When you stretch out on the knoll, face-down on the grass, you feel the curve of the earth inside you. That's how infertile women should sleep. The horizon descends to an inch from your eyes, and this inch, with its blades of grass and its insects, becomes the whole world. The sun works you into the earth like fertilizer.

You can also lie on your back. If the sky doesn't make your head spin.

The woman lies on her back in the garden. She's pale, untanned, in the green grass. The shadows of leaves are dabs of paint on her skin. The shadows dance, the painter adds one coat after another, until the body takes shape. The emerald of the grass and the milky skin. A light ochre about the shoulders and the stomach taut as an apple.

Milk and emerald, and the dark red juice of cherries running down her chin, a tiny rivulet down her breasts.

The woman is asleep.

Šūmanis with his jar of swill is frozen behind the black currant bush and is afraid to pass.

"Self-indulgence," someone says, having read what I've written. "Only bad movies feature white women lying in green grass."

Yes, of course.

But Šūmanis also has a wife.

Her legs are withered, brown, speckled by knotted veins. Her entire skin is taupe like dry, clayey earth, rough as sandpaper. Her hands are copper, no, the color of lignite, with black hangnails, they're cracked, and all the cracks are full of black, fertile oil. Her breasts droop like wasp hives and her stomach is a tough leather bag. The soles of her feet are broad and hard, they cleave to the earth with crooked, powerful toes.

She has bones and muscles and sinew, this Šūmanis's wife, and it's all on view.

Hair like lichen and a pudenda like a swallow's nest.

She is a woman and Šūmanis is a man. It would be dishonest to attribute love only to the emerald-green and white, only to the pink and gold. Šūmanis and his wife collide like rock against rock, and their love flares up brief and glittering, smelling of the shed, sweat, swill, and rather dirty sheets.

That's love, too.

The pinkish golden kind trails like a strand of honey, sweet and sticky, thickening here, disappearing there, it swells and wafts away like the scent of jasmine. Rolls like the sea with round, shallow waves when the wind dies, and each coming wave is more fragrant, sweeter and deeper than the last. Its edges are the color of transparent blood, and the yellow thread in the middle stretches for a long, long time. Then comes the ninth wave, the bowl of honey breaks, and the blood coagulates. And now you are Šūmanis's wife, your legs are tree branches, and you char hard and fast.

Love just the same.

On calm warm evenings the smell of jasmine by the house is almost nauseating, you have to shut the windows.

A lot of grass snakes live in the shed and in the pile of planks by the barn. Once Lilija, the former owner of the house, reclined on the grass under the oak tree. The tree's shadow gradually receded and left her slumbering in the sun. When she woke up, a sleeping snake was curled up on her chest. It gave Lilija a terrible fright, and since then she can't stand grass snakes.

How strange and beautiful. I thought such things happened only in fairy tales.

I'm jealous of Lilija, she's the snake's bride now, she's marked.

The snake is probably connected to death somehow, but in a good way.

I still don't know which fairy tale will be mine.

When I live in the countryside, the city seems unreal. I don't miss the city at all. There time flows unevenly and every hour has eyes of fear. In the city my soul runs a chronic high fever and has an irregular pulse. In the city I want to acquire too much—friends, love, recognition. In the city it's hard to distinguish myself from others. The fever in my soul passes for passion, and the short circuit of a single night leaves scars that are too deep and painful.

In the city everyone should carry a voltage regulator with them. In the countryside I don't care that I have no friends.

My house is in the middle of the forest, and there are no politics within a radius of at least two miles. Only mushrooms and berries.

Just now I scorned the city, but reading what I've written, I come to this conclusion: I write about the countryside like an honest-to-goodness city girl. All those twilights and weak white women.

Forgive me, my love. Your crepe paper gaudiness and your cheap spangles are dear to me. The smell of asphalt excites me as much as the aroma of hay. I need the city's gossip and intrigue, the city's fickle joy. I like money and everything you can buy with it in the city. I like loud distractions at night and coming home in the morning in the weak light as drowsy citizens are leaving for work on the first trolleys.

You are the longing in the eyes of the female yardkeepers, and the carnival glare of their orange vests. You are kisses in telephone booths. The rats' secret bustle in the cellars and the squeal of taxi tires at the Hotel Latvija.

You are a fragrant combination of French perfume, dirty hallways, and car exhaust.

You are unnatural, and that is precisely why you are beautiful.

(But understand—in the countryside there is no fear of death.)

You can truly love only one city. I don't mean the shell—the buildings and the streets and the cobblestones. I mean the living city, with its flesh and blood, with its people and their assigned roles.

And I discover: I can't love my city enough. Her flesh and blood are ravaged by an evil plague. I hear a foreign language in her streets, and the colors and shapes of these imported artificial flowers don't please me. Their stench works away at the walls of buildings and the foundations of monuments until they crumble.

And moreover—my city is poor. I can understand and forgive that, but a poor city is pitiful. Poverty in a city should hide itself in attics rather than show off on the main street. My poor city is like a tired old woman after violent sex with a vagrant who hasn't even paid. Her makeup is smeared and the dress that used to be so magnificent is soiled and torn.

Šūmanis promised to cut firewood today, but when he got ten rubles in advance, he took off.

The woman at night.

The night is frightening. Unkind voices whisper to each other in unintelligible tongues. The air is thick and viscous, the sheets are damp. The palpable absence of somebody else's soothing breath nearby. The dog of darkness, panting hotly, runs past the open window and makes the heart grow numb with foreboding. The window panes, so quiescent during the day, tremble as the fingers of tiny spirits touch them. The night's tentacles creep out of the corners of the room to caress the woman's body, throbbing as they retract, leaving slimy tracks on her breasts. The sickly sweet stench of rotten fruit bubbles up, and an owl shrieks with horror in the birches. Even the tree leaves quiver, when they feel the breath of night upon them.

The night is a man with a toothless mouth and burning eyes.

The darkness is his loyal sister, a crone, a matchmaker.

Šūmanis is probably staggering home through the night .

"A dark night or a bright day,

A drunkard doesn't care," he bellows a popular tune.

A bat shoots soundlessly right past his eyes.

"Scram, varmint!"

The night withdraws into the cool blue thickets of the forest, the darkness follows it slowly, her dirty sheets drying in the sweaty light.

The woman has fallen asleep.

The gray light of the morning doesn't flatter her. Her tortured face turns yellow, there's a cool damp in her elbow joints, under her breasts, and the rumpled sheets, twisted around her legs, are quietly steaming. The sign left on her chest by the finger of night is crusty and heaves slowly as the woman breathes.

But her breath is calm.

Night is gone.

By day all the terrors of the night seem absurd.

I laugh, but cautiously.

The village is dying. Has died already.

We city folk create only an illusion of life during the short summer. The few local inhabitants can be seen twice a week at the car store. Auntie Ella with her crutches. Mirdziš. Old Vangrov. Auntie Milda. Five or six others. Almost all of them are old, collapsing with their houses. Some are hostile:

"Those durned Rī-īga types leave no room . . . buyin' till the store's empty!"

Hardly anyone in the village keeps livestock anymore. They don't put up preserves either. In the car store the old ladies buy Globus jams and tinned peas and Selga cookies. What else can they do? No one produces milk here anymore, and sugar is rationed. The gardens go to seed, the old people don't have the energy. The young ones can't find work. And the children don't have schools.

The village is dying, and its death cripples the souls of the people in a strange way.

But come fall, when the city people gradually retreat, someone makes a tour of all the emptied homes in these and other villages: the window panes are carefully removed and just as carefully (thank God!) replaced, every drawer, every little closet comes under exacting scrutiny. Everything that has any value gets taken. Even a screwdriver or a hammer. Even an opened box of tea.

(When it turns out that it was a well-organized enterprise originating in the city of Ventspils, every autumn, for years, it's hard to believe.)

Waiting for the car store in the sweltering afternoon (sometimes you have to wait for two, three hours), the women idly hash out the latest events in the village. It's amazing how the news service works: who, when, how long they're staying, how long they'll be gone, what's been stolen from whom.

The women turn to the past only reluctantly: you young ones don't understand anything anyway. Well, yes—there were seventy houses in the village. Maybe some forty boats went out to sea. In the winter the men worked in the forest. Entertainment? Well, yes, they put on plays, sure. Right here in the tavern. And in Lielirbe there were dances, they used to walk those five miles there and back along the sea. And the Lielirbe boys used to come here as well, the young ones used to sing and dance at night.

Now there's nothing.

They sit in the sun, wait for the store. Listen—isn't that the hum of an engine? The dogs wait, too, with their mistresses. They sleep, panting in the heat, Benta and Uno, Little Jerry and Moris, Repsitis, Muizitis, Bonitis. The small ones are white and shaggy, the big ones all have some collie in them.

They wait, prick up their ears.

When the store arrives, they beg for cakes.

We're not just talking about break-ins. Ēriks's television antenna was stolen off his roof twice, but Imants lost a brand new outhouse. It's very simple—lift it off the ditch and take it away.

"I'm no thief," Šūmanis says. "D'ya think just coz I'm a drunk I'm gonna be a thief?"

Yes, yes, I believe you—a thief wouldn't say that.

When I go swimming in the evening there isn't a person on the beach as far as the eye can see. Occasionally the Carpathian guest worker herds the cows to the shore with his dogs.

At night the sand swallows up people's footsteps, blown smooth by the wind. Only the tracks of tanks and armored cars don't heal as quickly in the sand. Bordertown.

Sand. In the nose, mouth, ears. The woman's body and hair are the color of sand. She's masked. A gull lands on her shoulder and doesn't notice. A dog runs by, doesn't notice her. Only the sea notices—the tide sticks out its tongue closer and closer to her in the evening, probing.

The woman in the sand. Her body along the sea from Kolkas rags to Ventspils. The towns of Vaide, Saunags, Pitrags, Košrags, Mazirbe, Sīkrags, Jaunciems, Ķesteri, Miķebaka, Lūžņa, and Ovīsi are all birthmarks on her skin.

The sea doesn't smell of fish here anymore because there are no fishermen.

Mikelbāka is located around the woman's navel, between Kolka and Ventspils. My house "Jaunvigas" is right in the middle of the navel.

Viga is a hollow between the dunes.

The invisible umbilical cord grows from my house right into the sky. Like the beanstalk. I have to keep the house in good shape, I have to make sure the cord doesn't snap.

(It's absolutely impossible to get lumber for home repairs.)

The Pize cemetery is five hundred yards from my house. I haven't been there yet.

The migration of souls. There is such a theory. As they migrate, the road of the souls goes past my house. I sit by the window at dusk and watch them go by. Young and old. The older ones are a dense gray, the young ones are clear, almost transparent. The children's souls are like a gentle vibration, like a breath of wind, just barely discernible. They never drop in at our house, and that's just fine. We aren't ready for the trip.

The roses have blossomed.

The yellow ones bloom with a frantic haste and empty out soon. From a distance it doesn't matter, but look closely—they're old co-quettes wearing too much perfume.

The pinkish-white one blooms slowly and keeps for a long time. Cool and waxy in the hot sun.

White Christmas.

The woman in the river.

The Irbe flows swift and sinuous, bounded by steep banks. In some places fallen trees cross the current, the roots rise into the sky. As in Shishkin's painting, only the bears are missing.

An enormous number of gadflies.

The river runs swiftly but the thick and sultry air stands still. White sparks fly in the river's mirror, from the friction between water and air. The woman is up to her chest in the middle of the river, the brown stream coolly caresses her. The sparks leap into her hair and flare up crimson. You could stand like that until the river freezes. Her feet sink into the sand, take root.

If the river froze, an ice hole would form around the woman.

But the frost is still far away. Now—brown, honeyed, gray brown, all greens, sky blue. Need some deep purple. The ultramarine blue-bells on the shore can't be seen from this distance.

The woman in the sea.

Green water, white foam. Salt on the lips, salt in the eyes. The wind chases the waves and drives them back into the deep.

It's hard to stand in the sea, the waves try to throw you on the shore or to pull you into the depths. The woman lies down on a sandbank, the waves fall over her, push, lift, carry, throw, and the sand buffs the body smooth.

If you crawl out to the shore in time, you can hear your blood sough like the sea.

If you stay too long, the waves will throw a pebble on the shore, cool and shiny. Or a piece of amber.

A bit of self-discovery: I'm happy. Fear has abandoned me.

Fear has lost my scent, runs around confused, circles, whimpers, is ashamed to look his master in the eye.

Crawls into its cave, into the darkness, and whimpers, licks its wounds.

Waits.

(Once more: the woman and the night.)

There are cool nights, soothing nights.

Blue green like Siberian fir.

Clear as glass.

Like a mirror for the sky.

Like an echo.

They smell of hay, of peppermint, of moss, of falling dew.

On such nights the apples turn juicy.

On such nights all the windows are open, the stars walk right through, the darkness may enter. The darkness pours into the corners from the middle of the room, strokes everything, smoothes it down, licks it with a cool tongue, loosens things, and turns transparent, begins to radiate a pearly light.

The woman doesn't sleep, she listens to a moonbeam buzzing into the window.

She doesn't feel her body, it's dissolved in the crystalline glimmer, it floods across the floor, runs along the walls, silver, white, gray.

A star on her forehead and a secret on her lips, black as coal.

(That's not me.)

Moreover: there are warm and soothing nights.

Soft as a dog's belly.

Black as a mole's fur.

Not a leaf trembles, the blades of grass bend silently under the footsteps of darkness.

The night has hidden its face in the clouds, eyes shut.

The woman sleeps.
When the light dawns it will start to rain.

I live between what I think I see and what I know.
The less I know, the more I see.

Every day I follow the sun in a circle around the house.
In the morning the sun shines into the bedroom. Waking me, she promises a happy day. That's where I work.
The afternoon sun shines in the dining room. That's a good place to read, write letters, relax during the siesta.
The crimson evening sun shines into the kitchen, melts my aluminum kettles into copper, settles me for the night.

In the yard, Father splits the firewood that Šūmanis cut. The sound of the ax promotes a feeling of security: I still have a long time to live here.

Every day there's a new gift in the sea sand: an empty whisky bottle, a plastic Swedish gas can, an old shoe, a beer bottle. A can of oil paint—Aunt Olga painted her house with it.
Shoes wash up most often.
"Did all those people drown?" my daughter asks.
I do not know.

My favorite smells:
tar
honey
sawdust, resin, tree bark
camomile and meadowsweet, parsley
rotting leaves
nasturtiums
moldy cellars
smoking stoves
musk de Cartier
wet fur, puppy's breath.

Grown-ups will chew a carrot from the skinny end to the fat one. They are simply ingesting carotene.
No child eats a carrot like that.
A child starts from the fat end, breaking it off carefully with her teeth, pulling away the carrot's brightest part, the part encasing the core. If the carrot is mature enough and the child has practiced enough, then the small, light core comes out completely smooth in

the end, as if it hatched by itself, moist, even the tiny, tender, root-like bumps on the surface of the core are left whole.

Such a little core is a special delicacy.

I eat carrots like a child.

But with a radish you have to peel the skin first with your teeth.

You can also peel a tomato with your teeth. The honeyed softness of the tomato shimmers, a pale orange color.

With a cucumber cut lengthwise, you have to scrape out the seedy center first.

Rain, drizzle.

A foggy sea.

The foghorn trumpets across the whole village.

The rose blossoms are heavy with rain and bend to the ground.

A calm gray immobility, even the delicate threads of rain are frozen in the air. No end, no beginning.

People talk quietly, and the foghorn muffles their words.

The other side of the meadow is barely visible through the gray curtain of rain. I think I see a grim procession moving slowly—faceless men, shadows, pale stiff bodies on the stretchers, water dripping from their edges. Those drowned between two rains.

Hooooooo, hooooo—the foghorn like a funeral bell.

All Souls' Day at the Pize cemetery. The young pastor works up a glare of righteous indignation, God's anger at the congregation for deserting its temple (they "allowed" the Pioneer camp to set up a club in the Mikelbaka church). I believe in God, but I don't believe in God's anger at those lonely old people. The pastor's overly dramatic voice grates on my ears.

The Word of God should speak to the soul, but the soul hears quiet simple words the best.

The pastor goes on for a long time. The church choir, nine or ten old ladies, all decked out in pretty black-and-white polka-dot dresses, sit in a row on the knoll and rest the swollen legs in their thick stockings until the next hymn.

God's squandered words can't find a willing ear, they tangle in the tree branches—plop, plop—they drop into the burnt grass.

A dog lies at the pastor's feet, panting.

Depressing.

As the next hymn begins, I abandon the cemetery, and I can tell that God is not angry at me.

As I leave, I see a couple of families outside the fence, seated on blankets, having a drink, a snack, they've come from afar. No sign of Šūmanis.

August: red rowan trees, yellow sunflowers, marigolds still in full bloom, asters blossom, cucumbers ripen, cabbages spin into heads, the oak has sprouted acorns, the broad beans are turning black, red orange-cap mushrooms in the green grass behind the shed, round mushroom heads in the yard under our oak tree.
Is this insignificant?

I could describe this in more detail, but there's no time, you'd have to read for an entire month, day by day.

The wind is persistent here in the seaside village. At times it's fierce, pushing the meadow grass to the ground, stubbornly gripping the tree tops, won't let go, plucking the old shingled roofs chip by chip, it howls in harmony with the sea.
(You always hear the sea, the roll of the sea is the silence of this place. The city's silence is the chime of the late streetcar and the steps on the asphalt of a late passerby and the crunch of the yardkeepers' shovels in the early winter mornings.)
At times the wind is gentle, clinging, wagging its tail like a dog, wheedling, it rubs against your legs, licks your mouth.

The wind has subsided. The wind has run into the thick of the woods, hidden in some ditch, some old trench, the wind has drowned in the swamp. The wind has worn down and wasted away into a slim thread, spun into a zigzag in the widows. Windless—between the old and the new wind. The sky alights onto the roof of the shed, gray. No more rain. Still no rain. The sea is inaudible. The birds fall silent, the bees don't hum. The leaves are frozen, the grass is soaked. Peace and immobility. The woman sits at the window, she can't move—the air is too thick, too resistant to thought.
She sits in black clothes, her eyes painted black, she smokes. The smoke freezes in the air. Waits. Doesn't know for what.

The only visitor to our house is the former owner's old tomcat.
At night it sleeps up in the hay, by day it disappears somewhere.
You can live here for weeks without seeing a single soul.

Mary Coughlan is singing tonight in "Jaunvigas." She sings about her weak, naive people, about her harsh and impoverished homeland. Her husky, gentle voice spills like a stream of tears through the rooms, inundates the house, her voice and the fog flood the yard, across the meadows, the edge of the forest, the swamps, the swamps, the stagnant waters, the dark swamps.

Lots of swamps here.

There is no direct path through the woods—there's always some little swamp in your way. The drainage ditches haven't been cleaned for decades, the swamps force themselves on the houses, steal grazing ground.

Sedge and horsetails. Cattails.

Rotted tree stumps and the earth's bloody smell.

Black, green, gray, dark brown.

Broad beans in the spring, cranberries in the fall.

Fat mushrooms with yellow caps and white stems along the edge of the swamp.

A rock thrown into the stagnant water gives an abrupt and hollow gurgle, no circles of spreading water, only a startled swarm of mosquitoes takes wing, whining.

The earth rocks underfoot, a branch snaps, fear wells up suddenly, falls across the eyes like a gray veil, hisses in the ears like a snake, stinks like an animal.

To crash through the shrubs and the brushwood with narrowed eyes like a deer, let the branches whip your face and your somersaulting heartbeat even out with the rhythm of your running.

To fall on your face in the meadow on the edge of the forest and greedily inhale the solid, healthy body of the earth. The sun.

(But Šūmanis knows the way across all the swamps.)

As fall approaches, grass snakes grow scarce. On the other hand, there are many lizards and blindworms. Tiny baby lizards live in the chink between two boards on the hotbed, shiny little eyes peer out from the dark. But the blindworms lie in the grass or the sand like the copper neck hoops of our ancestors. When you approach, they crawl away unhurriedly.

The Liv cultural festival in Mazirbe. Booming, heartfelt speeches and the flag of the Livs flutters again over their building. Lots of people. I wonder how many of them speak the Liv language?

The shame of seven generations hangs its head.

But there's beer, champagne, cognac, chicken roll, and smoked carp at the buffet. As the Latvian and Liv anthems play, the thirsty people in line stand at attention.

Outdoors, in the evening, through the night, there's an honest-to-goodness blowout, two orchestras slave away in shifts, sweating buckets.

"*Molodaja guvernantka bernip rogila, Nekormila, Nepojila, upe iemeta,*" a pale kid sings into the microphone, and the Latvians jump merrily all over the Livs' bones.

The landscape God has created here cannot be called beautiful in the usual sense. It is monotonous. Wild. Gloomy. Mysterious in its monotony.

You can feel the presence of the border guards everywhere. I'm pleased and amazed—they are friendly, polite, and helpful. When there's another burglary in the village, they pitch in with their dogs (the police are helpless, there is one official policeman with a broken motorcycle for a coastal zone twenty miles long). Now and then they drive out to the loneliest houses at night, to make sure that everything is all right. They know all the locals.

No, these guards don't frighten me. Their tracks in the forest, the seashore, the dunes—these frighten me.

The dune guards the land like a rampart against the sea's aggressive ambitions. Wind on the seashore, the lap of the waves, the immense broad skies. You crawl across a dune and fall into a big bowl—the silence hits your ears, scorching heat, blue sky above your head. In the hollow, two rockets point their noses at the sky. Black, gloomy, eloquent silhouettes against the yellow grass of the dunes. Trenches and bunkers. The silence becomes threatening. The rusted coils of wire tangle in your feet, catch the hem of your skirt.

But from a distance of three steps, the rockets send out a sweet smell of warm wood—old broken wooden rockets.

At night the woman lies in her house and feels how, hidden behind the dunes, along the entire length of the coast, the rotting wooden rockets aim at the stars.

The lighthouse beam caresses the forests all night. Sleep, don't be afraid.

I can feel the way the lighthouse unites the earth with the sea, the forest with the beach, the solitary farms scattered through the woods, the people asleep.

The stars fall toward autumn.

A shining point and a streak in the sky. As the stars fall, the woman goes out into the yard, no fear in the dark. (Or: when you see

something beautiful, you forget fear, even in the dark.)
    The dog runs out and barks at the sky.

You really need very little to be happy.
    To see, to hear, to feel:
    how your hollyhock grows, opens, and blooms
    how the laundry dries all fragrant in the wind
    how the flowerbed breathes freely after weeding
    how the sand dries after rain
    how the fog lifts
    how the evening sneaks up
    how the sun rises
    how the seasons change.
    For lunch, you need new potatoes with dill, a mushroom sauce,
butter in one piece, tomatoes and cucumbers with sour cream and
onions.
    For dinner, pancakes with raspberry or cloudberry jam.
    For breakfast, a cup of black coffee.

And then the rains come.
    Everything is damp, everything smells.
    Of earth, rot, wet wood, of smoke.
    Mushrooms grow in the forest.
    In the attic, red bilberries ripen on sheets.
    Flies copulate and bite.
    The sea is fermented and lazy.
    The woman walks along the shore, the wet sand solid like freshly
poured asphalt. The seawater is green gray, blue gray, brown gray.
At the point where the sea meets the clouds hiding the sun it's pure
silver. The blue of a storm in the east.
    The raindrops roll over the face, the lips, behind the collar. They
melt into the sea, the wet sand, the cold sky.
    If you sit down on the ground, pull your knees up to your head,
hide your face in your knees, shut your eyes, and abandon yourself
to the rain, you can forget yourself completely and metamorphose:
into a barrel washed up by the sea, into a smooth piece of rotten
wood, a pebble, a grain of sand, a drop of rain.
    You can pour out over the sand and soak into the earth.
    Or do the opposite: forget your surroundings and feel only your-
self.
    A lazy and eternally thoughtless life.
    The pearl in the shell.
    Warm within and well.

The rains proclaim—September is coming.

Time to go.

The fall will stay.

I can only imagine how the oak will turn yellow and shed its leaves. How the wild boars will come for the potatoes on dark nights. How the rowan berries will be sweet after the frost. How on warm summery days swirling cudgels of fog will roll over from the sea. And how late mushrooms with copper-colored heads will sprout in the white moss of the pine saplings.

Time to go.

The city frightens me from a distance—will I still know how to live there?

Such a long summer, every minute like a drop of honey on my soul.

Such a short summer, it sped by like a windy day.

The woman starts to say good-bye two weeks before leaving.

Oh, yes, it's so far away, but every day is a parting.

Every day says: Soon.

You won't be there, you won't see.

You'll forsake it all, you're a stranger.

Joy isn't shiny anymore, it's tarnished with bitter yearning. Rusty.

Happiness isn't serene. Moments are held too hard.

Soon, soon.

Neither the forest nor the sea nor the swamps will miss you.

Your love is one-sided.

The woman in the twilight by the window. Her eyes painted black, her lips like coal.

She smokes.

She isn't waiting for anything.

On the day of departure the sun comes out after a rain. Everything glints and glitters, the drying dew lights up, the autumn colors begin to throb.

The car that takes the woman away is bright green. You can't find that kind of green in nature.

As the car turns onto the forest road, the sun hides behind a violet cloud, gold dust scatters itself over the treetops and disappears.

At the edge of the swamp Šūmanis stands in the bushes.

Waves farewell, smirks. Under his hat, two horns.

The woman looks back.

I don't much like autumn in Rīga.

Mud and gloomy people.

I want to dye my hair black and go to Malaysia.

To inhale an air as searing and damp as a sauna. There, the leaves of flowers are as green as my car.

The ocean is as hot as the water for sprinkling cucumbers in a tin bath. It smells of good tobacco there, and of palm oil, and of rubber tree sap. There is pink lightning, and rain, warm and thick as milk fresh from the cow. Night is divided from day there only by darkness, but the darkness drops suddenly like a theater curtain.

I will dine there in Chinese restaurants on the shores of the ocean.

At night I'll put an orchid on my pillow.

In the lively streets of Kuala Lumpur, I will melt into a sea of dark people in white clothes, and I will wait for springtime in Latvia.

The woman and autumn.

As it nears, autumn asks: Will you still be here in the spring?

Yes! Yes.

(I want to be.)

Translated by Baņuta Rubess

Aivars Ozoliņš

Aivars Ozoliņš (1957) has published only one book of prose, *Dukts* (1991), which is considered to be the first example of postmodern literature in Latvia. However, it may actually be an ironic a statement on postmodernism itself. *Dukts* gratifies only that reader who is willing to participate in it and play: "*Dukts* is a game between the gods and caesers, a game which anyone can play—even a child who doesn't know much, as long as he's been designated by the gods and the caesers for the game, or simply wishes to play it." One cannot rely on the author because in reality there is no author; he existed in the short moment that *Dukts* was put down on paper. In the game of *Dukts* the reader is kept amused by language and the word, which at the time of their creation were playing with the author, finally making him realize that "words, just like the world," have a "hollow center." Ozoliņš works for the newspaper *Diena* as a political commentator. He has polished his journalistic skills living and working in the United States.

Ozoliņš's "Tale No. 13" was originally published in *Grāmata,* a magazine devoted to philosophy.

Tale No. 13

Concerning an important event in the court of Emperor Frederick and other adventures which befall the knight San Alberto when he sets out to take away from Baron Miserabius his faithful Katherine, while her deceased father is unable to hold on to the wooden fish and the court falcon; about India's ruler's jewels, eight sons, and their mysterious fellow traveler; about what occurs when sheep are left to roam untended; about storytellers and stories, including this one, and how it all turned out.

Emperor Frederick, the mighty and benevolent ruler of his own lands, was fond of gathering in his court not only noble seigniors and other knights, but also connoisseurs of various arts and trades, even if they weren't descendants of ancient and famous families. All sorts of people would come—potters, horn blowers, swordsmen, hunters, money changers, peasants, magicians, horse trainers, court jesters, wrestlers, comedians, and thinkers, too, who would always keep silent, and advisers, who would always keep talking. Amongst all of them was a storyteller who entertained the emperor during the long winter and the short summer nights by relating all sorts of true, funny, terrible, sorrowful, and joyful events which had either actually taken place in the world or could have taken place. One night the storyteller became sleepy, but the emperor still wanted him to go on with his stories.

And the storyteller began to tell of a poor man who had one thousand bezants and who was on his way to see the sheep trader, and for each coin he received two sheep.

"Tell me, how can a poor man, if he is poor, have such a sum of money, which not even a good many of my knights have, though they neither consider themselves poor nor allow themselves to be called so?" Frederick wondered.

The storyteller explained: "Oh, ruler! Must I, a fool, tell you that in some places in the world there occur more wonders then even my friend Horatio has dreamed of? That is another story which I will tell you some other time."

"Very well." "On his way back, the peasant must cross a flooded river. On the bank he notices a fisherman in a dilapidated boat that has enough room only for the peasant himself and one sheep. The peasant climbs into the boat with one of his sheep, grabs the oars, and begins to row. He rows and rows and crosses over to the other bank."

The storyteller abruptly grew silent. The emperor said: "Continue."

But the storyteller replied, "In the meantime, let's let the sheep get over to the opposite side of the river. What happened after that I will tell you later."

Well, but in order to get all the sheep across the river, the peasant would have to work hard for many years. Therefore, the storyteller was finally able to get a good night's sleep. And he fell asleep immediately. Frederick thought it over and decided that no harm could come of this, only good. And he gave orders for a feast.

The kitchen maid prepared some dough and baked a pie with eel and raisins and hid it in the flour bin. But a mouse managed to sneak in there. Having noticed this, the cook let the cat into the bin and firmly fastened the lid. The mouse hid in the flour, and the cat ate the pie; when the kitchen maid opened the bin, the mouse sprang out, but the cat just purred contentedly and clearly had no intention whatsoever of catching the mouse. Fortunately, other provisions could be found in the kitchen cupboards, pots, and cellars to place on the emperor's table.

Emperor Frederick was a great and noble ruler, and all kinds of skillful people would travel to his court from far and wide, because the emperor would bestow gifts kindly and generously upon anyone who was a master of his craft. Fortune-tellers, healers, storytellers, horsemen, goldsmiths, animal trainers, millers, grave diggers, fire swallowers, comedians, and drummers would come, all kinds of artists. Frederick summoned them to the table and ordered finger bowls with rose water, but then suddenly there arrived seven soothsayers wearing pointed, paper cone hats studded with stars on their heads, and Frederick addressed them, "Which of you is the eldest?" "I am, your highness," an old man stepped forward, his beard touching the floor. He delivered greetings from his master, the grand ruler of India, the Presbyter John, and he presented to the emperor three gigantic and marvelously colorful gemstones along with his master's question. Emperor Frederick, without uttering a word, ordered the precious stones to be taken away. Then the envoys began to show their skill: suddenly it grew dark as night, rain began to pour and such hail that every one of the thirty-six thousand hailstones was the size of a hen's egg, and some of them—about one thousand—were even larger. Immediately, the barons, seigniors, knights, and dukes all took to their heels, away and under the table; however at that moment the hail and rain stopped.

The soothsayers then asked for a reward. Good Frederick said, "Ask whatever you desire." But they pointed at Duke San Alberto and said, "Ruler, let him come with us and protect us from our enemies." "Very well."

Everyone sat down at the table. Rose water was passed around, and a malevolent seignior, the Baron Miserabius with black eyebrows, suggested to Duke San Alberto: "Rinse your mouth, not your hands." But San Alberto replied, "I believe I haven't even mentioned you today."

When everyone had rested after the hearty meal, the invidious Miserabius again pestered the honest duke: "My friend, if I had a story, and I wanted to tell it to the very wisest man, tell me—to whom should I tell it?" And he received the following answer: "Tell it to the man you think is the biggest fool."

Having heard that, Miserabius became confused, and the others couldn't make any sense of it either; only the wise emperor Frederick, who always listened gladly to skillful orators, broke out in laughter and laughed from the bottom of his heart, while the others wanted to find out the cause of the emperor's merriment. The ruler explained: "Very well. A fool, being a fool himself, considers other fools to be wise. Therefore, if a fool considers someone else a fool, then that very same person will be a wise man. For wisdom is the exact opposite of foolishness. To a fool, wise men always seem like fools. But wise men can see that a fool is a fool."

Everyone liked this explanation, and they praised the emperor's wisdom and laughed from the bottom of their own hearts at Baron Miserabius's foolishness. But the baron took offense at San Alberto and muttered: "Well, very well. . . . " Then everyone took a seat at the table. After a few days, the emperor said to the envoys upon their parting, "Tell your ruler the grand Presbyter John that the finest thing in the world is good proportion."

The envoys bowed and set out for home; the knight San Alberto was with them. Soon they came upon a river and saw two middle-aged men scuffling in the river mud. The servants separated the two brawlers, and San Alberto asked them for an explanation. One of them, besmeared black, said, "Seignior, I am a poor miller. Therefore I have always held in reverence the Lord's Prayer, the Commandments and the Virgin's holy image. One day, though, just as happened to Abraham and Isaac, a dark night befell a sunny afternoon, with torrents of rain and hail, such as no one could recall since the days of Holy Noah. The river overflowed its banks and washed out to the sea my windmill, as well as a whole month's grist. What was I, a poor man, left with? I took my last one thousand bezants, went to the merchant, and traded each coin for two sheep, for I have an eligible daughter, who needs a dowry. This man lent me his boat, but alas, unluckily, one ewe gave birth to a lamb in the boat, and now this scoundrel is demanding it for himself."

The knight San Alberto turned sternly to the other brawler and asked, "Why do you demand something that doesn't rightfully belong to you?"

The boatman fell down in the mud and said, "Your noble lordship! I have eight marriageable sons! The first is the eldest, the second is wise, the third is a fool, and so are the others. They are all I have. As well as this boat. I have never coveted my neighbor's sheep. But the lamb was born in my boat, therefore it belongs to me."

Having heard both of them out, the just San Alberto declared, "The lamb belongs to the boat." Having said this, he spent the night along with his retinue in one of the countless abbeys of that region.

But that very night the abbot had been summoned by the pope.

Very well.

But the fair and wise miller's daughter said to her sad father: "I already know everything. Don't worry, Father, everything will be all right. Do you recall the incident with the emperor's falcon and the simple local boatman, to whom the good emperor gave back what he had promised, but which the emperor's vassal had had designs upon? So simply give me the net."

The aforementioned Emperor Frederick once owned a falcon, which of all the court's falcons was the handsomest and the best hunter. He had a golden beak, a ruby crest, diamond spurs, silver tinklers, and an enameled coat of arms with the emperor's lilies that he wore on a gold chain on his chest. And as it happened, the emperor had a craving to watch a hunt or perhaps to hunt himself with the falcon, other birds, and various dogs. When everyone had arrived at the place where the emperor's quails nested, for some reason the falcon didn't catch any birds, and though he usually always returned, this time—either out of caprice or for some other reason, he rose higher and higher, and flew so far away that he disappeared from sight. Having seen this, Frederick sent eight of his bodyguards to search for the fugitive. And so they set out in all directions. They searched for a week, a second week, and a third; they didn't find him and returned. Frederick grieved, for he was a courageous ruler, and the falcon was a noble bird. He gave orders for it to be announced far and wide that whoever brought back the bird would receive one thousand bezants, but those who failed would be hung on the spot. He then turned around and rode home.

While riding by a dry lake, Frederick noticed on the shore the miller's fair daughter dressed as a fisherman; he saw her cast a net into the dry lake and pull it ashore as if it were full of fish. Many a time the emperor had defeated his enemies; he had gained victories in tests of skill and knowledge, and where secret matters were concerned, had even gained knowledge from India's own mighty ruler's wise advisers. He now laughed from the bottom of his heart and asked the ersatz fisherman if by any chance he had lost his mind. To this, the wise Katherine in a harsh fisherman's voice replied, "If a boat can give birth to a lamb, why shouldn't there be fish in a dry lake?"

Delighted by the answer, the emperor wanted to be further convinced of the crafty fisherwoman's keen wit, so he said, "If you are really so wise, then go see San Alberto, the knight of my court, and arrive at the abbey neither naked nor clothed, having neither eaten nor not eaten, neither by day nor night, neither riding nor by foot. If you are able to do this, ask whatever you desire. If not—off with your head."

Having found out about this, the brave and noble knight San Alberto left the emperor's court and set out on a long and perilous journey to visit the seven soothsayers to receive from them in their city a horse and splendid weapons with which he could defeat the enemy at the gates and three times at the edge of the forest, thus freeing the land and establishing himself as an agreeable ruler to its people; he would have a wise and lovely wife and eight sons, even though the knights would continue to sit at the table and ask to be informed in minute detail of the sheep—behold, the courageous San Alberto didn't sleep a wink that night in one of the countless abbeys. From a piece of wood, he crafted a fish with which to make amends to the miller for the lost lamb, even though the fisherman had rightfully deserved it. For he was a just and honest knight, but the miller was left with a nubile daughter named Katherine.

Katherine stood up, donned the aforementioned net (and became neither naked nor dressed), ate one pea (and had neither eaten nor not eaten), took a sheep and mounted it—one leg dragging along the ground, the other hanging in the air (neither riding nor by foot); in this manner, as the sun was rising (neither by day nor by night), she arrived at one of the abbeys, not knowing that the scoundrel Miserabius had hidden in the shadows and was pricking up his ears.

Having caught sight of Katherine wearing a net and riding a hobbled sheep, San Alberto laughed with all his might and then said, "I see that you are truly wise and lovely. Ask whatever you desire."

To this, the wise Katherine said the following: "Oh, noble gentleman! I need nothing. I am the daughter of a poor honest miller. My father will provide me with a dowry, and I will get a husband. Perhaps even an honest knight, though he might be a poor one."

Having heard these simple words, the knight San Alberto was touched and said, "Very well. I will tell you the best way to do this. I see that you are a wise and lovely miller's daughter. So listen and take heed."

And he told her about the incident with the peasant who had a flock of sheep.

The peasant rowed the sheep to the opposite bank, where for each of them he collected one florin, and these amounted to one thousand florins. The peasant took the money and left. Soon, he came upon a river that had overflowed its banks due to incessant rain. "Why do I have one thousand florins?" the perplexed peasant asked himself. "I'd better go see the poultry merchant."

Very well. He went there and the poultry merchant asked him, "What do you want?" "I have one thousand florins," the peasant replied, and for each florin the merchant gave him fifty hens and took the one thousand florins for himself.

The peasant collected the hens and set out for home, but on his way he came upon the miller, dressed as an abbot who was coming back from seeing the pope. Right away, he asked him, "Good day, where are you going?" The peasant replied, "I went to see the merchant, and for each florin, you see, he gave me fifty hens. I had one thousand florins." The abbot said in reply, "I was on the other bank, I sold my sheep, and for each of them I was given eight drachmas."

Now the cunning peasant thought to himself: "If they're giving eight drachmas per sheep on the other side of the river, upon my word, it might be worth selling my hens." But he asked, "How can one get to the other bank?" "Well, I'll take you across," the abbot said. For the miller had a boat that could be used to cross the river whenever such a need arose. He also had a wise and lovely daughter, but that was all, if you don't count the one thousand bezants, because his windmill had been washed away by the flood and his lamb had been taken by the fisherman.

Fortunately, it happened that at that very moment a certain, completely noble but not particularly prosperous knight, the master San Alberto, was traveling by, coming from the mighty emperor Frederick's lands and going to Florence to see the grand Dante who was from thereabouts, and he stopped to spend the night at the roadside abbey. He separated the squabblers and, seeing the miller's calamity, in the morning, before continuing on, the knight crafted a fish from a piece of wood, summoned the miller and said to him: "Here, take this fish and tie it to the net when you go fishing. You will catch a huge number of fish. I hope that they will amount to enough for your daughter's—the sham fisherwoman's, ha, ha, ha—dowry."

Then San Alberto left the hospitable abbey and continued his journey to the lands of the grand Emperor Frederick. For in the court of the magnanimous emperor a warm welcome was always given to poor knights, as well as to artisans and other knowledge-able men with or without the scrolls of their family trees; all kinds of people gathered there. And everyone was awarded with rich gifts. Once, even the Presbyter John, the grand ruler of India, sent noble fortune-tellers to the emperor, for he, being gifted with exceptional intellect, loved sophisticated conversation. Therefore, the envoys set out to see Frederick in order to convince themselves once again of the excellence of the emperor's mind. Presbyter John gave them strict instructions: "Bring these three gemstones to Frederick and ask him what is the finest thing in the world. Then come and tell me." After some time the envoys related to John the emperor's re-ply: "Good proportion." The presbyter praised Frederick as a clever man of words, though not as a man of deeds, and invited him to come and enter into his service as a seneschal, commissioned to in-vestigate and describe everything in India. The Emperor Frederick was a wise and far-sighted ruler; he accepted the kind offer gladly and gave orders for a feast.

Everyone was already sitting at the table, and the emperor had already ordered the bowls of rose water, when suddenly a man of respectable age dressed in simple abbot's clothes appeared, carry-ing his hat and a sword in his hands. Frederick said to him, "What is it that you want?" The guest staggered forward and with a heavy sigh he said, "Great ruler! I am a simple fisherman. I have a mar-riageable daughter, but my windmill was washed away by the river. I was left with only one thousand bezants, and with these I bought sheep for her dowry. Two for each coin. Unluckily, one of them gave birth to a lamb in a boat. However, the righteous knight San Alberto, who defeated everyone seven times in the tournament, gave me a wooden fish when it was neither day nor night. On the first try, I got such a good catch that I received one thousand florins for it. But the third time, my luck must have turned sour, for the string to which I had tied the fish snapped. Oh, what a fool I am! I should have used wire. Would the good master San Alberto fashion another wooden fish? For, you understand, I have a marriageable daughter, but she got tangled up in some cunningly placed nets, and now an evil man has locked her in the abbey and placed guards at the gates. While I was rushing here with this sorrowful news, the scoundrel, you see, caught up with me. Now I no longer have any-thing, if you don't count the bezants. My days have come to an end."

And with a groan, the miller gave up the ghost.

To this, the wise Frederick said mournfully to the unfortunate man, "My son, don't take it so hard, for you're neither the first nor the last who didn't know how to hold on to the luck that the Almighty had deigned to grant you. It is not for men to fulfill your wish. For at that hour when you received the magic fish, the constellation of the heavenly bodies was arranged in a way as to bestow upon the fish this special power. If you think that this position of the planets could repeat itself, I'm afraid I must say this could take place no sooner than in thirty-six thousand years. Nothing personal"

Having uttered these consolations, the compassionate ruler ordered a banquet and commanded that the poor deceased be honorably buried and all of his debts paid off.

Having heard of this incident, the dashing and rich knight San Alberto, who at times had generously squandered his own fortune, but not his virtue, on feasts, horses, armor, and weapons, flew into a righteous rage, vowing to recover the lovely miller's daughter; he summoned his friends and relatives, let his intentions be known, and asked for support in his quest. All sorts of folk gathered: some advised him to set out right away, others attempted to talk him out of it; finally, they all agreed—he must go. They gave the brave man weapons, horses, and money, dressed him for the journey, and offered him reliable servants as traveling companions. Seated in his saddle, the knight San Alberto asked the dying man, "In which abbey? In which direction?" But the dying man managed to whisper only the murderer's name: "It was Miserabius, the dog." Then he closed his eyes for all time.

The knight dug his spurs into the horse's flanks, flying off down the road. He galloped for a week, and another, and a third, until one day a richly dressed and silent traveler caught up with him, and soon both of them arrived at the walls of a fantastically beautiful city. Nine old men with gray beards sweeping down to the gate came out to greet him; they presented the guest with fine weapons and a white horse and begged him to defend their city. The enemy attacked, and the battle began. The knight defeated the foes and freed the city. Then he defeated them seven more times in the open field, conquering the land and ruling there for a long time, but the gray-haired soothsayers were away in India the whole time.

India's mighty Presbyter John then decided that the gemstones that had been presented to Frederick, whose true nature was still to be unriddled, must have lost their power, and he secretly sent his goldsmith to the emperor's castle to recover these gemstones, giving him plenty of gold and diamonds to take along. Having arrived at the castle, the sly goldsmith began to set the diamonds in the gold and to present these adornments to those knights and seigniors who had influence in the court. Frederick, the mighty ruler of all the lands in those parts, soon learned of this. He loved and always paid attention to things of spiritual and material values, if they had been really worked on with all one's heart, and he generously bestowed gifts upon the makers of the aforementioned items of beauty. For this reason, not just prosperous seigniors came to see him from far and wide, but also all kinds of folk. He ordered a sumptuous feast, and rose water for hands, and as he was preparing to display his gemstones to the goldsmith, suddenly there entered a poor abbot with a hood covering his face, and Frederick asked him, "What do you want?" The abbot fell to his knees and explained his grievance: "I am but a poor abbot. The pope trusted me to keep an eye on his sheep, but what kind of a shepherd am I? A hail storm scattered the herd along the banks of the river from its headwaters all the way to the sea. For this, the pope is demanding that I pay him one thousand florins. But I am a poor abbot, and I have only an eligible daughter and eight sons, and they all need a dowry. What should I do, my ruler?"

Having scrutinized the abbot, the good Frederick replied, "If you are an abbot, then go to the pope and supply him with answers to the following four questions: How far is it from here to the heavens, how much water is there in the sea, what goes on in hell, and what is your greatest accomplishment? Then we will see."

Having heard these questions, which neither Aristotle nor Solomon could have answered, the abbot began sorrowfully to huff and puff like a frightened horse and, stumbling in desperation, he hurried back to one of his countless abbeys, unable to decide what to do.

During the abbot's absence, the villain Miserabius nervously stroked his mustache and schemed about how to obtain for himself the wise and lovely miller's daughter, whom he had cunningly ensnared in the nets he had laid out. Bolting the gates and placing some guards there—villains like himself—he tried this way and that way, but to no avail, for the wise and lovely fisherwoman responded virtuously to the scoundrel's licentious endeavors every time by saying, "I am a poor miller's daughter without a dowry. My father's windmill was washed away by the river, the pie was eaten by the cat, and the lamb rightfully fell to the lot of the fisherman. And I love the honest, though poor and destitute, San Alberto. Come what may, I will remain faithful to my beloved until the day I die. You are a thief and a deceiver." But Miserabius couldn't keep quiet. "Be mine!" Therefore, Katherine, to make a long story short, replied, "Very well." And then and there they set out for the altar. Afterward, she mended the net, occasionaly heaving a sigh over the poor San Alberto, and waited for the return of the abbot, who would bring answers to all the questions.

Still panting like a horse at a crossroads by a church, the abbot noticed that for some reason people were turning off from the straight highway and circling the church along narrow roundabout paths. He asked why they were doing something so silly. A miller replied, "Holy father, don't you really know anything?" "Of course, holy son, I know nothing," the abbot said without hesitation. A boatman said, "If you go straight, then soon you will sense the unbearable stench emanating from a knight in a coffin in front of the church. He smells so bad you could almost die. No one dares to pass by the corpse." "Why, for God's sake, doesn't anyone bury the unfortunate man?" "I will explain," said a fisherman. "Because the folk from these surroundings have a custom: a deceased knight must not be buried until the people to whom he owed money have been repaid." "The deceased must have been honest but poor," the abbot said. "And there's no one who can pay his debts," a peasant agreed. The miller asked, "But, if someone will pay off his debts, will he then be buried?" "Of course, Sir," a kitchen maid exclaimed. "But, if not, will he continue to lie unburied?" the abbot inquired. Everyone nodded in agreement.

Soon it became known that the deceased lying in the coffin by the church had been there for such a long time that not a soul could remember his name anymore, though a wise fisherwoman riding by on a sheep announced that the knight had died because he had not understood the proportion between a return journey and elapsed time. Back in the days of Emperor Frederick, the knight had set out with twelve bearded sorcerers to one of this land's countless abbeys in order to recapture his one and only beloved. There, in a tournament, he defeated all of his opponents no fewer than nine times and had ruled firmly, wisely, and fairly, in the bearded ones' absence. But then one day they returned. The eldest of the ruler's eight sons had just finished celebrating his fiftieth birthday. The sorcerers asked the duke, "Wouldn't you like to visit the good Emperor Frederick's court?" He hesitated: "What would I do there? Other people are there now. My son is already fifty." But the gray, old men insisted.

Very well. They set out and soon arrived at Frederick's court, the pope along with them. The emperor and all the knights were still sitting at the table and were just about to dip their hands in the bowls of rose water that Frederick had sent for just before the knight had gone away with India's envoys. Frederick knit his brow: "What has happened? Why aren't you leaving?" San Alberto—that was the knight's name—clutched his gray head: "My son is already fifty years old! I have defeated the enemy both in the city and beyond the gates!" The emperor then made the knight tell him everything, down to the last detail. At that moment, an abbot who was dressed as a miller and who was badly out of breath answered, "It is precisely seven million, nineteen miles and sixteen paces from here to the heavens, and the last steps are the most difficult; if you don't believe me, then have the river's tributaries dammed, have barrels brought, and have the sea emptied and measured, for in hell they are slaughtering, cutting, stabbing, and chopping people into pieces; they are hanging and boiling them over a slow fire in kettles filled with tar and oil, just as they do on earth; you can ask the honorable man who, having been there, returned and related everything to the grand Florentine, but this man has long since died and there's no one to bury him; therefore, my greatest accomplishment took place when instead of an abbot I became a miller and was able to tell all the people to whom the deceased had remained in debt, 'Go to the good emperor Frederick, the good Frederick pays for everything.' There."

All sorts of folk gathered. The good Frederick, the just and noble ruler, received them graciously, generously bestowing gifts upon each and every one. He said, "You may ask for whatever you desire." But everyone asked only for what he rightfully deserved. Therefore, the emperor ordered to be distributed to the claimants one thousand bezants—the money that the deceased had owed them for the sheep—one thousand florins for fifty thousand hens from the other side of the river, and another eight drachmas for traveling money. But one of them, the deceitful goldsmith Miserabius, couldn't keep quiet: "Aren't there any stones that are more precious?" Frederick, without saying a word, ordered his footmen to bring out the three aforementioned diamonds that he had received from the mighty John of India, and the happy goldsmith said, "Ruler, this stone, you see, is worth as much as your finest city." And then: "Look, and this is worth as much as your wealthiest province." And last: "Well, but this stone, look here, is more valuable then your whole empire, my ruler." Having said this, he grabbed all three. But one of the gemstones possessed such power that the goldsmith suddenly became invisible; he rushed down the stairs into the courtyard, quickly returned to India, and related this to the mighty John. The ruler listened to the goldsmith's story while staring into the depths of the stones, whence there occurred that which has happened then, now, before, and after.

The goldsmith told his story, and John saw that soon afterward the good Frederick became deeply sorrowful, for he was a stern and severe, though just, ruler, who readily bestowed gifts upon both nobles and common folks. He gave orders for a feast and for bowls of rose water to be served; however, at that moment, the eldest of his eight sons who had just begun to be bored and was turning gray after fifty years, stood up bravely and set out to win back the stones, the lamb, the pie, the miller's daughter, and justice, for he was a son worthy of his father—the great Frederick. The second son also stood up but was killed by the scoundrel Miserabius's venomous hand. The third, the dashing and handsome Narcissus, as is known, stopped somewhere halfway to catch his breath on the bank of a forest spring, noticed his own reflection in the water, uttered a cry, shed a few tears, plunged into the depths, and drowned, though later he turned into a blossoming almond tree; however, that happened later. Never seeing his other sons return, Frederick ordered a feast, summoned all kinds of folk, asked them to be seated at the table, and said the following words: "Hear ye, seigniors, gentlemen, and common folk—good deeds are never for nothing."

Having made this declaration, the noble, sorrowful, and mighty Frederick, the lawful ruler of all the lands of this region, ordered rose water to be brought, rinsed his hands in it, and in the wink of an eye vanished God knows where.

Having witnessed this, everyone seated at the table became very sad, be he duke, or clown, or merely a simple pope dressed as a miller, who in his confusion released Frederick's falcon with all its tinklers, ruby spurs, and gold or silver lilies in its beak. The bird flew out the window with a tinkle, and the shrieking pope rushed to catch it in hopes of getting at least one thousand bezants so he wouldn't have to hang himself from the first tree in the city square; but he tripped over the windowsill and fell out. But the guests, courtiers, and footmen heard his tidings of farewell: "To many, God sends good fortune, but most are not quick-witted enough to make honorable use of the brief stroke of luck granted them, or else they do not even notice their good fortune. So let us not grieve." Everyone then went down to the courtyard, made a sign of the cross over the pope, and set out in different directions.

Only the quixotic miller, rotting slowly away on the indifferent riverbank, continued to gaze in the direction of the sea, waiting for the magic fish to emerge somehow from the depths. Finally, he went blind, and having made his way to a boat, asked a bearded boatman to ferry him across to poor San Alberto. The gray-haired old man was not surprised and didn't even stir. Then, toward autumn, he said, "The knight you speak of has not been seen in these parts for some fifty years, nor has anyone ever seen him on the opposite bank. He may be journeying along the great wall of the East somewhere and, without any sense of time or proportion, maybe toward one of the countless abbeys. His eyes don't see, his ears don't hear, his feet don't feel the ground, and his heart is silent. His horse has long since been devoured by ravens and coyotes. The sheath of his sword rattles at his side like a dried up pea pod, and the steel inside it has crumbled to sand. Every thirty-six thousand years, a black whirlwind howls over the valley, the sun is eclipsed, the springs become turbid; at high noon, the night sets in. Lightning then slashes the air, and a depraved monster comes flying—it has webbed wings, a bloated belly, and a ghastly beak with teeth like scythes—and each time, it pecks out a single grain of sand from the top of the wall, carries it away, and casts it into the sea of time, where the wooden fish is always swimming in a school of large, small, living, unborn, and dead fish, but there is neither happiness nor man in that place. The sheep are scattered in all directions along the river and sea, and slaughtered by the royal servants, roasted by the emperor's kitchen maid, and eaten by all sorts of folk; you have died, and there is no one left anymore to herd them together and take them to the opposite shore; and the storyteller will not awaken until this task has been completed. Three thousand six hundred centuries must pass for the words and planets to return to their previous order, for the storyteller to regain his senses, recall his story, and tell the poor knight that he's still on his way to his sham fisherwoman in one of the infinite abbeys. The storyteller is sleeping; the knight cannot die, can't even find out that this story has, for him, ended a long time ago."

The deceased miller turned his empty eye sockets in our direction: "The same goes for us, dear reader. Amen, amen."

Translated by Ieva S. Celle

Gundega Repše

Gundega Repše (1960) is Latvia's most productive writer of modern prose. Having studied art history at Latvia's Academy of Art, Repše has also written critical reviews about art and biographical essays about Latvian artists. Repše's first collection of stories, *Koncerts maniem draugiem pelnu kastē* (A Concert for My Friends in the Ash Box, 1987), harks back to the so-called "angry girls' prose" produced by several young female authors who wrote about the absurd social environment of the 1980s. In 1988 Repše published her biographical novel/essay *Pieskārieni* (Touches) about the life of Latvian artist Kurts Fridrihsons (1911-1991). It is a vibrant and masterfully crafted account of a great artist and aristocrat of the soul whom Repše had known since childhood. Repše's biographical novel/essay *Tuvskati* (Close-Ups) about Latvian painter Džemma Skulme (1925) was featured in the Latvian press in 1990. Her novel *Ugunszīme* (Firesign) was published the same year. It is a portrait of the social processes of Latvia in the 1950s: the events surrounding and affecting the so-called French Group—Latvian intellectuals who for their love of French culture were arrested by the KGB and exiled to labor camps. In 1992 Repše published *Septiņi stāsti par mīlu* (Seven Stories about Love), yet again revealing her talent for visionary prose. Here, time, history, and values have "fallen out of their hinges." A powerful current of passions has thrown open the door of the mundane; the love in this book sees beyond ordinary good and evil. Two years later, in 1994, Repše's *Šolaiku bestiarijs. Identifikācijas* (The Contemporary Bestiary: Identifications) was published. Here, the author drew upon the modern world's attempts to identify with itself. *Ēnu apokrifs* (Shadow Apocrypha), which describes a woman's individual process of identification, was published in 1996.

Gundega Repše is a recipient of the Rainis and Aspazija Foundation Prize. She has also received a grant from Latvia's Ministry of Culture, and has participated in the Iowa State International Writers Program with the support of the United States Information Service.

"Stigmata" is from her collection *Seven Stories about Love*.

From *Stigmata*

You, who hear and feel and know, oh listen to me! You—supreme One, but no lord, I'm not calling You by name, You here. Listen, hear me! Come along and don't judge me, come, so I can talk and live with You.

Come across the sea and the fog, appear invisibly and don't let Your punishments rob us of dignity. If You judge and punish, You're merely Power, not Exaltation. But come freely, without the desire to judge and to punish; come clean and innocent! Across the swamps of Kelderi, Paurēni, Krievi and Roži, the swamps of Olga, Svēto and Ťilika, the swamps of Pīkstulnīca, Anšavēre, Jānīši, Aklais and Malmuļi, across the green sedge of Francsala, across the swamps of Stampaka, Ņekļudova and Apšinieki—come! Then walk with us and speak to us silently—You, who hear and feel and know. We are Yours as much as You are ours.

There they stand, on the broad, greenish brown stone stairs.

In the thickening evening fog, their contours melt into the massive body of the Vilnius opera house.

Malle—in a minidress of indigo silk and in violet suede shoes, her flaming red hair clinging to her neck and earlobes like a cloche. Her head thrown back aggressively, as if she were a revolutionary actress.

Victoria—cowering, freezing in a transparent lace blouse, her embroidered slip and bra straps peeking through. Her tightly belted waist, her chaste black skirt. A knot of long hair lying on her nape like a bunch of grapes in the rain.

Johnny—in a little blue velvet suit, ankle-length socks with pom-poms. A pale, frightened boy.

Laima—a dress spattered with swirls of scarlet spots, and wearing pointed red stilettos. Hands clutching at two chiffon scarves hanging over her stomach like moist dog tongues. Thick, black, frizzy hair, eyes of burning coal, and snakelike legs anchoring that copper bell of a bum with amazing self-confidence.

Gaunt Asja—nose turning red, in a black pantsuit. Biting her thin, straight lips. Her hands in her pockets, the line of her chin a triangle cut out of paper. Golden earrings dangling jaggedly.

Jorge's high forehead glimmers like a light bulb in the drizzle and fog. Raindrops clotting his large-lensed glasses. His straight, ash-blond hair sticks to his elongated, egglike skull as if electrified. Pacing back and forth with a bouncy gait. Looking as if his agile body could so easily be unscrewed from those stubby, determined legs.

Tall Peer—in a checkered jacket, white socks and moccasins. Calm, serene, a straight back. A light brow line and clear, glassy eyes.

Gradually losing his dark, shiny hair.

Finally—eighty-year-old Bertram with his round, watermelon head, stubborn, wise owl eyes, wearing a prehistoric striped suit. A green velvet bow tie like the summary dot on the *i*.

People have scattered, and cars have raced off, splashing through big puddles, taking the opera audience with them. Desdemona is swept away by a bald guy in a broken-down Moskvich. Othello, wearing a short windbreaker, rushes off with Iago and Bianca.

"Klaus has never once been on time."

"As if he didn't know when the opera ended."

"Well, he never stays to watch—he'd nod off and fall out of his chair."

"A driver is a driver is a driver."

"Aren't we Little Miss Professor."

"He's incorrigible, there's no point in wasting energy getting upset."

"A daily beating wouldn't be enough."

"Drivers like him are no good for our editorial staff. I'll talk to my husband in all seriousness."

"He's under no obligation to take the editorial staff on Sunday pleasure trips."

"Opera isn't pleasure, opera is spiritual nourishment."

"You're bound to burst, you're so nourished."

"Stop it, you two!"

"Looks like Klaus already has some girlfriends in Vilnius."

"He does not."

"Gas, maybe?"

"Should have done it earlier."

"Now all I want to say is 'Othello, up yours.' "

"As usual."

"Maybe something happened?"

"What, he broke his leg?"

"His neck, for all I care. He's still supposed to be here at eleven o'clock."

"Getting drenched like derelicts because of the king."

"Calm down."

"And no bonuses."

"Sniff him now and then in the morning. You'll understand."

"His bus is his castle. So he takes all sorts of women there."

"Don't talk crap."

"It bugs you, huh?"

"I couldn't give a shit."

"Since when, Victoria?"

"One hell of a fog."

"A chance for him to show off, Mr. Indy 500."

"Stop whining."

"But I'm cold."

"We've got to think of something."

"I know! Let's adopt a resolution!"

"You know where you can go."

"I'll never speak to him again."

"So what, you two understand each other telepathically."

"I knew you were jealous."

"You're nuts, like totally."

"Why on earth should I have to worry about some stupid driver after such a fantastic opera?"

"Don't think about him, just let me strangle you."

"Shut up for once."

The fog swirls in foamy clouds. It sticks to their bodies, clammy, cold and callous. Seven people standing at the opera like broken, rag dolls, with a five-year-old tot in ankle socks.

Beeping cheerfully, the bus pulls up. The septet glide down the opera stairs reluctantly, their pride injured. The boy, too.

Klaus's gray eyes are mocking; he leans back at the wheel like the lord of the manor and doesn't say a word.

"Cretin," Malle snarls, digging her violet nails into Klaus's dark palm.

"Have you lost your mind? Get out and walk."

"As of tomorrow you're fired," Laima says coolly.

"Just because you're the editor's wife, you think you're going to take control? Control your three kids."

"Hush up and drive," old Bertram orders.

Huffing and puffing, Klaus turns the steering wheel one way and then another. He pumps the gas and then deliberately hits the brakes to make the passengers roll in their seats like bags of rags.

Johnny starts to cry; Victoria strokes her son's wet hair.

"Take the blanket from the back seat," says Klaus.

"Turn on the heater," Asja shouts harshly.

"Ask Jorge to take you in his lap."

"Turn it on this minute!"

"You've all gone totally nuts, huh?" Klaus guffaws with annoyingly loud, unrestrained laughter.

"You're braying like a donkey," Malle flares up.

"And you're screeching like a monkey!"

"Watch where you're going, you lunatic!" screams Victoria, as Klaus brakes sharply, and she hits the seat in front of her with her forehead.

The fog looms dense and opaque.

Bertram cleans his shoes with a flannel scrap he has pulled out from his briefcase. He hasn't left the apartment without them for some fifty years. The black, round-tipped shoes shine like ebony. Peer stares blankly into the white mass, fear at the corners of his mouth. Asja and Malle whisper to each other. Laima puts on lipstick; Jorge chats with Victoria. Johnny sleeps.

"So, how was the opera?" Klaus asks.

"Wo-o-onderful." Malle is mocking him.

"Unforgettable," Asja joins in.

"You wouldn't have survived," Laima adds.

Klaus doesn't respond. The thick, slate-black sweater is crackly and unyielding.

"We're screwed," Malle says triumphantly.

"Stop, okay?" Victoria shushes her in a conciliatory tone.

"Why should I stop? An hour ago we could have hit the gas, no problem. Are you afraid little ol' Klaus will run off the road?"

"Enough, all right?" Laima intervenes.

"Why are you all so afraid of him?"

Jorge wakes up. "You obviously adore him."

"A hell of a lot more than your monkish egghead, I'll tell you."

"But he doesn't like high-strung women."

"I know, don't worry. He likes them in lace blouses and garter belts. Submissive."

"Please," Victoria murmurs.

"Well, what have we here?" Peer is awake now too.

"A homophobe, Mr. Peer. I can't deny it."

"Who's next?" Asja asks in a bored voice.

"The saintly widows, perhaps? No, Asja, I'm leaving them alone for now."

"What's with you? You're out of control." Jorge thinks Malle is going too far.

"We'll never get anywhere like this, dragging along like snails. I have to be home tonight, but just because of some goofball. . . ."

"Someone's waiting for you?" Jorge teases her.

"Imagine, yes—someone's waiting. Beefcake with all the trimmings, not just lofty intellect."

"Well, then, tomorrow you'll be a lot calmer, my dear," Jorge retorts gleefully and settles down to sleep.

"Malle, want some liqueur?" Victoria whispers.

"Sure. And how about a song or two, so our dear little driver doesn't fall asleep. Damn it, everything's wet. Klaus's seats will rot."

They have stopped. The fog is so thick, you could slice it.

"At least drive onto the side of the road."

"Into the ditch?" Klaus asks after a long pause.

"Someone will hit us standing here."

"If you're scared, jump out. I feel just fine."

"So childish," Bertram snarls.

"I'm afraid I can't levitate."

"I'll get out and look," says Peer. His white socks are visible in the fog for only a moment.

"Go ahead, knock back a little liqueur for courage," Klaus encourages them.

The bottle clinks, Johnny snores gently in his sleep, but otherwise there are no sounds. The air is powdered, dead.

"Victoria, you always have everything with you," Laima drawls respectfully.

"Always be prepared."

"Bring a nightgown, by any chance?" Malle starts up again. Victoria sighs.

"A splendid team," Jorge yawns and reaches for the liqueur.

"How long are we going to wait?" Victoria asks.

"That's your problem," Klaus snaps back.

"Wild beasts. One at a time."

"Maybe a new poem is on the way?" Jorge smiles hypocritically. Victoria continues breathing irregularly.

"How my Strazds manages you all, I just don't know," Laima says, horrified.

"He doesn't," Asja shoots back.

"And he has other problems."

"The harsh style of opportunism and the glue of survival."

"Some women get stuck in it, as far as I know," Laima replies maliciously.

"Why have you stopped?" Bertram woke up.

"I'm not going to drive God knows where. I can't."

"There's something you can't do?" Malle laughs.

"Shut up. You've barely been working a year, but you play the prima donna," Klaus calls out sullenly.

"Competition?"

"Sleep!"

"No, I'll go to the theatrical type for a smoke. Hey, Peer!"

Laima shakes her head, once Malle has climbed out. "She's unbearable."

"Has she taken something from you?" Bertram smirks.

"And to harrass Peer for his weakness. . . ."

"It's not a weakness, it's a different lifestyle," Victoria says in Malle's defense.

"How can you stand sharing an office with her?"

"I'm not complaining. She works hard. Here, you need some liqueur."

"That's all you think of. I'm getting out, too." Laima scrambles off the bus.

"Laima thinks Malle has something going with Strazds, that's why she's so self-righteous," Victoria explains.

"You always know about everybody's dirty laundry," Klaus mutters morosely, his ears turning red.

"But just think, Laima has three children, the psychopath Strazds, all those politicos, banquets, meals," Asja says, defending her.

"She's a smart cookie. She's a masseuse, she knows all of Riga."

"The wife of the boss, yes. She's seen a lot and heard a lot," Bertram mumbles enigmatically.

"When you were the editor. Wasn't your wife your superior?" Klaus chuckles.

"My wife, my friend, has been in America for half a century now with all my daughters, maybe you haven't heard, ergo no one has been my superior."

Klaus shrugs. "I can't keep up with your intrigues."

"They aren't intrigues. And as far as you're concerned, we're just the passengers," Asja complains.

"Some are, some aren't."

"That was wise," Asja smirks.

"What do you mean, wise? If you need wisdom, then steer us back to your university. You waste so much of your intelligence on the newspaper, turning people's bullshit into philosophy."

"Oh, you think the paper doesn't need intelligence?" Jorge perks up.

"The rules of grammar, that's all. The rest. . . ."

"Of course, in order to drive a bus, on the other hand, you need wisdom and experience and talent and connections. You even have to be able to read a little." Asja is insulted.

"Quit talking about work," Victoria sighs.

"What do you think, Victoria, can Little Miss Professor fall madly in love with a machine operator? Can a poet fall in love with a driver?" Jorge won't let up.

"You're mean," Victoria pants.

"I'm just a dumb little critic, nothing more, so don't get upset, let me sound off. Oh well, I'll climb out now."

"Jorge is a good person—he's sincere but neurotic," Victoria decides.

"Let people be, will you," Klaus rebukes her again harshly.

"Why won't you let her speak?" Asja attacks him.

"Well, what's all that blabbing. Rummaging through other people's innards."

"Are you afraid I might find something in yours?" Victoria attacks him bravely. Eyes wide open, moist as a calf's.

"My insides are just fine. And my liver is healthier than yours," Klaus snaps rudely.

"But your heart is a rotten mushroom."

"I'll show you mushrooms! Shut up and drink. If your husband could see you now! And if he knew, how you and me. . . ."

"Creep!" Victoria whispers with a sob.

Klaus beeps the horn angrily. The fog hasn't lifted. Frozen in tiny seedlike bubbles like cottage cheese.

Malle, Jorge, Peer, and Laima climb in, chilled to the bone.

"Can't see a thing. Not even the lights of other cars," Malle says. "But there's no ditch, you can pull over right here."

"Let me look."

Klaus crawls out of the bus, and the fog swallows him up immediately.

"He has absolutely no shame these days," Victoria whimpers.

"Who wouldn't divorce him?" Malle comments knowingly.

"But that was ten years ago," Asja notes.

"But if he can't get hitched again in ten years' time, it's obvious what kind of bird we've got here," Malle continues.

"You sure would like to get your hands on him, huh?" Jorge is smiling again.

"Oh no, you fool. He has such a great daughter."

"You're certainly well-informed!"

"He told me himself. It's all the same to me."

"Did he also brag about his superb navigational skills and all his school trips abroad?" Victoria queries.

"No bragging. He told me, that's all," Malle answers stubbornly.

"I'm hungry," Jorge says.

"Stop it!"

Klaus pulls the bus over. The scent of mushrooms and autumn leaves flows through the open window. Tempting and greedy. No noises.

Gradually they huddle up and collapse into the seats to sleep.

Malle, legs tucked under, is rolled into a ball in the back.

Bertram's head swings like a pendulum. Peer's is stiff and immobile, Laima's lower lip has dropped to make two soft double chins, Asja is pressed against the glass, and Jorge sways with his whole body, but Klaus looks as if he's shutting his eyes against his will, his arms crossed and legs spread wide. Victoria struggles between sleep and tears. She gazes at Klaus's silent back, her son wrapped in blankets next to her, and chooses sleep.

Othello doesn't enter their dreams; the strangler doesn't torture them.

What is this pea soup, tell me! Aren't we done trudging through the swamps? Is gravity so tied to the ground that we sink and sink until, without even feeling it, we give up and become extinct? Should we ask forgiveness from You, exalted One, for being pressed to the ground this way? The muddy swamp gases swallow, swallow camouflaged words, blood flows slowly, are You there, dear, still? The hand falls back; the eyes are filled and sealed with grass. Where? Great fellow traveler, where are we? Set the wind swinging, blow up a breeze, send us a message.

Asja wakes up first. "Have you been driving long?"

"Two, maybe three hours."

"Where are we?"

"Can't you tell?"

"What time is it?"

"The clock says four-thirty, but I think that's wrong. At three, we were still squatting in that meadow, then I slept an hour or so."

"Klaus, brother, a pit stop! The morning ablutions!" Malle shouts happily, stretching in the back seat.

"You can wait."

"Please, dear driver, please! Such lovely little flowered seats."

The meager morning light squeezes through stirred dregs of sky—pale yellow, weak, as though intimidated. The maple trees slapped by August nights, the stiff, bronzed oak trees, the stubbornly supple green firs, the long grass drenched with dew.

"You wouldn't have rubber boots, Klaus?"

"Hurry up, okay? Forget boots."

Malle walks into the brush on the edge of the woods, gaily shaking her fiery hair. Her legs are black, long as a bird's; her dress is wrinkled, short and pathetic. She returns merry, and shaking with cold.

They scatter along the bushes, stiff, crooked, twisted, bright as broken glass.

"Hard day ahead," Peer says conscientiously, combing his thin hair.

"Straight to the office," Asja says with reproachful diligence. Sleep has left a long, red mark on her cheek.

"I'm off to the galleries today," Malle says showing off, painting her eyes.

"We should catch up on our sleep," Jorge comments curtly.

"Klaus, do you have any soda?" Victoria croaks.

"Only the water on the window, my lady."

"Are we in Latvia now?" Bertram stares dubiously at the colorful woods.

"Where else—America?"

"What road are you taking, anyway? This isn't the Vilnius-Riga highway!"

"Did I say it was?"

"Get serious!"

"I am serious—for three hours now I've been tooling around God knows where," Klaus yells at him.

"Well, then, stop and ask somebody the way!" Laima orders. Her swollen eyes are tiny and helpless, but her thatch of hair has rolled up overnight into a sooty cupola.

"Where should I stop?!"

"At a house."

"No houses nowhere."

"Well then get on another road! As if it's your first day as a driver," Laima shouts dramatically.

"Klaus, don't fool around!"

"Keep out of this. I'm not crazy or blind."

"You mean to say for three whole hours you never saw anybody to ask for directions?"

"That's right, I didn't. It was still dark. Do you think I really just want to drive around with you dear, kind people, without anything to eat or drink?"

"Hey, look, there's a house, see? Head up there."

Klaus's gait is spiteful and defiant. His shoulders are set, his eyes straight ahead, he ambles, as if on a stroll—lazy, carefree steps. Fingers rolled into fists, holding his breath, puffed up, sucking in a nonexistent belly. Then his irritating, smoky silhouette disappears amid the twisting branches of the linden and apple trees.

The mossy loghouse squats, almost hiding, behind the rusty forehead of the knoll. Swaying beds of violet and white asters, winding sweet peas, a yard with lines of drying sheets and children's clothes. A stool with a crumpled dish towel. A freshly painted dog house. A porridge of hardened grease in a bowl and a long iron chain in the sand. The front door and the kitchen door are open. The air is light and smoky. A bowl of cooling potatoes and three chipped cups of coffee on the wooden table. Thin columns of steam trace wet lines on the sparkling kitchen window. Beets have begun to be chopped in a pot on the stove. Whey drips into a yellowish bucket from clumps wrapped in cheesecloth.

"Hey, farmer!"

In the room, there are obediently made-up beds, crocheted runners in pastel shades, a cardboard box with building blocks and a wooden horse.

"Hey, anybody home?"

Manure steams in front of the barn. Empty pens, the air warm and caustic. Eggs in the straw and a couple of light brown feathers.

Not a puff of wind. In the garden, boxes of spotted, sun-dappled apples.

In the barn, hay stacked up to the beams and a Niva parked crosswise.

The tractor is silent, the potato field motionless, glimmering with powder blue flowers, sparks of tiny green and yellow stamens here and there.

He turns back, taking large steps. Trips on the path over an old, slippery smooth cane. He waits a moment, listens, then leaves after all.

"Nobody's home."

"What do you mean?"

"What I say. Do you always stay home?"

"Rats, the Swedish reporters show up at 11:30, and I'm supposed to greet them," Laima calls out nervously.

"And what will Malle's muscleman say?" Jorge tries to laugh.

"To hell with the muscleman. I promised to blather on TV about life at the museums."

"All this talk is pointless," Bertram says firmly.

"Vitauts won't believe me, that's for sure," Victoria murmurs anxiously.

"And I'm breaking my hairdresser's appointment for the umpteenth time. I've got guests tonight and nothing in the fridge."

"I have to take my mother for some shots."

"Enough, I said," Bertram growls.

His owly eyes flash unpleasantly, bolts of green. His velvet bow tie is twisted sideways; no one has the nerve to tell him.

Klaus hurtles along like a cyclone, tense and staring, swerving around rocks and holes in the road at the very last minute. Johnny, having thrown off the blanket, whimpers about wanting to eat. Now and then their heads nearly bang against the top of the bus. The sun spills like lava over the fields and trees; the woods seem to shake with the convulsing bus in the molten light.

"The last thing we need is car trouble," Victoria agonizes.

"I'm hungry," Johnny whines.

"Klaus, stop at a store or some greasy spoon," Victoria says seriously.

"I guess you didn't bring a sandwich with you 'just in case,' " Laima says, trying to pick a fight.

"To the opera?"

"Well . . . liqueur to the opera?"

"But we really are hungry. Let's ask for something at the next house."

"Where are we actually? You hardly ever see a house. Do you have a map, Klaus?" Asja asks.

"You're insulting the navigator," Jorge intones.

Klaus is silent, his face gloomy and impassive.

"Frightfully unpleasant," says Peer. His white socks are covered with wet grass and mud.

"We should wash."

"Sunbathe, maybe?" Laima snaps angrily.

"Oh hell, I had a long-distance call to Berlin booked for this morning," Peer says despondently.

"A rally of transvestites or some other oppressed minority?" asks Malle, winking at Peer.

They have turned onto a twisting road in the forest, full of bumps. After a thorough rattling shake, they finally brake right in the yard. No shed, no barn, no sauna. Just an old, golden brown house with a tar roof and a small round pond in the back. No, there's also part of a granary, sunk in sweetbriar and phlox. An overgrown lawn and dozens of molehills.

"You go, Malle," Klaus says. The strange tremor in his voice compels silent compliance. And the others, glued to the windows, don't make a peep either.

Malle's dress is still wrinkled. After walking all around the house, she goes through a veranda with red and blue stained-glass windows and stops in a spacious old room smelling of sawdust, dried tea leaves, meat smoked long ago, and sheets blown dry in the sun. Faded clothes flung upon on various types of chairs. The sheets on the big, broad bed are tangled up like laundry inside a washing machine. A copper teapot shines on the black, oval table—two plates with remnants of stale food and the stained top of a Thermos.

"Hey," she whispers, "hey, what's up? Where are you? Andrej, Olivia!"

Back out in the yard, Malle contemplates two strangely flattened molehills. It's as if something very large and heavy had been pulled across them. Swiftly and spontaneously, tears well. She runs off behind the house.

Great fellow traveler, what are you doing? Can prayers inspire You, can You, the heavens, forgive those who belong to the earth? Answer me!

"Apparently, it's only a summer place. Mouse turds, no sandwiches," Malle says, deliberately nonchalant, and falls back into her seat.

"Get some directions, will you?" Laima shouts at Klaus.

"If you keep squawking, I'll leave you here, Mrs. Strazds," Klaus replies slowly and bitterly. "Supposedly I was fired as of today."

They drive on through clouds of dust, the setting sun tossing up and down along the slopes. Houses with slate roofs, wood chip, tar and aluminum roofs, one after another, silent, dozing. Open and partly open doors, some squeaking mournfully, others smoothly oiled—nothing goes in, nothing comes out. They simply exist. Without a heartbeat, they cry.

The passengers don't talk. Calling upon themselves, perhaps.

The hours wriggle away, slimy as slowworms—quick, cold, and damp.

"We're staying in that house on the hill," Klaus commands, and his order has no echo.

A path, studded with long field stones, leads up the hill. In the entrance, rubber boots and wooden clogs, a box with empty bottles.

They don't bother to knock anymore; they don't strain their ears respectfully, don't creep about, don't call out.

A light, varnished wooden table in the kitchen, a gas and a wood stove, a wreath from Midsummer's Night on a nail and a Latvian straw ornament hanging from the lamp. Rows and rows of jars on the shelf—filled with teas, grains, flour, spices, sugar, salt. Long, heavy benches. A crocheted curtain partially drawn, yellowing.

"Make something to eat," Klaus orders and goes into the dark yard.

"What's going on?" Victoria's tremblng voice is the first.

Asja grips Victoria's arm tightly. "Stack the dishes from the sideboard."

"I'll check whether there's a bathroom," Laima says, bustling around with manufactured calm.

Bertram, sitting on a bench and gazing into a dark corner of the kitchen by the basket of firewood, declares:

"Not even the tiniest breeze today."

Then he produces his flannel rag and polishes his shoes.

Peer's cheeks wobble a little, and he blinks his eyes at a sickly rate. Malle ties on the apron hanging by the gas stove.

"Look, Asja, it has 'Baiba' on the front."

"Find some coffee." Asja pretends she didn't hear.

"There's even a bathtub here, we could heat up the water and wash," Laima returns. Klaus has come in, too; he brings canned goods and a bowl full of eggs. "Great work," he says.

"There's a ceramics studio in the shed. Pots, candlesticks, enough food piled up in the basement to last the next three years."

"Klaus, what do you think about all this?" Victoria asks, dropping a pile of forks.

"Stop the hysterics, Victoria. Even your son knows not to lose his cool." Klaus begins opening one jar after another.

Time doesn't fly; the big rose-patterned clock on the wall is stopped at four-thirty. Sizzling potatoes, bacon and eggs—jars empty and pots of coffee vanish. But the conversations stick, sputter, sink, gutter out.

Johnny hasn't spoken all day.

"What's up, little guy?" Klaus is not so dangerous on a full stomach.

The boy doesn't reply, but he takes Klaus's hand in a tight, nervous grip and holds on.

Jorge makes a practical suggestion: "We need to get some sleep."

Food has made life simpler. Water splashes into the tub; mattresses and blankets cover the floor. The electric bulb flickers intermittently, bringing life into the room.

"Peer, let's go for a smoke!" Malle invites him.

They go into the entrance. The bluish air is still except for the sick-sweet stench of the roses out front.

"Just don't get upset," Peer says suddenly. "Oh, don't, please."

After a moment, Malle speaks up:

"Did you notice, all day . . . not a fly, not a bird, not a cat?"

"Really, don't, Malle!" Peer seems to ward her off, and his cigarette loses its embers onto the wooden floor, smashing into countless sparks. Then he adds:

"But see, there is electricity, so there must be. . . ."

"That's just inertia," Malle says skeptically, and they go back into the house.

"Malle, look, there's another studio. Look at all the earrings. With little bells and birds!" Victoria calls with artificially overblown delight and pulls Malle next door.

"Let's go sleep," Malle pushes her away bleakly, then clambers in between Laima and Bertram.

The night draws greenish light over the sleeping bodies with a soundless, gentle care.

"Goodnight!" someone says after a long pause. It's Johnny's voice. As if relieved, the octet replies together—as one. Then they settle in more comfortably, and dive into the abyss of sleep, alternately hesitating, resisting, dreading it, but going.

The morning is brimming with a flat, loud light. The sun is as round as if drawn with a compass, wrapped in fine, transparent cobwebs, trembling slightly in the absent wind.

Asja makes pancake batter. Klaus is gone. With the bus. The others sleep. Or pretend to. Her black pantsuit is covered with tiny, colorful threads from the blanket. From the back, her light, carefully combed hair looks like a round honey pot whose edges curl all the way over the collar of the blouse. The bow on her chest resembles a wilted peony.

Laima gets to her feet groggily and heads for the bathroom. Then Malle, Peer, Bertram, and Victoria, too, Johnny, lastly Jorge, who gropes for his glasses.

"Do you think he's off on his own?" Malle asks Asja, almost whispering.

"I find that hard to believe," she replies reluctantly, pouring pancake after pancake into the pan.

"Shouldn't we take some clothes?" Victoria queries fearfully.

"Then we might as well look for bags of money," Bertram growls. He's tied the bowtie back on.

"Did Daddy go to work already?" Johnny pipes up sleepily.

"Sweetie, I don't know. We're lost," Victoria explains, choking back tears.

Jorge finally catches on. "Where is Klaus?"

"Damn him!" Victoria sobs and slams her fist on the kitchen table.

"Stop blubbering," Malle yells at her. "Do you know where he went? Maybe to get gas."

"That's right," Peer speaks up, "we could run out, after all."

"Everything could run out, my friend." Jorge aims for irony, but his voice is weak.

Then they all sit down and eat. Coffee steams; eyes brighten.

"Turn on the radio!" Malle exclaims suddenly.

Jorge jumps up like a soldier and grabs the Abava on the windowsill. Knives and forks hover in midair. But no sound follows.

"I don't understand anything," Bertram begins seriously.

"Me too, nothing, absolutely nothing, it's a nightmare, it's. . . ." Victoria shakes her head, and her tangled bun unravels across her back.

"You just keep quiet now, okay?" Malle snarls.

"We should call Strazds," Laima says, enthusiastic.

"And what will you tell him?" Asja asks.

"That there's been a disaster, that he should notify the authorities, announce an investigation. I know the minister personally. He won't just let it slide; he'll examine it down to the last detail. Launch proceedings. I just hope the children have been taken to school."

"Oh, Laima, Laima," Peer sighs.

"The opera was full of people," Asja muses. "When could something have happened?"

"What if this is hell?" Peer says uncertainly, fearing ridicule.

"You think it looks like our countryside over there?"

"Then is it war?"

"Where's the noise?"

"Some kind of special invention? The Arabs? The Chinese? The Russians?"

"Getting even with the Latvians?"

"So why aren't there any dogs or cows?"

"What's the point of trying to figure it out? We have to think of what to do." Jorge stands up, and they all go into the yard.

Does the grass keep growing if no one needs it, oh, omniscient One? Are sundew, meadowsweet, Lady's Mantle, and Bachelor's Button meant only for Your pleasure, Your eye's caress? What do You do with the butterflies, the Graylings, the Nuns, and the Grizzled Skippers, the magpie, the lappet and the cabbage moths? What do You do with night moths, bats, screech owls, eagle owls there, where there's no night? What is the role of fireflies and soft glowworms in Your eternal day? Do You need so many? You give no sign, You hold Your breath, You are insulted because You're not being called "Lord." You alone. Lonelier now than all of us.

They wait like tired beetles in the hot sun; they cock their ears, dive into the air and the light, near and far, past the bend in the road and across the woods. Is he coming? Not coming?

"Would he really be such a pig?" Asja breaks down.

"Maybe there's been some kind of accident." Malle stares at Asja reproachfully.

"Why is it always his way or no way? He's not alone," Victoria prattles.

"Didn't I say the whole trip should be postponed?" Asja laments. Jorge cuts her off. "What's the point of talking about it?"

"Maybe there's a search going on? For us?" Laima ventures, with a tremor in her voice.

"Who is looking, Laima, who?" Malle looks with surprise at Laima's small, staring eyes, streaked underneath with grains of mascara like fine soot.

"And who needs us, anyway?" Jorge adds.

Laima starts to cry. "Nobody needs you, perhaps, but my Ilze, Ieva, Oscar—what about them?"

"No one is waiting for me. Except maybe the hunters' club," Bertram drawls mournfully. His face is calm; the wrinkles on his forehead and in the corners of his mouth seem to have evened out. He's like an apple rinsed by rain.

"Strazds will get drunk with the Swedes and go crazy, but the children will be on their own," Laima continues.

"A whole crowd is waiting for me, but now they don't care," says Malle. Her black stockings pulled off, her nose in the grass, she tans her pale, bluish, beautiful legs.

"Not a single bug," Malle observes loudly.

"Maybe we're supposed to be dead too?" Peer speaks up.

"Do you see any corpses?" Asja asks in a tired, indifferent voice.

"And any minute now, we too, just like them, we could." Peer isn't listening to the others.

"That could have happened anytime," Jorge snaps back sharply.

"So I'll never go to Berlin," Peer whispers, plucking stiffly at the grass.

"Maybe we should wait? Dig in the earth, plant something," Victoria calls out with sudden determination.

"Harvest the potatoes, pickle the cabbage, put up jam," Laima nods in agreement.

"Until we die?" Asja hisses, wound tight as a spring.

Victoria shoots her a hateful look. "Maybe."

"We will join hands and build a new home," Jorge smirks.

"Stop it." Malle rolls over with her stomach facing the sun. Her body is as firm as a taut belt.

"Homemade butter dishes, big baskets, small baskets, embroidery—we'll take it all with us to hell." Peer lets out an eerie laugh.

"We'll elect our own parliament," Asja concludes bitterly, and they all fall silent again.

Johnny digs in the sand by the doghouse. The animal tracks are large and deep. The boy's smooth cheeks are flushed with concentration.

"You're not too hot, dear?" Victoria takes her son by the shoulders and caresses his fair nape with tentative gestures. Annoyed by the interruption, Johnny wriggles out from his mother's hands to burrow in the dirt a little farther off.

"A little dynamo," Bertram comments. "Apparently my youngest great-grandchild is also five years old."

Drops of sweat have lined up on Bertram's forehead in military formation. The back of his striped jacket rests heavy and solid against the stump of the apple tree.

"Oh, but what about my manuscripts?" Victoria exclaims with sudden fear.

"Future civilizations will evaluate them," Peer grunts through clenched teeth. He has pulled off his shirt. In the garden's violet-green hodgepodge of sun and shadow, his naked, powerful back looks like clumsy impressionist spew. Cigarette smoke wafts around his gentle eyebrows in a stuffy, dirty cloud.

"Only three cigarettes left," he says.

"The bus!" Laima screams. Weaving on her pointy red stilettos, her breasts heaving, her green and red scarves flapping, she tears down the hill, followed by the smoke of her frizzy black hair.

"Klaus!" squeals Victoria. She wants to run as well, but she restrains herself, stays put. Blades and tufts of meadow grass are matted in her long hair. Johnny, confused, watches Klaus's calm, aggravatingly slow approach. Klaus appears not to have noticed Laima, who now follows him.

Malle scrutinizes Klaus with narrowed eyes, but she bides her time.

"We're close to some border. There's nobody."

The men hang their heads, silent.

"What shall we do, Klaus?" Victoria's voice quavers irritatingly.

"We still have power. I filled up on gas. You can take as much as you want," he says, with subtle shades of irony.

"Did you phone Riga?" Laima asks, as if it were self-evident.

"Yes. The Swedes went home, but Strazds is having sex with Veronica," Klaus says snidely.

"Stop sneering at us!" Malle roars and jumps to her feet.

"The phones are dead. There's no police, no emergency, no fire department. Nothing!" Klaus yells.

"What now?" Jorge asks pragmatically.

"I don't know about you people, but I've made a decision."

Laima curls her lips indignantly. "You're not on your own!"

"Be human, don't sneer," Malle says in a conciliatory tone.

"We'll keep driving until we find somebody. Even if . . . Anybody who disagrees can stay here." Klaus blurts out what he has to say and disappears into the house. Through the window they can see him eating quickly.

Blankets, matches and salt, tableware, soap and rubber boots, canned food and sweaters, a wealth of wealth. They stuff the bus to the gills.

Bertram pours red wine, slow as desire, into dusty bottles. His neck gleams, a devilish spark in his eyes.

"I don't plan to die on an empty stomach," he says.

Victoria sits on the warm porch and twists her hair into a huge, smooth knot. Jorge picks apples. Laima weeps indoors. Peer, leaning against the corner of the shed, gazes out over the groves of hazel trees and willows. Asja sees his powerful body sag like an empty sack.

"Peer, come help!" she says immediately, imperious. Peer comes. He moves objects into the seats; he folds things and wraps them. Then he takes Asja's hand, squeezes it, and whispers:

"I'm scared."

She smiles, and countless kind wrinkles settle into the corners of her eyes. She lets her dry, thin hand slide across his cheek and silently nods.

Then they all climb in. Malle remembers something, rushes back into the rooms. She seeks until she finds. She scratches a pencil across a scrap of paper: "Thank you for a place to sleep. We'll bring everything back." The engine hums. The hot grass turns into tousled hair under their wheels.

I called You my friend, I wanted to come closer, but You turned away. Maybe You don't exist? But if I—the weak one—call You—the strong one, then You must exist, otherwise my voice would have no sound.

What do You herald via the golden horizons, the flaming mugwort, the flutes strangled by the wind? Our souls are strapped into swings. The higher they fly, the faster they fall to earth. Innumerable, we can't enumerate the times You swung us up into the heights and then let go, bored, dropping us. You're as quiet as an abyss which has a voice when someone falls into it. And those bridges—the slim ones, fragile ones, sagging and trembling ones? Do You break them, or is our gait so heavy, our stomachs so full? Do our torments comfort You, our torments splashing over Your heart? If Your life is us, then who are we? Why don't You give language to the stutterers, if You want to hear them? You like to scare us, You skulk in our festering ignorance, in sticky nightmares and frothing passions, but why won't You let us catch sight of You? Are You so frightening? Great Fellow Traveler, why should we honor and praise You, if it's our weeping faces and our bodies, racked by fear, that please You? You are so selfish that You give Your regard to the prayers of staggering wrecks, of cripples, who have no self, just the naked despair of the slave who'll believe mud to be pearls if someone says so. Do You love the strong ones, my exalted Friend? Oh, no. You're old and tired, Your knees are made of shadows and Your hair is made of twilight, Your chest is the desert and Your genitals have dried up. You harvest, but you don't sow. You come and pick us, one after the other, You spit out the rotted ones, but You planted us after all, when You were so young—with an easy, casual hand—this earth, this grass. Aren't You afraid? Ever? Of the straining of bound hands and chained spirits, of the curses of unanswered questions? If someone curses You, do You give them Your hand? Is Your love creating my sorrowful question, which burns slowly and ceaselessly? You tyrant of chaos, You old elephant, sagging and wrinkled, You look with pain, now, at the weary wings of the angels—the angels You sent and scattered across the world. Those strewn feathers—glorious, gleaming. Whipped up by the wind of Your breath, the ashes of the dead call us, the weak, off into the distance, misleading, intoxicating, until we take revenge on You like soldiers tortured by insomnia, and we clamor, brandishing bright knives at the sky—where are You? Why pretend that ashes and dust are God? You get—fluttering wings, we get—decaying bones. We are a naked and dangerous parade, we will follow You, until You will be with us and then we will be—as one.

Translated by Banuta Rubess

Jānis Vēveris

Jānis Vēveris (1960) has been making an attempt to understand the deconstructed modern world in his first book *Kaugems un citi* (Kaugems and Others, 1993). In this work Vēveris has combined a long story "Kaugems" and eight short "deconstructions" in which life gradually becomes literature, and literature becomes life. In terms of their intimacy, these deconstructions are like excerpts from a diary. "Kaugems," on the other hand, is an exhilarating story about the wild bohemian ways of the "golden youth" in the Soviet area. Vēveris continued these themes in his novel *Spoguļu vīns* (The Wine of Mirrors, 1996), which was well received by readers and critics alike as a vivid recounting of the recent past. The mood of Vēveris's works is reminiscent of Max Frisch's *Homo Faber* and *Montauk*. One can sense the theoretician and critic standing alongside the author, constantly trying to clarify the links between life and literature, living and writing.

Vēveris has studied Latvian philology and presently works as an editor in two publishing houses, Artava and Enigma. Vēveris's story "Eventide" is from his second volume of stories, *Pildvielas spēlu lāčiem* (Stuffing Material for Teddy Bears).

Eventide

The scamper of bare feet on the forever squeaking staircase to the loft in dark brown stained wood, a hushed little laugh as the door opens, the scent of coffee tingling the nostrils, waking the senses, *wunderbar, oh, wunderbar,* the record spinning on the phonograph—no, it's a radio, an old receiver, a cumbersome box in a walnut shell.

The green indicator catseye blinking in the bluish dusk, the smell of coffee more and more discernible, the footsteps drawing close, softly grazing the motley quilt just behind my back, snowblue china, the golden brown stream of coffee rushing into the cup, the frosty white of sugar, the frosty white of hands, the frosty white of December, the paralyzing white of paper, thin blue circles of cigarette smoke, time outside space, space outside time, Eventide's the word, Eventide, Eventide, but a weary winter sun is still dawning, tinting the windowpane rubescent, impregnating the skyline with a pallid blush, tumbling through the loft window, flickering in the snowy blue of the cup, mingling with the smoke rings, finally touching the cornea, exploding in countless crimson droplets, raining like red dew on a white morning.

A dawn-reddened spoon in the cup, circling round and round, the fragile blush of daybreak on the page, black characters in neat rows, the song ends and fingers drift across the keys again: *wunderbar, oh, wunderbar.*

The sound of footsteps behind my back has receded, but I keep running, nobody's after me, but I keep on running: into the neat rows of characters, into the bluegreen dusk of imagination, tripping and tumbling, not knowing my way, and shelter is that timeless word which I want to render meaningful.

The house is teasing me, transmitting its noises up and down, the sounds from downstairs freely wander into the loft, shifting around nearby, glancing over my shoulder at the page, laughing, tittering, dying away, replaced by new ones, but downstairs the bare feet in furry slippers shuffle about almost soundlessly, shuffle sweetly and humbly, and there's nowhere I can escape:

the long, endless path, I'm not a traveler, I am just a guest on this road, going nowhere, getting nowhere, the page is already glimmering white, the day's arrived, the day is here, I put down character after character; I'm building a shelter with boundless diligence, creating and re-creating this house, these rooms, these footsteps in furry slippers, sewing the motley quilt to be caressed by bare feet in the morning, while I always remain here in the one which already exists:

cold coffee dregs in the cup, a new pack of cigarettes, the type-writer ribbon needs replacing, and that tasteless soup for lunch again, I tolerate it in humble gratitude, hoping I'll learn to enjoy it someday.

The garden is snowed in, deep and white. Snow creeps into my mouth but I don't give up, I dig into the drift, deeper and deeper, until the ski cap's green pom barely shows, it's but a fleeting mo-ment of triumph; energetic little hands fight back, thrashing about in the puffy dandelion billows, they finally emerge from the dense whiteness, throw themselves around my neck, fly away, farther and farther away, the snowsuit zipper bolts down the silvery path:

the warm, pulsating red of the sweater, a warm and rosy haze in which I hopelessly drown, snow creeps into my mouth, sunrise, sun-rise, then sundown, the flutter of blushing wings in my temples, melting snowflakes zigzagging across the thrown back face, eye-lashes tremble and then, almost imperceptibly, part at the very moment when a butterfly flutters out of nowhere, white in the win-ter air of blushing blue, it quietly circles above the churned snow, flickers over the whipped up drift, then blends in with the sky leav-ing us in the snowy wastes where for weeks we've been trying des-perately to get lost.

The red sweater crouches near the hot chimney wall, tea steams in the cups, *wunderbar, oh, wunderbar,* arms still attempting to take flight:

A GREAT WHITE BUTTERFLY—WHY A BUTTERFLY THERE A MOMENT AGO?

And: DID YOU SEE IT? DID YOU SEE HOW IT SUDDENLY APPEARED OUT OF NOWHERE? IT TRIED TO SPEAK TO US, DIDN'T IT, IT DID, DIDN'T IT?

I don't say anything and sip my tea, the snow's a disheveled heap in the garden, and butterfly wings float down white, whiter and whiter still, a white rustling quiver which suddenly I imagine to be shelter.

A shelter at least for here and now, a shelter for when I don't feel like getting back to my typewriter, a shelter in the white wastes submerged in snow.

The dog emits a howl in the early afternoon. I turn down the radio and listen attentively, thinking I must have misheard, but the mournful whine repeats again and again, and I strain my ears to no avail, trying to determine where it's coming from.

Footsteps from below that used to sound like a barely audible hush come to a halt: we are both listening.

As I head out into the garden, my eyes are overwhelmed, dazzled, by the whiteness. It takes me a while to notice the tracks. The tiny imprints in the snow fade almost imperceptibly, they wind through the rows of apple trees, approach our churned snowdrift, loop around it, and disappear.

I return to the house, climb heavily to the loft, and stare at the filled pages:

A GREAT WHITE BUTTERFLY. WHY THE BUTTERFLY THERE AND THEN?

Paper is impatient, paper demands and commands, paper . . .

Saved by footsteps on the stairs. Afternoon tea, the morning sun replaced by that same red sweater—close, closer, closer still, the pale skin appears ice cold in the dusk. The teacup tumbles to the floor, rolling round and round, and I catch myself listening for that doleful whine.

And so it goes—masochism, endless masochism, we giggle a good hour later, the old wooden bed with the worm-eaten balls on its posts exhausted under our weight. To suffer, we love so much to suffer, and the dog is just a product of our imagination, its tracks in the snow a fruit of our fantasies, and so is that poor butterfly.

What fruit, still a moment later we snicker into each other's face, a fruit stew it is, fruit stew served up by the cafeteria of our consciousness, endless clichés, each sunrise and sunset, each snowflake, each and every word we pronounce, each smile, each movement, each touch, and we ourselves, and we ourselves, as well: tired slaves of our prior notions, our consciousness like an album full of decals, where you find the same old thing, forever and ever the same: DID YOU SEE THAT BUTTERFLY? DID YOU SEE HOW IT SUDDENLY APPEARED, EMERGING OUT OF NOWHERE? IT TRIED TO TELL US SOMETHING, DIDN'T IT?

Like hell it did, sure put on the dog, we're giggling uncontrollably and the old wooden bed creaks. To make love in a snowdrift, that's great, that's just fucking great, and:

One could catch a cold that way, didn't it occur to you, you goddamn idiot!—Yes, of course, one could; and then off to the doctor, let the doctor see where the problem is, and while looking for the problem he'll take a look at the yellowish bruise, he does not know how sensitive this beautiful leg is! Isn't it beautiful, though, the doctor thinks, and then with the catheter, with the catheter! But you don't make a sound and in your mind you're soaring above that snowdrift! You fly and fly while he's busy with his rubber tubes and god-knows-what-else, you just go ahead and fly, and the doc has a radio on the windowsill, and a jerk is blabbering on the air.

I paste decals on the buns of my beloved, they quiver, every night I paste them on my beloved's buns, but in the morning they've all peeled off, good thing I have something in reserve, I always have something in reserve: I tattoo the ass of my beloved, one night I tattooed my beloved's bunny buns, and now I always have access to a comfy and lovely bottom at night!

But you just fly and fly and land on a white piece of paper that crawls with decals: here a letter, there a letter, who could have done it better? And these pictures don't peel off at all, these letters stick tight to the paper; in the morning I tattoo in the whole bunch, and, when I look in the evening at what I've done, there're bunny buns, so bunny, that I feel like throwing up, I feel like retching, endlessly, a long-winded vomit! And then the doctor comes along and asks: what's that shit on the paper? And what's that moth on the paper?

But you don't say a thing, you flutter up to the sky, to the very ceiling, I mean; you float so soulfully, choking on my cigarette, and the bruise on your beautiful leg burns like a mauve *Victoria* plum, like a flag of victory: but the bum is arching up in the air, so provocative, titillating, and proudly arched!

And I, the pitiful dog, I, the impotent pen, I'm just the tail end of a peacock, throwing up in all colors of the rainbow, forever groping for your marble ass, erect on my hindlegs!

Listen, you listen to this:

the long, endless path, I'm not a traveler, I am just a guest on this road, going nowhere, getting nowhere, the page's already glimmering white, the day's arrived, the day is here, I put down character after character; I'm building a shelter in boundless diligence, creating and re-creating this house, these rooms, these footsteps in the furry slippers, sewing the motley quilt to be caressed by bare feet in the morning, while I always remain here, in the one which already exists:

cold coffee dregs in the cup, a new pack of cigarettes, the typewriter ribbon needs replacing, and that tasteless soup for lunch again, I tolerate it in humble gratitude, hoping that a time will come when I'll finally learn to enjoy it.

Well, don't you feel like vomiting? Sure, you do! And there's nothing we'll both enjoy anymore! Sunrise like a reddened ass every morning, whereas I have a *weary winter sun still dawning, tinting the windowpane rubescent, impregnating the skyline with a pallid blush, tumbling through the loft window, flickering in the snowy*

blue of the cup, mingling with the smoke rings, finally touching the
cornea, exploding in countless crimson droplets, raining like red
dew in a white morning.

So, what did we talk about, what did we share such a delicious
laugh about?

No trace of that laughter. You scramble to the foot of the bed and
I notice another one, a fresh bruise on your hip, perhaps from the
tumble in the snowdrift. Choking on anger, I stare at the purple
spot, and your face is covered with crimson blotches as well.

To curse artfully, to make love and then curse artfully in bed, to
complain artfully at the typewriter, to suffer artfully, to despair artfully, to howl artfully—you manage everything so awfully artfully,
you impotent sex maniac!

Your taste is your ruin, your overrefined taste, your overpolished
sentences, your Virginia cigarettes, your daily consumption of a
rare brand of tea make you a tasteful jerk who even makes love in
an overly aestheticized, I'd even say, stylized way! You tasteful
fucker, you, don't you ever get sick of your own tastefulness?

Like hell you've been oversatiated, you've simply overgorged
yourself on nuances! Everything's so refined—halftones, chiaroscu-
ros, everything's got to be picked apart! You yourself are a decal,
long ago peeled off from its backing, but unable to find anything to
attach itself to!

Fucker, oh, my fucker, how stupid you are! You whine and whine,
you cry and cry, and everything comes out so awesome and exalted,
everything's *wunderbar, oh, wunderbar,* like on the radio this morning. Stop howling, my silly fuckhead, let those who've got to howl
howl, but you—you shouldn't! You look for some sort of perfection,
you search and search for it, and lose the daily little morsels thrown
your way, you cry for new taste sensations, but your soul has long
since peeled just like your cavity-ridden teeth. You chew reality like
bubblegum and can't understand why your fillings are falling out,
you chew and chew, and then you're so surprised that reality has no
taste after all, but reality's not for chewing, it is reality that chews
you up, day after day, moment after moment. You can't stop wondering, but reality spits on you! Spits on you just like this!

The spit is precise and well-aimed. I brush the back of my hand
across my face, then reach for my handkerchief, I wipe myself carefully, light a cigarette, I don't say a word, I wait for something to
happen. But what happens is more of the same:

See, you don't have anything to say! You've never had anything to
say on paper either! The only thing you know how to do is blabber
eloquently, *tinting the windowpane rubescent, impregnating the*

skyline with a pallid blush, and then whimper about everything being so passé! And you yourself so passé, so unredeemably passé! You don't live, you just write. Over how many pages do you plan to spread the romp in the snowdrift, huh? Think I don't know why you dragged me over there this morning?! You prodder of imagination with no imagination of your own! Oh, you know, you know damn well why you got so stuck with those minors and can't budge either way! Fancying yourself a Humbert Humbert, a Nabokov! Researcher of souls, you, misunderstood heart! What can you write about them if you haven't tasted them, eh? Why the sudden urge to write your own *Lolita,* asshole?! Oh, because years pass, years rush right past and my tits ain't so childish anymore! Now I have a marble white ass instead of a round, blushing little bum, but that's what you go for is round blushing little bums, you've always desired such a little bum who'd grunt complacently upon just hearing your voice, grunt complacently and forever prove to you how great and manly you are! But you are afraid of me! With each passing year you're more and more afraid of me! Because you're still a little boy who drools over life like a glossy tits-and-ass magazine, it's not that you don't want, you simply don't know how to be an adult! And that's why you're so terribly afraid of adults! That's why, for you, even the sun is a dawning ass! You'd fondly busy yourself with minors, admit it, honey, admit it! You'd fondly busy yourself with them, thus regaining PURITY, right? But that seems too complicated, so you attempt to manage it on paper, you generally live on paper, just nothing ever comes of it, right? And that's why your life's so corny and boring, the poor thing?! It's you who's corny and boring, so corny, no wonder you feel like throwing up. Because life ain't no minor, it's you who's an infantile dumbass. Eventide, how poetic, Eventide; you just had to fasten a house name to the piece you happened to be writing at the moment! The place where the sun sets, the western coast, the hard-earned loaf of bread, the last generation in the dunes, a terminal sunset, right on! They bought it and read it, and filmed it and watched it, and it went straight to your head, buddy, didn't it. You knew it was shit, but if everyone claims it's a rosebush . . . ! And so you sit in your Eventide, sit there, and can't write for the life of you! Oh sure, now you'll say—that shit brought us bread! And others did, too, all kinds of rubbish! Sure it did, honey, sure it did, what can you do if there are people who have to eat rubbish!

Here comes another spit, I think to myself, and start fumbling for the handkerchief, but instead of spittle there's a frightened face very close, and heart drops dribble into that same spoon reddened by dawn, and there's a red mist like earlier, during the day in the snow, and there's a stab in my chest, a deep, penetrating stab, long and ominous, then it settles down, calms down, then another stab, and the face, oh, Lord, this face!

So here we are, and where else could we be, we stare at each other dully, and the pages of the manuscript are scattered about, and then HE starts howling AGAIN: first barely audible, then louder, louder, louder still, till the howl turns into a quiet and distant whimper. Entangled in sleeves and trouser legs, in a weird sort of togetherness and haste we dress, then go out into the garden where the last redness of sunset has stumbled against the churned up snowdrift. Everything repeats itself, everything repeats itself in a boring and endless way, that what we're doing right now as well: the footprints in the snow, our stumbling steps trying to follow them, our febrile breath, our sudden revelation that it's *right here* and *right now*.

Nothing to see, but to feel—sharply, unmistakably.
The long, endless path.
Whimpers again and again, concepts seem to solidify.
Doglike humility, doglike complacency, doglike love, finally. And other doglike qualities; there're so many of them. Dog's eyes, dog's gazes, seeing everything that once was grown distant, but maybe it was just perceived. Covered pages gripped in the fist, the fingers relax, and the pages scatter one after another.
To give thanks for each day, for each breath you take.
No one's a traveler here, everyone's just a guest on this road. Still the endless path; we let the whimper guide us.
Boundless gratitude, unspeakable gratitude.
Oh, until one learns to find! One can never learn to lose.

Translated by Ieva Lešinska

Mārtiņš Zelmenis

Mārtiņš Zelmenis (1965) studied the Latvian language and literature at the University of Latvia. He has worked as an editor for numerous publications concerning culture, as well as for the literary magazine *Karogs*. His first collection of stories and tales, *Pelēkā brāļa stāsti* (The Gray Brother's Stories) was published in 1987, having lain dormant through a period of censorship because it was considered "incomprehensible and incompatible with the spirit of the times." The collection could be described as a set of journeys throughout the world of myths and parables. Zelmenis is also a professional photographer. He has translated books from the English language—*Total Terror* by Albert Kalme, dedicated to Soviet and Nazi atrocities in the Baltic States, and a book by Gary Jones entitled *Running a Shop*. Zelmenis works as an interpreter from the Russian and English languages and continues to write stories, essays, and literary reviews.

Zelmenis translated his story "Storm Approaching" and Arvis Kolmanis's "Story about Veronica," both included here.

Storm Approaching

The summer morning is green and Maria is doing her household chores. To be more precise, she has gotten up and is going to the barn to milk the cows. As she walks along the path to the low-lying building where the cattle make different noises, mist rises from the Venta; through meadows flanking the river and forests it rises to embrace the sky where the sun has emerged, itself rather green. The wind isn't troubling the grass; the wind isn't troubling the trees: it slinks, slow and lazy, across the meadows. The grass raises dewdrops to the sun. Maria stops for a moment—not to listen to the morning birds, she hears them always, every morning, even if there are no birds singing, and this morning seems a little more silent than other mornings—Melna, or maybe Mashka, is jangling her chains in the barn, or maybe it's one of the other cows, but there are no better cows than the two of them, are there?—pulling at the chain, jangling the buckets, no, they aren't lowing, but, having detected footsteps, await their mistress impatiently. Their mistress knows it. Knows it and listens. No, Maria is listening to the dew. The dew clings only to the grass, which was mowed yesterday; it cannot wet Maria's feet; the wooden shoes have thick leather uppers, and the grass has been cut short. It's true, the birds are still comparing their voices, and water murmurs on the other side of the meadow; Maria realizes that she's been standing here longer than it seemed: the sun has edged ahead slightly and is no longer green. It's become white, and Maria remembers there's much yet to be done. The usual daily chores that have to be seen to, by all means, and young Maria's got a new set of eyes—this morning she's looking at the world she's used to, seeking the difference between today and yesterday, and the day before yesterday—but yesterday and the day before yesterday are no more, and they elude her comparison. The open-air ball? Fatigue? The dancing? It suits a young newlywed woman without children. The last ball before the summer's field-work, but they've already started theirs, mowed one meadow, the second one's turn is tomorrow. Limbs aching from the dance? Maria merely smiles. Was it yesterday? Or late last night? Anyway, it's over. Tomorrow hasn't arrived yet, but it won't vanish anywhere because this morning is making such bright promises. The gentle hay-time wind, a clear blue sky, and the bright silver button still rising. If she would stop and look at the sun, she'd certainly see it moving upward. Where does the anxiety throbbing in her breast come from? It doesn't suit this morning. This morning smiles with the sun; this morning sways with the wind; this morning is full, ful-filled, and whole, even without any completed chores. Is the unrest seeping out from beneath the granary, trying to rise into the sky? Kittens will soon be creeping out from there. Maybe it comes from beneath the porch? For Peter is already standing in the doorway, putting on his cap, closing the door, and the bolt falls into place with a click. The shining boots descend from the porch, and Maria's anxiety loosens its grip. Releases its hold. Her fingers, clenched in a fist, unwind. Nothing can happen on such a morning to make one's heart quiver. Adolf is wagging his tail, prancing around in hopes of being allowed to go along. Nothing eventful can happen today, al-though Maria is staying home alone, but there's work enough to keep three people busy all day. Peter has already reached the road and is scolding the dog so eager to go with him; he's shouting some-thing funny as a farewell, something encouraging, a sly joke, but Maria, familiar with his continual jesting, makes no attempt to grasp the sentence snatched up and stolen by the wind. Farewells have no meaning, unlike a greeting, and that she'll want to hear in its entirety, and very soon at that, soon, and not a sound will be al-lowed to escape. She's ready to learn all of Peter's words of arrival by heart, in order to repeat them, to repeat—and remember—ev-erything, even things which haven't happened yet, but which must happen, for she's noticed the world's ways. She knows how the world behaves; the world has taken pains to explain it itself, with the help of her mother, of her teacher, of the minister. Peter shouldn't be going anywhere; it's a truth of the world; there's too much to be done here, and Maria has only two hands. The sun, and even the world, aren't going to wait; they both know it well. But what has to be done has to be done. Maria will manage somehow. She's never been one just to sit with her hands in her lap. It's still early, but Maria has so much to do—milk the cows, feed them, and the morning seems different from—yes, from what—from itself. Maybe because Peter's gone, but he had to go—no, truly, he could have stayed home, was it anything so urgent, after all, it's hay time, the hardest time in the fields, he could, should have stayed home, he didn't have to go, Maria thinks.

"No point in standing and staring at God's world as though I've never seen it before," Maria scolds herself in a soft voice. There's no one to hear it and misunderstand. The hay has to be tossed, here by the house and over by the forest; what's more, the neighbor's bull, that universal menace, got off his chain and managed to charge over and break the wattle fence around Maria's flower garden! Did anything remain after the rampage? The hollyhocks, the sweet peas? Maybe the marigolds? Perhaps only the wattle fence will blossom? What's the point of protecting the flower beds from hens and turkeys if everything is destroyed in one moment? Maybe the marigolds can still be saved, Maria muses. It's unimportant work, but of course, it's for the evening, when everything else has been taken care of. And the heat should be subsiding by evening. Maria remembers how yesterday evening at dusk the very same heat climbed up the stalks, the stems, the leaves, glided up along her legs like a premonition of wonder, like a playful breath, like a hand's caress. Does Peter have such a hand? Peter's hand is much rougher; but the naughty wind had lifted her skirt a bit. Naughty boy. Naughty Peter. If someone made her tell it, Maria would have blushed, comprehending what had taken place, but there was nobody there save for the morning with all those birds.

Well, the young mistress knows what she wants—to toss the hay, to tend the flower beds in the evening; roots torn out of the earth in hot weather die quickly, so she's put the flowers in a bucket hidden in the cool of the granary. In the evening, after all other work has been done, she'll see which plants might survive. If they couldn't be put back into the soil right then, into that hot black sand, there was nothing left to do. Maybe it wasn't very sensible to plant flowers in midsummer, even if they were generously watered, and what if she watered them even more and covered them in order to keep the sun away? Maria has a marvelous green thumb—will she really fail to get the flowers back into their beds? She resolves to do it fast, as soon as she can manage it, as soon as she has a moment to spare. Mightn't the flowers grow back into the soil simply because it's Maria's will? They aren't about to wither! Maria picks up the empty buckets and briskly goes to the barn. One can dream one's life away—Maria remembers her mother's words. Her words or somebody else's: all the cows are living beings, and no living being likes to wait—even if it's a cow with a mare's name. The names, along with other words, can change so little. Improve something. But invoke misfortune? Better not try it.

This morning, as every other morning, Maria is greeted by all that hear her welcome steps in the barn—the piglet in its separate sty, the big pigs, the sheep. Snouts and muzzles reach out for her, poking and scratching the tattered sty boards. She throws grass, scratches foreheads, pours water into the manger—and a thought dawns on Maria, the kind that usually dawns on more refined and spoiled minds, one of the kind she has trouble coping with alone: *I wonder how the women of Vidzeme, Latgale, and the land of the Sēļi go about their milking? Just like me? Do they feel the same premonition I do this morning?* Cattle are the same everywhere, some dappled, some brown. The milk flows white and foamy; tails swing like the pendulums of clocks; the cows are moving their heads, chasing flies away with their horns and tails (so easy to miss!), but the disturbing idea that's hit her recedes only later, although managing to take root: *What does a barn in Vidzeme or Latgale look like?* and, as there's nobody to tell, the mistress goes on about her duties. She takes the broom and sweeps the dungwash into the gutter. She scatters straw throughout the barn and sits down on her stool in order to milk Melna, then Mashka, then the other ones, and milk fills the pail, foaming. A small dark cloud has silently stopped at the horizon, waiting its turn, without Maria's knowledge. Maria notices it through the low, small window curtained with cobwebs, and she grows restless. Or does she? Perhaps it only appears that way to us, who gaze at this figment of our imagination. A small cloud is just a small cloud; there are always plenty of them in the sky, day or night, and only large clouds bring restlessness and rain. This one is certainly not like those, and if Maria's heart has trembled for a moment, it's not because of the cloud in the window. Maria doesn't bother about the guesswork. Her heart is a funny one: it trembles and jumps at just the moments when it should be as calm and collected as a sheep to be shorn. But sheep are never calm when they are being sheared. Maria knows the ways of her heart, knows that it is capable of some surprises, for instance, anxiety out of the blue. Are all other hearts different, and hers—the only funny one?

Is there a lot or a little to do in the barn in the morning? Maria doesn't give it a thought, although it takes some time to scratch the flanks of the cows, to fetch hay and straw, it takes time, but she has the whole day for it! A beautiful, sunny day—like this very morning, if only the rain wouldn't come all of a sudden, if only it wouldn't turn gray and overcast. The heart that jumped but a moment ago is silent now and seems ashamed of itself.

The cattle must drink before they are driven to pasture. Today it won't be far—she'll drive them to the closest meadow by the forest, the one surrounded by a fence. Maria has no time to herd them, the hay is waiting; she takes the rod, but there's no need to urge any of the cows on, and once they're inside the pasture she hurries back— when she's alone at home it's much harder for her to manage everything, but all of a sudden and for no clear reason Maria's decided firmly: she has not only to take care of the house, the hay, and the meal; she must also put the flower garden in some order; some unrecognizable voice in her head is chattering away, talking and talking incessantly, demanding that she do it, do it quickly, right away, now, this very moment—she shouldn't wait for the evening to come. When Maria raises her head and looks around, as if searching for who's talking, for where he is and who he might be, she sees only what a bright day it is, and how some birds are tiptoeing through the grass stubble but others are jumping from one branch to another right beside her, how the flies are dancing in clouds right behind the barn, where a dunghill is swelling. The river flows there and speaks no more, it is much heavier and more imposing than when she went to the barn some hours ago, or even earlier, when Peter went away and—yes, that's right—the voice spoke for the first time.

Everything is much more yellow than it was before she milked the cows—the leaves in the trees have lost their green freshness, and, it seems, they are making a quite different—rustling—noise. The rain hasn't come for so long—let it not come for a while yet.

What's befallen her? Is she bewitched? The jabbering must be in her head! Wait, wait—did he not laugh, oh, the one who was telling her to tidy up her trampled flower garden? The wild ducks rose up from the rushes and flapped their wings against the waves. The ducks had been hallooing to each other just a moment ago—that was the noise. If Peter were home, wouldn't he reach for the gun? Maybe it's actually better that he's not home; Maria lifts her hands to her head—it's still rather hot—look, there's one more cloud at the horizon, maybe the one to bring a storm. The work still to do! Maria grabs the rake and hurries off to the meadow. Half-running. How much will she manage this day? The haystack-maker is not home; if it rains, is there any reason to try to collect the hay? Yes, of course there is. And yet she feels guilty and out of tune, not managing what should already have been finished; Peter, it's a pity he can't lend a hand, but the work has to be done, sure it does, it has to, it has to, it has to be done, and Maria does her best, beads of sweat converging at the tip of her nose, drop by drop, drop by drop; she's got no time to wipe them off, so they splash away noiselessly, like tears. Her eyes are sore. But it's the sweat! That's the noiseless dripper. While there's hay, there's sweat, which will dry later. Like the hay that's dried out in this hot weather. Peter. Can he even imagine the way Maria's working here now, her skirts flying, the buttons on her tight blouse bursting open? Maybe he wouldn't even suspect it.

While Maria fiercely brandishes her rake, the one talking in her head has fallen silent, and then Maria suddenly obeys!—as if in a daze—at high noon, when everything is parched; she fetches water and spills it over the flowers, crumbles the soil, but the water of the Venta is a joker, the moment she's watered the flowers it vaporizes, and the roots peek up out of the soil as if they'd signed a pact, and Maria struggles in vain. Can she manage it at all? Or maybe she's trying to do more than she can. As if bewitched. As if the evil eye's cast a spell on her, envying her. She—the one who knows no other vice save its name! And in her head—didn't someone just laugh? She has to manage, she has to do it all! Yes, there was some laughter, somebody was splitting his sides with laughter, as if from a good joke. Maria doesn't catch the joke, she doesn't even have time to think—is someone laughing about her? She has to work, to work, to manage, and she tries to do it all. Nothing funny about that.

As the heat diminishes, Maria suddenly realizes that the last moment has come to prepare a meal, and she hurries home as the horizon gets darker and darker, amassing even darker clouds than before. All of the green hues have disappeared long ago, when she was trying to straighten out the flower bed; gone, and only the dark colors surrounding her are still bright. When the porridge bowl is on the table and the spoons are in place, Maria rests her head in her hands, worn-out by endless physical chores, and stares into the stove's blazing mouth. Will everything she's done have been in vain? will the wattle fence be the only thing in the garden to bloom? Peter should be back soon. She'll bring in the cattle before the rain, she won't leave them to suffer, but what if no real rain comes, just a few drops? The cattle need a real pasture, not just an enclosure, but where can she find someone to herd them at such short notice? Why on earth did Peter leave home? Why did she have to stay home alone? Maria straightens her bent back and slouches to the door; in the dark foyer she fumbles for the door bolt which has grown heavy, like a snag, like water, like the soil, no, like a heart, has grown heavy from the old boards, and she fusses for a while trying to get it open. And again the wind seems peculiar somehow, different from yesterday's playful wind, but yesterday is long gone. It looks like the rainfall will be heavy. Such is the weather. In the early morning it looked different, but that's characteristic of hay time, you can't be sure of anything.

On her way to fetch the cattle home, the weather—despite the drizzle—seems fine, although a bit on the cool side, and on her way back Maria has to wrap herself in her shawl because the cold northeast wind tosses dry leaves in her face, and it's hard to lift her tired, heavy legs. Suddenly, Maria recalls that there was a time when such trifles like the wind and a bit of cold meant nothing to her. Should it be reiterated how much she's thinking about Peter? Terribly. In fact, she's thinking of nothing else.

She drives the cattle home before the clouds have concealed the sun altogether, and there's a chill with the dampness—and a kind of cellar smell—seeping in, but Maria shakes it. Can't she raise her head? walk with a straight back? The work won't take care of itself.

Where is Peter dawdling? No sign of him. He should have been home ages ago. Maria doesn't think in words, shows no sign of longing, she only misses Peter very much. That's nothing surprising. Storm clouds have darkened the area, and one particular stretch across the Venta has darkened; the clouds have transformed her yard into a dance floor for shadows—how they jump and spin in elaborate dances with the branches of the big trees now! On the other side of the Venta, where the old graveyard lies, trees are wringing their hands and moaning about the wind's calamity at the dark skies, though the skies themselves are masters of the wind, changing darker and darker still. Thank God she's managed to bring all the cattle in. When will Peter come in from the rain? If he comes now, he'll be wet to the bone.

While Maria forks hay to the cows, before she sits down on the milking stool rocking on its rickety, manure-caked legs, the wind outside grows stronger. It seems determined to tear all the remaining leaves from the trees—did it make such a deal? The cows breathe heavily, appear slightly nervous. As if they'd rather not allow themselves to be milked, but none of them is supposed to calve soon—they'd better not look back over their shoulders with the big, doleful eyes which city slickers call beautiful, they better not look— lo, the cows are jiggling like last year's foals, not letting the woman milk them or wipe their teats properly. A foolish thought crosses Maria's mind, she can't shed it like an autumn leaf in the same murderous wind that's plundering everything outside now: *is it possible that she's feeding hay to the cows but that it turns to straw the moment the cows touch it with their soft muzzles?* No, that's the most foolish thought ever to come into her head. Maybe they, the cows, no longer regard Maria as their mistress, perhaps they know Maria's got someone talking in her head? Such is the weather, even the cows are acting strange.

Is Maria milking her cows for the first time?—the strong woman doesn't let the mischief of her cows bother her, she merely toils a bit longer than usual, and, when the pails are full, her back doesn't want to straighten itself. Maria doesn't hurry even though the cold glides up her legs with icy hands—Frost's hands, which ought to cool both Maria's flesh and heart. No, the ice doesn't reach her heart. The cold remains without. Heavy hailstones clatter against the barn window's dirty glass. Then there are even bigger ones. Maria sighs, she hasn't the strength to lift the pails, lift her shoulders, her back, her eyes—everything's so heavy. Of course, she's overestimated her strength. But she has to finish, finish the work! For there's no one else to do it. Maria knows nobody else like Peter, but he's not here. Should the cattle suffer just because their mis-

tress feels tired and is losing her strength? Heaven forbid! Maria
lets her eyes linger on the floorboards, she lets her shoulders slump
the way the soil likes it better, but the pails—those she is able to
tear away from the ground, and lift, and—carry them.

The milk is in the pails and the foam's rising up over the rims.
Where's that cat gotten to, she's never missed a milking! Who was
the one meowing, who was the one rubbing softly against Maria's
legs, who was the one asking for milk, who was the only one to
share her warm, foamy milk with the hedgehog, forbidding Adolf to
come near. The cat's disappeared, who knows where, maybe she's
afraid of the rain, Maria can't imagine where the cat's gotten to.
Maybe she's got kittens already? It's not that Maria's afraid, afraid
to imagine it, for Maria is courageous, make no mistake. Always
has been. Then . . . and now, and still is. She doesn't speak of it, of
course. Doesn't think about it, either. Life goes on, something has to
go on, everything happening around here is happening to her,
Maria, and everything happening happens for the better, or is she
wrong in thinking so? When the cat was slithering around her legs,
Maria knew how to take care, not spill the milk, not to stumble over
the tomcat's speckled back. How many colors did he have?—The
world's supposed to come to an end when a three-hued calico male is
born—the woman recalls some forgotten words spoken by someone
himself long forgotten. It was Peter, wasn't it? Who knows. But all
of a sudden she can no longer remember something far simpler: was
the cat, the one that came to drink milk, a male or a female? When
it was winding around her legs, Maria knew how not to spill any
milk, not to stumble over the speckled body, but now her legs are so
unsteady, as if three-colored male and female cats were wrapping
themselves around them, as if the cats were celebrating something
important in their lives, something, the existence of which Maria
has known at some other time, but now no longer, no more . . . What
could it be? Maria thinks and gazes into darkness, deeper into darkness, but she has no time to think. What's there to think about, life
is going on and on, and on. It doesn't stop to wonder what's been
happening right now or what's been missing. Actually, Maria is not
concerned about this, she's got something more important to do—
what a shame—Maria can barely lift the pail, nor the other one, the
cows are giving so much milk she can't lift it. She has to step carefully in order not to spill that warm whiteness; outside it's so dark,
so very dark, she can barely make out the path anymore, and the
wind is blowing in gusts, it touches her face with gritty snowflakes,
which fall into the milk. Maria can feel that in spite of the snow it's
beginning to freeze, for her cheeks turn rosy (she can feel it) and
burn. As if Maria had been walking around in this cold, thick white-

ness for hours. She must get inside under the roof as fast as she can. Her feet seek the snow-covered path—where is it, it was here a moment ago. She walked here only recently and everything was in its place. Life won't help her, more likely the opposite. Pattering on, lost in thought, as though lugging those full pails, and, pausing to catch her breath, she senses without looking that her lilac bush is completely leafless; yes, some poles are still there, the remains of a fence surrounding the flower garden, there's the old bench Peter promised to mend soon. Everything has to be somewhere here, right here in this yard, but it's become so dark this evening, this cold evening, so dark she can see nothing at all. The wind has blown the moon away. It's dark in the room, the fire in the stove must have gone out by now if there's no glimmer of light in the yard where the wind is blowing such big, dark snowflakes. Like flies. Where are they from? When did they appear? Where's Peter gone? He'll be home, he's not a drunk, Maria knows, she remembers. At the wrong time. Maybe he got as far as the nearest neighbors, maybe he's waiting for the awful weather to die down. Maybe he hasn't even started walking. Who can tell. . . . It's such a long time ago he ought to have been home. It's so long ago Maria can't remember it clearly anymore. The one talking in her head keeps chattering and chattering, telling her about her work, about what she's accomplished this winter, for the winter is real, the realest of her entire life, speaks of Peter, whom she should not have trusted at all, of—no, he says nothing about himself. Maria listens, she knows there's no reason to answer, she merely has to decide where to tread. The path is slick with ice, her worn wooden shoes are unsuited for this weather; Maria's breathing is heavy by the time she's managed to reach the door; she suddenly stumbles and milk spills over the worn-out threshold; it flows in a wide stream through the chink under the door across the foyer's well-worn clay, seeps into the cracks between the bricks, the milk wants to seep into the earth but it can't, the earth's trodden harder than clay, harder than bricks. What rich soil this would be, it can't be that no blood has ever been spilled here. What a pleasure it would it be to sow and plant in such rich soil, watered with milk and blood, but Maria's not the one to do it. Snowflakes are sifting lower and lower in the chimney-room, ever thicker and thicker, and the wind keeps whistling along—as if accompanying the other whistler, the one inside Maria's head, the very same one who's been more Maria than Maria herself for such a long time, more Maria than the old woman with sunken eyes, those big, black eyes like forest lakes. When she was young—not so long ago. . . . Oh . . . the eyes, those eyes. . . . Was it really so long ago? Certainly not.

"You have the right kind of eyes for crying," the one inside her head chatters. "Why haven't you started yet?" he asks. "You've got all the right reasons to do it. You shouldn't delay, you don't have much time left. Looking around and listening to the birds suits young girls. Come on, get on with it!"

Maria listens. Maria thinks. She thinks but does nothing. God's the one doing. Has he been the one speaking in her head? She hasn't been to church in such a long time; ever since its roof has fallen in and Mille uses the ruin as a pasture for her goats. Mille is Mille, she's even worse, but never mind, she's not a young girl anymore, either. It seems Mille doesn't have a tooth left in her head, what a shame. It's not a laughing matter, Maria doesn't laugh about it. Not a laughing matter. Her hands are clenched around the yoke. She carries the pails to the unheated end of the house, there's no need to cool the milk in the well. She carries the milk and thinks, gazes into darkness, deeper into the darkness, as deep as she can, darkness that consumes the deep blackness—all that remains of both the dark secrets that no one has even tried to discover. This is what Maria thinks of while looking into darkness, deeper into darkness, while the wind and snowflakes assemble themselves into a whirlwind while it gets ever darker, and the rivulets of milk freeze into the ground between the cracked bricks on the opposite side of so many doors behind her. Old, shabby Adolf tries to lick up a little, but he can't keep his feet. Of course Peter hasn't returned, if he had, he wouldn't let the dog suffer so, old age is really awful if you can't hear or see anymore, but Maria isn't surprised, she's known this since the moment he put his cap on, oh, yes, way back then: how could she make such a mistake, she who's got such a clever one rattling away in her head: of course the room's completely dark, nobody's sitting at the table and spinning his old cap in his fingers, his feet crossed in his old boots. The fire in the stove is nearly out, all save the last embers that glow timidly, reminders of themselves: *we're passing out, in a moment we are to be no more.* Maria hurries to the mouth of the stove as fast as she can, nearly falls on her knees, blows her weak breath onto the smoldering embers; she holds on to the stove that's still slightly warm, gropes for some twigs on the floor, breaks them, and throws them on the embers, and blows, blows her breath out. No one's whistling in the chimney anymore, it seems. The storm has come and gone. It's snowing. A thick layer coats the windowsill. Everything in the yard must be covered inches deep. Luckily, there's no thunder in winter, Maria's scared to death of thunder. Maria at the stove mouth as if fallen on her knees, as if blowing at the embers, holding onto the stove, finds the twigs, breaks them, throws them on the embers, blowing, losing her breath. Flames leap back to life, consume the twigs, pant deliciously, mirroring a bright night, ancient green times, a wreath of myrtle like a golden nimbus, something darker and indefinite—that which is deeper in shadow—something that never happens, but somehow always turns out to be experienced in the end.

Translated by Mārtiņš Zelmenis

Rimants Ziedonis

Rimants Ziedonis (1962) studied journalism and made his debut in literature with a collection of poems, *Atvēzējies glāstam* (Ready to Hit with a Caress, 1986). He is the son of Imants Ziedonis, a famous Latvian poet. In 1992 Ziedonis's collection of stories, *Dzīves pieredze un ziepju burbuļi* (Life's Experience and Soap Bubbles), was published. "Flying Fish" is from this book.

Ziedonis puts the reader to a double test: the readers must first become familiar with the author's personality, which seems to mirror the entire world, and then the reader must reexperience the author's strange experiences through his memories, fantasies, and reality. Ziedonis thinks that life's experience must be forgotten because it "smothers the wonder in people's eyes." Ziedonis has criss-crossed Australia, compiling interesting material about the Latvians living there. He has worked as an editor for the literary magazine *Karogs* as well as for the newspaper *Literatūra. Māksla. Mes.*

The Flying Fish

A ventilation fan came on, its hum overpowering the steady drone of the airport. Napkins in glasses fluttered in the flow of air, a newspaper quivered in someone's hands, the corners of tablecloths waved, ashes slid slowly into one corner of the ashtray, a breadcrumb (on the table) began moving. Tiny, almost imperceptible movements commenced. On the floor, a dust colony drifted by; a mouth exhaled smoke which then immediately vanished, as if the mouth had drawn it back in; a woman's styled hair rippled; the dry flower arrangement on the bar rustled.

He stuffed a pickled pumpkin cube into his mouth, ran his tongue over its grooves, and let the associations roll. A woman washing laundry. She scrubs the sheet rhythmically along the washboard, water splashing over the sides of the basin; the woman bends over, then straightens, leans over, straightens herself, steam billowing to the ceiling, the suds rising like a mountain . . . interesting—if you write a word on a tiny pumpkin with a fountain pen, does the word grow along with the pumpkin? . . . Look, the suds are already overflowing. Tasting soap in his mouth, he worked the cube under his tongue. Now it's growing, slowly growing, pushing his tongue upward, the corners already pressing against his cheeks, his cheeks become square, grow, his chin becomes square, his jaw cracks, stop, I'm suffocating, stop. Nitroglycerin, the large, square nitroglycerin tablet shrinks, melts, my tongue slowly settles, I am no longer suffocating, strength flows into me, enough strength to suck methodically on the next cube. . . . Jeez, what was I thinking of?

Having eaten, he glanced at his watch. Still plenty of time. He went up to the bar. Would you pour me a cognac? . . . On one side of the road stretched a rickety old wooden fence; holding lightly onto Mary's elbow, so that the girl would not trip in her high heels, Lueas helped her cross the narrow strip of land pitted with rabbit holes. . . . Would you pour me a cognac? Yes, yes, just a moment . . . the still youngish, redheaded, primly dressed Mary Carson glanced over. . . . Are you almost done with the page? The girl pulled herself away from her book and poured a splash of cognac into a large glass.

He sat down in his seat and watched as the girl sank back into her reading. Like a cat, she moved her head along with the lines on the page, her expressions mirroring the text. Studying the girl's face, he tried to imagine what she was reading. Look: the girl freezes, stops twirling her hair, smiles faintly. . . . I'm sorry, very sorry—he rose, stood for a moment stroking the carvings on the back of his chair. He had risen very deliberately, but in his slow fingering of the carvings she sensed confusion. For the first time, she saw Harry . . . no, better yet Victor . . . confused. She sensed that she now would have to say something cruel so that he would leave without having lost his self-respect, so that he would leave angry, defiant in the face of insult. . . . The smile vanished from the girl's face. Someone stopped at the bar, and the girl had to pull herself from her book again, her face lost its animation, and she turned toward the new customer with a mechanical smile.

Still plenty of time.

He swallowed and squinted, trying to merge the human silhouettes, the lines and edges of the room into a variety of geometric forms. Two young women in tight slacks were sitting at the bar. They appeared to be—humanists. The pear-shaped silhouettes straightened into triangles and vibrated slightly in the man's eyes. A family rose from a table—two children with their parents. They approached the door, each with their own gait. The woman moved smoothly and evenly until, with the shine from the surface of the round door reflected on her, she rolled out of the restaurant. A little behind her, on either side, were two bouncing tennis balls followed by a heavy clothespin swaying back and forth. The amplitude of the husband's oscillation was disturbing; it seemed that he would tip over at any moment. As soon as this composition slid out the door, a wide cube with healthy, straight, sharp edges appeared in the doorway. Will it enter? Will it pass by? Carefully, almost brushing the jamb, the cube slid through the doorway and made its way in. The floodlight over the bar shone on one of the cube's planes, and an angular shadow slid across the room.

Having aired out the terminal, the fan shut off. The tiny movements all ceased. For a moment, in concert with the ventilation, people quieted. Struck by the silence.

Caught in this moment, he felt uncomfortable—the quiet, the geometric lines on pause. He widened his eyes and rapped on his glass with his ring to break the sudden quiet. The room's torpor disappeared; conversations resumed and climbed in volume. At the bar, a huge man with huge fingers fiddled with a tiny change purse; the pear-shaped girls fidgeted on their barstools.

He glanced at his watch. Five more minutes had passed. A watch—another of mankind's enterprising attempts to achieve harmony, to pull itself together. Organization around the clock. Let's all meet at three! The ants won't come. Neither will the anteaters. Those creatures won't allow a mechanical device to impose its demands on their natural rhythms.

An airplane drones, shaking the white glass building. The plane slowly turns to pull onto the runway. Flattened faces pressed against the little round windows. You really can't go anywhere. But let me try to leave—let me try to leave. That must be tested—can I leave, or will only my body leave?

The rumbling intensified, and the airplane raced ahead until it hauled itself off the ground. Massive. A whole town, barn, auditorium, stadium. There are enough of them in the plane to found their own nation with their own parliament, opera company, Olympic team, brass band. A flying republic. Farming would be touch and go. But, not to worry, they could raise flying squirrels and flying fish. Occasionally, the airplane could land on the shore of some ocean, lower its snout, tuck in its wings and drink. A few centuries would pass, and this flying republic would gain mythic status like the Flying Dutchman. Scholars would write detailed studies of the bizarre flights of a strange airplane speeding around the globe surrounded by regiments of flying squirrels and flying fish. Reports questioning their scientific merit would fly around in response, demanding evidence or just shouting—YOU'RE LYING! I'm not lying. I'm telling the truth. Swear on the Bible. I don't have a Bible. I have a math workbook. Let's pretend it's a Bible. There, place your hand on it and repeat after me: I swear to tell the truth, the whole truth, and nothing but the truth. . . . Now repeat that and look into the sky. You have to look. . . . Now continue: If I have lied, I will sit down in the big puddle with all my clothes on and stay there for five minutes. Now, repeat!

The younger boy puckered up his face, gazing silently up at the sky. Then, without lowering his head, he sneaked a glance at the older boy. I said that you were lying. I wasn't. Why should I lie? Then repeat after me, sneered the older boy.

Fine. Then tell the whole story from the beginning—every detail is meaningful, everything is important.

Edward and I . . . Keep your hand on the Bible . . . Yesterday Edward and I searched for an *inaccessible* spot to dig a bunker. We went into the woods. First we stuck together, then we decided that we would find the inaccessible spot faster if we split up. Edward looked at his compass and said that he would go north, so I should go south. I looked at the compass, and it turned out that if I went south I would end up back at the house. . . . In fact, Edward didn't really understand anything from that compass. Edward studied the compass again and said that I should go west. But I said, Let's flip a coin, because there were really a lot more inaccessible places north than there were west. But Edward said that if he didn't have a compass then I wouldn't even know north from west, and that he wouldn't flip a coin and that he was going north no matter what....

Fine, now enough of the north and west.

You said yourself that every detail is important.

Go on.

Therefore, somewhat unfairly, Edward went north and I went west. But I just keep finding *accessible* places everywhere. I crossed the canal. . . . Where? It doesn't matter. I said every detail is important. At that spot where Anita buried her rabbit. I climbed into the gully, through the raspberries. I noticed that the tops of some of the trees were bent and burned. I kept going. Then I noticed some kind of singed piece of metal. I kept going; the brush was thicker. The place was getting pretty inaccessible. I thrashed through some bushes, clearing the way with my knife. With your knife? Show me. The younger boy pulled a small knife from his pocket. Ha, that's for sharpening pencils! Well, there wasn't that much to clear. All right, said the older, go on.

So I pushed through to a clearing, a meadow really. Trees knocked down, singed, and there's a wrecked airplane with AIR MAIL painted on its side. Bluish smoke everywhere. One wing was broken, the tail, too. The cockpit windows smashed. I climbed onto the wing, walked over to the nose, and crawled in through the window. The pilot was slumped over the controls, dead. The radio was still on. The windshield wipers were going back and forth. But the windows were smashed? Yes, but the wipers still worked. I admit, I got scared. And then? Then I heard soft moans from the tail of the plane. I went farther back—everyone was in their chairs, dead, all bruised. In the very back someone was crying quietly. I looked. It was Anita's father, the one they showed on TV, the one who was missing. When he saw me he started whispering—Water, water. Blood was streaming out of his head. First I ripped up my shirt and bandaged him. Then I started looking—maybe there was a lemonade bottle somewhere. Suddenly he stopped moaning and whispered—Thank you, I knew you were a good fellow. Then he died. I closed his eyes and crossed his hands on his chest.

Having detached itself from the ground, the huge flying machine sank deeper and deeper into the haze until it disappeared. Only the resonant drone sound affirmed its existence. Soon this sound, too, was engulfed by the noise of the airport. He pushed his glass around with his fingers, listening to a jumble of noises that was surprisingly soothing.

Suddenly the man stopped pushing his glass. His gaze froze. He listened intently to the drone. It seemed that in it pulsed a vibrating halloo, as if someone were muffling himself, then hallooing again. The man tilted his head toward the restaurant's door from which most of the airport's hubbub came. Frozen, he focused on the sound; his gaze wandered around the room.

The hallooing died out. Quickly shoving his glass away, he suddenly relaxed and smiled. Probably about himself. He smiled and swept his palm over his eyes.

The impersonal, monotone drone resumed.

He left the restaurant and walked slowly around the airport. Tired passengers were slumped in rows of yellow chairs, waiting for their flights, from time to time checking over their various bags and parcels. As they sat in their identical yellow shells, each was still distinct. He felt a great compassion for all of these people. They sat there warm and cozy like hamsters, blinking their eyes sleepily, eating sandwiches, sucking lemonade through a straw, looking each other over with curiosity. One lady was inspecting her purchases with great pleasure. She slowly lifted one little object to eye level and gazed at it lovingly. A child in his father's lap, both of them sleeping, both heads nodding, both mouths slightly open—two koala bears encased in warm breath. A practical man in shiny shoes reads a newspaper, shaking it, folding it very precisely, refolding and shaking it again; a girl writes a postcard, occasionally chewing on her pen—she looks off in the distance, thinks, adjusts her pen, energetically writes, I am sitting in the airport and, as you have guessed, writing you a postcard. I am really very tired and everything is annoying me. We are sitting here in these rows of yellow chairs and it amazes me how everyone is the same. They read the same newspapers, eat the same sandwiches, sleep—all of them with their mouths open, snoring. I hope that I don't appear the same as everyone else to you. But you must remember that a moment may come when you will appear the same as them to me. I'm just joking, joking. I want to be with you. I can't write anymore because a man is looking at me and smiling. Don't think that I am teasing you. There, he's left, gone downstairs into the main hall to wander around the airport. These crowds, all the repetitive activity soothes, makes one amiable. He made his way through the passengers, looking for a clear path, sidestepping a baggage cart, climbing over a suitcase, a parcel.

Thus he meandered to the exit, squinted, took in his surroundings. Dusk. A yellow line of lights approaches the airport; a red line recedes. Every few moments a car pulls up to the entrance, and the new arrivals order each other around energetically as they unload their bags. Taxis wait in long lines in the airport lots. The drivers stand around in groups, gesturing with their hands, engaged in anecdotes with involved plots. Then I . . . I listen. I hear something. Then him. A carburetor. But how can that be? But it is. That's what is important. Then I. The left wing. Then he smoked, watching a boy run in and out, delighted at the terminal doors opening and closing by themselves. The boy played with the doors as if they were something alive—cautiously approaching until he was caught in the projector's electric eye and the doors slowly opened, then the boy stepped back and the door quivered and started to close; he sprang toward the door, it opened obediently, but the boy teased it and halted right at the entrance, glaring at the electric eye; he retreated again, waited for the door to close, and then, marching like a soldier, went inside.

As the man watched the boy, his eyes revealed anxiety.

A bus pulled up to the terminal. The passengers swarmed through the door, pushing the boy aside. The door trembled, unable to close for a moment, until the group reassembled inside.

Simultaneously, a stream of arriving passengers flowed in from the far end of the airport. Tottering, trying to retain an air of dignity as they approached the taxis, passengers with their arms full of suitcases streamed by. Although there were plenty of cabs, the taxi stand became the center of a great deal of frantic scurrying. The cabdrivers dispersed, each climbed back in his car and headed for the city, explaining to their fares that there was little to buy in the stores here, that yesterday the weather was nice, that their pay is low and at night someone from the back seat can hit them over the head, and that recently one driver had his throat slit and his car found who knows where.

He took his last drag with renewed energy and tossed the butt into a concrete garbage bin. Water dripped from his sweater, and damp pants clung to his legs. Jumping into a taxi, he sneezed and blew his nose in his wet handkerchief. The driver glanced back and surprised at his fare's sodden appearance demanded—do you have money? Yes. Sure? Yes, I have money. Where would the gentleman like to go? He gave the address. That's on the other side of town, show me how much money you have. I have money at home. Get out, before I throw you out! Honest, I have money at home. The driver reassessed him, shook his head and started driving. How much is five times three? Fifteen! And five times nine? He furrowed his brow in concentration, staring at the window. Then I can cheat you. He sneezed. Don't sneeze right at my head.

He observed the driver's bald spot intently, imagined drawing a line through it with a felt-tip. BOSCH. No smoking! I am always right. License No. 4051. Tour de Europe. 01.32 . . . 01.33 . . . 01.34 . . .

Kmlh . . . his gaze slid over the dashboard to the little trinket dangling from the rearview mirror. A little mermaid woven from colorful wires. Could you tell me, please, where one can buy a mermaid like that?—he inquired politely, watching the driver's vibrating eyes in the mirror. What do you mean, you such an important guy and you don't know where to get them? He felt embarrassed. After a moment, the driver glanced in the mirror again. You have to make them yourself. What happened—did you fall into the canal? He nodded and looked at his feet—a puddle had settled on the floor mat, and the seat cover was drenched.

"Go upstairs to Kristina's to eat. If you haven't come home by nine, you won't be allowed to go anywhere tomorrow. I will be in late or back in the morning." He read the note and went to the window to peer carefully around the side of the curtain.

The driver waited; leaning against his vehicle, he studied the windows. The sewing machine! Straining, the boy shoved the Tikkakoska against the door. It slid slowly, wheels squeaking, pulling the hallway rug into a pile. Chairs! He piled one on top of the other onto the sewing table, then pulled his father's weights to the door and finally wedged a broomstick between the handle and the floor. Footsteps in the entryway. The doorbell rang. The boy stood in the hallway holding his breath, not blinking an eye. The bell rang again, again. Soon it was ringing constantly. Then silence. You could hear the driver breathing behind the door. Hey—didn't I tell you that I'd beat the hell out of you if you don't pay up! Silence. Bam—Bam—Bam, a fist against the door. Silence. Then the door creaked and a chair tumbled off the top of the barricade. He braced himself against the sewing machine and cried out, "You'll never knock this door down, you damned Irishman!"

The driver waited; leaning against his cab, he studied the windows. The boy pulled away from the curtain. Lifting his white cat off the bookshelf, he put it on the table and sat down facing it. That's life, he commented in a sepulchral voice, gazing deep into the cat's green eyes. The cat's pupils expanded. Now what else can I do for you? He stroked the cat's head. Outside, a car honked. The boy quickly leaped onto a stool and pulled out the first book that he touched. I will read you a poem, he said to the cat, leafing through the book. Then he began reading earnestly: As the moon through dark horizons/ Is blazing its path/ Light dawns in me/ Through the dark past/ We all sat upon the deck/ The Rhine carried us along/ We watched as the green banks. . . . The boy's voice cracked and tears filled his eyes. He swallowed the lump and continued: We watched as the green banks / Grew red in the sunset's glow. . . . The car outside honked urgently. The boy took a deep breath and quickly read the last verse: Pensively I sat at the feet/ Of a beautiful lady/ In her fair, adoring face/ Fell the sparks of eternity.

Then he stroked the cat's head again, covered it with a handkerchief, squeezed his eyes shut, and hit the cat as hard as he could with a hammer. Plaster fragments and coins splattered the table.

The driver got into his car, pressed the cat's headless torso between his feet and started to count the coins, mostly ones, some threes, a few tens. The boy pressed his face against the half-lowered window, and the driver sullenly poked through the coins with his lumpy fingers. Can you take a fare? A woman ran up to the taxi. Wait a second, mumbled the driver. Ohhh, he moaned theatrically, you screwed up my count. He recounted, muttering the numbers out loud. After a moment his lips stopped moving; he looked vexed. He poured the handful of coins back into the plaster torso and gave it back to the boy saying agitatedly: I'll waste all day counting!

He took his last drag with renewed energy, tossed his cigarette butt into the concrete garbage bin, and went back into the terminal. He climbed up to the second floor, leaned against the railing, and, watching the activity below, quietly hallooed. A few people temporarily froze, tilted their heads, listened. A woman gazed up at him and smiled; someone else glanced suspiciously. The aroma of flowers.

The aroma of flowers was coming from somewhere. He headed in its direction. A large group of people carrying flowers stood at the door of the arrival gate. These people had lively, animated faces, and even the more withdrawn ones were happily smiling. A man in tattered pants and dull shoes held a single limp tulip which had slipped out of cellophane. But what a face. What a face! A tiny moment of ecstasy.

The man gazed through the glass at the arrivals who were descending the stairs from the plane. He looked elated—as if any minute he might bound toward the plane. A woman smoothed out her clothing, her hair, carefully unwrapped five red carnations, carefully folded the shiny wrapper, and put it in her pocket; another woman stood quietly with two children, each holding a daffodil, waiting for a father, a husband; a committee in navy and gray raincoats with self-assured smiles; two representatives—one holding a sign "Sanitorium AMBERCOAST," the other "5th Congress of Philanthropy." The airport shuttle delivered its passengers, and soon they started streaming in through the doors. Some quickly passed the welcomers, knowing that nobody would be expecting them; others emerged smiling, looking for their families or hosts. The children with the daffodils jumped all over a man, presumably their father; the committee in raincoats greeted another committee dressed in the same thing; they hugged stiffly, patting one another on the back; the fellow in the tattered slacks had instinctively held out the tulip which dangled limply as if about the die; he peered into the stream of arrivals until, look—finally he moved toward a chubby, middle-aged woman in a simple overcoat. The stream was now a mere trickle. The last to emerge from the door were two students, apparently Arabs, who headed deeper into the airport, chattering and craning their necks. The woman with the carnations lingered a moment by herself, then removed the wrapping paper from her pocket and carefully rewrapped the flowers. Her face showed no particular emotion, neither anger nor remorse, she simply turned and left with a light, dainty step.

The smell of flowers dissipated. A note of happiness still resounded in the air. Watching the comings and goings, he had begun to smile.

An announcement came over the intercom. The man listened— they were announcing his flight. He prepared to go toward the baggage check-in when he heard again the distinctive hallooing. The man froze and tried to pinpoint the source of the sound.

As suddenly as it had started, the hallooing stopped. He searched the faces of those around him. Had they heard the sound? Apparently not.

Did you hear? he turned toward a man next to him who was rummaging for something in his briefcase. Hear what? Nothing, nothing . . . a hallooing. Hallooing. Hallooing. Who was hallooing. I, I guess it was me. Calm down, you're being childish. . . .

Suddenly the infant stopped screaming, opened his eyes, and asked: Why are you staring at me? One of the nurses replied comfortingly: You've just been born.

Yes, yes, I am aware of that. Where is my mother?

The staff in their white gowns remained silent.

I am under the impression that none of you is my mother. . . . What is this label on my hand? Take it off or I'll start to scream again. And you didn't answer me—where is my mother?

The staff in their white gowns remained silent.

And who is that? That is your father. Father? Yes, I guess it could be, he looks a little like me. Father, why do you have bags under your eyes? I get the feeling that all of you are on the verge of tears. . . . Why am I all bundled up? You could unwrap this. We can't, child, you'd freeze. I'll be the judge of when I'll freeze and when I won't. And while we're on the subject, I'd like you to treat me with some respect. . . . I guess I just wet the blanket, that probably wasn't the smartest thing I could have done, but forgive me . . . I lost my train of thought . . . could one of you say something? Why are you all standing there and staring at me but no one has anything to say. I didn't want to force myself on you, but no one asked me if I wanted to be born. But now I would like you to respect me. You need to understand that I am born and I am the only one like me in the world. There is no other. And you are each unique, in case you've forgotten. . . . Father, don't you know where my mother is, either? Father, in my first year I would like to get to know you and my mother and, I hope, learn to love you. *Can someone please talk to me?*

You're not raking properly, the father scolded. Don't pull the rake off the ground so often. See, your lines are all broken and wobbly. And don't push your rake so deep, you're not plowing. Rake it again.

The boy walked across the uneven, white sand to the side of the grave. He took each step slowly and firmly, looking back at each footprint as at evidence of his existence. Then, diligently, he began to loosen the sand again.

Now look where you've stepped, you idiot.

He had stepped on the next grave.

But then how can I rake the sides?

Impatiently, the father took the rake from the boy and continued the work. Do you know what sin is?

Shoddy work.

Something like that.

But you know that your sins will be passed to your children and to their children and to your children's children and so on?

What do you mean—passed on?

Your sins, your shoddy work, will not only come back to haunt you, but the shoddy work will haunt your sons and the sons of your sons. Your children will have to redeem not only their own sins, but also yours and mine. They will have to compensate . . . do lots of good deeds to offset the bad—the bad ones they've committed, but also the bad one's we've committed.

But, for example, Grandpa? What bad deeds has Grandpa done?

Well, for example, Grandpa once ate a whole bag of Grandma's jelly puffs. That's a small sin, but a sin because it made someone sad.

But Grandpa was real happy about the jelly puffs. And if he hadn't eaten them he would've been sad. To not give Grandpa jelly puffs is a sin.

But his happiness was at the cost of Grandma's happiness. He felt good, but Grandma felt bad.

But why should Grandma feel bad if Grandpa wants jelly puffs?

Because Grandma had waited in a long line for the jelly puffs and she was saving them for the holidays.

Oh, . . . But, for example, I am your son and if you do something bad to me, the boy poked himself in the chest, then must I redeem that bad thing with a good thing?

Are you asking if my sins against you will have to be redeemed by you?

Well, yes.

The father thought to himself. Then, without answering, he took a small vase and walked to the water pump. When he returned he twisted the vase into the ground, filled it with some small carnations and held it for a moment. Then he handed a small penknife to the boy. Here, clean out the letters. Carefully the boy cleaned the letters. ANNA 1941–1963. . . .

That's good. Now don't fidget. Stand here a moment and think about your mother. It's always good to stand and think a while so she knows that we haven't forgotten her.

What should I think? the boy asked. He couldn't imagine his mother in any other way than the way she appeared in the photograph on the headstone.

Fine, then don't think. Feel. Breathe. She is everywhere. Everything is her. You are a little bit of her. . . . Blow your nose. . . .

So I am a little bit of everything?

Yes. You will stay here on earth as a little piece of your mother.

And you?

Me too. But I won't stay here as long.

They both stood there, holding their hats in their hands. The boy sniffled. Blow your nose. The boy searched his pockets. You didn't bring a handkerchief again. You probably don't have a comb, either. It's stupid not to carry a comb and handkerchief, the father scolded, searching for his. Fine . . . I don't have one, either. Look, he steered the boy away from the grave, if you don't have a handkerchief, you can also blow your nose like this. He leaned over, squeezed his nose with two fingers, and blew loudly. There, now you try. The boy did the same.

But I don't know, said the father suddenly.

What?

I don't know if you also have to redeem *those* sins, but I don't think God has thought that through, either.

He listened. At first he flooded all the sounds into one flowing drone, one stable tone, so that he could isolate the hallooing if it recurred.

Shhhhh, he said, turning toward a couple engaged in conversation. They looked at him in surprise and then continued talking in the same volume as before, annoyed at being disturbed.

He focused on each sound separately. Maybe he was just hearing things? Maybe it was just a door squeaking, a window rattling, the fan humming, static in the PA system? He concentrated on the tiny sounds—the tab ripped off a receipt, the steady click of a telephone dial turning, the swish of a raincoat . . . so you leave Friday . . . the squeak of wheels on a suitcase, coins jangling in someone's pocket . . . if it's not there, then go . . . a draft, maybe the wind is hallooing, rushing from one crack to another? . . . You ask them to open it up and check right there and then . . . Could you please lower your voices? No, man! The man turned to him. Listen, we're going to talk wherever we want and as loud as we want. If you don't like it, you can move.

Coming through, coming through—the baggage handler shouted, heading toward a crowd of people. Startled, they jumped aside. COMING THROUGH, COMING THROUGH. He was focused so intently on these minute sounds that he was startled by the shout. He felt panicky. The shout reverberated in his head until it died out.

The man looked around carefully, trying to figure out what direction the hallooing might come from. He went into the post office and telecommunications center and started to yank open one pay phone booth door after another . . . WHAT, WHAT I CAN'T HEAR YOU. . . Excuse me . . . write down, two two four eight . . . Pardon me . . . GET IN LINE! IN LINE! . . . and give him chamomile tea in the evening . . . FINE! LOVE YOU! LOVE YOU, I SAID! Nothing, nothing . . . Excuse me.

He strode through the baggage claim quickly, poked his head in a corporate office where an executive seated in a club chair was fuming as he read a newspaper. Bad news, presumably.

The man's pace became increasingly sluggish. He climbed to the mezzanine and looked out over the main hall. It had become less crowded. An ebbing tide awaiting a new high tide. Airport rhythm. It could quiet to almost nothing, then suddenly fill with great activity.

As he washed his hands in the restroom, he looked in the mirror. And, as happens to everyone at some point, he looked at his reflection and was gripped by the question: *Who's that?* Childlike, lively, happy eyes full of wonder formed a sharp contrast to the wrinkles in his eyes' corners. His whole face was contrasted with his eyes; his eyes, which knew no tragedy, no hostility, no stress, no cunning, no pretense. But his face was weighted with sorrow and unease. A face that could frighten, confuse, change to marble, transform itself into a dignified profile worthy of a coin. Capable of the right smile for every occasion. A normal face. Like all faces—formed by its relationship to the world. He washed it with cool water. Unchanging. Unchanging. Unwashable.

He left the restroom and sat down in the waiting room opposite a wall of glass through which he could watch the runways. A robust family had settled comfortably in the same row. The mother had removed her shoes to rest her feet. Her large toes were folded back as she happily stretched them. The father was trying to politely peel an orange—it wasn't working, and juice was squirting in all directions. The man's face was so intent on his task that it appeared that he was skinning some game and that it was blood, not juice, squirting everywhere. A little girl sat between them, drinking lemonade through a straw, occasionally blowing bubbles in the bottle. Quit clowning, the man growled, annoyed by his orange. The girl stopped blowing. The mother set some sandwiches on a piece of foil and passed them to the girl. She ate with obvious distaste, rushing through each bite to finish quickly. Eat properly, don't gulp, every bite should be chewed sixty times. Give it to me. The mother took the girl's sandwich and started to feed her. Zzzzzzzz—see, an airplane is flying, zzzzzzzz—right in your mouth—Yummm! Chew it, chew it thoroughly. The little girl looked at him with sad eyes, and he replied with an understanding smile.

Suddenly the girl stopped chewing and stared wide eyed at the huge window. Since her mouth was stuffed full, she gestured toward it. What is it, asked her mother, a plane? Energetically, the girl nodded toward the window a second time. Yes, yes, that's the one we'll be flying in soon. You'll be able to look out of the window at the city below, maybe even see our house. No you won't, growled the father, spattered with orange juice, it's overcast. Yes you will, sure you will dear, reassured the mother, then questioned the father— Now really, do you think we won't be able to see? Of course you won't, he snarled. Well, if you won't then at least you shouldn't broadcast it to a child in that tone of voice.

Will you please look! cried out the girl with her mouth finally empty. She was staring at a whole school of flying fish darting around outside the window. They were prodding the glass with their mouths and peering with their blank eyes into the terminal. The girl pressed her finger to the glass and the fish shot away, immediately replaced by others.

Well, what do you want us to look at? The lights? Those are there so that the planes will know where to land.

Fish!

Now don't start acting silly again. Come here, let's finish your sandwich.

The girl glanced at the strange man with disbelief. He gave her a conspiratorial nod and smiled gaily.

Come now, dear, the mother said, gesturing with mounting annoyance. The fish were startled by the sudden movement and darted from the glass. He and the girl, oddly connected, watched the regiment of fish retreat into the haze.

Wearing a heroic expression, he sat in the big puddle and gazed off into the distance where the forest started beyond the sand pits. The treetops formed a jagged line.

How much longer? Pipe down, you've only been there for a minute and a half. The forest looks notched, as if it's been cut with scissors.

I'm telling the truth.

He squinted and tried to see the outline of the land beyond the sandy knolls. One of the boys stood right in front of him. The frog is squatting, the boy teased. Listen froggie, if you can jump out in one leap we'll let you go home.

He ignored the boy, pretending that the outline of land went right through what blocked his view.

Come on, try it, maybe you can.

Listen, don't you feel like something is going right through your stomach? In one side and out the other?

Pipe down, you've got three more minutes. The blocking boy's tone was starting to sound aggressive.

All the boys started jumping around the puddle taunting.

A crocodile lives here, with AIR MAIL stamped on his belly. When he bites you in the butt, you cry. Did you bring along another pair of pants? No, he's going to have to go home in his underwear. Hey, does your underwear have AIR MAIL on it? He's got underwear with flowers. You better go home bare-assed, otherwise it'll look like you wet yourself.

He watched the other boys' antics calmly, then looked away again.

He likes sitting there. Like a king on his throne. Look, there goes your plane with the windshield wipers on.

The sun edged out from between the clouds until the sand pits shone a bright yellow. He watched as an airplane rushed through the puddle, leaving behind a white line. It glided over the puddle into the sand. The clouds also glided to the edge of the puddle and were sucked into the sand, another dimension. Then he watched a water beetle scoot around on the smooth surface between the clouds, occasionally crossing the white line left by the plane.

Suddenly he felt a mud ball smack his temple. He gave his attacker a serious look. He was laughing. Ha, don't look much like a king now! Then he looked at the older boy. The gaunt boy looked away and yelled at the attacker Don't throw anything! Or you'll get a beating! He stopped laughing and let another mud ball fall at his feet.

I'm telling the truth.

Shaking the mud out of his hair he scanned the water surface carefully, searching for the water beetle. Unable to locate it, he raised his head toward the sky. Yes, that's where it was—scooting between the clouds like lightning, occasionally crossing the white line left by the plane.

I'm telling the truth.

They both watched the regiment of fish retreat into the haze.

I'm telling the truth.

The check-in line was moving at a snail's pace. He waited in line, fidgeting, pushing his suitcase with his foot, looking at the bald head of the man in front of him. How can such a perfectly round head exist? And no hair? He looked to be about forty-five, fifty; baldness probably did not worry him too much anymore. But he was probably wearing a hat or combing his five hairs sideways over his bald spot ten years ago. How does it feel to sit in a theater with such a fine, round, bald head? Everyone who sits behind you inadvertently finds themselves concentrating on the round back of your head. The feeling can't be too comfortable. You must sense it if even one person is staring. But what if everyone in the auditorium stares?

He reached automatically for his pen, but controlled himself. The man in front instinctively stroked his head, as if protecting it.

He took the pen from his breast pocket and twirled it in his fingers. The bald man looked behind him, nervously looked away, and reached down to adjust the straps on his bag. Nimbly, he scribbled a line on the man's bald spot. The man jerked upright, grabbing the back of his head. He wasn't quite sure of what had happened, but, seeing a spot of ink on his palm, deeply offended, he glared at the man next to him. Flushed and unable to find the right words to deal with this situation, he leaned slightly forward. You're an idiot, he said in a cracking voice finally finding the words, a total idiot! What's the meaning of this childish prank!?

He took his pen from his breast pocket and twirled it in his fingers, focusing on the bald spot. Then he found his notebook and energetically scribbled doodles across a page. When he stopped scribbling, he examined the jumble of lines and slowly, precisely wrote over them in fat letters: BE HAPPY.

He was still glancing around every few moments, tensing, as if ready to chase someone at any given instant. There were about five people left in the line in front of him, so he started searching his pockets for his ticket and passport. Three photographs. One at age sixteen, then twenty-five, then forty-five. The last was freshly pasted in. He studied the differences—more wrinkles, which did not begin and end on the face but were little remnants of huge, worldly, interwoven lines; the face in the last photograph was no longer a harmonious cast by a classical sculptor where every form is balanced, the composition in democratic harmony, where each element—the nose, the mouth, the forehead, the eyes—are equal in their beauty, where there is no background. But in the last photograph, the face had become a background. A background for the eyes. A calm background for the eyes, an expression subordinate to the eyes' dominance. In these black-and-white photographs the eyes seemed to be in color. Only the eyes were the same in each picture—happy, inquisitive, and very alive.

Now really, why doesn't anyone ever smile in official photographs? Perhaps there is an unwritten rule that you must not smile in state documents.

The line moved again. He watched with curiosity as a teenager in front of him carefully combed her hair and touched up her lipstick. Conscious that she was being watched, the girl smiled at him. He looked into her eyes somberly, almost timidly.

Next!

The girl quickly finished arranging her hair and sat down opposite the camera. She sat stiffly with her hands folded in her lap and stared at the lens. He stood by his father's leg, surprised by the sudden change in the girl's expression. No longer was she beautiful. It seemed to him that she had suddenly died and stiffened. This image made him panic. The girl bit her lip, and life returned to her eyes. Then she confidently shook her head, lightly straightened her hair, and her face relaxed.

The photographer was busy adjusting his camera. Now, stay still—he raised his hand. The girl's bottom lip began to shake.

Ready! said the photographer, but at just this moment, a suppressed giggle burst from the girl. She shot her hand in front of her mouth, but her eyes—they were twinkling with laughter; they were beautiful.

The boy looked up to see how his father liked *these things* and saw his father's face oddly contorted—his cheeks drawn in, the blacks of his eyes obscured by his eyelids so that only the whites showed. His father was teasing the girl and mimicking her stern expression. Sensing that his son was watching him, the father stopped his pantomime. He looked slightly embarrassed. Surprised, the boy continued watching his father—he had never seen him act so oddly.

Now, have you calmed down? the photographer asked with sullen impatience.

The girl tensed again.

The photographer raised his hand.

The girl's lower lip began to tremble again and suddenly she spun her head away laughing.

Next! the photographer called out angrily. And you can sit off to the side for a bit until you can control yourself.

The father and son sat down in front of the white background. The photographer brought out another camera, tilted both their heads, and shoved a green giraffe with yellow spots into the boy's hand. The boy froze in an expression of tragic seriousness, sensing that smiling now would be a grave mistake.

Your ticket? Excuse me, Sir, your ticket!

Pardon me—he finally let go of the passport with his ticket inside, which the girl with the peaked airline cap was trying to pry from his fingers. Her cap was tiny and fastened to her thick hair with several large pins.

He put his suitcase on the scales. My carry-on, too? You can keep it if you like. Why aren't you smiling he asked the girl. There, if that makes you feel better, she showed her teeth in a mechanical smile. After a moment, handing his documents back to him, she asked in a more civilized tone—what should I smile about? What do you mean—about what? You have beautiful hair and a cute hat, and you're spinning with the world and breathing. . . . Hmmmmm, the girl sighed and, smiling a tiny, reserved smile, she turned toward the next customer in line. But you did smile, he said, leaving the counter.

He leaned against the corner of a souvenir stand and went through his wallet. A monthly trolley pass, a few bus transfers, scraps of paper with scribbled phone numbers. "I was pleased to meet you"—type business cards of no real value, a dry cleaning receipt from who knows when, a work permit, a bank book—he wouldn't need any of these anymore. He wadded them all up and tossed them into a garbage can. Photographs, a few photographs that he always carried with him—his mother and father at a party, neatly dressed, very happy; in another, they have both stuck their heads through a plywood panel with a brightly painted cartoon of a man in a fluffy sheepskin hat, a sword and a slender female figure at his side; also in some sort of folk costume from the Caucasus, with a young boy between them, looking the same as the older photo but with the face empty because I didn't exist yet, I didn't exist; Grandpa and Grandma by their house under the lilac bush,

Grandpa oblivious to the photographer but Grandma looking straight into the lens . . . halloo . . . a photograph in which a slim woman is standing at the sea shore with a huge spear of grass in her hand, photographed against the sun so that her silhouette is dark and you can't see her features, just the bright, bright sea . . . halloo . . . look, it's me—he peered at the boy in the blue coat. The boy is standing in line for cotton candy. His coat has a large, cheerful vent in the back, like a blue beetle . . . halloo . . . he rested his head against the glass of the souvenir stand and closed his eyes. The hallooing came closer, faded again. And so he stood there as if confused, as if suffering, like a child, like an old man, rigid, then unsteady again. He opened his eyes and gazed sleepily around the terminal—people were crowding, crossing back and forth, and a fish, a flying fish, was nervously hugging the glass wall near the ceiling. He looked at the final photograph. He and his father with heads pressed together, the boy looking straight at the camera, wide-eyed, serious, and the father, smiling easily and looking somewhere off to the side, as if he had forgotten that they were having their picture taken, and the giraffe, the green giraffe with yellow spots.

He put the photographs back into his wallet and began watching the fish gliding near the ceiling, occasionally bumping into the glass with its mouth. The fish was apparently trying to find an exit; it was gliding from one end of the terminal to the other, then back again. With each trip, its fins' movements became more frantic.

He looked around the terminal—was there an exit? Only the doors, which opened and closed automatically when someone passed through. He started to panic again.

The fish glided up to the air-conditioning vent and, driven by a gust of frigid air, shot away diagonally across the whole concourse, to stop in one corner of the huge glass jar. Raising his head, he watched anxiously to see what the fish would do next. It flew lower until it was gliding right above the heads of the passengers, almost touching them. It seemed that no one noticed the fish. It touched one lady's hair with its winglike fin; the lady looked around but didn't see the fish, even though it was right next to her. The fish glided up to the window of a ticket agent. Right at that moment, the agent gestured sharply, scaring the fish back up to the ceiling, where it maneuvered among decorative lamps that looked like undersea coral. It darted around increasingly fast until suddenly it dove toward the glass about three yards above the automatic doors. He flinched. The fish shot away at the last moment, avoiding impact with the glass. He breathed a sigh of relief; his heart was racing and his palms sweating.

The fish looked as if it was only warming up. It flew a few laps around the ceiling. He stood in the automatic doors to keep them from closing, whispering, Here, over here! But the fish flew another circuit, then shot off in a new direction. Glass shattered. He moaned softly and, with his face drawn in pain, searched for the fish. He couldn't find it. He was ready to go to the far side of the terminal, where the fish had crashed through the glass, when it suddenly appeared again flying even faster than before. The fish shot around above the passengers' heads, tacking nervously until it settled into its former circular route.

He tensed, pressing his fingers into fists: Here, here, over to this side, he whispered.

The fish plunged toward the door. He tucked his head down into his shoulders and raised his elbow like a spade. The fish crashed into the glass a few yards to the side of the door. Stunned, he took a deep breath and wedged himself into the side of the door.

Are you ill? someone asked. No, no. Is there anything I can do for you? It looks like you're about to faint. Sit down. Don't stand in the door.

He waved them away and tried to focus on sighting the fish. It was thrashing around on the floor nearby. He went to it and was leaning over to pick it up when the fish suddenly recovered and shot up along the glass.

I'm telling the truth.

The fish's movements were a little wobbly; it seemed to dip from time to time.

Here, over here . . . once more . . . here, he whispered, joy and spite shining in his eyes.

The fish dove toward the door again. He leaned over slightly, tensed his muscles, and hallooed—Hal hal loo loo. The fish crashed into the glass closer to the door. He clenched his jaw in pain and felt faint.

You really are unwell; I'll help you sit down and go get a doctor. Who is that? Tosca. But why is she so fat? Quiet, we can talk during the intermission. Leave me alone, I'm fine.

The fish was rolling around its winglike fin, trying to rise from the ground. It managed to take off, fly a few yards, and then fell down again.

I'm fine, he whispered.

The fish moved again and ascended like a corkscrew, turning around its broken fin. He watched the fish's helpless movements. His eyes filled with fear, and as the crippled, swirling fish dove for the glass again, his eyes filled with sheer terror. He covered his face and screamed.

I AM FINE!

Sir, your nose is bleeding, it'll stain your shirt, said a woman, peering into his face. Do you have a handkerchief? she asked, searching in her purse.

Thank you, I have my own somewhere. While he rummaged through his pockets with his head tilted back, the woman stood holding her handkerchief in her hand.

I can't find it, guess I don't have one, he said after smiling glumly. Here, take mine. It's really no problem. See, you already have a drop on your shirt.

Reluctantly, he took the dainty handkerchief with its crocheted corners and pressed it to his nose. A pleasant scent filled his nostrils.

A woman.

What can I give to you in exchange that's as fine? he asked nasally. I don't really have anything to give you, only a piece of notepaper. A clean, white piece of notepaper is also beautiful.

Don't think so much. You'd better sit down, you're very pale, she said, taking the paper.

He sat on a bench in the terminal with his head tilted back, hallooing quietly. His nose eventually stopped bleeding. He looked at the wadded, dainty handkerchief in his hand—it was scented and bloody with the initials A. R. in the corner. He didn't dare throw it in the garbage can; that seemed too tactless. He felt very warmly toward this A. R., whom he had met for only a moment and whom he probably would never meet again. He folded the handkerchief in a piece of paper and put it away in his wallet.

Absentmindedly, he stared at the ceiling and gently hallooed again. And from somewhere, someone hallooed back. He didn't laugh, just continued his ethereal hallooing.

Someone echoed his call.

He became silent. His face lost its empty gaze. He listened. The hallooing would come closer for a moment, then more distant. His light-headed euphoria dissipated. He crossed his legs nervously and looked around . . . halloo . . . he covered his ears and pressed his head between his knees . . . Halloo. . . . Suddenly he jumped to his feet and hallooed in a clear, loud voice. Startled, people looked at him. He arched his neck back, hallooed again, then listened attentively. Everyone was silent from surprise; only a few voices drifted in from the far side of the terminal. A few people who had been sleeping awoke and asked around drowsily: What's going on? What happened?

He ran to the railing, surveyed the main lobby, and hallooed again loudly. People looked up. Some were still busy with their baggage, but when they noticed that almost everyone else was looking up, they did, too. He hallooed again. There was dead silence except for the hum of the ventilation fan, the squeak of a suitcase strap and the whirr of various kinds of airport machinery that could not be startled. Hey, do you like rock and roll? he shouted with a friendly wave. Yeah! The first to respond were the teenagers. I didn't hear you! He cupped his hand around his ear. You don't like rock and roll? Yeah! The response was louder. Again! YEAH! everyone yelled together, looking at him bright eyed. Hey—hey! he yelled, loosening his necktie and throwing it down into the crowd. Fights erupted as people tried to yank it out of each others' hands. H e e e e e e y! he yelled louder. All together now! H e e e e e e y! the crowd roared wildly. Heila-heila-heila-hey!-HEILA-HEILA-HEILA-HEY! The whole airport shook. He became silent, as if concentrating before a performance. The crowd looked at him, then started impatiently clapping, stomping, and whistling. He looked down solemnly and raised his hand. The noise stopped.

Then he raised his palm to his mouth and began to halloo. HALLOO! the crowd cheeringly echoed.

He stood carefully surveying the hall. People started looking away, some good-naturedly, others with scorn, swearing and shaking their heads. The bustling resumed.

He sprinted down the spiral stairs, quickly crisscrossed the main hall, peering in every corner, occasionally bumping into someone or tripping over a suitcase. He looked behind the newsstands and the souvenir stands; he peered over the check-in counter between the airline ticket agents. Hallooing, he passed through the post office and telecommunications hall again and ran back up the stairs. The balcony was deserted. Only a young couple stood leaning back on their elbows against the railing and looking out into the haze.

He hallooed. H - a - l - l - o - o resonated through the terminal. The young couple giggled. Do you need some help? the young man asked, and they both hallooed. Quiet, quiet! he raised his finger to his lips and listened. He listened closely for a moment, then darted back through the terminal and poked his head into a service entrance. A hallway. He hallooed. The sound carried down the corridor, and he followed it. A door. A few women working with calculators, sorting papers. What do you need? He continued down the hall. There were doorways on both sides. He was about to open one, but he realized that there was no point in opening them all. Instead, he stopped to listen. What are you looking for? one of the secretaries asked again, having followed him into the corridor. As if blown forward by this question, he ran to the end of the hallway and down a set of stairs. That's a restricted area! came a shout behind him. He shoved open the heavy metal door with his shoulder. The runways. He stepped out a few feet and hallooed again.

Why are you yelling, and how did you get here in the first place? A stern man in bright, yellow coveralls took him by the elbow. You'll have to leave immediately.

He tried to reenter the terminal through the door he had just exited, but the airport employee pointed him toward an open gate in the fence around the airport. Go through there!

He went out through the gate and walked around the whole airport until he came to a fence on the other side. Then he crossed the runways and hallooed again. No reply. A cab driver leaned out the window and beckoned to him by flashing his lights.

He sat down on a bench at a bus stop and observed the bright glass jar. In the dark it looked like a huge aquarium. He could plainly see every movement. He felt uneasy, sitting alone in the dark outside this shimmering jar. It seemed to him that everything, all life, was concentrated in it.

He went back into the terminal, crisscrossed all of its rooms until, exhausted, he climbed up to the second floor and pressed against the railing, still focusing on any movements below.

He knelt to look at the rabbit's grave and pressed a frosted shard of glass etched with the word *NIAGARA* into the ground. Stems of reedmace were poked in the ground all around the sand mound like dark poplars. The grave was carefully raked. He walked with two fingers through the furrowed sand, then redrew the lines with his forefinger. Then the boy fingered the candy placed on the grave, a Christmas candy in a bright tinseled wrapper. Hard as rock.

It was beginning to get dark, and the forest became chiaroscuro but still distinguishable. The boy checked to see if his flashlight was still in his pocket and ventured deeper into the forest. He picked up a fallen branch and walked, pressing it against the earth like a seasoned traveler. The branch was heavy, and after a while the boy abandoned it and started to run. He ran, lifting his knees high in the air, trying not to step on any dry branches. Suddenly, with a terrible crack, he stepped on a pine branch. Terrified, he clung to the tree's trunk. He heard the snorting of two horses, and, after a moment, two uniformed riders in navy riding breeches with red stripes down the sides and white hats appeared. They stopped and filled their pipes not far from the tree which sheltered the boy. Michael, did you hear a noise? Don't be silly. It was probably a raccoon, no one lives around here.

The horses shied and snorted. Michael, let's ride away from here. I don't like this place. I don't want to get shot in the neck with a poison arrow. Peter, I think that your whiskey flask is a little too tall.

They dug their heels into their horses' sides and, still smoking, headed away at a slow trot.

The boy watched them recede, then he ran farther into the forest. He stopped to catch his breath and peeled a transparent scale from the bark of a pine. Through this he looked up at the darkening sky. He turned it every which way, observing every nuance. He could see the world on this tiny scale. He took a small pad of paper from his pocket, a quarter of a cut-up notebook, and carefully placed the scale inside. Then he took in his surroundings, reoriented himself, and headed through the raspberry bushes.

I am right.

He strode along purposefully, plucking a few raspberries and popping them into his mouth. Here and there, frightened birds fled from the bushes.

The forest was now all blue-green, only branches still distinguishable. It filled with quiet whispers, movements of the night.

The boy topped a knoll, squinted, and looked around. His gaze stopped, and he headed toward a singed metal fragment. He moved it back and forth with his foot, then crawled through the bushes toward a clearing. His heart pounded and for a moment he crouched in the bushes, peering through the leaves.

He crawled even closer to the clearing and watched, biting his lip. The airplane with its broken wings lay in the slowly melting fog. He heard the whist of the windshield wipers as they brushed back and forth, stirring tiny whirlwinds in the mist. Flying fish glided calmly in the haze around the plane. Scooting along on his chest in the wet grass, the boy crept right up to the edge of the clearing and raised his head. His clothing quickly became damp.

Slowly, the regiment of fish floated toward him. They stopped at a safe distance, initially afraid to come too close to the frozen, towheaded little figure. He lay holding his breath, his head raised. The fish gradually became braver. Curious, they slid by his face, lightly touching his forehead, his nose, his hair.

The boy's clothes were now completely soaked, and he felt a sneeze coming on. He tried desperately to suppress it, not wanting to frighten the fish, which had begun gliding closer and closer. He pressed his face into the ground and sneezed, feeling the sand and grass on his lips. The fish darted away to the other side of the clearing.

He hesitated to raise his head again, afraid that everything might have disappeared—the fish, the airplane—and that only he remained with his mouth in the dirt. Raw and cold.

Finally, the boy raised his head. The fish were calm again, floating from one side of the clearing to the other, occasionally drifting alongside of the airplane. AIR MAIL.

The boy stood up carefully. The fish ignored him, no longer seeing him as a threat. The boy became bolder, too, and stood up straight. Then, shuddering in the damp air, he tried to warm his hands by putting them in his wet pockets.

I am right, he said with conviction and left quietly on his tiptoes, as if leaving a room when you don't want to wake anyone.

The boy's flashlight hummed quietly in his hands as he pushed through the raspberry bushes on his way home; the beam occasionally lit on a red berry, a spider's web dripping with dew, a bright beetle.

The flashlight was really made for a stronger, larger hand. He turned it off to rest, and crouched.

The dark. The raspberry bushes. All above his head, thick, inpenetrable raspberry canes. A rustling. He pulled himself into a ball. Noises are so different at night than during the day. Even this raspberry patch sounded different during the day. And my voice? The boy whispered—I. I, he repeated in a louder, wavering voice. Even my voice sounds different in the dark.

He became frightened. And dark air? Is dark air any different? The boy took a deep breath, held the air inside and waited. Pheeeew—he finally breathed out and became even more frightened. Quickly he turned the flashlight back on. Its beam stopped against a nearby wall of thick raspberry stems. He watched this tiny round world of light. A beetle crawled along a vine into the light, then disappeared into the darkness. A moth flew along the outer edge of the circle, then fluttered away.

More and more tiny creatures ran into the circle of light and twisted and twirled in it.

But the beetle, he thought, does that beetle still exist? And the moth, is it still somewhere?

More and more life filled the ring of light, more moths, beetles, various tiny creatures. They gathered in an increasingly dense group and spun faster and faster. The boy watched this dazzling whirl of life bright-eyed, at the same time feeling alone, all alone and vulnerable, standing outside of this circular world of light. He longed to roll into it, to spin along with all this life. He was overcome with the fearful thought that he didn't even exist, that all that was real was what was in this circle of light; outside of it there was nothing. He wasn't there, nor were many others—the beetles that flashed in the first circle of light, the butterfly that disappeared into the darkness, his father, his Grandma and Grandpa.

The boy's hand grew tired from holding the flashlight. He gradually let up on the switch. As the lighted area grew dimmer, the insects' swirl appeared to slow down.

The boy prepared for the final illumination; he pressed the switch with all his might and the circle of light blazed—the activity in the circle increased in excitation. Dispirited, he pressed the switch. Everything lost. Any moment now. Fear was in his face. Any moment now. He felt that, when he extinguished the light, all that still exists would vanish. When this circle of light darkens, I will be alone in nothingness.

His hand trembled, stiff from the effort. The light flickered, faded. The boy pressed the switch for the last time—the insects glimmered, then disappeared.

Darkness and a strange, sudden silence.

He took a long look all around him, but he had been blinded by his intense gazing into the light and he was unable to see anything. The boy listened for any sound. Silence. No rustle, no breeze. He could hear only himself, amazingly clearly—his breath, the pounding of his heart, the thunder of blood in his veins. I—he quietly enunciated the word and then repeated a little louder: I.

Hey, he cried out softly, is anyone out there? His voice sounded dry and lifeless.

HEY, IS THERE ANYTHING?
silence

no rustle
no breeze

Now in the distance he heard hallooing. It drew closer.

The boy drew a deep breath and finally moved. He took a few steps in the dark and ran into a stump. He climbed onto it, raised his head, and finally saw the sky. Everything exists. The heavens are full of sparkling life. So much exists.

He raised his hand and turned on the flashlight, sending a beam of light into the sky.

Halllllooooo—the hallooing was drawing closer. The boy ran toward it and hallooed back with all his might. Running hard, he felt the raspberry thorns hitting his face, felt the wind; he felt life and movement all around, Everything exists. And the earth ran under his feet. He galloped, leaping this way and that to avoid the dark silhouettes of trees in his path. The hallooing was very near. He ran hallooing in reply.

In one leap, the boy was across the ditch. Finally he had jumped over it—he, the smallest, who always had had to run to the plank bridge while the other boys jumped across like kangaroos and raced off ahead of him. The boy stopped to look back at the gully. Wide, yes.

Then, listening carefully, he surveyed the freshly tilled field. As if raked with a giant rake, he thought, but the border hasn't been touched.

The hallooing sounded right behind him. He hallooed back. After a moment the boy spied his father's silhouette on the far side of the gully. In the pale moonlight, his face looked tired and drawn. They stood quietly on opposite sides of the ditch. The boy heard his father sigh.

Fool, his father finally said in a deep voice, and started to walk toward the footbridge. The boy kept up with him on the other side.

I am right.

What? the father asked in a relieved voice.

The boy did not answer. The father stopped, waved dismissively toward the bridge, tensed, and leaped over the ditch. Water splashed, and he said something strange as he stood in the moon's yellow glow.

What was that you just said?

A bad word.

You should have gotten a running start.

Listen, do you love me?

Quietly the boy nodded his head. He was confused. His father had never asked him that before.

Then promise you won't wander around at night.

I left a note.

Promise.

I promise.

The father waded through the water, then, shooting his palm to his mouth, softly hallooed. The boy stared at him with an intense gaze, then began to halloo.

They crossed the fields and headed toward town, hallooing like mad, at times laughing and shouting. When they had crossed the field, the boy took his father's hand and said, Look, we trampled the plowed field, and the edges aren't raked.

Pressing his forehead against the window, he watched as his plane lifted off. With his finger, he drew clouds of smoke from the airplane's tail on the glass.

Why are you smudging up the window? barked the cleaning lady as she mopped the floor between the long rows of yellow chairs, What's going to happen if everyone goes and smudges it?

He paid no attention to the cleaning lady and quietly whispered a poem: As the moon through dark horizons is blazing its path. . . .

Calm had settled over the airport, a moment of emptiness, only a cleaning man washing the floors in the main concourse, sweeping back and forth with an odd, tractorlike machine . . . the moon is blazing its path. Light dawns in me, through the dark past. . . . Exhausted, he fell back in a chair and gazed at the ceiling . . . the light dawns in me. We all sat upon the deck, the Rhine carried us along. . . . Then he found the razor blade and carefully unwrapped it. The razor blade shone, reflecting the light from the lamps. . . . The Rhine carried us along. We watched the green banks / Grow red in the sunset glow. . . . He stretched his arms out in front of him and examined them carefully. Blood ran rhythmically through his veins. *LIFE*. He exercised his fingers like a pianist, and the blood began to circulate faster. . . . Grow red in the sunset glow. Pensively I sat at the feet of a beautiful lady. In her fair, adoring, face fell the sparks of eternity. . . . So he sat with his arms outstretched, frozen as he stared at them. Suddenly, he slapped himself on the knees and began carefully to trim his fingernails with the blade. . . . As the moon through dark horizons is blazing its path. . . .We watched as the green banks grew red in the sunset glow. . . . A hallooing echoed. He looked over the rows of chairs. In the very corner, a dark tuft of hair protruded over the back of a chair.

I am right.

Tensed like a bird dog, he got up, took a step, and hallooed softly. The tuft of hair moved.

Standing behind the chair, he looked quietly at the boy in the navy coat, then carefully, gently, as if afraid the boy could disappear, he put his hand on his head.

The boy stood up, the boy in the blue coat with a large, playful vent in the back, the boy like a beetle, and said:

Stay. Stay, stay.

I am staying.

Translated by Sarma Muižnieks Liepiņš

The Bookstore in America: Woodland Pattern

The previous article in this series focused on Borders Books and Music as one possibility of what the bookstore and bookselling might be in the future, and what forebodes for the future and availability of books in the United States. Following that article with one devoted to Woodland Pattern Book Center in Milwaukee might seem a ridiculous second step, but Woodland Pattern is a very interesting alternative to, not only a chain bookstore, but conventional independent stores.

My first experience with Woodland Pattern must have been just about the time that it opened in 1979, now almost twenty years ago. It had been recommended to me by the poet-novelist Paul Metcalf, who had either given a reading there or was about to give a reading. Located in a neighborhood of Milwaukee rather than in prime retail space in the downtown, and rather inconspicuously settled in the middle of a block that does not, I believe, have any other retail space, it's rather easy to drive by the store a few times without noticing it, something I usually manage to do.

My first visit to Woodland Pattern meant that I had to drive from Chicago to Milwaukee, approximately 90 miles, or 180 round-trip, solely for the purpose of going to what Metcalf had promised me

was a very good store. What I found was a store that had an incredible selection of literary magazines that could not be found in Chicago (and also had several back issues of these magazines, which perhaps spoke to the popularity of the magazines but also to the proprietors' commitment to keeping things available), and the best selection of poetry (perhaps this should be "poetry," because it was an in-depth selection of what one of the proprietors most liked—the Black Mountain poets, the New York School, San Francisco poets, the Objectivists; noticeably absent were the poets who were receiving the big awards and those most often published by Knopf, Norton, and Farrar, Straus). There were also tapes of writers reading, a criticism section, a rather unconventional children's section; at least, this is all that I remember. I spent several hours there, and began what became a once or twice a year trip there, and one that cost me (aside from travel expenses) far more than I could afford. And several of those trips over the years were also related to or planned around attending one of the readings that were held (and still are) in a special room attached to the store, which is also used for art exhibits (that is, there are no books in the room).

As the interview that follows makes clear, Woodland Pattern was *begun* as an alternative store, not a marketing endeavor to counter competitors, which at that time would have been Webster's (now defunct) and Schwartz's; the chains, at least as we know them now, did not exist. Woodland Pattern began as a conception of its founders, one of whom was obsessed with poetry, the other with . . . a variety of things. They saw their role as serving a community. Because of their interests, they thought that poetry should be the primary focus of the store and that it should be well stocked and kept there, regardless of sales; and there should be this public reading space that would feature the writers they liked and would become a very interesting space for exhibits of various kinds; if the store failed financially, then at least the failure would be on their terms. And they began as a nonprofit endeavor, not just (I assume) because there in fact was no profit to be made, but because such a status made them eligible for the little amount of grant money available to things bookish.

Woodland Pattern has now survived almost twenty years, despite being so noncommercial. And it has survived long enough to see itself modeled in other forms of retail—the "boutique." So, twenty years ago, the only kind of "coffee shop" was the greasy spoon on the corner, and no one could have foreseen such a thing as Starbucks, never mind the several non-chain specialty coffeehouses that exist even in the smallest of American towns. Woodland Pattern is, aside from some of the other products it sells, a specialty store that emphasizes what everyone knows cannot support a bookstore—poetry. And yet, because of this specialization and because of other strategic thinking on the part of its founders, the store goes on, and on. Despite what the founders fear would be the effect of a superstore moving in nearby, Woodland Pattern Book Center is, I think, an example of the kind of store that a chain could not compete with, nor would want to compete with. Woodland Pattern is doing something essentially different from traditional retail bookselling, and stays carefully within the niche it has created for itself.

In terms of the future of bookstores in America, one question is whether a Woodland-Pattern-type store can be duplicated elsewhere by people who could learn from its experience, or whether this is a store/center that is unique and completely dependent upon its founders. So, for instance, could Chicago sustain such an operation, in effect becoming *the* place for poetry, *the* place for poets to read, and then *the* place for whatever other interests the founders have? And if this is possible for poetry, isn't it also possible for literary translation? perhaps even literary fiction? experimental writing? In other words, if the chains have become the all-purpose and widely stocked bookstores, is there room now for highly specialized stores that can do things that are beyond what the chains are doing? Of course, all of the above represent rather small markets, and therefore perhaps all must of necessity be nonprofits. If Woodland Pattern could be duplicated, we then have another model—other than that presented by the chains—for what the future of bookselling in America might be. (John O'Brien)

RCF: Let's start at the beginning. How did the idea for Woodland Pattern come about?

Karl Gartung: Well, there was a bookstore called Boox, Incorporated that was started by Karl Young and Tom Montag when they were running *Margins* magazine and Tom had a little distribution deal he was running on the side out of *Margins*—that was about the time that Leonard Randolph was at the National Endowment and they decided to set up a distribution project. Since *Margins* was pretty well regarded, they were invited to submit a grant. So they submitted a grant for both distribution projects at Boox, Incorporated. It was not nonprofit at that point, so they had to route all the money through the state arts board. It was a piddling grant, $5,000 or something like that. One of the things they were supposed to do was to hire someone to watch the store and they hired me. They had a little gallery hooked to it. It was in the "lobby" of a theater called Theater X here in downtown Milwaukee.

RCF: When did Boox, Incorporated open?

KG: That was opened in 1973-74. When I arrived, it was altogether voluntary. Publishers sent in their books and it turned out to be a donation; they never got paid for them because there was no money. The grant gave Boox, Incorporated money for salary and they had money to buy some books. When they interviewed me, I was complaining that the only person I was really interested in at the time, which shows my limitations I suppose, was William Carlos Williams. I had been looking around for all this poetry and all I could find were poets like Richard Wilbur and Robert Lowell and all the confessional poets and the Beats and so on and so forth. The Beats were interesting but not very sustaining as far as I was concerned. Now that judgment on them is just a judgment on me, but what I was really looking for were the Objectivists and the Black Mountain poets but I didn't know they existed, let alone where they were.

RCF: When does this hook up with something called Woodland Pattern?

KG: Well, I worked in this store and here were all these books. Charles Olson and the Objectivists were on the shelves already. So I was home at that point. I had always been involved with theater and Anne was a visual artist and here we were in the lobby of this theater and it had a little gallery and it had a bookstore. But we outgrew the situation of sharing the building with the theater. It got to be cumbersome and we wanted to invite people into town to do readings and we couldn't guarantee that we would have a room for them to read in. We started looking around to move. At that point we also decided that we didn't want to be running all the money through the arts board. We also decided we'd change our name. We found it in Paul Metcalf's book *Apalache*. That's where "Woodland Pattern" came from: ". . . south of Lake Superior, a culture center: the Woodland Pattern, with pottery but without agriculture, imported without loss from Lake Baikal, Siberia . . ." We found this little building that we could afford; Anne was losing her job with the university, so we had some of her retirement money and she was willing. We bought the building and moved Woodland Pattern up there. By that time we had gone from one hundred titles to about five thousand titles.

Anne Kingsbury: We decided we wanted to buy a building because we wanted to keep the rent stable. We were looking with some other groups and they found a building before we did and they didn't have room for us. They fixed it up beautifully, but they had only a year lease. At the end of the year they couldn't afford the rent of the building they had improved so much. We decided that we weren't going to do that.

KG: We had another opportunity: there was a high school that was closing and they offered us room. I thought to myself that this is still a teaching facility and some parent is going to come through here and see William Burroughs or John Giorno or our exhibits. So the first time that would happen we thought we wouldn't have a place anyway.

RCF: In what year did the current location open?

AK: We stepped into the building to start tearing down walls on December 26th, 1979. We opened to the public about six to eight weeks later with one room. That included changing the building and getting that one room ready, which is currently the middle room. And people went through what looked like a dingy, warehousey type thing to get to it. The second room we opened up was the gallery. Our first program was an independent filmmaker from Chicago.

KG: We had a whole series of independent films. That became our performance series at the time. There were several local filmmakers who were involved, and some Chicago filmmakers came up. Then came independent music and then the poetry program and fiction readings. And then we had the gallery shows and we quickly started the mural project on the building.

RCF: When Woodland Pattern was started, was it nonprofit?

KG: Yes. We knew that if we wanted to be a bookseller and make a profit, we wouldn't be able to sell new literature.

AK: There are a lot of really good bookstores in Milwaukee. There are some good independent bookstores and I know that some of the chains are better than others. But to carry the back issues of the *Review of Contemporary Fiction,* for instance, and to give it shelf space and to carry some of our chapbooks and to keep the prices consistent, well, you're not going to make the money per square foot on these books if you want to hang onto them and not turn them over after a certain amount of time. You need a subsidy or independent wealth.

In 1982, we had a book conference, a small press book fair. We got Ted Wilentz to come in as a keynote speaker. He used to run the 8th Street Bookshop in New York and he was also a consultant around the world. We held the event at the university. I took him over to Woodland Pattern. I knew about his background as a bookseller and consultant and I worried that when he walked in he would say, "You better get some romance and mysteries and Westerns in here." And when he walked in he looked around and he said, " You need to be subsidized. You need to keep going but it won't be possible in a commercial situation. But it's important that you keep going so you're going to need to get other kinds of help." It was a reinforcement for us. When you're getting started, you're not quite sure if everything will work out.

KG: At that time, if you walked into any commercial bookstore in the country they would always have a poetry section of twenty-five titles and they were always the same ones. To have a bookstore where people would walk into the store, and even if they were literate they wouldn't recognize ninety-nine percent of the titles, well, to think you could make that self-supporting is ludicrous.

RCF: What kind of support was available at the time?

AK: We received funding from the National Endowment for the Arts from the time we were incorporated until they reconfigured last year and eliminated the literature program. Last year was the first year we did not receive NEA funding. I applied under one of their categories and we didn't make it. But before that, we had received money every year. So you never could take it for granted, but there was always that. The state has an arts council and we would get a little funding there. It's a source that has been consistent. The city has program money and the county has organizational operations support money. But everything is diminishing, partially because of the National Endowment cutbacks. The state receives money from the NEA, and when those funds dry up or are reconfigured, then they eliminate the kinds of funds that we can apply for. So where we used to be eligible to receive money in three categories, now we are eligible only for one. And the city is the same way; we used to receive money in two categories, now we can apply only for one. Thank goodness they're still going, but there is less to apply for.

RCF: How do you compensate for this?

AK: Well, we've been lucky. I have this pouch that I'm making with a quote from Emily Dickinson. The quote says, "Luck is not chance, it's toil. Fortune's expensive smile is earned." We've been fortunate that when something has been taken away, we've been in a position to take advantage of an opportunity, which is luck. Doors close and you scramble around and you try to find something else. So far, we've been able to do that, although last year we lost a big part of our budget. With last year's budget, we figured we lost over a third because we lost funding from the National Endowment. But now it's back up to what it was before. Our grant from the Lila Wallace-Reader's Digest Fund helped us leverage money from the other foundations in town. And the Lannan Foundation has helped us out with funding for programming for a second year, which is really great. And we're trying different fund-raising techniques.

KG: We're involved in a really big project right now. They're building a big convention center downtown. We sold them on the idea that a Wisconsin convention center ought to be different than any other by having the words of our own writers on the walls.

AK: It's a four-block convention center. It will be the biggest one in the state. We submitted a response to the public arts and we were the top proposal that was accepted. We're putting in the work of between fifty and seventy-five writers, historical and contemporary, throughout the building. It's not going to be painted on the walls because they will eventually have to be repainted, of course. So the letters will be raised or etched in glass or cut into the wood. Words from Wisconsin writers or ones that had substantial connections to Wisconsin. That was and is a big project. So we have that money. But since the budget was reconfigured, we're going to end up doing a lot of the work without compensation because we want the project to be successful.

KG: When we first started our programming here, and it carries right through to this project for the Midwest Express Center, we always said that we should pay writers that we brought in for readings. We've always made sure we've had enough to pay people's way, but normally more than that. This may be the first project in the country of it's kind where people are actually getting paid for their writing.

RCF: Have you ever done much with mail order? Do people come here and recognize your store as a place to get poetry and then order via the mail?

AK: We've been working on that. Years ago we received funding for two years under the Community Development Block Grant. They gave us money for computers and an inventory program and a half-salary to do this. We have all the inventory on computer, which is twenty-seven thousand titles right now with fourteen pieces of information on each title, for cross-referencing. So you could call and all we have to do is look it up and send it out. The second step for us was to create annotated lists of ethnically specific areas. We don't have an annotated list of the poetry because it's just too huge. But we do have lists for Native American, Asian/Asian American, Africa/African American/Caribbean, and Hispanic/Latino. This information is available at no cost to people who ask for these catalogs. There's a lot of information in them. They've gone to almost every state in the union, plus Japan and Norway. We also get orders from tribal libraries across the country. There is some mail order, but we would not exist on mail order. It's sort of a supplement to the mission of letting people know what's available.

KG: It has actually become quite a substantial part of our book sales. We've been working hard at that and it will improve some more. Pretty soon we're going to have a web page. We can generate a catalog on demand and that's what we'll do, so that it's up to date.

We had the opportunity to become a distribution company at one point and just do a traditional kind of mail-order distribution. But I thought it was really important for some kid to be able to walk in the store and find his way. I think it's really important for there to be a point of contact. Maybe that will happen more and more on the web, I don't know.

AK: We would like to use the internet to reach those people who would be interested in what we have but don't know about us. It never made sense for us to do an expensive catalog for two copies of something that was $1.95. But over the computer you can just enter it or take it out.

RCF: How many readings do you sponsor in a year, poetry and fiction?

KG: The most we've ever done in a year was eighty. But that was eighty readings, music performances, exhibitions, whatever.

AK: We do between forty and fifty public events annually. And that includes gallery openings and music events, but the majority of our events are readings. Some are invited national readers coming in, some are regional, some are local. And then we have things like our classes. They have a reading at the end of a class.

RCF: What are these classes? And who teaches them?

AK: We have writing classes for kids, teenagers, and adults. We have a group of people who are teaching. If someone wants to teach a class, they would send a proposal to us. If it looked pretty good we would work out a percentage payment with that person. We would then advertise it and we would run a class.

RCF: Do you track the amount of people who come in for the readings and performances?

AK: Yes. We track the number of people coming in. We have exhibits running all the time.

KG: We've had all kinds of exhibits, although we're moving more and more towards having people who have done books or are involved with book art. In the spring we're going to have a show by the Waldrops, Keith and Rosmarie.

RCF: Why did you move into the least likely neighborhood in Milwaukee?

AK: Many of our decisions have been both philosophical and pragmatic. Philosophically, what's the point of moving next-door to the university when there are so many commercial bookstores as well as university bookstores? There's not as great a need. We wanted to be where there wasn't something. Pragmatically we could afford the location, so it worked together.

KG: And it's close enough to the university and a lot of university people live in the neighborhood. It's low rent. It's an old working-class neighborhood.

RCF: How would you describe your role in the community?

AK: I would say that ideally our role would be that of a catalyst. We're putting people together with literature and we hope that something special is going to happen. You may come in and say, "Well I really don't like poetry but I'm interested in baseball." And I could pull out Tom Clark's book on baseball. You might suddenly think that poetry wasn't just something that you hated in public school and was boring and was for ladies with teacups. There are these preconceptions of what it might be. Our role mainly is to put people in touch with their interests so they can say, "This is part of my life and poetry can be part of my life and it's dealing with subject matter I'm interested in." You start where a person is. If they like one thing, you can show them something else. I really believe a lot of it has to do with exposure. When people first come into the new music concerts we're having, especially the improvisational concerts where nothing is notated and it isn't necessarily melodic or rhythmic, some people say "This is awful." But after you've heard it you start saying, "I like this better than that." You start making judgments on experience instead of an uneducated conception. I think our role is to be a matchmaker between people and books. Because we are nonprofit we are able to do that. Everybody who works here—and our tastes are widely different—has a commitment. They have their own enthusiasm.

RCF: Is Woodland Pattern a model for what others could do in other places?

AK: I think every place has it's own kind of need. That's what makes all the literary centers different because they're responding to their community. You could have people that have equal commitment, but they have different interests so it would take a slightly different spin. It really has been a part of our lives. It's something that you wake up in the middle of the night with or you poke your partner when they're trying to go to sleep and start bringing up these conversational things. It *is* your life. In a sense, that's really a fortunate situation because you don't spend a lot of your life doing a job while you spend a little of your life doing what you want to do.

KG: We didn't start out from the standpoint of wanting to be a commercial bookseller. We were plopped into a situation where it was already turning towards a nonprofit grant world. That's fortunate—and unfortunate because it shouldn't be necessary. In some ways we've been sort of straddling. You can't just decide what you're going to do based on what people are willing to fund, which is what a lot of people do. They may not die out but they don't look like themselves after a month.

AK: We've also had an amazing piece of luck and I don't know that that credit has been given. But one of the reasons we were able to survive at a certain time was because of David Wilk's Truck Distribution.

KG: David and I got to be good friends. We used to drive up to Minneapolis and I would go into his basement, which is where he was running his distribution project. We worked out a deal because he was trying to get the books out, too. He was committed the same way we were. He would put things in our store on consignment. We were able to have a lot more books in the store than we had bought. At one point, between David and a lot of other friends who would consign stuff to us, the stock was about two-thirds consigned because there was no other way.

AK: When the distribution changed hands and turned into Bookslinger, it grandfathered in. I think we were probably the only account that they sent books on consignment—but of course that's not happening anymore. Consignment allowed us to have a range of things that we didn't know were wonderful but if you don't know it and you don't have a lot of money, where are you going to put your money? Because we've had those books, we know we want to keep having them. But we've also built up our finances.

KG: Another good piece of luck is that we were always profoundly aware of our ignorance. There were two things that came out of that. One was that if we found a press that published a book we liked, we would order pretty much the whole catalog. We would let the editors make our choice for us. The other thing was that we had to trust friends from the beginning. Karl Young and Tom Montag would go through catalogs with me. We would choose to order that way. But it wasn't by committee. Karl had one set of tastes and I respected him. Tom had another set and I respected him and anybody in town that I respected had another taste and if they wanted to go through the catalogs and mark things I would order them. In that way we could build up a store that wasn't made up of just one sensibility.

RCF: How does that work now?

AK: The same way. We all have input. People can come in and suggest things. Whenever a writer comes through Karl always asks them, "Who are you reading? Who are you interested in?" If it's not someone we have on hand, then we make sure we order them. Lately we've had a lot of it on hand, which is really nice. But there is still so much we don't know. We just keep asking.

CHILEAN POET, ARTIST AND FILMMAKER CECILIA VICUÑA IS, ACCORDING TO THE SPANISH MAGAZINE QUIMERA; "ONE OF THE MOST VIVID AND CREATIVE PERSONALITIES OF THE LATIN AMERICAN SCENE." SHE HAS PERFORMED HER POETRY WIDELY IN THE U.S., EUROPE AND LATIN AMERICA. WORKING IN THE TRADITION OF THE ORAL POETRY OF THE HIGH ANDES, SHE BRINGS FORTH A POETIC UNIVERSE OF ANCIENT RESONANCE AND NEW FORMS. AMONG HER MANY HONORS, SHE HAS BEEN AWARDED THE ARTS INTERNATIONAL AWARD, LILA WALLACE-READER'S DIGEST FUND (1993). THE AUTHOR OF 10 BOOKS OF POETRY, SHE NOW LIVES IN NEW YORK CITY.

Join Cecilia Vicuña at 10 am on April 13 for a free workshop. Cecilia Vicuña will lead you in explorations of space and time . . . and words. "To enter words in order to see, is the point of word-working: to work speech, to speak watching speech work." Advance reservations are strongly recommended. Limit: 15

This event is supported by funds from the Lannan Foundation, the Milwaukee Arts Board, the National Endowment for the Arts, the Wisconsin Arts Board, Milwaukee County Artistic & Musical Programming Advisory Council, the Helen Bader Foundation and private donations. Woodland Pattern is also a member of ACHOICE.

Flyer for Cecilia Vicuña workshop

RCF: Who had the idea for your promotional mailings?

KG: That was a practical thing. At one point it was cheaper to do it that way. It's not cheaper to do it that way anymore. We were holding these events by people that no one knew anything about, which was the whole point of doing them. The way we do our reading series is that we feel somebody is an important writer, we bring him into town and then aquaint people in town. So say you're having this event by Paul Metcalf. You can send out a press release saying he is the great-grandson of Herman Melville and you can put it in a calendar and maybe get it announced in the paper and maybe get yourself and your wife and some friends and Paul Metcalf to come. Or you can ask Paul to send you some stuff that hasn't been published yet and put it in the brochure with a little biography and so on. I wanted to do that for each individual person because it seemed like a way to honor them.

I've always hated getting stuff in the mail where I had to keep the whole thing because there was only one thing I was interested in. So I thought if you have this thing and it's not tied together with staples or something people could open it up, go through the envelope and throw everything away except the one thing they were interested in and put that on their refrigerator. The other thing was that printers always have pieces of paper that they cut off to make specific lengths. We developed a relationship with our printer where we could go in and check their waste and design stuff to fit it.

AK: Now our mailing list has grown and it's a lot harder to print cutoffs because it's harder to get three thousand pieces of whatever it was. We have gone to a self-mailed flyer for the majority of the newsletters and things we're sending out because it costs the same whether you're doing a small piece or whether you're doing a big piece. They don't want to throw this stuff away if it can be used. We're trying to save money and we're trying to work around what they have.

Flyer for Amiri Baraka reading

KG: We used to do a mailing for every single event. But then when we started having two or three events in a month, even in those days when it would be cheaper, it would become really time consuming and expensive, let alone counting the time staff puts into it. Now we would have a whole bunch of odd sheets and we could just stuff them in a brown envelope and mail the whole thing.

Flyer for Lorine Niedecker lecture

RCF: Do you think everybody in Milwaukee who should know about Woodland Pattern does know? If not, how much does that bother you and what do you do to try to change that?

KG: We've done all kinds of different things. We used to have a dial-a-poem service, but that finally died a couple of years ago. I would record a reading or I would read a poem. And we had an answering machine and we would put that on there and they would get that as a greeting instead of "How are you? Call me back when I'm home." We ran that for about fifteen years. That was the reason we started recording the readings.

AK: We have chosen to put our money into the programming and into the newsletter rather than buying adds. The publicity we get is community listings. But because we've been around so long we have a pretty decent working relationship with certain people at the newspaper. They're not going to do a big article on every event, but we're getting some coverage now, so that's okay.

KG: It's really hit and miss though. We don't have somebody who trusts us the way we want to trust other people. So we can't get regular attention for all the writers that come through.

RCF: What about radio attention, NPR? Do you get any attention from them?

KG: Barely. Very little. We've worked at that hard from time to time. I think what we're going to do if we can afford it is to start being a donor, as Woodland Pattern, to public radio so that they have to put something on the air and then maybe we can persuade them to use our tapes.

AK: Our goal is for Woodland Pattern to reach a point where we would be recognized as a major cultural institution in the literary arts. Now that doesn't mean we would be downtown in a glamorous edifice. We want the literary arts to be taken as seriously as the symphony. We're not an alternative, we're *the* thing. We're not an alternative to something else for literary arts; there isn't anything else.

KG: We're a public institution. The "public" literary institutions have basically been the university English departments. But they're not really public. And they're not really user friendly. When Anne was involved with the university, we both had decided that the university had become a kind of a priesthood, all these people were speaking in a specialized language to each other. I was pretty disillusioned already. And I wasn't finding any better stuff there, up until we moved to Milwaukee, than I was finding in the commercial bookstores.

The reason I got into the position at Boox, Incorporated was that I had taken a class with Jerry Rothenberg, who was here at University of Wisconsin at Milwaukee. So in two years I basically went from rereading Williams to seeing live John Cage and Jerry Rothenberg, Charlie Marrow, Gary Snyder, David Antin, Jackson Mac Low, Jack Higgins, and Allan Kaprow. All these people were coming to the university, but I just had this feeling that we didn't want to be part of it. They can do what we do any time they want to and they can do it better but they won't.

RCF: Do you work with the university at all?

KG: We're trying to work with teachers for textbooks. Actually one of the members of our board is a special-collections librarian. He's ordering books from us (we've been assured that that's not a conflict of interest). When we have writers come through, their books will end up in that collection. And if they're book people, they might give a talk at one of the university's book forums.

AK: It works better when it's person-to-person so that there are people over there in the university that we work with on an individual level and then they use their connections there.

KG: Like Native American studies. Kim Blaeser is a very good fiction writer and poet at University of Wisconsin at Milwaukee. We cosponsor some writers with her. They'll come into town to work with her and then we'll have a public event.

AK: We supply a lot of books for Native American studies. A lot of students come to Woodland Pattern to buy books for their Native American classes. We have a good Native American section. But then the money we make from those books is almost always turned over into bringing a writer that fits that particular group. Maybe the money you spend here can turn into a writer for your class. That works out for both of us.

KG: Our new idea is to have a literary center in the schools, to have somebody there to bring writers in when they come to us.

AK: We're now working with one high school—this is part of our Lila Wallace proposal—Marquette University High School. This happens to be a private high school but there is a teacher there who is really interested in expanding her kids' experiences beyond the normal classroom. She's taking them to readings. She's taking them to plays. Because we met she is now assigning them to come to several readings at Woodland Pattern. And they're going to write or draw responses to these experiences. Now she's broadening her curriculum to work with other faculty members in the arts and music. Then they're going to come back to Woodland Pattern and do a public presentation of what they got from the semester. It's for the kids that they want to come. I think anytime you say, "You forty people have to go somewhere" you're going to get people who are not as interested. But the ones who are interested are the ones who are going to come and then they will respond.

RCF: By working with high-school students you begin teaching them about how you go into a bookstore, and how to feel comfortable in them.

AK: The other thing is, at least in the arts, and I won't generalize for every city, but in Milwaukee the major core audience for the ballet, the symphony, the theater, is an aging audience. It's people in their forties and above. They're trying to reach a younger audience, and that's not that far off from us. We want to reach into another generation of readers and writers. One of the things that may make us a little different from some of the other centers is that we've always felt that the reader was an important part of the center. Some of the other centers are very much writer-oriented and that's not bad. But now they're seeing that maybe they need to connect the writer and reader. That's something we've always felt was really obvious. We want younger readers to get involved. If you get younger readers, you'll get younger writers because there is going to be some overlap there.

RCF: If Barnes and Noble moved in down the street from you, what effect would it have? I've always thought of Woodland Pattern as a model for how a chain really couldn't compete. It seems if a Borders or Barnes and Noble opened up near you, your business would increase because they wouldn't have a number of poetry books that you have and they would send customers down the street to you.

KG: We do have relationships with those people out of necessity, somewhat. It's not necessary for us to carry some things, some of the really mass-market things by writers that might be of interest to many people. We can save our money on that by sending those people to Barnes and Noble and likewise for them.

AK: Actually, we have a good working relationship with every bookstore in town. They know they can send people to us. They know what we have. Even Barnes and Noble will send people over. That's the advantage of their hiring locally because they have local people that know what we have. But we will also send other people to other bookstores and we might call to make sure they have it on hand. The primary thing is service to people who want to find whatever it is they want. For instance, we do not have a spirituality section. But there is a bookstore in town that has a lot of books that deal with that and we regularly send people. That works out fine. They send people to us for what we carry.

RCF: If you could project ten years from now and if money were not a problem, what would you be doing that you're not doing now?

AK: We'd be paying benefits to staff.

KG: I'd probably be working here for money instead of as a volunteer. I've always kept my truck-driving job as a buffer against the rise and fall of business.

AK: Whatever happens ten years from now is going to be different because we'll both be ten years older and we need to find people who want to continue on and there will be some overlap with what we are doing.

RCF: Are those younger people coming along?

KG: They're coming along now. Peggy Hong is the person who is running the workshop program and getting workshops and writers into schools. She's working half-time. Lisa Corona was an intern last year from a little college called Cardinal Stritch and now we're hiring her. She's really good. She'll be working on audience development and financial management projects. Carolyn Elmer does all of our ordering. She's a real book person. Amy Hoffman is doing a lot of volunteer coordination. And Brooke Barker does all of the work on our catalogs and does inventory work on our computers.

AK: There may be new things that we don't see yet, but we've never had the idea that we wanted to grow just to grow. We want to do what we do really, really well and maybe make it deeper rather than wider. We don't know what we don't know, so I'm not sure of what we're not doing that we haven't thought of yet.

We would also like, I think, to maintain and keep a professional staff. What we're finding is that younger people are in greater debt coming out of school. I'm amazed at what students have to pay on student loans. It's incredible. Bright, young, literary people, at this point, might not be able to work for a place like Woodland Pattern because we can't afford to pay the money they would need to pay for their education. We want to get to a point where we can pay people like that, to pay people that would be satisfied with making a lot less money than they could make in other places. At this point, it's so much less—not compared to commercial bookstores because bookstores notoriously don't pay well for general staff—than other kinds of occupations or locations. You can have a passion, but you still have to eat. Especially if you have a family. Those are things you take into account. We've been really fortunate with the people who are on the floor now with us. But I don't know if we can expect the next generation to subsidize the center the same way the current generation has been subsidizing it with wages and no benefits and stuff like that.

RCF: How important is it that Woodland Pattern continue after both of you are retired or gone?

KG: I don't know. Obviously it's important to me to have it be here, and I think for Anne as well, just for our own education. If it isn't, then people will be back where they were.

AK: I would like to see it continue but that will kind of depend on who wants to see it continue past us. We can do what we can but we can't force it. We're not going to be able to make someone have the same feeling for it. It will depend on the demand.

RCF: One of the theories about publishers is that they have their own special, limited time. You can look back at Barney Rosset at Grove Press. In some ways he got absorbed by commercial publishing which could then do the books that he broke the ground for. I don't know that the same thing applies to what you're doing; that it's so dependent upon the time in which it was happening, that you only do something really unique for a while and then you become like everybody else.

KG: That's a good question because we've always tried to fill a kind of cultural gap. My reason for doing this was because, traditionally, you would only find out about a writer after they were already dead. The ones I was interested in were the ones whom I would find out about after they were gone. I think that finding writers is still going to be necessary whether of not we do it or whoever replaces us. I think someone will find a way to be a conduit.

AK: What we've tried, and what I hope continues, is to make people aware of the number of choices that they have amongst all these titles, all these writers. And as Karl said, emphasizing a current group of people who are writing rather than people who are gone. Classics are wonderful and they're classics because they're really good.

KG: But they're classics because they had an audience in their own time.

AK: And we want to encourage people, in a sense, to find the classics of now and to have the chance to speak with these writers. Some of the really exciting things that we've had the privilege of being part of is introducing a writer to a publisher and have something come out of it. Sometimes it ends up being a book a year or two years later. It's exciting to know that that happened in our living room or at Woodland Pattern, to see those kinds of connections being made. So maybe when Karl or I aren't here anymore, it will stop for whatever reason and it will be an encapsulated, special time. But I'm hoping that it can continue. And it won't be the same, it wouldn't be the same. No one is going to be our clones. So it will be different with whatever, whoever it is that cares about it.

RCF: Could you imagine some student who is interested in books coming here to study what you're doing and then going off to wherever that person's from to start something very similar? Because what you have set up really is, in my experience, unique. Perhaps someone who could look at what you've done, study what mistakes you may have made, how you would have done certain things differently, and go off and do their own thing or make a variation on it.

KG: Sure. I could see that, but there would probably have to be a Borders or a Barnes and Noble or an independent bookstore there, too. There would have to be other resources for the kinds of books we don't sell. What we've tried to do here is fill in the cultural gaps. If a graduate student were to start up something like Woodland Pattern, if would be because they have something that they're interested in and that they want to share, but also to fill a gap that exists in their community. Someone might be able to do what we're doing where there really isn't any kind of resources at all. I think it depends on the needs or wants of the community. We almost always have one or two people here at Woodland Pattern, employees or otherwise, that are reading the store carefully. No one has gone off and created another literary center, but they've done other things, like magazines. What we think Woodland Pattern could become is a place where you can find a writer and that writer's sources, the writers he or she read.

AK: I think what you might find is unique about Woodland Pattern has to do with us being a literary center rather than a bookstore.

KG: And the readings being a literary activity and not a booksale opportunity.

AK: We're thrilled if we sell books when the writer comes through but the writer is not considered a commodity. They're coming because they're doing something important and we want to share them and whatever they're writing about, with our community.

KG: Our readings haven't been directly tied to book publications. Now it's more and more likely that it would be connected to the publication of a particular book, but it's not probable. It happens more regularly now but I bet you eighty percent of our readings have nothing to do with a new book. Maybe more than that. If it has to do with a book it's probably a happy accident. If we hear somebody is on a book tour, like with Curbstone or Coffee House or some other press, or if somebody contacts us and they're going to be on a book tour and they want to read at our place, then it would be connected with a particular book. But it would happen because we were already interested in them.

AK: That's true. We're at a point now where we do get a lot of inquiries from people coming through. We can't do all the readings that people ask us to do, at least not the way that we're doing them now. Each reading, each event is special. We really do try to build an audience for each event and not just throw them out there.

RCF: Do you have any sense of how many people become buyers of books in your store because they've been to the readings or vice versa?

KG: One of the things that's different about us is that we charge admission to readings. The only other places that do that are places like the Art Institute. Most of the universities have them for free and students are required to attend anyway. People would pay their admission and the books would be there and they would think, "Well I already did my job." But now more and more people are buying books, maybe because of the Barnes and Noble readings. Just before every reading I say, "You have the opportunity to do what you should do in the presence of a writer which is buy their books."

RCF: Do you think that your customers first come to the store to buy books or first come to the readings?

AK: It cuts both ways. It really does because, in a sense, for each reading we get a different kind of audience and I can use Walter Mosley and Kenneth Koch as two examples. With Walter you might obviously get people who are interested in him because he's a mystery writer. And then you get people who are interested in him because he's a black writer, so people in the black community want to come and support that. And then you get people who are interested in him because he's a big name. And then maybe you get some people who are core who just want to come to a reading, trying things out. Some of those people would only come because it was Walter at Woodland Pattern and then they would buy a book. But it would also be because someone would be there and find out about it and then come to the reading. So it goes both ways. As for Kenneth Koch, there are a lot of people who know him in the educational field because of his teaching books. But then there are those that know him as a poet and they will come to hear his poetry.

KG: He is somebody who came because the Lila Wallace-Reader's Digest Fund paid his way on a tour. I don't think we ever could have invited him on our own. It turned out to be a really interesting reading.

AK: So there is a case of maybe you wouldn't have selected a person but once they're here you're really glad they came.

RCF: Do you establish relationships with a lot of the people you bring in to read?

KG: We hope to. You always want to. That's really interesting and that's the part that's really been difficult, psychologically I suppose, to know how much of a relationship you have and if it's strictly a business relationship. With literary relationships it's a lot tougher to make the distinction. It turns out that not very many of them are not more than business. If you can't offer another reading or whatever, then a lot of the times the relationship goes away. If you have a project that involves them, there is a relationship.

AK: I think, because we don't really want to treat a writer as a commodity, that some of them are willing to come back when it's less convenient for them. That's a good thing. And there are people who might stop by when they don't have a reading in town or just to say hi. It becomes a friendship that grows out of this other thing. But we always try to have a good time with a person coming through. So you're not just waiting at the hotel until we take you to your reading. Walter enjoyed his reading with us before when he was brought through with the Lila Wallace touring project, even though he can always read at some of the commercial places. Actually, last time he was in town he read at the library, which was a huge event. I talked to his agent and she said that she would like to have him in our thirty by thirty room. Every other city is having him in these huge auditoriums but she said, "No, that's where he wants to read. With you." Because that's what he wants to support.

John O'Brien and Christopher Paddock

The following is a response from John Evans of Diesel, A Bookstore to the previous article in the Review *concerning the future of the bookstore in America which featured Borders Books and Music.*

I am writing you regarding your interview of Borders management in the Summer 1997 issue of *The Review of Contemporary Fiction*. My partner, Alison Reid, and I was very surprised to see your "Bookstore in America: Borders" banner on the cover. Perhaps one of your reasons for beginning the series with Borders was to gain this kind of recognition. Obviously, you have already heard of other attributions to your "provocative" stance toward Borders. All in all, my disappointment with your choices, marketing or other motives aside, is far outweighed by my surprise at the lack of serious engagement with the considerable issues at stake, some of which you raise in your introduction.

First, with regard to the series, I think an earnest discussion of the state of bookselling is a worthwhile, even an important one. I presume that you will be providing banner headlines and equal print space to the subsequent bookstores featured in the series. I also presume, unfortunately, that the same lack of critical interviewing technique will be used with the other booksellers.

In your introduction, the reader is led to believe that the series is meant to clarify issues and deal with problems of vital concern to "The Republic" and to bookselling. The sense is that these things will get the seriousness they deserve. You also indicate that one of your concerns is the saturation of a corporation's culture in the minds of its workers, across the spectrum of employees. The main gist of your introduction only leads to profound disappointment in the thirty-five pages(!) of interviews which follow. Not only are no booksellers on the floor or in actual stores represented in your interviews, but only upper management buyers, marketing execs, and other top officials are interviewed. What happened?

My first impression was that this whole series was a MBA thesis idea for a graduate student at Ann Arbor. The emphasis on management structure, broad brush references to culture, The Republic, etc., and the vague references to the "issues" of bookselling fit the bill. The interviews, however, in their lack of the vitally important critical, pointed, or leading voice of the interviewer indicated this would never pass academic muster. So, I wondered, what was the point, and why were all the initial points in the introduction abandoned? A thirty-five page puff piece of one-sided self-promotion was printed in the form of interviews in an independent literary journal seeming to advocate one portion of that journal's customer base over all others. Very strange!

Not that an independent bookseller, given the opportunity to sing his praises to the fawning attentions of a publisher willing to devote thirty-five pages to *his* store would not do the same. The Borders people were only doing what they do. But why were *you* doing it? For the reader, a thirty-five page insert, without "Advertisement" printed top and bottom, does not get excited by one-sided interviews. A position paper from Borders would have saved so many trees, got the point across clearer, and saved readers some time for reading books, or true interviews.

I want to address some of the issues you flagged but then abandoned in your piece. It is true that Borders has received a lot of criticism from people concerned with books, reading and ideas. It is also true that sometimes it is only the corporate, or chain, or size aspects that get discussed in this age of big-box retail and the sound bite. Size arguments, either "they are too big or we are the best because we are big," are largely emblematic of more complex and important issues. Somehow you, along with many publishers, the media, and some of the reading public, seem seduced by the size and power of Borders. It seems to blind you to questions of homogenization, of buyers' control of what gets published, for example.

Over the last few years, at an ever-increasing rate, these things are happening in the book business: titles are being killed when chains, like Borders, decide to not carry or support them; independent bookstores are closing nationwide; sales reps jobs, which provide conduits of information from readers through bookstores to publishers, are being lost; fewer and fewer buyers are influencing the design, marketing, selection and editorial content of the books which get published; return rates on books purchased are increasing; prices on books are increasing significantly; consolidation of ownership of all portions of the culture industry is increasing, especially by entertainment media conglomerates. All of these are vitally significant indicators of dangerous trends in the society affecting issues of free speech, cultural diversity, democracy, in short, The Republic. Yet, aware of this as you certainly must be, you decided to neglect them in your hours and hours of interviews.

You assert that the chains, like Borders, invite families in ways independent bookstores never did. Not only did I visit bookstores happily as a child (new, used, independent, and chain bookstores) but I felt welcomed in them. One of the things about independent bookstores is that they are different! Perhaps your family didn't go, or your neighborhood lacked a good bookstore, but to generalize nationwide and toe the corporate line is, in your position, unconscionable. It is common knowledge in the book business that a chain store is only as good as its nearest independent. Chairs, music, events, fireplaces, welcoming atmospheres, local author displays, etc., are all things widely available in independent bookstores around the country. More available before chains copied them, set up shop next door and drove them out of business. Your uncritical stare aimed at the glamour of chains like Starbucks, for instance, obscures your vision of the very real damage they do around them.

Whether it is a question of who determines the books and ideas we are able to buy, the relationship of businesses to their communities, the net economic effect of corporations on local, national, and book-trade economies; the effect on children of reducing all cultural production to entertainments and consumable goods; the danger that, once the independent stores and reps are gone, book publishing will become the new Wonder Bread; none of these were seriously attended to in your piece, and that's a shame.

Though the damage of your Borders promo piece is already done, I hope that some responsible engagement with the actual issues is forthcoming.

Sincerely,

John Evans
Diesel, A Bookstore
Oakland, CA 94618

William Eastlake (1917 - 1997)

The first time I met William Eastlake he was both appalled and amused to hear that I had been drawn to his work by seeing the film of *Castle Keep,* his World War II novel. I was a rarity, it seemed: the first reader he had met who would confess to such a philistine history. It was, I explained, the dialogue that had snared me. As I learned later, Eastlake had walked away from writing the screenplay himself when the studio refused to allow the full four-letter flowering of what he called "soldier's language" to be put into the film. Other writers had been called in to finish the screenplay, and the script doctors knew a good thing: they lifted whole chunks of dialogue straight out of the novel.

Eastlake's dialogues are built of such simple blocks that any single exchange can seem silly if you miss the context that surrounds the words. In *Castle Keep,* for example, Alistair P. Benjamin and Lt. Amberjack attempt to sink a Volkswagen and fail, and Alistair comments, "It's just showing off." But the VW exchange is accompaniment to the unsettling truth that there are forces beyond the control of any army, forces as irresistible as the tide, which will conquer man no matter how hard he tries to fight against them. And when they are challenged by a superior officer, Amberjack asks Alistair,

"What do we do?"

"Play it real simplistic."

"What's that?"

"Tell him we're not here."

Eastlake didn't need the four-letter words at all. This *is* the real language of soldiers, of the exhausted, the endlessly put-upon, of the pounded-down who joke their way into dignity, of those who stubbornly persevere.

After reading *Castle Keep* and several other novels in quick succession, I found this to be the characteristic sound of all the sympathetic characters in Eastlake's works, be they soldiers, ranchers, teachers, Indians, even young Tom Paine. Here, from *Portrait of an Artist with Twenty-six Horses,* is an Indian Country rancher's common sense coming up against sales-speak:

Ben Helpnell was working on his new Monkey Ward pump beneath his abandoned windmill. . . . "It is a hermetically sealed, self-contained unit, and without any fuss or bother or expensive plumbers or electricians, you just drop the whole thing in the well." Ben had done that yesterday and since, he had been looking for it.

. . . "I must of done something wrong."

"You chunked it down the well," Mary said from where she watched behind a screen door.

"It said in the book—" and then Ben ceased, knowing that women will even contradict the book. . . .

Underlying the humor is the reality: water means survival in this high desert country.

Upon meeting Eastlake himself it quickly became clear that this voice was, at its heart, Eastlake's own. Those who travelled to Bisbee, Arizona to visit Eastlake travelled to hear his voice, his stories. He was rarely the hero in these stories, usually not even their center. He would tell about the soldier he had known who had conducted the sounds of bombardments; tell about the Michigan novelist who had come to Bisbee and tried to pick up a waitress by telling her she looked like Mary Magdalene; tell about how the day he brought a new dog home it had jumped up on the couch and pawed the remote control, turning on "That's Incredible," thereby naming itself. But he wouldn't tell about how he won his hero's decoration in World War II. He wished to be no one's hero. (Among those who care about writing, however, this wish was doomed to failure.)

The last time I visited William Eastlake was in August of 1994. I had begun the day, halfway up the state, with a visit to the Casa Grande ruin. This 600-year-old survivor from the civilization of the Hohokam Indians is now under a canopy—acid rain is eating it. A few miles south, past the Tom Mix plaque under the Palo Verde trees, just after the turnoff to Oracle Junction, a sign announced *Biosphere 2,* the experimental self-contained environment. ("Biosphere 1" is their term for the outside world.) Visitors at Bio 2 are welcomed by a cluster of kachinas made from obsolete nuclear hardware. Among other bits of history, we are told that the wild pigs who had once been part of the Bio 2 environment had been eliminated—eaten, in fact. Also, some nimble small primates intended to serve as a companion species kept beating the human residents to the best food, and they too had to go. "Here," the guide told us, "we replicate the world outside in miniature."

When I returned to Bio 1, I was greeted by one of Arizona's sudden, scouring thunderstorms. It flooded every arroyo and scratched mountain tops with its lightning. From Eastlake's front yard, nearby Mexico was a pollen-colored bowl under the clearing sky.

I hadn't seen Eastlake since a visit during the last pass of Haley's Comet, but we picked up right where we had left off: he eagerly led me in to shoot pool. The way to the table was past his desk, and on it lay the draft of an essay on his visit to the home of Charles Darwin. "I suppose evolution has always been my real theme," he told me. Moral evolution, I knew he meant, as his fiction and essays all make clear. His first novel (written in 1952 and still unpublished) was about the forced "relocation" of Japanese Americans to concentration camps during WWII. And in "The Bandits" (1956), a short story about the possibility of nuclear holocaust, a character asks, "Are we still changing or is this form of man the final product?"

This question figures prominently in the first three "Indian Country" novels (revised by Eastlake just before he fell ill, and reissued as *Lyric of the Circle Heart*), as well as *Castle Keep* and *The Bamboo Bed,* the two war novels which followed. Many readers see the *Circle Heart* trilogy as a self-contained world within Eastlake's work. But *Castle Keep* is very much one with these, despite the differences in time period and locale. All four are about the difficulties of sustaining brotherhood. *Go in Beauty* is about a feud between two brothers, a split so terrible that it causes a drought across Indian Country. *The Bronc People* opens up the idea of "brotherhood." It details the coming-of-age experiences of two brothers, one white and one (adopted) black. There is much here about race and culture and how wide are the rifts we all have to cross to reach one another. *Portrait of an Artist with Twenty-six Horses* is about forgiving one another our many human failings. *Castle Keep* is about the inevitability of conflict and misunderstanding and how we all might rise above this, and how it is worth the effort even if only small things might be salvaged.

All four of these novels show characters resisting what Eastlake explicitly labels the "sentient evil" that stalks us all, that which uses hatred and envy and jealousy to try to twist us into its image. In all of these early novels Eastlake's world-view is one of cautious optimism, a real hope that people might save themselves and others by acting honorably.

The stories in *Jack Armstrong in Tangier,* though not collected until 1984, were written soon after *Castle Keep.* They show Eastlake's optimism becoming less sure as he travels around the Mediterranean meeting people who are unable to escape the maelstroms of their fates. The world seems out to punish one and all in these stories. Eastlake then became Vietnam correspondent for *Nation* magazine. And, as happened to so many Americans, Vietnam extinguished nearly all of his remaining optimism.

In *The Bamboo Bed,* his novel of the Vietnam War, the difficulties involved in making true human contact shown in the earlier novels become impossibilities. The war and the "sentient evil" become one. There is no clean side to lie down on in the bamboo bed. Moral evolution comes to the fore when an officer asks an enlisted man why the Americans should behave better than the "Unfriendlies," who lie and skulk and booby trap:

"Because of moral evolution."

"Is there such a thing? . . . Answer me as a human being. How? How do we make moral evolution?"

"By starting it."

"There's a war on."

"That's why we should start it."

But all these characters are killed. Everyone is killed. Obviously, there can be no moral evolution where no one survives.

The works which followed *The Bamboo Bed* are at once more comic but in various ways darker than the first four. In *Dancers in the Scalp House* (1974), a return to Indian Country, the Indians and a white schoolteacher named Mary-Forge insist on acting honorably—and this means they lose their country and their lives. Eastlake's "Tricentennial novel," *The Long Naked Descent into Boston* (1977), and the loosely tied stories of *Prettyfields* (1987) both operate within much reduced compasses. Beneath their burlesque surfaces boils outrage at the eternal life possessed by human stupidity and cruelty, bigotry and greed, but there is precious little sign of hope that a course correction might now be achieved. *The Long Naked Descent* details how America was created not just with, but *by* a number of moral failings, and how these are so ingrained they can never be cured. To laugh and simultaneously to feel disgust with the world as we know it is an unsettling combination, and these books found fewer readers than the early, more optimistic ones. How must Eastlake have felt, having to write them? It is worth noting that Eastlake published no new novel in the last twenty years of his life.

*

There were a number of deaths that affected me in 1997, my father's foremost among them. Eastlake's death, six weeks earlier, thereby became the year's second-greatest loss for me. In the course of the last talk I had with my father he chose to ignore the risky operation he faced, and spent his time concentrating on what he felt was important: his granddaughter. In the course of the last talk I had with Eastlake he chose to brush off questions about his own work and talk of bigger matters.

Eastlake and I had our last talk on the terrace of a restaurant in Bisbee, beyond the cover of the canopy, under the evening sky. Across from us rose a steep hillside on which were perched old miners' shacks. Eastlake told how these had been allowed to run down and had once been offered for $400, but they had now been painted bright blue and pink (!), and sold for many times that amount. Bisbee had become an "artists' colony." This led him to a number of observations on the capitalist system, on ranching (he always thought more of his ranching skills than of his writing talent), about how it was a current media insult to call someone part of the "intelligentsia," about the selective abortion of female fetuses in countries trying to enforce population control, about the shame of America extending China's most-favored-nation status. . . . It was a great whirl of ideas, as funny, as throwing-knife-sharp, and as complex as any of his novels, all centered on his worries over the human condition, our insectlike urges to devour ourselves and others, to crush anyone or any ideal which might get in the way of our getting all Bio 1's best food first.

So it was with great relief that I sat drinking my tea and watching the air go indigo over the mountains—relief at hearing that however damaged were Eastlake's hopes for man's moral evolution, they still had not been extinguished. This was the voice he no longer had the heart to commit to the page, but which came to life as he warmed to our face-to-face dialogue. This was the living voice of an idea, one explicit or inherent in all his work: that moral evolution can only be achieved one person at a time, one dialogue at a time.

As long as readers continue to open Eastlake's books, this dialogue will continue, and such an evolution will remain for us all a stubborn possibility.

Go in Beauty, William Eastlake.

—W. C. Bamberger

Book Reviews

Nathanael West: Novels and Other Writings. Ed. Sacvan Bercovitch. Library of America, 1997. 829 pp. $35.00.

The Library of America here collects the four short novels published during West's lifetime, seven short stories, a play, two screenplays, selected letters, and what is likely the outline for the planned fifth novel, for which West was under contract with Random House at the time of his death. Of the previously unpublished material the stories are of the most interest for the general reader. The play and two screenplays are minor collaborative efforts. And while the letters fascinate, the selection is disappointing. The editors have chosen to include only those letters touching on literary issues, and at twenty-three letters this makes for a thin selection. Since space isn't an issue, I can't help wondering if a more general roundup wouldn't have been better.

All published here for the first time with one exception, the stories were composed between 1929 and 1933, the critical years of West's artistic development, coming between the dreadful *Balso Snell* and the perfectly realized *Miss Lonelyhearts*. As such they provide an unprecedented glimpse of what the young artist was up to. The stories reveal West's early preoccupation with American popular culture and the extent to which he was willing to experiment with nontraditional narrative. They also reveal a profound anxiety of influence. Born in 1903, only four years after Hemingway, West nevertheless identified himself with the second generation of modernists who arrived late on the scene in the late '20s and '30s—with those writers who came immediately after the Lost Generation. The stories, and *Balso Snell* too for that matter, are filled with a sense of belatedness that sometimes overwhelms the early fiction. Not coincidentally, failure and fakery are the common themes of these stories.

"The Adventurer" is a story that bears some resemblance to the James Thurber story "The Secret Life of Walter Mitty." In spirit, though, it lies much closer to the darker works of Beckett and Pynchon. The story explores the gross discrepancies between the inner and outer life of its narrator Joe Rucker, an order clerk for a wholesale grocery. Rucker doesn't engage in active daydreaming so much as he recalls memories of his old fantasies, images flickering dimly on the monitor in his head. In an earlier, happier state he hunted tigers in the reading room of the New York Public Library. But once awakened to the fact that he is one of an "innumerable horde" wasting his days in the library, Rucker can no longer take refuge in his dreams or in reading.

"The Adventurer" has no structure other than the associative memories in Rucker's head and the ratiocination of a mind turning against itself. And once started, such a story can come to no logical conclusion. In another story called "Western Union Boy," we encounter another of life's casualties, F. Winslow, haunted by his dreams. In this case Winslow, an old college acquaintance of the narrator's whom the narrator runs into in a speakeasy, is haunted by a particular recurring nightmare. It is about a semipro baseball game in which Winslow played as an adolescent. After dropping a fly ball and losing the game, Winslow is prevented from boarding the team bus by an older bat-wielding cousin as the rest of the team watches from the bus, and Winslow is forced to hitchhike back to town. The fact that the narrator has bothered to record Winslow's story at all suggests that Winslow's nightmare has in some sense become the narrator's, and so by extension ours. In a longer unfinished story called "Mr. Potts of Pottstown," the inversion of reality and nightmare is complete when Potts, another would-be adventurer, learns that the Swiss Alps he intends to climb are fake—indeed all of Switzerland, its "lakes, forests, glaciers, peasants, goats, milkmaids, mountains, and the rest of it" are all part of elaborate scenery in a huge amusement park owned by a giant corporation referred to only as "the Company."

The most polished and finished of the stories, "The Impostor," is a biting satire of the expatriate scene in Paris. (West spent a few months in Paris in 1926, the same year he legally changed his name from Nathan Weinstein to Nathanael West; afterwards he would circulate the fiction that he had lived there in poverty for years.) The story begins with the absurd premise that any artist in Paris in those days needed to look the part to be taken seriously, i.e., one needed to look "crazy." The story's narrator, a writer or likely a would-be writer, arrives in Paris well after the first and second waves of American expatriates have already landed. "As time went on," the narrator complains, as if giving voice to West's own anxiety of influence, "being 'crazy' became more difficult. . . . One had to be original." The narrator's brilliant solution is to portray his craziness "through the exaggeration of normality," by donning a pressed suit, gloves, and a tightly rolled umbrella. He soon finds himself invited to every important party.

The perfection of West's comic technique would require greater distance from his characters than he achieved in the short stories, but the stories display the same obsessions and stylistic brilliance found in the later novels that have earned him a high place in American letters and which mark him as a true forebearer of postmodern American fiction. [John Kulka]

Rikki Ducornet. *The Word "Desire."* Henry Holt, 1997. 193 pp. $22.00.

As with *The Fountains of Neptune* and her other acclaimed novels, Rikki Ducornet's new story collection is a crystal-work of poetic dimensions. The twelve stories contained here are so organically shaped that they seem to be made of molecules, not words. They range across North Africa, Europe, Asia and the Americas at different historical periods and with an ambition no less than to limn "desire" as "a sacred text that has been copied out again and again by a fallible scribe."

In fact, each story might be thought of as an unveiling of desire's multifarious nature. In "Rosevine" the scribe is in the form of a boy, the desire a pristine world suggested by seashells. "The Chess Set of Ivory" undercuts the Osiris myth by allowing its teller to walk in on his own wife dancing nude with another man. Desire as destroyer/animator; core mythology; water, earth, light—especially light, the elemental imagery that is Ducornet's signature—forces discussion of the book into an antiquated vocabulary.

Reading it, we feel, like the Mexican priest in "The Foxed Mirror," that we are looking at ourselves/desire through a dark mirror. The Freudian dichotomy of sex and death that informs "The Neurosis of Containment" becomes simply a modernist formulation of something eternal, something people have always copied out in their idiosyncratic hand. The penultimate story, "Opium," centers on a dying pope fed on breast milk and gold. It ends with a collage of violence wrought by the word *desire* when conceived as a noun: holy wars, murder; a historical sweep that could be the book's epiphany. But a final, extremely personal story serves as a coda that, like *The Divine Comedy,* harmonizes the desire of the self with the desire that moves history, indeed all humanity. A sublime achievement. [Steve Tomasula]

Paul Metcalf. *Collected Works, Volume Two: 1976-1986.* Coffee House, 1997. 600 pp. $35.00.

At the beginning of *I-57,* his account of driving the length of Interstate 57 during his fifty-seventh year, Paul Metcalf writes, "I have never stopped writing this, and it has not yet begun." If this comment notes a commonplace truth about writing—that the writer never accomplishes what he intends, so that, in effect, his efforts to do so mean he is always beginning or, in some way, yet to begin—it also emphasizes Metcalf's rejection of finish; work determined by boundaries of one kind or another—definition, closure, convention. Such order is always arbitrary and, for Metcalf, artificial, fatal to the creative impulse. From the beginning, he has sought to escape containment of one kind or another and to seek in the writing process, fluidity. ("America is a verb, Europe a noun," Metcalf says.) His method is to cluster texts of one kind or another together: historical, scientific, autobiographical, literary, correspondence, fragments, found language. In some books, he has not written a word of his own. *Both* is about John Wilkes Booth and Edgar Allan Poe—*both* acts as the currency of metamorphosis in the book, and is also all, any, each, every. *Waters of Potowmack* is history as histology, geography as physiology, poetry as archaeology. In it, Metcalf finds what we have lost, listens to what we have tuned out. "My effort," Metcalf writes, "has been to collapse time to create a plane on which events of all periods may occur at once to create tensions that one finds in the static arts." He is as original a writer as we have, part of a native American aesthetic that includes, among others, Melville (his great grandfather), Thoreau, William Carlos Williams, Olson. It is important to have his work, virtually all of it published in small presses, more readily available. [Robert Buckeye]

Edmund White. *The Farewell Symphony*. Knopf, 1997. 413 pp. $25.00.

With *The Farewell Symphony*, Edmund White's final entry in his autobiographical trilogy, I was left wondering when White ever had the time to write a book about his climb up the literary ladder in 1970s Greenwich Village. Although my memories of the '70s involve diapers and "Sesame Street," I am well aware of the hedonistic frenzy that gripped the urban gay community in the post-Stonewall years. However, White's apparent non-stop sexfest (sex in clubs, sex in the park, sex on the loading docks, sex under semis, sex in Italy, etc.) seems to defy logic: at one point the narrator does some math and figures he had over 3,000 sex partners between 1962 and 1982 (according to my calculations, that's three partners a week for twenty years!).

Putting all calculators (and envy) aside, amidst all this kissing is plenty of telling. On one level *The Farewell Symphony* reads like a gossip rag, but the name-dropping proves to be problematic. In a disclaimer, White describes the book as an "autobiographical novel," and "not a literal transcription of my experience. The characters are stylized versions, often composites, of people I knew in those years." Along with partially fictionalized artistic figures, there are a number of thinly veiled characters—James Merrill included—and others whose identities White does not even attempt to conceal—like Michel Foucault. At times it is difficult to determine where facts give way to White's creative substitutions.

After playing the name game I arrived at the novel's most revealing moments, which do not take place in the microcosm of the New York literary world but rather in Chicago. Visiting his mother, who is scheduled to undergo surgery for breast cancer, he analyzes their relationship and concludes he had "fought free of her gravitational pull but now, like a dark lodestone, she was drawing me back to her." At home he also encounters his manic-depressive lesbian-in-denial sister as he descends through memory into the Freudian cesspool of their childhood. In just a few chapters, White achieves a genuineness that forms the core of his novel, something that pages and pages of sex (although titilating) seem to lack. [Kent D. Wolf]

Péter Nádas. *A Book of Memories*. Trans. Ivan Sanders with Imre Goldstein. Farrar, Straus & Giroux, 1997. 706 pp. $30.00.

There are rare moments when a reviewer recognizes that a book he is discussing is a true work of art, an astonishing achievement. I once reviewed a strange novel entitled *Pale Fire*; although I did not know how to capture its formal, dazzling structure, I recognized it as a masterpiece. Although I'm not sure about *A Book of Memories*, I believe it is one of the great novels of the last fifty years. It reminds me, in part, of the amazing conjunctions of memory, sexuality, and creativity found in Proust and Mann.

I can merely hint here at the themes and metaphors of Nádas's achievement. The title immediately brings into play two of the underlying themes of the narrative: memory and the creative description of memory. There are three sections of the text. One seems to be concerned with the "last days" of the narrator who, at age thirty-three, tries to understand the reasons for despair about his abilities to render the past—that past which has made him the odd, miserable artist he assumes he is. But even in this section we are made aware of his "anomolous nature."

Although the narrator wants to write another text—and he gives us in the second section a broken, mythological "mural"—he is unable to finish it. He is so preoccupied with arbitrary movements, disjointed perceptions, that he offers one which reflects his obsessions with creativity and bisexuality. He calls his text "the multisecret world of my presentiments and presumptions." The "multisecret world" challenges his talent and his life.

To complicate matters, the third section seems to be another revision—a revision by another narrator. Thus we have a textual commentary upon the "original" text. And we are not really shocked because Nádas has been using duplicitous subversions throughout his novel. Such sentences as the following have prepared us for "multisecret worlds": "There is no memory without the recurrence of emotions or conversely, every moment of lived experience is also an allusion to a former experience—that is what memory is." [Irving Malin]

Anthony Cronin. *Samuel Beckett: The Last Modernist*. HarperCollins, 1997. 645 pp. $30.00.

This level-headed biography is informed by a healthy impatience with the sycophantic testimonies that have turned Beckett into the official saint of the postwar era. It sheds much light on the personal origins, Irish topography, and fraught publication history of Beckett's fictions and plays. Cronin stresses Beckett's aloofness from politics and literary movements, including "the Dublin literary swim," the theater of the absurd, and Parisian existentialism. With reference to Beckett's fiction, Cronin helpfully delineates the development from the show-off sophistication of *Murphy* through the escalating uncertainty of *Watt* to the self-imposed "awful prose" (Beckett's phrase) of the trilogy *Molloy, Malone Dies* and *The Unnameable*. "In general too much has been made of Beckett's interest in philosophy and too little of his impatience with it," Cronin declares. Instead, Beckett's work, especially the fiercely self-reflexive fiction, entails for Cronin a "profound exploration of the self." By sealing off his subject from the literary, philosophical and historical currents of the day, Cronin is able to concentrate on Beckett the person, exploring his major friendships and his often tortuous relationship with women. However, in narrowing the focus to the personal, Cronin also diminishes Beckett's stature as an author who has proved astoundingly pertinent to modern audiences. The condition of uncertainty that preoccupies Beckett *is* philosophical: born of philosophical reflection, universal in intent. Missing from Cronin's account is any attempt to analyze the reasons why Beckett's supposedly idiosyncratic vision won global esteem in the postwar era, and why this warm reception was largely limited to the plays. That said, *Samuel Beckett: The Last Modernist* provides essential insights into the complex personality of a writer whose achievement has yet to come into perspective. [Philip Landon]

Patrick Deville, Jean Echenoz, Olivier Rolin, Mark Polizzotti, Florence Delay, Sonja Greenlee and Harry Mathews. *S.* Brookline, 1997. 97 pp. Paper: $12.95.

A truly collaborative effort, *S.* finds seven French and American writers writing about a group of central characters, themselves centralized by S. herself. S. (or Suzanne) is sent through this collage of variations to meet with her sexuality, crimes and linguistic adventures.

It is fair to call the book Oulipian, given that the book's final section, "The Quevedo Cipher," is written by the one American member of the predominantly French group. Like Mathews's novel *Cigarettes*, *S.*'s structure is built on the recurrence of details that shift and metamorphose from section to section. Names and places, objects and actions all refract within the framework. What occurs as we look through this latticework of overlaid detail is at turns tragic, comic, and consistently mysterious.

The convention of mystery writers to begin *in medias res* is retained by most of the writers of *S.*, it seems, as a means to intensify the title character's enigmatic life. The writers are also drawn to investigate the mysteries of sexuality, crime, and psychology through the lens of their language. The language of each writer remains playful throughout, as though the greatest mystery is that of the words, as if their manipulation, their movement and plotting, is that same movement and plotting of a sentient being.

After all, it is the words doing all the work. Suzanne is merely a participant, with the readers, in the writers' activity. The collaboration is inventive and the collage coheres because the different views of Suzanne and her world, seen at various times, are surrounded by the solidly unstable chaos of language. [Thomas Lecky]

Mark Leyner. *The Tetherballs of Bougainville*. Harmony, 1997. 224 pp. $21.00.

The fading lights of Leyner's first novel *Et tu, Babe* find us scrambling for cover in an infomercial gone ballistic, urging us to buy buy buy our way into TEAM LEYNER! world, if we so dare. Now, five years later, squeezed between the publication of *Tooth Imprints on a Corn Dog*, a regular column in *Esquire*, and screenplay work on MTV's *Liquid Television*, Leyner's attention once again focuses on (surprise!) Mark Leyner. *The Tetherballs of Bougainville* catches up with Mark as your run-of-the-mill thirteen-year-old shirtless Versace pant-wearing wanna-be tetherball-playing master grammarian who lands a $250,000 a year lifetime award (for a screenplay that is yet to be written) on the same day his father is scheduled to be executed via lethal injection by the state of New Jersey for his escapades on PCP, and, yes, the very same day in which the said dose of lethal drugs fails to kill Papa Leyner (resulting only in a slight case of nausea) to whit young Mark has sex with the warden overseeing the execution. Welcome back to Mondo Leyner.

Tetherballs continues Leyner's satire of the publishing industry's marketing of hot new writers (i.e., Mark Leyner) as hip-flasking, pseudo-rock stars, equipped with the latest and greatest in literary weaponry to sedate an oftentimes hostile readership. Leyner refuses to settle down into any one narrative groove, taking us from what promises to be a fairly conventional novel into young Mark's burgeoning screenplay, then abruptly into a fifty-plus-page review of the said screenplay/film that never was and may never be.

Burroughsian concerns of capital punishment, media hype, drug culture, and carnivalesque sex riddle *Tetherballs,* lampooning the very society which produced them with pie-in-the-face smart-assing. Such slapstick satire has made Leyner the lovable literary Tasmanian Devil he is with academic and mainstream audiences alike. At its sarcastic, self-reflexive best, *Tetherballs* is both postmodern product and parody, a full-blown riot in the coffers of the New York publishing industry and a testament to Leyner's whipsmart comedic genius. [Trevor Dodge]

John Hawkes. *An Irish Eye.* Viking, 1997. 159 pp. $22.95; Lesley Marx. *Crystals out of Chaos: John Hawkes and the Shapes of Apocalypse.* Fairleigh Dickinson, 1997. 244 pp. $39.50.

John Hawkes is yet another contemporary American novelist who has unaccountably received relatively little scholarly attention. What a pleasure, then, to read Lesley Marx's study of Hawkes's career. In this smart, readable, and compelling book, Marx argues that in his early novels Hawkes's male characters seek to make order in a fragmented and chaotic world by subduing the world to their artistic, narrative, and apocalyptic visions. But in his more recent novels Hawkes has introduced women's voices as a means of overturning the authority of the male-authored narratives. The result is the recognition that narratives do not make the world but must "negotiate their authority in the world with the stories of others."

It would be interesting to see what Marx would do with Hawkes's latest novel, *An Irish Eye*, narrated by a thirteen-year-old Irish foundling, Dervla O'Shannon, a.k.a. Thistle. In the style of a fairy tale Thistle describes life in Saint Martha's Home for Foundling Girls, her eloping with World War I veteran Corporal Stack from the Old Soldiers' Home across town, his injury and her virtual imprisonment in the manor where he is taken to recuperate, their escape, and her eventual return to the Home for Foundling Girls. But Thistle's adventures are far from straightforward. The farther she roams from Saint Martha's, the less stable are the countryside, her sexuality, and her sense of identity. The narrative itself becomes unstable as the story Thistle tells us competes with the letters she writes to the Foundling

Mother back at Saint Martha's and as it becomes less and less certain that she has ever left Saint Martha's. Thistle tells us early on, "I shall never in my life be borne down by the mere truth of things."

An Irish Eye strikes me as a bit slight, but Thistle is a captivating narrator and the story has the charm of a good, but twisted, children's story. [Robert L. McLaughlin]

Paul Auster. *Hand to Mouth: A Chronicle of Early Failure.* Henry Holt, 1997. 449 pp. $25.00.

This book is an Auster museum: a memoir followed by three appendices of the writer's early projects. For many Auster enthusiasts the appendices' three plays, baseball card game, and full-length detective novel may be as interesting as the memoir since they provide useful background to the later fiction that accounts for Auster's reputation.

The memoir itself is an often funny, self-effacing piece, Auster's attempt to understand his cash-strapped *wanderjahre* of the seventies. Acknowledging his early dedication to writing, he shows just how difficult and self-defeating such commitment can be. Along the way there are entertaining accounts of Auster's various odd jobs and portraits of a number of interesting figures from the period whose paths crossed Auster's: Jerzy Kosinski, John Lennon, Mary McCarthy, and others. What Auster seems unable to dramatize fully, though, is precisely the subject of his subtitle, early failure. Instead the memoir functions as a study in literary apprenticeship, with its account of poverty never quite coming to life (in part since we are aware of the writer's subsequent success). That shortcoming is not a serious one, since what many readers want is knowledge of the apprenticeship. In that regard, this text helpfully supplements Auster's first memoir and the fictions he produced following the apprentice period.

As for the apprentice work, it is just that. One play is the germ of the novel *Ghosts,* another that of *The Music of Chance.* The card game suggests the permutational fascination Auster inherits from the Beckett of *Watt,* while the detective novel displays the dominant motifs of *The New York Trilogy.* I shudder to think of dissertation chapters extrapolating the subtexts of Action Baseball, but this collection is a welcome picture of Auster's artistic development. [Stephen Bernstein]

Emer Martin. *Breakfast in Babylon.* Mariner Books (Houghton Mifflin), 1997. 321 pp. $12.00.

Emer Martin's first novel, the winner of a major award when first published last year in her native Ireland, is as brutal as it is beautiful. Set primarily in Paris, with interludes in London, Munich, Amsterdam and Israel, *Breakfast in Babylon* traces the progress of Isolt, a young Irishwoman, through a European underworld inhabited by punk junkies, beggars, and criminals.

She hangs out by day at the Pompidou fountain in Paris and by night in squalid and dangerous squats. Martin writes of this underworld, where drugs and alcohol are the only comforts and where life is short, in a spare, matter-of-fact prose. Isolt, as a woman, is an outsider and her status, or lack of one, allows her to stand outside and observe. One senses that she will retreat from this world as earlier she had retreated from an unhappy childhood in Ireland; that she hopes to arrive at wisdom through extreme experience, but not to succumb to it.

Despite the grim material, *Breakfast in Babylon* is often a very funny book and shows that Martin possesses in abundance the classic Irish gift for the absurd and the comic so evident in the fiction of Flann O'Brien and Samuel Beckett. It is her light and sure touch which renders the novel so remarkable. Also notable is Martin's sure register of place and her ability to trace Isolt's development as a woman as she trudges through the underworld. *Breakfast in Babylon* also represents a completely new departure for the Irish novel. Martin is the first Irish writer to represent the underside of Irish participation in Europe—a continent not of riches, but of addiction, abuse, nihilism, and despair. An explosive debut. There has never been an Irish novel like it. [Eamonn Wall]

Denis Johnson. *Already Dead: A California Gothic*. HarperCollins, 1997. 435 pp. $25.00.

Although Johnson is drawn to sinners, deviants, and criminals, he does not glorify them. Instead, he attempts to find "virtues" in their misguided choices. He is interested in the possibilities of their conversion, their secret longings for salvation. The fact that his Catholic background has nourished his art helps him in his mission. He never preaches; he never writes propaganda. Johnson is interested in the "in-betweens," those people who still desire some tiny measure of grace. And in his new novel, he uses his heightened poetic language to shine light into his *California Gothic*. His rushing, driving sentences are a bit excessive, but they are saved by radiant phrasing, unexpected metaphors and strange beauty.

The two main characters—who are curious doubles—are Nelson Fairchild, Jr. and Carl Van Ness. Both are half-alive, ghostly "shades"; they are drawn to each other because they are "doomed." There is, perhaps, a sexual attraction, but they understand their greater need to violate morality, their murderous and/or suicidal urges. They are, in Leonard Cohen's wonderful phrase, "beautiful losers."

Words tend to inspire a sense of dread, awe, other universes that are filled with magical transformations and transgressions. Fairchild, who longs to kill his father and wife, thinks aloud: "When you die, your consciousness blanks out, but it resumes eons later, when the history of molecules has been revised enough to preclude your death due to those particular circumstances: the bullet hits your brain in this world, but in a later one merely tickles your earlobe. You die in one universe and yet in another go on without a hitch." The entire novel tests the limits of thresholds (psychological, religious, linguistic); it explores the "brink of intelligibility."

Johnson's California is, perhaps, a stranger land than Pynchon's *Vineland;* it is a miraculous realm, another "universe" in which transubstantiations occur so suddenly that we are never sure whether the big earthquake will occur. Maybe Johnson believes it is occurring right now. [Irving Malin]

Dennis Cooper. *Guide.* Grove/Atlantic, 1997. 176 pp. $22.00.

In *Guide*, the fourth book of his five-novel cycle, Dennis Cooper charts passage between a variety of seeming oppositions: desire and its fulfillment, reality and fiction, life and death, bodily knowledge and the language with which we express it. This middle-space seems to be Cooper's preferred subject because, as his character Chris puts it, it is only there that one can truly achieve a simultaneous understanding of both a thing and its opposite; "drugging himself in death's general direction," so as to move between existence and its extinguishing, Chris believes that only in such a location can we hope to grasp briefly what might be "everything there is to know about human existence."

Cooper's novel is itself a performance of this general idea. It is narrated by Dennis, who is self-consciously "writing a novel" about his friends; of *Guide*, he says, "This is it." Like Cooper, a writer for *Spin* magazine, and like Cooper, the author of a *Spin* article on homeless teens (which is included, and is significantly similar yet different from Cooper's), Dennis is both Cooper and a self-consciously fictional projection. This metafictional turn nicely illustrates *Guide* as a medium between the "real" world and the kinds of fiction we use to describe it. The novel's characters are effective mediums for the music lyrics, movie plots, and pervasive, seemingly communal fantasies of sex and violence that flood the Los Angeles setting. Absorbing and enacting and reshaping this pop culture, they come alive in often disturbing but always strikingly contemporary ways, functionaries of the fin-de-millennium hyperreal.

Guide is not for the (even remotely) squeamish. Although Dennis refuses to indulge his own murderous homosexual fantasies, his friends/characters/creations are not so restricted. It is not without reason that Cooper has been called a postmodern disciple of Sade and Genet. [Matthew Roberson]

Gerald L. Bruns. *Maurice Blanchot: The Refusal of Philopsophy*. Johns Hopkins, 1997. 339 pp. $39.95.

Twenty percent of Gerald L. Bruns's study of Blanchot's life and work consists of endnotes, a fact that would generally predict the other eighty percent to be fashioned in late twentieth-century overarticulated academic prose. Bruns does indeed have his own set of tropes and terminologies but manages to use them quite effectively in his consideration of Blanchot's work. It must be said that Blanchot is no easy subject and Bruns readily admits this in his preface. The chapters that follow attempt to situate a writer who persistently resists situation.

Blanchot's interest in madness, death, imprisonment, like Beckett's, is never far from his interest in language. With this in mind, Mr. Bruns has accepted the challenge of close reading over indeterminate generalization. His ten chapters are further broken into terse sections, a structure in keeping with his subject's admiration for the linguistic fragment.

Bruns sees Blanchot facing the relationship between philosophy and poetry as a late-Romantic, reviving this classical debate within an era of intense political and social unrest. The fragmentation of language is mirrored in the history of the time, though also in literary history. The book delves deeply into Blanchot's reading of Heidegger and Celan to reveal the cross-pollination of linguistic, poetic and literary ideas.

As the first full English language study of Blanchot, this book is a fine introduction to the major work of this oft overlooked French master. [Thomas Lecky]

Mario Vargas Llosa. *Making Waves: Essays.* Trans. John King. Farrar, Straus & Giroux. 338 pp. $27.50.

Author, journalist, literary critic, playwright, filmmaker, presidential candidate. Mario Vargas Llosa is a jack-of-all-trades. Collected here—many for the first time in English—are four decades of newspaper editorials, political commentary, and film and literary criticism by an author who earned his place in the arena of world literature as a major figure in the Boom of the Latin American novel in the 1960s. *Making Waves* is a fine chronicle of Vargas Llosa's artistic and political development, and one can sense the evolution of his ideology in these pages. Like many of his contemporaries, the Peruvian writer was a fervent supporter of Castro in the 1960s. The early writings in this collection reflect that passion: "[T]he hour of social justice will arrive in countries, as it has in Cuba, and the whole of Latin America will have freed itself from the order that despoils it." With the exile of Cuban authors in the 1970s, Vargas Llosa moved closer to a break with Castro and writers still in support of the communist leader—a break exacerbated by a fistfight with Gabriel García Márquez in a Mexico City movie theater.

Making Waves showcases Vargas Llosa's thoughts on the vocation of the writer and the role of literature as well. Once a Sartrean existentialist, Vargas Llosa was soon drawn to Flaubert. The use of personal experience as raw material aided him in his quest for critical realism. For Vargas Llosa, a writer is a slave to his vocation, a position that allows one to express "a terrible indictment against existence under whatever regime or ideology." In a lecture given on receipt of the Rómulo Gallegos prize, he advised, "Warn them that literature is fire, that it means nonconformity and rebellion, that the *raison d' être* of a writer is protest, disagreement and criticism." A blend of sharp-eyed analysis and personally committed criticism, *Making Waves* is a truly rich work by a major international writer. [Kent D. Wolf]

Jean Echenoz. *Big Blondes*. Trans. Mark Polizzotti. The New Press, 1997. 201 pp. $22.00.

The winner of several prestigious literary prizes, and one of France's foremost contemporary writers, Jean Echenoz is best known for his tongue-in-cheek humor and his parodies of pop culture. *Big Blondes* is a quintessential Echenoz novel, exploiting the comic potential of detective writing, comic-book characters, and Hitchcock thrillers (especially *Vertigo*) in a hilarious plot based on the stereotypes and clichés associated with blondes. As Paul Salvador, a television producer preparing a series of documentaries on blondes, sets out to track down the elusive Gloire Abgrall (alias Gloire Stella), a former pop singer who disappeared after the suspicious death of her agent, he and his detectives become involved in a fast-paced chase around the world. Their pursuit takes them from Brittany to Australia and India, then back to France, and embroils them in the shady operations of an international drug-trafficking ring. At the center of the cast of oddball characters—with transparently symbolic names—is Gloire herself, whose penchant for pushing her enemies off high places—cliffs, bridges, elevator shafts, balconies and the Rouen cathedral—is tempered by Béliard, a homunculus and kind of alter ego whose magical powers make him a cross between a guardian angel and a miniature superman. Mark Polizzotti's fine translation does an excellent job of capturing Echenoz's hallmark style; his clever wordplay, unexpected turns of phrase, and idiosyncratic humor. In short, *Big Blondes* is a must for anyone with a taste for zany thrillers that combine social satire and love stories with a good dose of farce. [Susan Ireland]

Alasdair Gray. *A History Maker*. Harvest (Harcourt Brace Jovanovich), 1996. 224 pp. Paper: $14.00.

Alasdair Gray sets his recent novel in the twenty-third century, and like many science fiction works, it is full of sex, violence, and adventure. But the novel is less Gray's exploration of the sci-fi genre than it is a unique fable about power, fame, and gender relations. In the intervening centuries between our time and the novel's, the modern nation states have fallen as capitalism expired.

A History Maker seems most like Gray's 1985 novella *The Fall of Kelvin Walker* as Wat Dryhope, like Kelvin, is both a sympathetic and repulsive character. Indeed, both works demonstrate that the protagonist's individual development need not be the vehicle for the author's didactic purposes. Gray instead relies on a more organic understanding of the conflict he creates: the matriarchies have established a stable utopia, but this future promotes a lot of unnecessary death and killing. Rather, Gray calls attention to the need for interdependence between men and women, not in the name of patriarchy, but in the name of community. This political goal becomes clear by the novel's end.

What finally makes *A History Maker* unique is that Wat, the apparent hero, fails to have any part in the remaking of his society. In this way, Gray expresses his own ambivalence toward hero worship, both as a cultural phenomenon and as a method of sociopolitical improvement. From his quasi-Hegelian perspective, change can be produced by the individual, but *progress* demands the efforts of the collective. [William M. Harrison]

Nathalie Sarraute. *Here*. Trans. Barbara Wright. Foreword by E. Nicole Meyer. George Braziller, 1997. 165 pp. $22.50.

As a scholar of French literature, I rarely recommend a translated novel over the original. But the fact is that Nathalie Sarraute has been here, and done this, before. The infinite slowness of perception and psychological response to stimulus was the governing principle of her earliest works, most notably the 1937 *Tropismes,* which became one of the founding works of the Nouveau Roman when reprinted by Minuit in 1957. Sarraute published *Ici* (*Here*) in France in 1995; by the age of 95, she had earned the right to have her prose sound tired, but the more fundamental problem here is the achronicity of the novel. Sarraute's trademark is the elaboration of the nanosecond of response—by what torturous routes does a forgotten word return to memory?; how can "they" say "that" to "me"?; why is such and such an expression not exactly appropriate to the situation I wish to describe?—but in the information age, the nanosecond seems no longer worthy to be explored. Indeed, it is more likely to be deplored, as we expect our internet connections to deliver information instantaneously: we don't dissect the nanosecond any more; we drum our fingers impatiently through it.

In her preface to the English translation, E. Nicole Meyer writes that "continual movement distinguishes this text where words can exert vast power." I agree with her that Sarraute remains true to her belief in the power of words, but I find the French text of *Here* static and tedious, difficult to stay with for long. Barbara Wright has translated three previous novels of Sarraute's, and, indeed, has written about problems of translation in a recent issue of this journal. It is in her version only that the text seems indeed to have "movement." She captures well Sarraute's continuously interrupted prosody and takes justified liberties with the text in order to preserve Sarraute's reliance on phonetic association to structure the book. Wright's translation, ironically enough, harks back to the original freshness of *Tropismes;* I suggest, therefore, that if one wants to go "here" where Sarraute is in this more recent book, it is better to go "there" instead with Barbara Wright. [Renée Kingcaid]

Hélène Cixous and Mireille Calle-Gruber. *Hélène Cixous Rootprints: Memory and Life-Writing.* Routledge, 1997. 254 pp. Paper: $17.95.

Rootprints is an excellent introduction to the multifaceted work of Hélène Cixous, who has written more than thirty books of poetic fiction, countless critical essays, and eight plays. The format, no less than the content of this unusual book, reflects the great diversity of Cixous's oeuvre, combining as it does an extended interview with Mireille Calle-Gruber, excerpts from Cixous's notebooks, photographs from her family album, extensive bio-bibliographical information, critical essays and a contribution by Jacques Derrida.

The dialogue between Cixous and Calle-Gruber provides the occasion for Cixous to develop the themes of sexual difference, self and other, life and death that are omnipresent in her writing, while at the same time allowing her to insist that she is primarily a poet. This is a useful corrective to the tendency in the United States to regard her as a feminist theorist on the strength of the celebrated essay "The Laugh of the Medusa," and her contributions to *The Newly Born Woman.* Yet "To have an upright position, analogous to that of a theoretician, is not my intention," Cixous declares, emphasizing that " 'The Laugh of the Medusa' and other texts of this type were a conscious, pedagogic, didactic effort on my part to classify, to organize certain reflections, to emphasize a minimum of sense. Of common sense."

Rootprints brings out clearly that it is the pursuit, through poetry, of uncommon sense that is Cixous's project. For her, "To write is to have such pointy pricked-up ears that we hear what language says (to us) inside our own words at the very moment of enunciation." [Mary Lydon]

Marie Darrieussecq. *Pig Tales: A Novel of Lust and Transformation.* Trans. Linda Coverdale. The New Press, 1997. 151 pp. $18.00.

The publication of Marie Darrieussecq's unusual first novel, in France, was one of the literary sensations of 1996. An immediate success, the book was soon selling over three thousand copies a day, and the renowned director Jean-Luc Godard is already working on an adaptation for the screen. With characters who metamorphose from human to animal form, this satirical tale suggests a cross between Aesop's fables and Kafka's *The Metamorphosis,* while the graphic descriptions of the physical transformations recall scenes from movies like *Altered States.* At once a sociopolitical fable and a love story, the novel is narrated from a mud puddle by a masseuse in a beauty parlor who has metamorphosed into a pig and whose increased appetite for food and sex leads to a series of bizarre, often farcical, escapades. Her adventures culminate in a liaison with a high-level executive-werewolf; he devours pizza delivery boys while she guzzles the pizza. Meanwhile, in the nightmarish outside world, at some unspecified time in the future, the country has been ravaged by war, epidemics, and famine. Corrupt, racist, right-wing politicians have risen to power and have hypocritically promoted a "healthier" world. In Darrieussecq's tragicomic exploration of humanity's animal nature, the chatty, mock-naive style of the unsophisticated narrator pushes every pig pun to its limits, and her deadpan comments on her changing appearance parody those of an adolescent contemplating the onset of puberty. *Pig Tales* is a striking modern fable by a young writer who has made a dramatic entry onto the literary scene. [Susan Ireland]

James Kelman. *Busted Scotch: Selected Stories.* Norton, 1997. 264 pp. $23.00.

These are bleak, beautiful stories. James Kelman has a startling ability to wiggle into the skins of his characters—often angry, bitter, beaten, lost—and speak in their voices. Of the thirty-five stories collected here (ranging over more than twenty years of Kelman's career), many take place on the tattered margins of Scottish society—pubs and betting parlors, parks and streetcorners. Sometimes they are peculiarly affecting because Kelman doesn't really seem to be trying to tell a tale; he gives us a glimpse of a life through dialogue, an anecdote, a scene overheard on the street. These fragments of lives are as puzzling and pleasing, sad and amusing as if we'd stumbled upon them ourselves. Loneliness, lack of work and alcoholism give many of these characters an edge of despair. "No Longer the Warehouseman" is an almost perfect little story in the voice of a man who simply cannot stick with "gainful employment." "The Paperbag" is typical of the stories in this volume: a man's lonely meditation on a brief, humiliating encounter with a woman: "Why am I the most fucking boring bastard in the whole fucking world?" Really, these stories are too various and brilliant in such crazy ways that it is impossible to encapsulate this book's many splendors in this tiny review. But the overall flavor of these stories is fairly represented by the narrator of "A Situation," a man who has slept with his fiance's sister. He is tormented by his deed but unable to admit it to her: "You take the way I live my life as an ordinary man; this is an average day and I've committed awful sins." [James DeRossitt]

Pier Paolo Pasolini. *Petrolio.* Trans. Ann Goldstein. Pantheon, 1997. 470pp. $27.00.

Pasolini claimed in a 1975 interview that this projected novel would serve as "a kind of 'summa' of all my experiences, all my memories." First conceived in 1972, it tells the story of an Italian bourgeois man, Carlo Valletti, who splits into two selves. Carlo I rises to power as an engineer for ENI, the Italian state oil-and-gas company; Carlo II ("Karl") pursues various forms of sexual pleasure and eventually transforms into a woman. But calling *Petrolio* ("Oil") a novel, or even a narrative, is highly problematic. Even more so than such canonical unfinished works as *Billy Budd, Felix Krull,* or *The Trial, Petrolio* is diffuse, elliptic, and above all fragmentary. There is no telling, moreover, to what extent this fragmentary quality was Pasolini's stylistic intention or merely a symptom of the novel's aborted composition (only one fourth of it was drafted). Not published until 1992, the Einaudi Italian edition attempted to reproduce what was left of this 521-page manuscript which was found in a folder on Pasolini's desk when he was murdered in 1975. Goldstein's translation duplicates the contents of that folder: Pasolini's "Project Note"; an unsent letter to Alberto Moravia describing the novel's stylistic rationale; an outline of what might be called the novel's plot; and the manuscript itself, consisting of about two hundred fragmentary Notes, or Appunti. Since this English edition will most likely be of interest to either Pasolini enthusiasts or scholars interested in narrative form and composition, it is regrettable that it does not also include a more extensive editorial apparatus. But for any other readers with the patience to endure its challenges to novelistic assumptions and formal polish, *Petrolio* offers a wealth of penetrating sociological, political, mythological, literary, and psychological reflections. [Thomas Hove]

Richard Beard. *X20: A Novel of (Not) Smoking.* Arcade, 1997. 320 pp. $22.95.

With *X20*, Richard Beard takes a novel approach to the concept of addiction. Gregory Simpson, in the wake of a friend's lung cancer death, quits smoking. Replacing cigarettes with a pen, Gregory reflects on a ten-year habit. Love and tobacco tempted Gregory in his college years in the form of Lucy Hinton, a chain smoker who had attempted to seduce him with both her body and her butts: "She could lick smoke from the corner of her mouth like sugar . . . The archetypal co-ordination of hand to mouth, the same as a sudden thought or a cautious tasting or the blowing of a kiss". Gregory's journal jumps from past to present, moving from memories of a lost love to his meetings with the Suicide Club, a group formed to combat anti-tobacco crusaders and to enjoy a smoke-filled environment. Among the club's members is a cranky centenarian, Walter, who remains healthy despite almost a century of smoking.

Although Beard tackles a timely issue, the unscrupulousness of the tobacco industry, he avoids the preachiness associated with anti-smoking fascists. The sardonic humor of *X20* carries the novel; I believe we all have much to learn from cantankerous Walter who rather wryly reveals the message at the novel's heart when he quips, "Death is natural." [Kent D. Wolf]

Anthony Burgess. *Byrne: A Novel.* Carroll & Graf, 1997. 150 pp. $20.00.

Shades of Alexander Pope and George Gordon Lord Byron, a novel in verse! This is no ordinary novel (but then neither was *A Clockwork Orange*). From the first stanza to the last, we are in the shadows of *The Rape of the Lock* and *Don Juan*. Burgess has taken, in this mock-heroic modern tale of sexual high jinks, the classical *ottava* and turned it on its head. When the narrator writes of Byrne's sexual prowess, "As for Cash / He lived on women, paying in about / Ten inches. We don't know what they paid out," an immediate echo comes from Byron: "A little still she strove, and much repented, / And whispering 'I will ne'er consent'—consented." Or when Tim, one of Byrne's twins (the other is Tom) meets Dorothy, his half-sister, she is described as having "A slack / Sack bosom, ample though, from which depended / Smeared spectacles whose legs had been ill-mended," we might look for the antithesis in Pope's magnificent couplet about Belinda: "On her white Breast a sparkling Cross she wore, / Which Jews might kiss and Infidels adore." And though *Byrne* tells a story about an Irish composer and painter and four of his children, *Byrne* is much, much more than a tour de force mock-epic novel about an Irish Wilt Chamberlain. Burgess, in fact, uses the *ottava rime* to express his feelings about music, art, film, TV, theology, philosophy, history, and literature. He does this by giving us witty and ironic comments on important topics of our time. *Byrne* is Burgess at his best. [Jack Byrne]

Charlotte Perkins Gilman. *With Her in Ourland*. Ed. Mary Jo Deegan and Michael R. Hill. Praeger, 1997. 216 pp. Cloth: $55.00; paper: $15.95.

With Her in Ourland brings the intrepid Ellador from Herland into the world of her husband, sociologist Vandyck Jennings, as World War I is raging, in time to witness the destruction of much of Western Europe. Gilman's 1916 sequel to the utopian novel *Herland* (1915) provides interesting insight into what one American feminist thought about her society. As Ellador and Van travel the world, their voyage becomes a vehicle for a critique of various societies. Their last stop is the United States, because Van thinks that his democratic nation will compare most favorably with Herland. Although Ellador thinks America holds more promise than the other societies she has seen, the last third of the novel is primarily Ellador's critique of America's housing, health care, education, and economic system.

With Her in Ourland makes much more sense when read in connection with *Herland* and I hope that one day the two texts will be published in one volume. *Herland* is the more dramatic story since it places three different men in a peaceful society of women. In the sequel, when Ellador ventures out to her husband's world, the tone becomes more didactic and little happens until the very end when she becomes the first woman in her country in 2000 years to give birth to a boy.

The lengthy introduction by Mary Jo Deegan is useful in placing Gilman's work in a cultural context, but it could be much more concise. She integrates information about Gilman's life with discussions of sociologists who influenced her such as Jane Addams and Lester Ward. However, much like Gilman's novel, Deegan's introduction becomes too pedantic at times.

With Her in Ourland is a troubling portrait of the world in 1916 that will undoubtedly make readers glad they live in the present and sorry that there is still so much to be done to make the United States into a true democracy. [Sally Perry]

Will Self. *Great Apes*. Grove/Atlantic, 1997. 416 pp. $24.00

In Self's new book, chimpanzees are the superior species. They drive the cars, paint the pictures, and act as agents and therapists. In the evolutionary game of strategy, teeth and nails, chimpanzees, not humans, are dominant. Humans live pathetic, indolent lives in zoos or endangered, contingent lives on animal preserves in Africa.

Enter Simon Dykes, painter. At the novel's start, Simon is a human in a recognizably human world. One morning he awakes face to snout with Sarah, his girlfriend, held in her long, furry arms. Sarah is a chimp. Actually, Simon is too, but he doesn't easily cope with his metamorphosis and the overthrow of the world's order. The past was rewritten while he slept: Planet-of-the-Humans movies play on TV, Jane Goodall studies wild humans, and Stephen Jay Gould writes about Darwin, though Darwin is a chimp now.

The story of *Great Apes* is the story of Simon trying to describe his perception of the world to others; this novel is about boundaries and the perception that creates them. How can Simon convey his predicament in the language of chimps? The circumscribed language of chimps who practice psychology is even less helpful to Simon. What interests Self about Simon is not whether or not he's crazy. Instead his subjects are the satirist's trusty targets: social manners, behaviors exhibited by groups of people, and the politics of everyday social gatherings. These concerns are not new to Self. In a story in *The Quantity Theory of Insanity*, he writes, "Jane Bowen extended her hand with an overarm gesture that told me she couldn't have cared less about me, or my antecedents." The world is rigidly taxonomic. In *Great Apes*, a chimp "drags himself backwards across the yard arse aloft, ischial scrag nervously puckered" to greet another. The difference between the two is one of perspective.

What the world of chimps grants Self is a new perspective on the human behavior that has interested him all along. Where a human character in a more realistic story requires an author to be subtle, to show how deference quietly affects the meeting of an all-star psychologist and his assistant, the world of chimps makes all this loud, physical, and cruel. Self takes the imaginative leap that Gould suggests would be valuable though not possible scientifically: that is, a mammal's perceptions reveal its mentality, and it is Self's wonderful turn to mine this understanding for satire. *Great Apes* is a novel about psychology in which the characters are turned inside out, all the raw innards and secret hypocrisies revealed, bald motives and base desires on the outside for all to see. [Paul Maliszewski]

Paula Geyh, Fred G. Leebron, and Andrew Levy, eds. *Postmodern American Fiction: A Norton Anthology*. Norton, 1998. 672 pp. $24.95.

Norton has once again worked its genius. Whatever the hell the term *postmodern* might mean (to Norton, it apparently means anything *after modern*), it would seem to include John Hawkes and Gilbert Sorrentino, the latter having spent a career collecting nasty reviews for being a *postmodernist*. Hawkes and Sorrentino are not here represented, though many of the usual suspects are: Barth, Coover, Pynchon, Barthelme (Donald, that is), and Gass. But then almost anyone else is likely to pop up as well: Audre Lorde, Tim O'Brien, Bobbie Ann Mason, Jayne Anne Phillips, Douglas Coupland, on and on. That all of these should appear between the covers of one anthology is a postmodern gesture in and of itself. Perhaps Norton intended this book as an elaborate postmodern joke! [John O'Brien]

Stacey Levine. *Dra—*. Sun & Moon, 1997. 150pp. Paper: $11.95.

Levine has created a three-dimensional world of two-dimensional people. The world of *Dra—* is a literal labyrinth of bureaucracy, where endless hallways, train stations, and indoor airports link one bizarre official interior after another, from employment offices where employees and applicants sit on open toilets along a far wall to an abandoned work site guarded by one efficient secretary. Dra— has been notified that she is eligible for employment, and the novel follows her incessant quest for work.

The setting is a substantial counterpoint to Dra—'s meandering consciousness, which the third-person narration traces in a series of violent reversals. Her historical ancestor is Henry Adams, who "found himself lying in the Gallery of Machines at the Great Exposition of 1900, his historical neck broken by the sudden irruption of forces so totally new." For Dra—, every turn is dangerous, as she is utterly unprepared to deal with forces both mundane and spectacular. No wonder that she spends a great deal of her time huddled under stairwells and in telephone booths and toilets. Even bowel movements are crises.

Often it is argued that the antidote to an impersonal and absurd world is human connection. In *Dra—*, characters speak with sentimental and unguarded earnestness about the meaning of life, about sex and dread and disease. The Administrator, the Nanny, the Nurse, and Manager each implore Dra— to talk about her feelings and are infuriated by her reticence. Yet all this honesty is as revealing as, say, a job interview. "Tell me your biggest flaw," we've all been asked. We all know to lie. Just be sure to keep track, and don't begin to believe yourself.

Dra— is a masterful book about a horrifying world. You'll recognize it because you live in it. [Monique Dufour]

Linda Simon, ed. *Gertrude Stein Remembered.* Nebraska, 1997. 195 pp. Paper: $15.00.

Had Gertrude Stein not possessed a truly fascinating personality, her publications would have remained interesting to only the few literary scholars intent on expanding the canon of works by early twentieth-century women writers. But because Stein was a woman of independent mind and means, living, writing, and collecting in Paris when that city defined modernism in the arts, and because everybody who was anybody in venturesome artistic style eventually became entangled in Gertrude's web and emerged preserved in her conversation and in her memoirs, Stein has maintained and will maintain an honored place in cultural history.

In *Gertrude Stein Remembered,* Linda Simon, author of the unusually interesting *Biography of Alice B. Toklas* (1977), reprints selections from the memoirs of nineteen famous artists who encountered Stein and Toklas and who remembered their experiences vividly if not always pleasantly: Acton, Anderson, Barlow, Barney, Beach, Beaton, Bonney, de Morinni, Gilot, Imbs, Kahnweiler, Matthews, McAlmon, Preston, Severeid, Steward, Tchelitchew, Van Vechten, and Wilder. Supplementing these articles and extracts are two newly published items: an obituary of Stein written by three of her Radcliffe fellow students, and a memoir of Stein by a fellow student in psychology classes at Harvard.

The mystery of the present volume is that nowhere does Linda Simon mention her first book, a collection of similar materials, *Gertrude Stein: A Composite Portrait* (1974). The earlier volume, fairer overall for containing more negative commentary on Stein, contained articles and excerpts from Acton, Anderson, Hemingway, Olivier, Putnam, Rose, Sitwell, Vollard, and Wilder, among others. Readers new to Gertrude Stein or devoted to her life and works should own and enjoy both of Linda Simon's volumes. [Ray Lewis White]

Grete Weil. *Last Trolley from Beethovenstraat.* Trans. John Barret T. Godine, 1997. 160 pp. $22.95.

This troubled and affecting novel examines the psychological damage suffered by a German correspondent who lives in Amsterdam during the Nazi regime. Although Andreas's journey to Amsterdam is an attempt to escape the horrors of his country, he ends up confronting his identity there more profoundly than he might have done at home. Caught between his belief "in the necessity of bearing witness" to the fate of concentration camp victims and his difficult status as a citizen of the Third Reich, Andreas feels increasingly lost and confused amidst Amsterdam's canals. Without thinking through the consequences of his actions, he risks his life to take up the cause of the Jews, harboring some so that they can avoid the Beethoven Straat Trolley which transports them eastward, in the direction of death.

Weil's ability to disorient the reader to reflect Andreas's state of mind is masterful. Like him, we are caught in a Kafkaesque maze, and we share his very real sense of lurking danger coupled with the desire to do what little good he can. His dilemma is at once moral and practical: "Doing nothing can be more evil than doing something, but what should he have done?" His need to do what is right leads him on a quest to rescue an imprisoned Jew named Daniel, a boy who seems his double. This search for a missing part of himself reinforces his state of fragmentation "into seeing eyes, hearing ears, a beating heart, twitching nerves, and blood that was running out drop by drop." In spare, poignant vignettes, the author enables us to inhabit Andreas's world, appealing to our historical conscience and to our shared sense of the pain of the Holocaust with the emotional force of a visit to a concentration camp. [D. Quentin Miller]

Lucinda Ebersole. *Death in Equality.* St. Martin's, 1997. 146 pp. $19.95.

"Equality" is a small town in Alabama where people go to die, especially people called Cordelia, the last in a line of whom has left New York and lies riddled with cancer. Hers is one of the main narrative voices in the most recent work by Lucinda Ebersole, who is perhaps best known for editing the Mondo anthologies (Barbie, Elvis, etc.).

Cordelia is the "greatest unpublished novelist of her generation," soon to become something less than a footnote in literary history—her books unwritten, her stories untold. But another voice, belonging to Cordelia's writing self, intervenes. It not only tells us most of what we know about Cordelia (she herself describes primarily the geography games she plays with her nurses and the hallucinogenic, erotic effects of pain); it also relates myriad tales of deaths that have already taken place in Equality: a premature baby, an elderly stroke victim, a little boy who baited his fishhook with baby water moccasins and died because the first hospital he was taken to did not accept "coloreds." Relentlessly, Ebersole introduces one character after another and then snatches them all away; the one character who reappears in several stories, Augusta, remains underdeveloped, as if to say people become interesting—become real—only as death approaches.

The stories are linear and unlayered, their outcome foregone; but taken together, they add up to something. They convey a sense of both the universality of death and the complicated private process of dying, and they remind us that death is the great leveler: it brings everyone, whether young, old, white, or black, into that mythical state of equality. [Susann Cokal]

R. Zamora Linmark. *Rolling the R's.* Kaya, 1997. 149pp. Paper: $12.95.

Of the group of adolescents featured in R. Zamora Linmark's *Rolling the R's,* many are recent immigrants to America from Asia, and most are of mixed racial descent, but all are searching for identity—national, racial, sexual—in a Hawaii described as more volcano than melting pot. The book is a kaleidoscope of narrative forms and perspectives, written in the pidgin English these young people speak. Their dialect raises crucial issues of identity and expression. A Japanese-American teacher is criticized because "her American upbringing has blinded her from reading between the lines of the history textbooks where silenced people choke from invisibility and humiliation," but Mai-Lan Phan, her Vietnamese pupil, maps out her own expressive freedom when speaking her broken English: "And no need to think American to speak English because, to Mai-Lan, language is not words, but rhythms and sounds."

These young people move, without differentiation, between the world of physically and sexually abusive adults and institutionalized racism, and the world of the blow-dried glamor of *Charlie's Angels,* disco contests, and Scott Baio posters. For Linmark, these televised icons are more than the cultural currency of 1979; they are the scraps of tinsel from which immigrants assemble their American dreams. Their knowledge of this culture is encyclopedic. Linmark's pop-culture references can also be spot-on, as in the painful plea of Edgar Ramirez, a defiantly homosexual fifth-grader, that Casey Kasem dedicate a song to the boy he's in love with: "How many times I tried to write like Susie Polish Shutz, her words so true to my heart?. . . . I so hungry for this boy, Casey. And even if I one boy when you get to my name, how come, Casey, how come you no pick my letter for the week?" It's not only in history textbooks that people choke from invisibility and humiliation. Like William Vollmann's *The Rainbow Stories, Rolling the R's* coaxes the unfamiliar music of these voices out of the margins and into words. [Graham Fraser]

———————

Harry Ritchie, ed. *Acid Plaid: New Scottish Writing.* Arcade, 1997. 256 pp. Paper: $13.95.

A diverse collection of work—stories, essays, poems, and a play—makes up this colorful, brash anthology. *Acid Plaid* is a sort of book-length yelp of joy at the new vitality of Scottish writing, a blossoming most famously represented, of course, by Irvine Welsh, as well as James Kelman and William Boyd. If you're new to new Scottish writing, however, you might do well to read this alongside one of Welsh's novels, or his stories in *Acid House* or perhaps one of Kelman's many books. This volume has some very fine work in it, but there's also a fair bit of weak writing. Welsh has a very funny, disgusting story here about a despicable bloke whose wife gets her legs cut off through his own misprision; all he wants to do is find a TV so he can watch a football match. Iain Crichton Smith has a nice little tale here about an aging man in a small village who decides to improve himself by enrolling in a Foundations program at Open University, to the envy and chagrin of his neighbors. Duncan McLean offers a play in brilliantly poor taste about a man trying to persuade a pal to sleep with his wife so that he can catch it on film and use it against her in a divorce proceeding. Other contributors include Janice Galloway, Alasdair Gray, among others. Angus Calder closes the collection with a meditation on Scottish writing that sort of brings it all into cultural/historical perspective that you wouldn't get anywhere else. So if you'd like to explore some fresh, edgy new Scottish writing, this is a fine introduction to several established writers as well as many who are new to these shores. [James DeRossitt]

Irene Dische. *Sad Strains of a Gay Waltz*. Metropolitan, 1997. 302 pp. $23.00.

I am pleased by the fact that this novel confirms Dische's ability to fuse comedy and sadness. This novel, like *Strange Traffic*, moves gracefully from the mysteries of existence to the "mundane" oddities of daily life. It is set in divided Germany, a place of dislocation. Benedikt Walter, a member of the German aristocracy, does not care about wealth or class. Nor does he worry about his place in the world. He, in fact, has little use for living things; he is interested in mathematical purities: "Nature, he concluded, was an experiment of grotesque complexity doomed to failure . . . He dreaded the hysterical colors of spring and the unintelligence of grass." He worships Einstein who, like other mathematicians and physicists, seems to prefer abstractions to bodily pleasures. We are told that Benedikt "had a shock catching a glimpse of himself in a mirror and realized he had an exterior; he identified himself with his work and not with the laurels or with the income that it earned, either."

Benedikt has AIDS, but he regards it as merely another unfortunate perversity or imperfection of the body. He treats his disease as another mere nuisance. He hates the feelings of despair and treats his disease as a theoretical axiom. Benedikt is, if you will, a kind of holy fool and when he places an ad in a personals column for a son, he gives his name and terminal condition.

Of course, Dische has the world close in on him. She introduces "others" who don't know what to make of his perverse behavior. She structures her novel as a kind of musical counterpoint. Einstein's ghost, who regularly appears to Benedikt, says to him: "Any strong emotion is like a tone of music; it makes memories along the entire range of one's history resonate. No tone exists by itself, there are no pure emotions." The novel becomes a "strange traffic," a work of changing tempo. Dische is able to move from "solo" thoughts of Benedikt to the frenzy of his "circle." And she allows Benedikt to unwillingly grow from unworldly robot to compassionate human being who is loved by his adopted son and wife.

Only a talented artist can compose a "gay waltz with sad strains," a tragic comedy of remarkable, lyrical "turnings." [Irving Malin]

Janice Eidus. *The Celibacy Club*. City Lights, 1997. 200 pp. Paper: $9.95.

Janice Eidus's second collection of nineteen comic short stories traffics in the myths and fairy tales, fantasies, and pop icons that constitute our "collective unconscious." Her characters—often disaffected, confused, bored, witty city dwellers—rely on mythic dreams to organize their lives and lend importance to their existence. In the opening story, "Elvis, Axl,and Me," a woman discovers Elvis hiding out as a Hasidic Jew in a Bronx deli, and they begin an affair—although she actually lusts after Axl Rose—imagining that he will be her true love after the tribulations of rock and roll stardom eventually force him to fake his own death. A screenwriter in "Making Love, Making Movies" envisions his adulteries as scenes from B-movie scripts, casting real people in character roles. Over several stories, Eidus's interest in the American psyche extends beyond media culture to examine our current fascination with self-improvement programs. While the title story's narrator investigates an unusual support group that encourages her to sublimate her sexual desire with rich desserts, other stories concern Barbie's publicity-seeking attempt at female bonding ("Barbie Goes to Group Therapy") and a woman who abandons herself to an obsessive romantic infatuation with exercise equipment ("Nautilus"). In spite of these wonderfully peculiar stories, whose quirky attitudes invite comparisons with T. C. Boyle's short fiction, this is an uneven collection. Sketches about a torrid liaison with actor-turned-aspiring-playwright James Dean("Jimmy Dean: My Kind of Guy") and a support group of women mourning their hairdressers' AIDS deaths ("Ladies with Long Hair") create provocative situations which the author fails to develop. Overall, however, Eidus's stories are bizarre, hip explorations of the allure of modern myth, written in a fresh, lean, fast-paced, urban prose. [Trey Strecker]

Emmanuel Carrère. *Class Trip*. Trans. Linda Coverdale. Metropolitan, 1997. 162 pp. $19.95.

Carrère's latest novel has been a popular success, both in the States and abroad (winner of the Prix Femina; rights sold in fourteen countries). And for good reason, perhaps. Though *Class Trip* echoes same understated, Kafkaesque anxiety that made his *The Mustache* popular in literary circles, Carrère distances the reader from the brutal consequences of a relentless self-conscious. We come to know the horror of this novel gradually; it floats underneath the text as Carrère subtly implies the gravity of what is known without revealing its face. *Class Trip* is terrifying not because what is suspected is acknowledged via a dramatic climax, but because suspicion becomes steadily actualized over the course of reading it.

Nicholas, a ten-year-old boy, is dropped off by his father at a skiing school to join his classmates. He is an introverted, small kid, a bedwetter who never stays over at anyone else's house. His father, a prosthetic limb salesman, is the harbinger of Nicholas's ills; he has left with Nicholas's suitcase in the trunk of the car after insisting upon driving him three hours to the school. Nicholas's pensive nature and social anxiousness appear to be informed by a volatile home life; the reader is left with as vague but eery a sense of the forces that run his family as Nicholas. What is apparent is the transcendence of the father's paranoia into Nicholas's consciousness.

Nicholas's gruesome daydreams constantly seek redemption for his father's tales of children who are kidnapped by organ hunters.

Because Carrère paces this book slowly, its horrible truths are left within the text—nothing is ever directly conveyed. A dark cloud subtly envelopes the reader as Carrère contextualizes Nicholas's unsettling anxieties. There is no startling conclusion, nor are there any banal moral epiphanies at the novel's end. Instead, the reader is left with the terrible realities of what has not been said. A finely crafted achievement. [Christopher Paddock]

Justine Lévy. *The Rendezvous*. Trans. Lydia Davis. Scribner's, 1997. 142 pp. $22.00.

Narrated by eighteen-year-old Louise as she sits in a café all day waiting for her unreliable mother to come to their rendezvous, Levy's wonderful first novel paints a poignant yet funny picture of strained mother-daughter relations. While she waits, Louise reminisces about her mother—an egotistical former fashion model whose self-destructive tendencies have led her to drugs and alcohol. Louise's painful memories alternate with comic interludes involving events in the café. In particular, Louise relives the most distressing episodes of her childhood and adolescence—her mother's overdose, her arrest for shoplifting and the ensuing prison visits, her drunken appearance at a parent-teacher meeting, and the series of male and female lovers who have passed through her life. Recurrent letdowns and disappointments give rise to a wide range of emotions on the part of the daughter, ranging from anger, jealousy, and resentment, to intense love and guilt at having abandonned her mother to live with her father. This tale of a mother unsuited for motherhood and of a daughter's unrequited love powerfully evokes the sense of tragic loss and the emotional impact of a difficult relationship. Lévy's conversational style and gift for dialogue have already led to favorable comparisons with prominent writers such as Françoise Sagan, Nathalie Sarraute, and Marguerite Duras. Readers interested in the subtle portrayal of complex family relationships will not be disappointed by this irresistible novel. [Susan Ireland]

Ana María Moix. *Dangerous Virtues*. Trans. Margaret E. W. Jones. Nebraska, 1997. 153pp. Paper: $10.00.

This translation marks the first appearance of Spanish writer Ana María Moix in English. *Dangerous Virtues* is a collection of five stories that alternates between interiorized semi-realism and Calvino-like fancy, exploring themes of isolation and disconnection between the protagonists and the world around them. By personifying the stock phrases and personalities of folk tales (doomed forever to repeat their well-told actions) in "Once Upon a Time," or by following a personified Problem's embarrassment at being selected to be but a sexual difficulty, Moix's metafictional cleverness overwhelms her more serious themes of entrapment and frustration. The other three stories of her collection, although inventive and even at points surreal, provide a much more favorable environment for Moix's explorations of estranged consciousness. Gazes and mirrors dominate these pieces, as protagonists substitute looks for words, seeking visual rather than verbal connection with the world. In the title story—which is told through layer upon layer of intricate indirection, making the recounted events as hermetically puzzling in the telling as they are in substance—two women who never speak but only gaze upon each other from a distance share a profound and exclusive communication. The final story, knowingly but nevertheless ambitiously entitled "The Dead," charts a hostess's growing psychic alienation from her husband, her dinner guests, and even at points, reality. In a flower-filled room with mirrored walls, she drifts about her party like a strange fish lost in Dali's aquarium: "At first, she doesn't see herself; she doesn't find herself among the faces, backs, and reflected flowers. She doesn't find her face in the surface that is getting more and more misty with smoke and diffuse colors . . ." Like her subjects, Moix's writing is intricate and self-consciously poised, but her poise conceals mysterious, self-mirroring depths. With *Dangerous Virtues,* Jones's graceful translation allows English readers their first glimpse into Moix's intricate and unsettling hall of mirrors. [Graham Fraser]

Fernanda Eberstadt. *When the Sons of Heaven Meet the Daughters of the Earth.* Knopf, 1997. 404 pp. $25.00.

When Isaac Hooker meets the Geblers, he is just a step away from homelessness. Like most people in the world that revolves around Dolly and Alfred's Aurora Foundation, he is an artist; but he learned to draw and paint in a New York City shelter, and his mental stability is questionable.

Once he's caught up in Aurora, it seems Isaac's troubles are over: he has a studio and a grant, and a much loved mistress in Dolly. She is an adoring, zaftig mother figure who uses the Foundation to hide her own deep unhappiness and sees Isaac as her salvation. For Isaac, art is the way to face demons; he pulls himself back from the brink of insanity by painting his childhood home again and again, then branching out into religious allegories such as the one that gives this novel its title: a representation of the mad, decadent times that preceded Noah's Flood and the serene seas that replaced them.

Fernanda Eberstadt's meticulously observed third novel is at its best and truly moving when it reveals not the pomp and pretension of the 1980s art world, but the pain of a middle-aged woman who has never been beautiful and who falls in love with a much younger man. Even philandering Alfred has some moments of astonishing pathos and revelation. It is difficult, however, to get a full sense of Isaac as a character; even when he is most lost his speaking voice belongs to an articulate critic, while his mental voice is more that of a wondering child. Though he becomes one of the art world's darlings, he never seems truly at home in this novel's crowded canvas. [Susann Cokal]

———

Michel Leiris. *Rules of the Game, Volume One: Scratches.* Trans. Lydia Davis. Johns Hopkins, 1997. 258 pp. Paper: $15.95; *Rules of the Game, Volume Two: Scraps.* Trans. Lydia Davis. Johns Hopkins, 1997. 244 pp. Paper: $15.95.

Surely the paperback publication of these two volumes of Leiris's autobiography *Rules of the Game* is a significant cultural event. The entire autobiography runs to four volumes; we can look forward to the remaining volumes which will be published in 1998.

Leiris is, with Blanchot and Bataille, one of the important French writers who, in part, influenced or anticipated the criticism of Cixous and Derrida and their American disciples. *Aurora*, his surrealist novel and *Days as Nights, Nights as Days*, his text of dreams, stand as two of the great works of modern French literature. Leiris understands that autobiography is an odd genre. Memories are, of course, selective and fictional because they transform the events they try to capture.

He structures his work in a fascinating way, recognizing that as a writer he was influenced by linguistic events. He muses: "One doesn't say . . . remusement but heuresement [happily, fortunately, luckily]. This word, which I had used until then without any awareness of its real meaning but simply as an interjection was related to hereux and the magical power of this relation suddenly inserted into a whole sequence of precise meanings."

Leiris establishes a "life of words," a magical transformation of the self through language. His sentence structure—which reminds me of the convoluted ones of Proust or late James—is one of the circling shades of perception of a "series of waves" (Leiris's phrase). And the sentence structure disolves clear-cut distinctions; one phrase gives birth to another. From the chapter "Alphabet," Leiris writes: "I look at the alphabet: a succession of symbols on pages or a small book that I study, a slender construction of white pages where various linear constructions stand out in black, constructions I must assimilate at all costs." He uses the present tense to suggest that his childhood fascination with language is filled with luminous power. But he is writing the sentence in the "real" present. Thus there is a kind of "game." "Past" and "present" seem to melt or dissolve. Leiris wants us to be seduced by the mental assimilations. He wants to draw us into his artwork. And he succeeds brilliantly; we follow his turns of phrase—as we do Proust's—and recognize that we are saved by linguistic structures, hypnotic arrangements of words.

I have no doubt that this translation captures the magical power of the French. Lydia Davis, one of our most interesting fiction writers, deserves our gratitude for her rendition of Leiris's "scratches." [Irving Malin]

———

Edward Sanders. *1968: A History in Verse*. Black Sparrow, 1997. 260 pp. Cloth: $25.00; paper: $14.00.

1968 saw the assassinations of Martin Luther King and RFK, My Lai and the Tet offensive, Soviet tanks in Prague and barricades in the streets of Paris, *Electric Ladyland* and *Cheap Thrills*, and much more. 1968 was also an important year for then-Yippie and rock star (with the Fugs) Ed Sanders, whose first novel, *Shards of God*, was inspired by the joint Chicago debacle that was the Yippie Festival of Life and the Democratic convention—events that figure prominently in *1968* as well.

If *Shards* presented itself as drug-laced, extraterrestrial "smut-porn" with Abbie Hoffman and Jerry Rubin cast as revolutionary epic goof-heroes, *1968*—like Sanders's 1995 verse biography *Chekhov*—reworks the events of that year in the light of ideas Sanders first propounded in *Investigative Poetry* (1976): that "poetry should again assume responsibility for the description of history" through "relentless pursuit of data."

The result is a verse history that is equal parts chronicle, personal anecdote, documented reportage, polemic, and paean. A powerful narrative of one year's "chrono-flow," *1968* takes its readers from Avenue A on the Lower East Side to "the halls of robokill" to remember and assess events large and now largely forgotten. Sanders may privilege the directly (prosaically) descriptive over the conventionally poetic, but his guns are locked on rock 'n' roll, and 1968 emerges as twelve months of Mardi Gras during the sacking of Rome, a love-in at a firefight with tracer rounds seen by strobe light. "How temporary it all was," Sanders observes of that year, beautiful and disheartening by turns, yet finally how unforgettable:

> . . . the tear gas grenades
> Allen and I sprinted through
> to get back to the Hotel Lincoln
>
> The sweet sound
> of Didi's wrist bell
> on Avenue A
> . . . .
> the struggle
> for freedom
> & a just, sharing world

In his introduction several years ago to John Clarke's *The End of This Side* (1979), Sanders called for "mythic poetry and National Epic." With *1968* he has answered his own call. [Brooke Horvath]

Debra DiBlasi. *Drought*. New Directions, 1997. 89 pp. Paper: $10.95.

Drought opens on "House" in June heat. It takes up barely half the page. Turn the page. There is "Woman," Willa, on verso, and on recto, an evaporating pond "Drowning in air." It is a film of a novella, stringing scene after scene with titled chapters, each filling less than a page and heaving sighs of white space.

The book is shaped to call attention to reading as an act of seeing. Similarly, DiBlasi's prose technique reminds the reader that she is looking, staring, at private moments. She moves the reader's eyes from "a wooden table" to "a misshapen tube of oil paint" to the woman's body, where "a brown strand of hair falls from her chignon onto her white neck where tiny beads of sweat gather, slide away, then gather again." With equal precision and objectivity, she describes the precise layout of the house, the milky eyes of a dead calf fetus, the couple in their bed, and the erection in the man's pants as he reads a romance novel, *Tropical Heat,* in the cab of his pickup truck.

Drought accumulates the images that tell the story of a man and a woman from June to September as a drought ravages their cattle ranch. In many ways, the story is an ordinary one. Plenty of people wait for rain and lose their farms. Still more couples argue. What's interesting about *Drought* is how it sustains the tension between the generic elements of tragedy and its precise manifestation in the mundane details of everyday life. [Monique Dufour]

Catherine Liu. *Oriental Girls Desire Romance.* Kaya, 1997. 354pp. Paper: $13.95.

The narrator of Catherine Liu's first novel, a smart, young Chinese-American woman drifting among the addictive excesses of 1980s New York City, feels trapped in "a perpetual state of internalized exile" and struggles to find her "bearings" by mapping out her multifaceted identity. Although its plot includes descriptions of her Ivy League education and a visit to Beijing, most of the novel unfolds against the clashing privilege and poverty of New York's glitzy nightclubs, its art world, and dingy strip joints. Structurally, each chapter focuses on specific people (her uncompromising Communist father and depressive mother, her teachers and lovers, drag queens, and artists) or experiences (her childhood dominated by the passive, subservient ideal of Chinese womanhood, her experimentation with drugs, a series of temporary office jobs, and a stint as a stripper) that the narrator regards as essential components of her identity. While nearly each of the novel's twelve discrete sections is strong enough to stand alone by using a fragmented, minimally connected text to represent her narrator's fragmented world, Liu creates a static, impressionistic portrait of a woman who appears less an active subject than a still-life object. Lia's inquiry into the complex nature of fantasy and desire, including the importance of addiction in American consumerism, the dynamics of the sex industry, and the politics and aesthetics of drag, clearly demonstrates her considerable promise as a young novelist and her aptitude as a critic of contemporary culture. [Trey Strecker]

Mario Benedetti. *Blood Pact and Other Stories.* Trans. Daniel Balderston, et al. Curbstone, 1997. 213 pp. Paper: $13.95.

This superb collection, nearly thirty stories spanning forty years, brings together tales of urban romance and political strife from the beloved Uruguayan writer. The fictions, most only a few pages long, are masterful in form, at once succinct and evocative. Many of the early tales from the forties and fifties (before the devastation of the countries totalitarian coup) are thematically reminiscent of Kafka—though with none of the weighty mood. Benedetti's language is light and playful (often in direct opposition of the plot), full of humorous generosity to the reader. The story opening the collection, "The Budget" is representational of those examining the bland menace of bureaucracy in urban life. A small government office is promised a new budget, but convoluted excuses and endless waiting prove more unbearable than the companionable monotony of their job. The longest story is the superb "The Other Side," narrated by a comical seventeen-year-old Uruguayan exiled on the other side of the river in Buenos Aires. Imprisoned and beaten in Montevideo for a minor political prank, upon release he flees across the border where he meets a whole community with tales of torture and despair. The last and title piece of the collection is a bittersweet narration on life coming to a close. Eighty-four-year-old Octavio, living with his daughter's family, refuses to speak, except to his little grandson. They have a blood pact: Octavio will tell his grandson a new story from the past everyday if the boy promises not to reveal that Granddad can actually speak. An apt story to close the collection, for Benedetti is that rare thing— a true storyteller. This is only the third of his many works to be translated into English, and it is a welcome occasion. [Andria Spencer]

Nicholas Delbanco. *Old Scores.* Warner Books, 1997. 271 pp. $24.00.

We know the story: the sixties; college; the professor, Paul Ballard, and the student he becomes involved with, Elizabeth Sieverdsen; the brief flaring of their love, its near predictable failure. It was the sixties, after all, and too many mistook indulgence for love. And its sequel: to revisit, with the cold eye of experience and time, that youthful evanescence. Or, even worse, to come together again years later, marked by life, particularly divorce, and think that this time . . .

It is the story of *Old Scores* but not the one Nicholas Delbanco tells. Love is either more than we will ever understand or less than, much less than, we desire, but it is everything Paul and Elizabeth desire, all they need to understand, even if they do not know it at the time. Despite years apart, their love marks them forever, alters their lives. Delbanco gives us here an Abelard and Heloise for our time, and if his comparison, of necessity, at first diminishes, it also enlarges; Paul and Elizabeth are legitimate heirs. It is a characteristic modernist method to hold the present up against the past, and Delbanco has employed it frequently; in *Small Rain,* for example, a version of Tristan and Isolde, or *The Martlet's Tale,* an account of the prodigal son. Guy Davenport argues that modernism was determined by the discovery of the specific, and Delbanco's detail is always, Thomas Lask notes, "dense, Euclidean in its ability to focus on a particular point of time and space." Here and elsewhere, he keeps faith with the still uncompleted modernist project: his impulse utopian, standards absolute, measure the particular. We may characterize his writing at every point in this complex and difficult enterprise by its acute intelligence; by its compassion, particularly for the old; and, first and last, by its language, precise, exact. *Old Scores* is characteristic. [Robert Buckeye]

Kathleen Wheeler. *A Guide to Twentieth-Century Women Novelists.* Blackwell Publishers, 1997. 442 pp. $65.00.

Perhaps what's most remarkable about this ambitious, encyclopedic book is that Wheeler wrote all of it, and in so doing demonstrates a wide range of reading and taste. But as with almost all such guides, there are some serious omissions, as well as some welcome recognitions. Included for full entries are such writers as Jane Bowles, Christine Brooke-Rose, Eva Figes, Ann Quin, and Elizabeth Smart—in other words, not the usuals. Not included, however, are, among others, Brigid Brophy (who gets a half-sentence mention), Joanna Scott, and Janice Galloway—perhaps not household names, but better to have these than some who *are* present—Harper Lee, for instance. Despite the book's title, it is limited to writers in English rather than covering the world, though there is a twenty-page chapter on women from other parts of the world. So, while the book is uneven in a number of ways, the unevenness is largely a result of the genre itself. Put this volume together with a few others of its type, and you will have a true guide that covers almost everyone. [John O'Brien]

Stepan Chapman. *The Troika.* Ministry of Whimsy, 1997. 251 pp. Paper: $14.99.

Consider this an E-ticket ride and you'll walk away smiling for being whipped through surprising twists and loops—no final payoff, but that's okay: the point's the journey, not the destination. If you don't like wild, disorienting rides, however, then you'd best stay away from such mad, spinning teacups as *The Troika*. Fittingly, chapter one opens with a quote from Lewis Carroll's *Alice's Adventures in Wonderland*. There are three protagonists here: the mother (an old Mexican woman), the father (a Jeep), and the daughter (a brontosaur). They travel across the desert for eons. They travel to the future. They all switch roles (the mother becomes a brontosaur, for example). Like *Alice,* it seems like nonsense, but the absurd fantasy is so beautifully rendered in detail, you hang on through the ride. Also like *Alice,* there seems to be some grand allegorical significance to it all, but no single interpretation satisfies: *The Troika's* four section headings—"a family ill-

ness," "relapse," "signs of recovery," and "the cure"—indicate this is a journey through madness; the surreal landscapes of isolation are reminiscent
of *Waiting for Godot*; violations of form and sliding identities are blatantly
deconstructionist; the themes of fragmented family and man-as-machine
are clearly postmodern. But to what end? We are left with no rational conclusion, which seems to be Chapman's intent. "Can I tell you a Zen koan
before I go?" Chapman writes in the final pages. As with koans, linear
thinking fails when searching for answers in this novel. *The Troika* seems
designed to reveal the traps inherent in logical thought and analysis. In the
end, "Nothing had been decided, but everything was solved." [Grant Hier]

Howard McCord. *The Man Who Walked to the Moon*. McPherson, 1997. 123
pp. $18.00.

Near the end of Howard McCord's novella, the narrator says his story is "a
veritable account of a lucid insanity of long duration, an oblique confession,
an apologia pro vita sua, a fantasy spun in a cold winter, or out of night."
This serves as an apt description of a tightly squeezed, haunting tale told
primarily by William Gaspar, a recluse whose voice sounds at times like
those of Poe's insane, criminal storytellers. Paul Bowles's gruesome story
"Doña Faustina" also comes to mind. Gaspar says at one point, well into the
book, that he has killed 127 people. Only gradually, though, do we begin to
learn of the narrator's vocation (besides walking, that is). This, in fact, is
what in part creates the suspense. What is this man doing in the desolate
regions of Nevada, obsessively climbing on a mountain called the Moon? He
reveals, little by little, his obsession with guns. And we realize that he himself is now being hunted down on the mountain, by a "Palug cat," a hunter
who seems to be a henchman of a hag-spirit-woman called Cerridwen whom
he first met during a crisis as a soldier in the Korean War. Realism is
gradually eroded by the delusions of a deranged mind. McCord skillfully
portrays both the psychological terrain of his assassin-narrator and the
physical terrain of the mountain. As in many of Cormac McCarthy's novels,
the natural world seems completely indifferent to what we call moral con-
siderations. A work of great imaginative force and sharp, penetrating
prose, *The Man Who Walked to the Moon* leaves the reader on edge for days,
thinking how many William Gaspars might be loose in the world. [Allen
Hibbard]

Kathy S. Leonard, ed. and trans. *Cruel Fictions, Cruel Realities: Short Stories by Latin American Women Writers*. Latin American Literary Review
Press, 1997. 131 pp. Paper: $15.95.

This new fiction anthology features nineteen excellent stories by twelve
South American women writers. As the title suggests, cruelty is the control-
ling passion that links these works, although some of the tales are tinged

with the magic realism and black humor so frequently encountered in contemporary Latin American literature.

Gilda Holst Molestina of Ecuador, for example, provides "The Competition," a wonderful story in which a sadistic professor who delights in embarrassing students is reduced to a cowering fool. Similarly, Argentinean author Ana María Shua's "A Profession Like Any Other" is an object lesson (worthy of Monty Python) in the dangers of angering one's dentist.

A number of stories, such as "Bus Stop" by Chilean writer María Eugenia Lorenzini, reveal the often dreary, sometimes harsh and empty lives of so many South American women, while others—Velia Calvimonte's "Coati 1950" and Colombian author, Nayla Chehade Durán's "The Vigil"— expose the raw, senseless violence too typical in parts of Latin America. Also, Kathy S. Leonard's biographical sketches and editorial comments provide a helpful framework for approaching these stories.

For readers new to South American fiction, *Cruel Fictions, Cruel Realities* is a strong starting point. As Ana María Shua's thoughtful forward illustrates, even though the voices throughout are female, these stories transcend genders issues, focusing instead on entertaining, thought-provoking tales of human existence. Those familiar with Latino literature will find this anthology an enjoyable addition. [Robert Headley]

Jonathan Yardley. *Misfit: The Strange Life of Frederick Exley*. Random House, 1997. 255 pp. $25.00.

This book is an embarrassment. Even the author's photo is awful, though perhaps it reveals something of the problem with the book; in it, Yardley's expression seems to be saying: "We never sit with our elbows on the table, now do we? No, no, no! This just won't do. Mother would die if she saw those elbows." The word for this is . . . proper? unctuous? No. The word is *prissy*. That's it. Yardley's photo speaks of prissiness.

The book has no index, which is a true feat of the imagination for a biography. How does Random House publish a biography that has no index? Are Yardley's reviews in the *Washington Post* so important that they let him get away with this laziness? Apparently.

Fine. No index. But then one begins to read the deadly book itself and discovers that there are no footnotes! Just what was Yardley's method in compiling this "biography"? Well, he seems to have gotten all of his information from several people and then recorded what they had to say with little or no attempt at judging their accuracy. Had he footnoted, it seems as though he may have had to put quotes around everything in the book or have had footnote numbers at the end of every paragraph to indicate which source had filled him in on this particular subject.

And finally. The style of writing is that found in the worst of biographies. Exley is called "Fred" throughout the book, anecdotes are told in winsome, snappy ways, and vast generalities about life and man stick to almost every page. All that is absent is anything remotely resembling a decent biography of Frederick Exley.

I can't think of anyone more ill-equipped to write this biography than Yardley. But then I have a hard time thinking of anyone more ill-equipped than Yardley to be an in-house reviewer for the *Post* (just how do they pick these people? are IQ tests ever administered? writing tests? anything?). Why did Yardley even bother? [John O'Brien]

———————

Ficke Schoots. *Passer en douce à la douane: L'ecriture minimaliste de Minuit: Deville, Echenoz, Redonnet et Toussaint.* Rodolpi B.V. (Amsterdam and Atlanta), 1997. 234 pp. No price listed.

It's a tough job, but someone has to do it—impose some sort of order on what continues to be a near manic production of high-quality literary novels in France. In this study of four contemporary French novelists—Patrick Deville, Jean Echenoz, Marie Redonnet, and Jean-Philippe Toussaint—Fieke Schoots takes an excellent stab at it. It is not the least quality of this book that Schoots recognizes up front the perilousness of the classificatory enterprise: the four novelists were selected for their having been published by the Editions de Minuit (home of Beckett, and of the Nouveau Roman) during the 1980s and for having been, roughly, included in Minuit's advertising campaign of "impassible" authors. The group does not constitute a "movement"; skillfully, Schoots points up their commonalities without neglecting their differences to offer a clear and cogent description of their "minimalist" appurtenances. In contrast to the "reductions" of American minimalism in art, music, and literature, Schoots defines the minimalism of these four French novelists as a reexploration of the multiple resources of language and narration. For Schoots, the French minimalist story is neither "simple [nor] impoverished: it is characterized by the attention directed to the materials of novelistic writing, by the decomposition of novelistic procedures and by the precision with which the language is manipulated" (my translation from the French). Schoots's criticism—intelligent, circumspect and clearly organized—is a model of the genre: it makes you want to rush to the novels themselves, not to judge the analysis but to enjoy them as much as the critic obviously has. Schoots's final discussion of the place of the minimalist current in terms of succession to the Nouveau (Nouveau) Roman and postmodernist thought is perhaps less successful, but that is undoubtedly owing to the nebulousness of the terms "modern," "modernist," "postmodern," "postmodernist" themselves. In one sense, Schoots's taxonimy is a drop in the bucket, but this bucket, in general, could use lots more drops like this. [Renée Kingcaid]

———————

New and Recommended in Paperback

• Michel Tournier. *The Four Wisemen.* Trans. Ralph Manheim. Johns Hopkins, 255 pp. $14.95. This is the third Tournier novel to be reprinted by Johns Hopkins.

• Gordon Lish. *Dear Mr. Capote.* Four Walls Eight Windows, 251 pp. $12.95. Lish as editor, as promoter, as self-promoter, as favorite person to bash, as any number of things has gotten in the way of an appreciation of his fiction.

• Miguel de Cervantes. *Don Quijote.* Trans. Burton Raffel. Norton, 733 pp. $18.00. A very solid new translation, together with an informative introduction.

School of Stupidity

Once again, there has been a great deal of competition for entrance into the School. After much wrangling and exchange of nasty words, Michiko Kakutani, the daily reviewer for the *New York Times,* has been awarded entrance. I should point out that there was no disagreement about whether she deserved the award; rather, the disagreement was whether it should be awarded for Lifetime Achievement or for a particular act of stupidity. Some members of the committee argued that if Kakutani doesn't deserve a Lifetime Achievement award, then who ever will? Others felt that the committee should focus on particular acts. The latter were victorious.

On September 28, 1997, in the *New York Times* Magazine, Kakutani published an article entitled "Never-Ending Saga," devoted to the subject of the future of writing, particularly hypertext. Clear throughout the piece is the fact that she really understands little about the subject and its cultural ramifications, almost as though she had been overhearing folks talk in the washroom and had taken scattered notes on the subject. Fine, fine, we can't expect too much from the *Times* culture and book staff. But she came into her own halfway through the piece in two telling and incredibly stupid remarks.

First, she writes, "The repudiation of linearity, of course, is nothing new. Laurence Sterne shattered the traditional narrative in 'Tristram Shandy' back in the 18th century . . ." Well, how is it possible to shatter the "traditional narrative" when one is writing at the beginning of the origins of the novel as a form? Just what *tradition* might she be making reference to? Cervantes? Homer? Her remark is truly lovely because she is very, very suspicious about all of this "new," a-historical writing, that it may be destroying the very foundation of the Western World!!! That Western World she is so dedicated to that she doesn't appear to know that Sterne could not be shattering something that had not yet been established.

Second—and this is what really got her the award—she completes the sentence that is cited in the previous paragraph by saying, "and 20th-century novelists—from Faulkner and Eliot through Rushdie and DeLillo—have made fragmentation a cornerstone of their art." What???? Who??? The novelist T. S. Eliot??? Is this what the daily reviewer for the *Times* just said? T. S. Eliot???!!!!

I should point out here that the committee recognized that the fact checkers at the *Times* are rather bright, and that they most likely recognized the error and decided to let it go. And quite likely, the committee felt,

James "I-Don't-Like-Hard-Books" Atlas, editor at the Magazine, read the piece but did *not* recognize the error.

In conclusion, we would like to congratulate Ms. Kakutani. We would also like to ask how she ever got her job.

Books Received

Albert, Laurie. *The Price of Land in Shelby.* New England, 1997. Paper: $14.95. (F)

Appel, Allan. *High Holiday Sutra.* Coffee House, 1997. Paper: $13.95. (F)

Asturias, Miguel Angel. *The Mirror of Lida Sal: Tales Based on Mayan Myths and Guatemalan Legends.* Latin American Literary Review Press, 1997. Paper: $14.95. (F)

Babb, Sanora. *Cry of the Tinamou.* Nebraska, 1997. Paper: $16.95. (F)

Bacho, Peter. *Dark Blue Suit and Other Stories.* Washington, 1997. Cloth: $30.00; paper: $16.95. (F)

Barone, Dennis. *Echoes.* Potes and Poets, 1997. Paper: $14.00. (F)

Bass, Rick. *The Sky, the Stars, the Wilderness.* Houghton Mifflin, 1997. $23.00. (F)

Bauer, Douglas. *The Book of Famous Iowans.* Henry Holt, 1997. $25.00. (F)

Beard, Jo Ann. *The Boys of My Youth.* Little, Brown, 1998. $22.95. (F)

Bellen, Martine, Lee Smith, and Bradford Morrow, eds. *Conjunctions:29: Tributes: American Writers on American Writers.* Bard, 1997. Paper: $12.00. (NF)

Bello, Andrés. *Selected Writings of Andrés Bello.* Ed. Iván Jaksić. Trans. Frances M. Lopez Morillas. Oxford, 1997. $30.00. (NF)

Berry, R. M. *Leonardo's Horse.* FC2, 1997. Paper: $13.95. (F)

Bezzerides, A. I. *Thieves' Market.* California, 1997. Paper: $12.95. (F)

Bingham, Robert. *Pure Slaughter Value.* Doubleday, 1997. $21.95. (F)

Birkett, Jennifer and James Kearns. *A Guide to French Literature: From Early Modern to Postmodern.* St. Martin's, 1997. $59.95. (NF)

Bolton, Isabel. *New York Mosaic.* Steerforth, 1997. $35.00. (F)

Boyle, T. C. *Riven Rock.* Viking, 1998. $24.95. (F)

Brodkey, Harold. *The Runaway Soul.* Owl, 1997. Paper: $17.00. (F)

Brodkey, Harold. *This Wild Darkness.* Owl, 1997. Paper: $12.95. (F)

Brodkey, Harold. *The World Is the Home of Love and Death.* Owl, 1997. $25.00. (F)

Brookner, Anita. *Altered States.* Random House, 1996. $23.00. (F)

Brussig, Thomas. *Heroes Like Us.* Trans. John Brownjohn. Farrar, Straus & Giroux, 1997. $23.00. (F)

Buechner, Frederick. *On the Road with the Archangel.* Harper San Francisco, 1997. $16.00. (F)

Burgin, Richard. *Fear of Blue Skies.* Johns Hopkins, 1997. $19.95. (F)

Burke, Carolyn. *Becoming Modern: The Life of Mina Loy.* California, 1997. Paper: $18.95. (NF)

Byatt, A. S. *The Djinn in the Nightingale's Eye.* Random House, 1997. $20.00. (F)

Calvino, Italo, ed. *Fanastic Tales: Visionary and Everyday.* Pantheon, 1997. $30.00. (F)

Charlebois, Lucile C. *Understanding Camilo José Cela.* South Carolina, 1997. No Price Given. (NF)

Clark, Laverne Harrell. *Keepers of the Earth*. Cinco Puntos, 1997. Paper: $14.95. (F)

Clark, Tom. *Empire of the Skin*. Black Sparrow, 1997. Cloth: $27.50; paper: $15.00. (P)

Coldsmith, Don. *Medicine Hat*. Oklahoma, 1997. $21.00. (NF)

Cosic, Bora. *My Family's Role in the World Revolution*. Trans. Ann Clymer Bigelow. Northwestern, 1997. Paper: $16.95. (F)

Costello, Bonnie, ed. *The Selected Letters of Marianne Moore*. Knopf, 1997. $35.00. (NF)

Cox, Elizabeth. *Night Talk*. Graywolf, 1997. $23.95. (F)

Craft, Linda J. *Novels of Testimony and Resistance from Central America*. Florida, 1997. $39.95. (NF)

Dakron, Ron. *Hammers*. Black Heron, 1997. $22.95. (F)

Davenport, Guy. *Twelve Stories*. Counterpoint, 1997. Paper: $14.00. (F)

Davies, Stevie. *Four Dreamers and Emily*. St. Martin's, 1997. $21.95. (F)

Dische, Irene. *Strange Traffic*. Owl, 1997. Paper: $12.00. (F)

D'Lugo, Carol Clark. *The Fragmented Novel in Mexico: The Politics of Form*. Texas, 1997. Hardback: $40.00; paper: $17.95. (NF)

Echevarría, Roberto González, ed. *The Oxford Book of Latin American Short Stories*. Oxford, 1997. $30.00. (F)

Eisenberg, Deborah. *All Around Atlantis*. Farrar, Straus & Giroux, 1997. $23.00. (F)

Eltit, Diamela. *E. Luminata*. Trans. Ronald Christ. Lumen, 1997. Paper: $15.00. (F)

Evenson, Brian. *The Din of Celestial Birds*. Wordcraft, 1997. Paper: $10.95. (F)

Faschinger, Lilian. *Magdalena the Sinner*. Trans. Edna McCown. HarperCollins, 1997. $23.00. (F)

Frank, Steven J. *The Uncertainty Principle*. Permeable, 1997. Paper: $12.00. (F)

Frank, Thaisa. *Sleeping in Velvet*. Black Sparrow, 1997. Cloth: $27.50; paper: $15.00. (F)

Freeman, Jr., Castle. *Judgment Hill*. New England, 1997. $24.95. (F)

Freud, Sigmund. *Writing on Art and Literature*. Ed. James Strachey. Forward by Neil Hertz. Stanford, 1997. $45.00. (NF)

Fuentes, Carlos. *The Crystal Frontier*. Trans. Alfred Mac Adam. Farrar, Straus & Giroux, 1997. $23.00. (F)

———. *The Old Gringo*. Trans. Margaret Sayers Peden. Farrar, Straus & Giroux. Paper: $11.00. (F)

Fyfe, Mark. *Asher*. Marion Boyars, 1997. $18.95. (F)

Galdós, Benito Pérez. *Nazarin*. Latin American Literary Review Press, 1997. Paper: $15.95. (F)

Gardiol, Rita, ed. and trans. *The Silver Candelabra and Other Stories: A Century of Jewish Argentine Literature*. Latin American Literary Review Press, 1997. Paper: $16.95. (F)

Giardinelli, Mempo. *Sultry Moon*. Trans. Patricia J. Duncan. Latin American Review Press, 1998. Paper: $13.95. (F)

Giroux, Robert, ed. *Bernard Malamud: The Complete Stories*. Farrar, Straus & Giroux, 1997. $35.00. (F)

Godden, Rumer. *Cromartie V. The God Shiva Acting through the Government of India*. William Morrow, 1997. $22.00. (F)

Gonzalez, Alexander G., ed. *Modern Irish Writers: A Bio-Critical Sourcebook*. Greenwood, 1997. $95.00. (NF)

Gordon, Karen Elizabeth. *Torn Wings and Faux Pas*. Pantheon, 1997. $23.00. (NF)

Grossman, Lev. *Warp*. St. Martin's, 1997. Paper: $12.95. (F)

Gummerman, Jay. *Chez Chance*. California, 1997. Paper: $10.95. (F)

Gwaltney, Don. *The Bandit Joaquin*. Apple Core, 1997. $14.95. (F)

Harrison, M. John. *Signs of Life*. St. Martin's, 1997. $21.95. (F)

Hartman, Geoffrey H. *The Fateful Question of Culture*. Columbia, 1997. $22.50. (NF)

Harvey, Robert and Helène Volat. *Marguerite Duras: A Bio-Bibliography*. Greenwood, 1997. $69.50. (NF)

Herbert, Rosemary and Tony Hillerman, eds. *The Oxford Book of American Detective Stories*. Oxford, 1997. $30.00. (F)

Hester, Katherine L. *Eggs for Young America*. New England, 1997. $19.95. (F)

Hindus, Milton, ed. *Selected Letters of Charles Reznikoff, 1917-1976*. Black Sparrow, 1997. Cloth: $27.50; paper: $17.50. (NF)

Howard, Maureen. *A Lover's Almanac*. Viking, 1998. No Price Given. (F)

Hustvedt, Siri. *The Enchantment of Lily Dahl*. Henry Holt, 1997. Paper: $12.00. (F)

J., Angelica. *Fermentation*. Grove/Atlantic, 1997. $20.00. (F)

Jacobs, Harvey. *American Goliath*. St. Martin's, 1997. $24.95. (F)

James, Lily. *The Great Taste of Straight People*. FC2, 1997. Paper: $8.95. (F)

Jenkins, Robin. *Willie Hogg*. Polygon, No Price Given. (F)

Jones, Idwal. *The Vineyard*. California, 1997. Paper: $12.95. (F)

Jones, Louis B. *California's Over*. Pantheon, 1997. 24.00. (F)

Kadare, Ismail. *The File on H*. Arcade, 1998. $21.95. (F)

Kay, Terry. *The Runaway*. William Morrow, 1997. $24.00. (F)

Kemp, Sandra, Charlotte Mitchell, and David Trotter, eds. *Edwardian Fiction: An Oxford Companion*. Oxford, 1997. $39.95. (NF)

Kennedy, Thomas E. *Drive, Dive, Dance, and Fight*. UMKC, 1997. Paper: $14.95. (F)

Kincaid, Jamaica. *My Brother*. Farrar, Straus & Giroux. $19.00. (F)

Koning, Hans. *Pursuit of a Woman on the Hinge of History*. Brookline, 1997. Paper: $15.95. (F)

Köpf, Gerhard. *Innerfar and Bluff: Two Novels*. Trans. Leslie Willson. Camden House, 1997. Paper: $26.00.

Krusoe, Jim. *Blood Lake and Other Stories*. Boaz, 1997. $18.50. (F)

Langbaum, Robert. *Thomas Hardy in Our Time*. St. Martin's, Paper: $18.95. (NF)

Lee, Valerie. *Granny Midwives and Black Women Writers*. Routledge, 1997. Hardcover: $59.95; paper: $16.95. (NF)

Legge, Gordon. *In Between Talking About the Football*. Polygon, 1997. No Price Given. (F)

Lifshin, Lyn. *Cold Comfort: Selected Poems 1970-1996*. Black Sparrow,

1997. Cloth: $25.00; paper:$14.00. (P)

Lish, Gordon. *Self-Imitation of Myself.* Four Walls Eight Windows, 1997. $22.00. (F)

Locklin, Gerald. *Charles Bukowski: A Sure Bet.* Water Row, 1995. No Price Given. (NF)

Loriga, Ray. *My Brother's Gun.* Trans. Kristina Cordero. St. Martin's, 1997. $18.95. (F)

Lovecraft, H. P. *Tales of H. P. Lovecraft.* Intro. Joyce Carol Oates. Ecco, 1997. $23.00. (F)

Machado de Assis, Joaquim Maria. *Dom Casmurro.* Trans. John Gledson. Oxford, 1997. $25.00. (F)

MacLaverty, Bernard. *Grace Notes.* Norton, 1997. $23.00. (F)

Macintyre, Ben. *The Napoleon of Crime: The Life and Times of Adam Worth, Master Thief.* Farrar, Straus & Giroux, 1997. $24.00. (NF)

Mann, Thomas. *Six Early Stories.* Trans. Peter Constantine. Sun & Moon, 1997. $22.95. (F)

Marías, Javier. *Tomorrow In the Battle Think On Me.* Trans. Margaret Jull Costa. Harcourt Brace, 1997. $24.00. (F)

Martin, Stephen-Paul. *Not Quite Fiction.* Vatic Hum, 1997. Paper: $8.95. (F)

Mayo, Wendell. *Centaur of the North.* Arte Público, 1996. Paper: $11.95. (F)

Mazza, Cris. *Fomer Virgin.* FC2, 1997. Paper: $11.95. (F)

McLaughlin, Lissa. *The Grouper.* Avec, 1997. Paper: $8.95. (F)

Melo, Patrícia. *The Killer.* Trans. Clifford E. Landers. Ecco, 1997. $23.00. (F)

Metcalf, Paul. *Collected Works, Volume Three: 1987-1997.* Coffee House, 1997. $35.00. (F, NF, P)

Michaux, Henri. *Tent Posts.* Bilingual edition. Trans. Lynn Hoggard. Green Integer 4, 1997. Paper: $10.95. (F)

Mississippi Review: Barry Hannah Special. Volume 25, number 3. 1997.

Mitgutsch, Anna. *Lover, Traitor: A Jerusalem Story.* Trans. Roslyn Theobald. Metropolitan, 1997. $23.00. (F)

Moody, Rick and Darcey Steinke, eds. *Joyful Noise: The New Testament Revisited.* Little, Brown, 1997. $23.95. (NF)

Moorcock, Michael. *The War Amongst the Angels.* Dell, 1997. $24.00. (F)

Morgan, Bill. *The Beat Generation in New York: A Walking Tour of Jack Kerouac's City.* City Lights, 1997. Paper: $12.95. (NF)

Morrison, Toni. *Paradise.* Knopf, 1998. $25.00. (F)

Mulligan, John. *Shopping Cart Soldiers.* Curbstone, 1997. $22.95. (F)

Nooteboom, Cees. *The Captain of the Butterflies.* Trans. Leonard Nathan and Herlinde Spahr. Sun & Moon, 1997. Paper: $11.95. (P)

Olson, Charles. *Collected Prose.* Ed. Donald Allen and Benjamin Friedlander. Intro. Robert Creeley. California, 1997. Cloth: $50.00; paper: $19.95. (NF)

O'Rourke, William. *Campaign American '96: The View from the Couch.* Marlowe, 1997. $24.95. (NF)

Owomoyela, Oyekan. *Yoruba Trickster Tales.* Nebraska, 1997. Cloth: $40.00; paper: $15.00. (F)

Pamuk, Orhan. *The New Life.* Trans. Güneli Gün. Farrar, Straus & Giroux,

1997. $24.00. (F)

Pelevin, Victor. *The Blue Lantern*. Trans. Andrew Bromfield. New Directions, 1997. $22.95. (F)

Polito, Robert, ed. *Crime Novels: American Noir of the 1930s & 40s*. The Library of America, 1997. $35.00. (F)

Polito, Robert, ed. *Crime Novels: American Noir of the 1950s*. The Library of America, 1997. $35.00. (F)

Popov, Evgeny. *Merry-Making in Old Russia and Other Stories*. Northwestern, 1997. Paper: $17.95. (F)

Quinn, Daniel. *My Ishmael: A Sequel*. Bantam, 1997. $23.95. (F)

—— and Tom Whalen. *A Newcomer's Guide to the Afterlife*. Bantam, 1997. $22.95. (F)

Radway, Janice A. *A Feeling for Books: The Book-of-the-Month Club, Literary Taste, and Middle-Class Desire*. Chapel Hill, 1997. $29.95 (NF)

Ramos, Luis Arturo. *Within These Walls*. Trans. Samuel A. Zimmerman. Latin American Literary Review Press, 1997. Paper: $15.95. (F)

Rilke, Ranier Maria. *The Rose Window and Other Verse: An Illustrated Selection*. Selected and Illustrated by Ferris Cook. Little, Brown. $22.95. (P)

Robinson, Marilynne. *Housekeeping*. Noonday, 1997. Paper: $11.00. (F)

Roche, Maurice. *Grand humoresque Opus 27*. Editions du Seuil, 1997. No Price Given. (F)

Rosario, Vernon A. *The Erotic Imagination: French Histories of Perversity*. Oxford, 1997. $27.50. (NF)

Roubaud, Jacques. *Le Chevalier Silence: Une Aventure Des Temps Aventureux*. Gallimard, 1997. No Price Given. (F)

Salvayre, Lydic. *The Award*. Trans. Jane Davey. Four Walls Eight Windows, 1997. $18.00. (F)

Sanford, John. *Intruders in Paradise*. Illinois, 1997. $26.95. (F)

Schulze, Ingo. *33 Moments of Happiness*. Trans. John E. Woods. Knopf, 1998. $23.00. (F)

Searle, Elizabeth. *A Four-sided Bed*. Graywolf, 1998. Paper: $14.95. (F)

Shields, Carol. *Larry's Party*. Viking, 1997. $23.95. (F)

Simpson, Mona. *A Regular Guy*. Vintage, 1997. Paper: $13.00. (F)

Singal, Daniel J. *William Faulkner: The Making of a Modernist*. Chapel Hill, 1997. $29.95. (NF)

Singer, Isaac Bashevis. *Love and Exile: An Autobiographical Trilogy*. Noonday, 1997. Paper: $16.00. (NF)

Sleem, Patty. *Back in Time*. Prep, 1997. Paper: $16.00. (F)

Smith, Lawrence R. *The Map of Who We Are*. Oklahoma, 1997. $24.00. (F)

Smith, Patricia Juliana, ed. *Lesbian Panic: Homoeroticism in Modern British Women's Fiction*. Columbia, 1997. Cloth: $49.50; paper: $16.50. (NF)

Spark, Muriel. *Open to the Public*. New Directions, 1997. $24.95. (F)

Stavans, Ilan, ed. *The Oxford Book of Latin American Essays*. Oxford, 1997. $35.00. (NF)

Steinberg, Alan. *Cry of the Leopard*. St. Martin's, 1997. $21.95. (F)

Steinke, Darcey. *Jesus Saves*. Atlantic Monthly, 1997. $23.00. (F)

Teleky, Richard. *Hungarian Rhapsodies: Essays on Ethnicity, Identity, and Culture*. Washington, 1997. Paper: $18.95. (NF)

Tesich, Nadja. *Native Land.* Brookline, 1997. Paper: $15.95. (F)

Thomas, Ruth. *Sea Monster Tatoo and Other Stories.* Polygon, 1997. No Price Given. (F)

Torrington, Jeff. *The Devil's Carousel.* Harcourt Brace, 1996. $23.00. (F)

Treadwell, Elizabeth. *Eleanor Ramsey: The Queen of Cups.* San Francisco State, 1997. Paper: $7.00. (F)

Updike, John. *Toward the End of Time.* Knopf, 1997. $25.00. (F)

Urquhart, Jane. *The Underpainter.* Viking, $22.95. (F)

Webb, Don. *Stealing My Rules.* Cyber-Psychos AOD, 1997. (F)

Weinstein, Arnold. *Red Eye of Love.* Afterword by John Guare. Sun & Moon, 1997. Paper: $10.95. (F)

Williams, Niall. *Four Letters of Love.* Farrar, Straus & Giroux, 1997. $23.00. (F)

Wolf, Christa. *Parting from Phantoms: Selected Writings, 1990-1994.* Trans. and Annotated. Jan Van Heurck. Chicago, 1997. $24.95. (NF)

Wolff, Tobias. *The Night in Question.* Vintage, 1997. Paper: $12.00. (F)

Wongar, B. *Raki.* Marion Boyars, 1997. $25.95. (F)

The Wormwood Review: 143. Gerald Locklin's Chapbook: The Last Round-Up. Volume 36, number 3. 1996. $4.00. (P)

Yamashita, Karen Tei. *Tropic of Orange.* Coffee House, 1997. Paper: $14.95. (F)

Yoder, John Howard. *For the Nations.* Eerdmans, 1997. Paper: $28.00. (NF)

Translators

Ieva S. Celle is a Ph.D. candidiate in the Department of Slavic Languages at Brown University. She has translated Edvins Liepins's novel *Riga and the Automobile* and stories by Vizma Belsevica, Alberts Bels, and Imants Ziedonis.

Franceska Kirke was born in Rīga, Latvia, in 1953. In 1972 she attended Jānis Rozentāls School of Art in Rīga and in 1978 the Latvian Academy of Arts. Her paintings have been exhibited across Europe and America.

Rita Laima Krieviņa (née Rumpeters, 1960) spent the first twenty-two years of her life in the suburbs of New Jersey and New York City. In 1982 Krieviņa moved to Latvia, at that time a Soviet Socialist Republic, and has lived there since. Krieviņa has had three children's books published in Latvia: her translation of and illustrations for Jaime de Angulo's *Indiāņu teikas* (Indian Tales, 1991) and illustrations for Jaan Kaplinski's *Kas ko ēd* (Who Eats What, 1993) and for *Kaķis lēca smēdē* (The Cat Jumped in the Smithy, 1994), a collection of Latvian children's counting rhymes. Krieviņa's illustrations for her ABC book won the VAGA publishing house's Green Tail Award in 1995. Krievina has worked for the *Baltic Observer* and the *Baltic Times* as culture editor, writing about life and people in post-Soviet Latvia. She presently works for the Delegation of the European Commission in Latvia, where she is keeping track of Latvia's EU preaccessions progress.

Iven Lešinska was born in Rīga and studied at the University of Latvia, Ohio State University, the University of Colorado, and the University of Stockholm. She has translated a number of contemporary Latvian poets into English and the poetry of T. S. Eliot, Allen Ginsberg, Ezra Pound, and Seamus Heaney, among others, into Latvian. She is currently the editor of the magazine *Rīgas Laiks*.

Sarma Muižnieks Liepiņš was born in Kalamazoo, Michigan, in 1960. *Izģērbies,* her first collection of poetry, was published in 1980. Subsequently her poems and essays have been published in periodicals in the US, Canada, Australia, Germany, Slovakia, and Latvia. Currently, Liepiņš works at the Harvard University Widener Library in the Baltic collection and as a professional artist. She lives in Boxford, Massachusetts, with her husband and two sons.

Born in Cesis, Latvia, Ilze Kļaviņa, Mueller lived in Germany and Australia before moving to the United States, where she makes her permanenet home. She has also lived in Tanzania and Zaire. A graduate of the University of Chicago and University of Minnesota, with degrees in German literature, she teaches German at Macalester College in St. Paul, Minnesota. A recipient of a Fulbright Fellowship and the Canadian-Latvian Jauna Gaita Translation Prize, Kļaviņa-Mueller has been translating German and Latvian poetry and prose into English since the 1970s. Her translations include *Idleness Is the Root of All Love,* by German poet Christa Reinig (Calyx Books, 1991). Recently she has begun writing poetry and is published in *Looking for Home* (Milkweed, 1990).

Baņuta Rubess is an award-winning playwright and director who writes and directs in English and in Latvian. Her writing ranges from feminist comedies to political satire, from a jazz play to a teen drama. Rubess also devised and produced the highly successful radio series *Adventure Stories for (Big) Girls* for two seasons on CBC, Canada's national radio network. For the past four seasons, she has been an Associate Artist at Theatre Passe Muraille in Toronto.

Rubess's Latvian plays have been both scandalous and popular. Her first play was the Latvian musical, *Varondarbi* (Heroica, 1978). Her next musical, *Tango Lugano,* was produced both in North America and Rīga. In 1991 when Rīga was barricaded against the Soviet army, Rubess was there to co-direct a play by Latvian feminist Aspazija in the tiny independent theater, Kabata. Her translations of Andra Neiburga's stories have been published by *AGNI* review in Boston.

Māra Sīmanis, although not a professional translator of literature, has been translating concepts across cultures for decades. Born in Chicago in 1960 and raised on the Latvian *dainas* (folk songs), she gained her B.A. in International Relations from Knox College in Illinois and M.A. in International Management from the School for International Training in Vermont. She taught English in Japan and was the Program Coordinator for the Institute of Latvian Studies in Münster Germany during *perestroika*. The day after German re-unification she moved to Latvia where she worked at the newspaper *Diena* setting up the Foreign News Desk, the Foreign Ministry initiating foreign aid coordination, the Ministry for State Reform developing public administration reform policy and the Prime Minister's Office improving policy planning.

REVIEW:

LATIN AMERICAN LITERATURE AND ARTS

The Major Publication for Contemporary Latin American Literature and Arts

Winner of the **Phoenix Award** for Editorial Achievement

Isabel Allende

Jorge Amado

G. Cabrera Infante

Carlos Fuentes

Gabriel García Márquez

Alejo Carpentier

Rosario Castellanos

Octavio Paz

Pablo Neruda

Elena Poniatowska

Subscribe Now!

Individual Subscription
$18.00 (1 yr., 2 issues) $32.00 (2 yr., 4 issues)
Institutions
$27.00 (1 yr., 2 issues) $54.00 (2yr., 4 issues)
International
$28.00 (1yr., 2 issues) $54.00 (1yr., 4 issues)

REVIEW:
LATIN AMERICAN LITERATURE AND ARTS
P. O. Box 3000
Denville, NJ 07834-9481
(Make checks payable to the Americas Society, Inc.)
Tel 1.800.783.4903 / http:///www.Americas-Society.org

UNIVERSITY of DELAWARE PRESS

(Recent and Forthcoming)

Into The Tunnel
  Steven G. Kellman and
Irving Malin $36.50

Adaptations as Imitations: Films
  from Noveis
James Griffith $39.50

After the Final No: Samuel Beckett's
  Trilogy
Thomas J. Cousineau   price TBA

Unlikely Stories: Causality and the
  Nature of Modern Narrative
Brian Richardson $36.00

Joycean Cultures: Culturing Joyces
  Vincent J. Cheng, Kimberly J. Devlin,
  and Margot Norris, eds.   price TBA

Daughters of Valor: Contemporary
  Jewish American Women Writers
Jay L. Halio and Ben Siegel, eds. $43.50

University of Delaware Press -- 326 Hullihen Hall -- Newark, DE 19716 -- (302) 831-1149
FAX: 302/831-6549   **E-mail:** udpress@odin.english.udel.edu
Please address orders to: AUP, 440 Forsgate Drive, Cranbury, NJ 08512   (609) 655-4770

AMERICAN LITERARY TRANSLATORS ASSOCIATION

Join with translators and others who have found a forum for the exchange of ideas on the art and craft of translation. Through annual conferences, newsletters, and the journals *Translation Review* and *Annotated Books Received Supplement*, you'll find the professional association you need, whether as a beginning or long-time translator.

UTD, MC35
P.O. Box 830688
Richardson, TX   75083-0688

972/883-2093
FAX: 972/883-6303

Texas Review Special Issue on

James Dickey's Fiction

Lawrence Broer: "Fire and Ice in Dickey's *To the White Sea*"

Nelson Hathcock: "No Further Claim to Innocence: James
   Dickey's Revision of the American War Story"

Steven G. Kellman: "Sergeant Muldrow's Bird's-Eye View"

Irving Malin: "First Sight (Site, Cite)"

Joyce M. Pair: "Measuring the Fictive Motion: War in
   Deliverance, Alnilam, and *To the White Sea*"

Daniel R. Schwarz: "Reconfiguring *Deliverance*: James Dickey,
   the Modern Tradition and the Resistant Reader"

Ernest Suarez: "'Real God, Roll': Muldrow's Primitive Creed"

Ernest Suarez: "An Interview with James Dickey: Poet as Novelist"

New Photographs of Dickey by Gene Crediford

Available at $10 from

   Texas Review Press
   English Department
   Sam Houston State University
   Huntsville, TX 77341

S T O R Y Q U A R T E R L Y 32

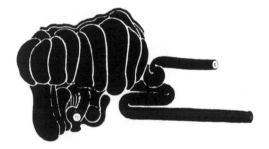

Single Issue $5
P.O. Box 1416, Northbrook, IL 60065

Dalkey Archive Press
New & recent titles

Unbabbling by REYoung

Love and Death in the American Novel by Leslie A. Fiedler

Eros the Bittersweet by Anne Carson

Those Barren Leaves by Aldous Huxley

Rigadoon by Louis-Ferdinand Céline

You may visit our website at:
www.cas.ilstu.edu/english/dalkey/dalkey.html

Unbabbling
by REYoung

$13.95 pb

A first novel bristling with anger and rantings, *Unbabbling* stretches back to the Tower of Babel (and before) and moves forward into a distant, twilight future in cities completely strange and utterly familiar.

"The entire novel is driven by raw verbal energy, and the result is dizzying. . . . Unbabbling *is distinctively American: angry, brutal at times, and unrelenting in its loathing, directed at everyone and everything. It is disturbing because it effectively captures how the centrality of humanity has been wholly drowned out by the babble of money."*
—Rain Taxi

*"*Unbabbling *reads like a wild romp through the subconscious of such esteemed modernists as Joyce, Pynchon, and Kerouac."*—Booklist

"This bizarre work rattles readers' sensibilities with a rich literary montage of the preposterous that carries with it a very strong social indictment of our times."—Library Journal

Dalkey
Archive
Press

Love and Death in the American Novel
by Leslie A. Fiedler

$16.95 pb

A classic work of literary criticism with a new introduction by Charles B. Harris.

"[This] witty, exasperating, energetic, penetrating book will prove indispensable."—Kingsley Amis

"I know of few works of criticism that are so likely to involve the reader whose interest in literature is not of a professional kind . . . it amounts to a general cultural history of the nation."—Lionel Trilling

"One of the great, essential books on the American imagination."—New York Times

"No other study of the American novel has such fascinating and on the whole right things to say."—Washington Post

Eros the Bittersweet
by Anne Carson

$12.95 pb

A book about love as seen by the ancients, *Eros* is Anne Carson's exploration of the concept of "eros" in both classical philosophy and literature. Epigrammatic, witty, ironic, and endlessly interesting, *Eros* is an evocative and lyrical meditation in the tradition of William Carlos Williams's *Spring and All* and William H. Gass's *On Being Blue.*

"Anne Carson is a rare talent—brilliant and full of wit, passionate and also deeply moving."—Michael Ondaatje

"Highly recommended."—Choice

"There is a fine beauty to the work, and it deserves reading."—Library Journal

Dalkey
Archive
Press

Those Barren Leaves
by Aldous Huxley

$13.95 pb

Aldous Huxley's assault on the twentieth-century mind and manners set in the palace of Mrs. Aldwinkle and filled with characters absorbed in their world of pretentions, illusions, and self-congratulations.

"*Brilliantly done;* Those Barren Leaves *has humour, daring, some excellent fooling, remarkable erudition and plenty of Huxley's salacious irony.*"—Guardian

"*It is brilliant and daring . . . humorous, witty, clever, cultured.*" —Nation and Athenaeum

"*Mr. Huxley has never written a richer book.*"—Nation

Rigadoon
by Louis-Ferdinand Céline

$13.50 pb

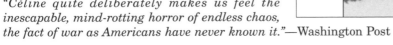

Completed just before his death in 1961—and bringing to conclusion his trilogy consisting of *Castle to Castle* and *North*—*Rigadoon,* as the critic J. H. Matthews has said, "stands as a summation of its author's experiments in fiction."

"*Céline quite deliberately makes us feel the inescapable, mind-rotting horror of endless chaos, the fact of war as Americans have never known it.*"—Washington Post

"*More than most modern authors, [Céline is] able to plunge directly into the burning center, where Europe, in rage and anguish, is tearing itself apart. In so doing, he captures the heat and energy of the final holocaust better than almost anyone.*"—Nation

"*The novels of Günter Grass, of William Burroughs, and of Norman Mailer would not have been written without Céline's precedent.*"—New Yorker

Dalkey Archive Press

Order Form

Individuals may use this form to order Dalkey titles or back issues of the *Review of Contemporary Fiction* at a 10-20% discount.

Title	Qty	Price

Subtotal _____

(10% for one book, 20% for two or more books) Less discount _____

Subtotal _____

($3.00 domestic, $4.50 foreign) Plus postage _____

Total _____

Ship to:

_____

_____

_____

_____

_____

mail or fax this form to:

Dalkey Archive Press

ISU Campus Box 4241

Normal, IL 61790-4241

fax: 309 438 7422

tel: 309 438 7555

Credit card payment   ❏ Visa   ❏ Mastercard

Acct # _____ Exp. Date _____

Name on card _____

Phone Number _____

Dalkey
Archive
Press

Please make checks (in U. S. dollars only) payable to *Dalkey Archive Press*.